K. B. PELLEGRINO

HIM, ME & PAULIE

DRUGS, MURDER, AND UNDERCOVER

©2019

Livres-Ici
PUBLISHING™

ISBN: 978-1-951012-00-7 (hc)
ISBN: 978-1-951012-01-4 (sc)
ISBN: 978-1-951012-02-1 (e)

Library of Congress Control Number: 2019909535

"I don't think lying to my mom or dad, or in this case to the police, is always a bad thing. If I am working to do the right thing and know that what I'm doing would frighten her, then I shouldn't tell her. Moms are supposed to be protective, but if what I'm doing is helping people, and the police and I think that I'm the best at doing it, then I have to lie to my mom or she will stop me. It's one of those situations my teacher told us about; when doing the right thing creates problems but not doing the right thing could really hurt people. I'm thinking that lying is sometimes the only solution, and in this case, it's just a little fib to the police."

Jackson Loyal to himself, 2018, "Him, Me and Paulie"

MAIN CHARACTERS

<u>Undercover-Boys aka Couriers of Information</u>
Him – Wayne Dion
Me – Jackson Loyal
Paulie – Paulo Santiago

<u>West Side Major Crimes Unit Detectives</u>
Captain Rudy Beauregard
Lieutenant Mason Smith
Lieutenant Petra Aylewood-Locke
Sergeant Ashton Lent
Sergeant Ted Torrington
Sergeant Lilly Tagliano
Sergeant Juan Flores

<u>Confidential Informant</u>
John McKinney

CONTENTS

CHAPTER 1   Deviations from the Good 1

CHAPTER 2   Ash Fights for his Life 12

CHAPTER 3   Undercover Informers! 23

CHAPTER 4   Revelations 34

CHAPTER 5   Stake-outs 41

CHAPTER 6   Beautiful Girl Dead 52

CHAPTER 7   Drugs and Murder 62

CHAPTER 8   Motives on Hold 71

CHAPTER 9   Faces and Friends 80

CHAPTER 10   Innocent Victims and Faces 88

CHAPTER 11   Two Problems Chased 97

CHAPTER 12   Herbie and His History 107

CHAPTER 13   Synthesizing Somewhat 114

CHAPTER 14   More Undercover Trouble 124

CHAPTER 15   What If? 132

CHAPTER 16   Serendipity 140

CHAPTER 17   Armistice Day Celebration 150

CHAPTER 18   Working Past Reports.................... 157

CHAPTER 19   Partying in Evergreen 168

CHAPTER 20   Therapy and Other Answers 175

CHAPTER 21   What People Know........................188

CHAPTER 22   Confabulation and Discovery 202

CHAPTER 23   Fitting the Puzzle Pieces 213

CHAPTER 24   Bits for the Fit..............................222

CHAPTER 25   Bitter – Bitter - End 232

1

Deviations from the Good

Teresa Loyal watched her eleven, almost twelve-year-old son, Jackson, from her kitchen window. Her heart beat faster as she studied the handsome face with his beautiful eyes resting on their Labrador Retriever. It surely was a case of first sight love for both the boy and his dog. As Jackson threw very long sticks, they enticed the dog, Widget, to run and run. The family had the puppy for a year and thank God, he was now settling down a little. *What would I have done if Jackson wasn't here? Neither Harry nor I have the patience to train Widget. Jackson's attention deficit disorder finally found a real job requiring his energy, other than video games, baseball, and soccer. Widget focused Jackson's life in a more grounded reality. The only quiet thing Jackson liked was art, probably because his two friends liked it.*

Teri, as her friends called her, well really everyone, washed the green beans in the colander and moved to quick fry them in olive oil. She had already browned organic grass-fed ground beef, which cost eight dollars a pound, with onions. She planned to steep them together with some beef broth and seasoning. Served over mashed potatoes, the dish was one of Harry and Jackson's favorite. She mixed the salad and pulled a peach torte from the oven. *My men will never starve from want of a home cooked meal. I try, for myself, to eat more vegetables, but have just given up. These men are carnivorous.*

Hearing Widget barking, almost in pain, Teri ran to the window, hoping against hope, Jackson had not hurt the dog. She believed boys were part animal until it was trained out of them by their mothers. Jackson was not the culprit today, however. Instead, Wayne Dion, a neighborhood boy, had torqued the long stick, flipping Widget in a spiral and clearly, from her view, had injured the dog. Jackson was now pummeling Wayne. Teri ran into the yard trying not to trip over the hose lying next to the pool, yelling, "Stop that! You're hurting Widget and each other."

Fifteen minutes later, after severely scolding both boys, she returned to her kitchen. Teri's heart was pounding. She brought Widget in the house and inspected his body. His heart was still pounding too as he continued to bark up a storm while he looked through the glass door out to the yard. *I've had enough of this. Every time Wayne is here, there is trouble. Chelsea can't stand him. Maybe it's because he's almost a year older than Jackson and he wants to be in position superior. The hell with this! I'm calling Jackson in for dinner. He can wait in here with me and tell me his side of the story.*

I have a plan. I've been watching those two, Jackson and Wayne, and together they are trouble. I can't blame Wayne all the time because often Jackson is the troublemaker, but today I think Wayne is the problem. I don't think they will ever be good together. It's too bad they are in the same year in school; although Wayne is five months older, five months makes a difference. For sure I'll certainly send Jackson to a different high school. Let them mature. I know in my heart kids can turn the wrong way at any age. You have to watch them. Look at twelve-year-old Anya, who killed all those children in West Side; and they say her mother watched her night and day. Sometimes all the care in the world is not enough.

Teri tried to call Jackson in, but he was nowhere to be found. She spotted his cell phone on the kitchen counter. She knew in her heart he left it there on purpose so she couldn't track him. She thought, *just what am I going to do with that boy? Now, I will worry until he comes home. Well, it's time to have a sit down with Jackson and Harry. Maybe Chelsea is right when she says we all spoil him. I don't really think that and if I do, I think I spoiled Chelsea even more when she was his age.*

Teri was thinking about their lovely home, aware the location was not far from the more negative side of town. She didn't love being near to small strip malls, restaurants, and two old time clubs that were originally ethnic clubs. She thought, *I had never been in either one of those clubs until the other night. The Puccini Club was named after the famous Italian composer and it was the setting of Nigel's 100ᵗʰ birthday party.*

Teri mused about Nigel. He was a gardener, originally from Jamaica, and according to him was brought to the U.S. in 1942 as part of a workforce for the military with the offer of work and eventual citizenship. He'd told Teri it was a wonderful opportunity for him, but he did like to go home every few years. He had some children there.

Her cell rang and her friend Liz Abernale, Nigel's employer, was calling with some gossip. Liz lived over on Evergreen in a gorgeous older home nestled within a beautiful West Side newer development. They discussed the party the other night and wondered why they didn't think to get Nigel's story on the news. After all, he was still working as a gardener, drove his own car, shared an apartment with a friend, and visited just about every small business in this section of West Side; probably got around more than Mayor Fitshler. He was one hundred years old and a busy man. Teri could not get her arms around how he could exhibit such agility and energy at his age. Liz changed the focus to the venue for the party; well not actually where it was held, but the surrounding neighborhood. Neither woman was familiar with the area before, prompting Liz to say, "Did you see the drug traffic there? I asked Nigel and he just shrugged his shoulders saying, 'It is everywhere today,' like he just accepts it. He's one hundred years old and he goes to the club regularly. I worry about him. You know he came to us when I purchased this house; like an inheritance. He's been the gardener here for forty years; not able to work now more than a couple hours at a time, but he'll work in ninety-degree heat. I make iced tea for him. He loves it. He's the one who keeps my vegetable garden going; the one whose work allows me to bring my surplus veggies to the women's club.

"I look forward to the days when he shows up; he is such an inspiration. Nigel also does the yard of the house just sold in my neighborhood. You know the big house with the really handsome and prosperous couple who drive the two Audis. I think their names are Janine and Raymond Losocala. I'm going to invite them to my next party. Raymond's company is supposedly a big vendor for security to the casino; and they used to live in Las Vegas. My husband says he spoke with Ray and he knew diddly-squat about Vegas; he says they couldn't have lived there for long. Anyway, Teri, don't you think the police should do something about that spot in town where the party was?"

Teri did. "You know Mona and Rudy Beauregard are my neighbors; although I only really socialize with Mona at all the potluck suppers and such. Anyway, Rudy is head of Major Crimes at the police department. Maybe I'll talk to him. He's not community patrol, so perhaps if there's not a murder in that region, he doesn't know how bad it is."

"Teri, he must know something about it, because the news reported there were two home invasions on the street next to the club, on Silvain Street. Mona stated he was on the case."

Teri did not answer immediately. Liz queried, "What's wrong, Teri? We're still connected. I can't hear you."

"Turn on your television, Liz, right now – on the news."

The news announced, "It's a sad day in this beautiful community of West Side. Two Major Crimes Unit Detectives, Ashton Lent and Theodore Toddington, have been gunned down on Spruce Street. They were taken to the hospital and this reporter was told Detective Ashton is in critical condition, while Detective Toddington is in serious condition. We will keep you updated."

Teri stated, "I'm hanging up. I'll call Mona. She'll know more. Beauregard will be crazy. This is awful and Spruce Street is the street the club is on. It backs up on Silvain Street. I'll call you later."

Mona clicked her cell and knew it was Teri. Her answer was, "Teri, I don't know any more than you do. Rudy is at work and I tried to call him. He didn't answer. I saw him in the TV coverage at the scene and he looks physically ill and awfully angry. The track on the bottom of the screen says Ash and Ted were on Spruce Street to question witnesses in the home invasion case and another shooting I hadn't heard about. I just don't understand this kind of crime. We're a suburban city. I'm so afraid for Ash and Ted. I'll call you when I know more."

The crime scene was visible to some residents in the houses next to number eight Spruce Street, where the two cops were shot. These residents stayed on their porches, not only for what was normal interest in a shooting, but because the street and, they heard, the surrounding whole quarter square mile, was filled with blues and detectives; not just with West Side police but police from Agawam, Westfield, Springfield, Holyoke, and the state police. One rather unsightly and rough looking resident was heard to say, "Not a day to screw around with them. You'd be dead before you knew what hit you. Stupid thugs, they should know better than trying to kill cops. It's a no-no. Now there'll be no traffic, neither customers nor suppliers here, and no moving of equipment. Business is shut down in this area for a while. I wonder where they'll move production."

Lieutenant Joe Stellato was there from Springfield's MCU along with West Side's Mayor Fitshler who was heard by just about everyone within a three-hundred-foot radius screaming at West Side's Chief of Police Coyne, "What the hell happened here! Toddington is my wife's brother. I told you to keep him safe. Since when do Major Crime's detectives get shot? I never heard of that before. I'm telling you, he had better recover or my marriage is over."

Captain Beauregard was heard to say in a louder voice than normal for him, "Mayor and Chief, I've sent Lieutenant Ayleward-Locke to the hospital. She will notify me on any changes. I believe Ted will recover. It's Detective Lent, whose current state is critical. He lost a great deal of blood at the scene. Just look at this site and you'll see how complicated this situation is. Ted got hit in the arm and chest; but he always wears a vest when he's out of the station, which saved his life for sure. Detective Smith and I are working the details of this case, but I am short detectives. There are just three of us now to work this case and our other cases. I need more detectives and I need them now. I'd like to move Officer Tagliano up as a temporary detective for this case with your support. I know her background, and frankly I think she's wasted in Vice."

Chief Coyne was surprised Rudy would do this in front of Mayor Fitshler but thought, *then again, what better time? The mayor has an iron in this fire and the ability to increase the budget to cover the transfer; a transfer I hope like hell we'll be able to retain.*

The Mayor assented, "Do what you have to do, Beauregard. In fact, pick another cop to move into the bureau. Life is changing round here; changing times need more cops. I get that. This is not what suburban living should look like; cops shot in the street just because they're interviewing someone. Do we know what happened here? Who did it? Was it drug related, because I've gotten several calls about this community policing section."

Beauregard did not answer, turned away, and tuned the two men out. He appeared to have no time for them or anyone who could not supply answers. Detective Mason Smith was there with his laptop doing drawings and organizing the uniforms. Beauregard asked Mason to have the uniforms record all license plates in a five-street square area. He met with the state police and staff from the medical examiner's office. This was a shooting of two detectives and anyone, who could get over to the site to help, did. The uniforms were having a difficult time keeping some kids out who knew the back entrance through some woods to the Club's parking lot. There were two kids on eight-hundred-dollar bikes who insisted they lived on the street, and when questioned, had the audacity to jump up onto the porch at the site with their bikes saying, "Hi, Dad" to an old man sitting there. Only problem is the boys were around twelve to thirteen years old and the old man was in his seventies and maybe Latino. The boys were Caucasian. Rather than move them out, Rudy told the uniform to just watch them. He thought, *what the hell are they doing here now? There isn't a kid in the world doesn't have a motive for what they do. I'm certain they're familiar with this area; they no doubt have been here before; how else would thy know how to access this spot from the woods? They don't belong here, but they know this place, and, damnit, I bet they live within a mile, more than likely in one of the nicer neighborhoods.* Rudy asked one of the uniforms to make sure the kids didn't leave until he could talk to them.

Mason approached him and said the most reliable story he heard so far was from a young housewife who was bringing in groceries when the excitement started. "Captain, she says there is a good-looking man, about forty to forty-five, who has been going in and out of the third-floor apartment in number eight Spruce Street for the past month. The house has an absentee landlord. She thinks a lot of stuff is going on in both the first and second floor apartments. I quote, 'they sell drugs out of the first floor by the side window which is very low. A guy sits in there two hours a day at random times.' The customers apparently know the random times so she thinks there's some sort of a signal for the customers to come. They don't let anyone hang around the street who is not known to them, but she didn't think they ever said anything, or had anything to do with the tenant on the third floor. She saw the third-floor tenant running through the back of the house after the shots. He always walked to the house when he visited and entered by way of the back of the house, not the front, so she figured he had a car on one of the other streets and didn't want it to be seen on Spruce Street."

Springfield's MCU Lieutenant Stellato assisted in taking statements aware that Mason was busy. Stellato had help. A uniform officer taped what he could when a witness allowed permission.

Beauregard caught a glimpse out of the corner of his eye of another boy, around the same age as the two already on the porch, jump from behind some bushes next to the house and position himself on the porch. It was clear the three boys knew each other. The uniform guarding the porch in front of the steps had turned his back and didn't notice the third kid get on the porch. Beauregard groaned at the sight thinking, *damn kids today are so agile and shrewd. Something has called all these kids together. Might be worth a conversation!*

Calling Mason over, they climbed the porch steps after telling the uniform officer to keep guard in case there was a runner and also reminding him he missed the new guy who had skipped onto the porch right behind him. The uniform officer would be doubly vigilant now as indicated by the brilliant red on his already nice Irish rosy cheeks. The kids were polite when asked why they were there but offered no reason. Beauregard thought one of the boys looked familiar and took out his pad and requested addresses. Only the third boy was willing to give his address. Mason stood tall hoping to intimidate and said, "Alright guys, Officer Timulty will watch your bikes, while I take you in. It won't be long before your parents will be looking for you; we'll find out who you are then." And he brought Officer Timulty up to the porch to guard the bikes. The officer had to look away to stop from laughing.

Jackson Loyal was not laughing. Instead he whispered to Wayne, "I'll get killed if they bring me to the station."

Wayne told him, "They can't do anything to us. We're kids."

Jackson decided, after a look of complete desolation at Wayne, that he must move forward to try making a deal with the detective. He thought, *manipulation works with my parents and my teachers. I hope he's not like Chelsea. Nothing works with her. I don't think lying to my mom or dad, or in this case to the police, is always a bad thing. If I am working to do the right thing and know that what I'm doing would frighten her, then I shouldn't tell her. Moms are supposed to be protective, but if what I'm doing is helping people and the police and I think that I'm the best at doing it, then I have to lie to my mom or she will stop me. It's one of those situations my teacher told us about; when doing the right thing creates problems but not doing the right thing could really hurt people. I'm thinking that lying is sometimes the only solution, and in this case, it's just a little fib to the police.*

Jackson turned to Detective Mason Smith and said, "We're not bad. We just heard about the shooting on Wayne's father's police scanner and we know the shortcut here. We come here all the time. There's a game store over in the second mall and sometimes they give out free games if you're a little kid. They want us addicted; that's what my sister Chelsea says. We also go to the woodworking shop for drawing/drafting paper for our art club. We've done nothing. We both know the guy who ran away. Wayne, Me and Paulie are good artists. We can draw a picture, can't we, guys?

"We know we can do it good enough, but the deal is you cops don't tell our parents. Santiago here is the best people artist, aren't you Paulie?"

Paulie had a different take on the situation, "Geez, are you guys nuts? They'll get their info from us and tell our parents anyway. Don't you know shit?"

Beauregard broke in, addressing Detective Mason Smith. "What do you think, Detective? Are these stand-up guys or just punks? Santiago here sounds like he doesn't trust the police. Two of our detectives have been shot and maybe will die, and these punks are telling bullshit stories. Bring them down to the station."

Jackson could see the situation was not going well. Although only almost thirteen years old, Jackson appeared to the others to be more confident as he acted as if he were in control. "Detective, I trust you to keep your word. Between the three of us, Him, Me and Paulie, I promise we can help; we can help you find this guy. No one has ever taken a picture of him. He looks normal except for his eyes. They would scare you; like glassy really blue and he looks around suspiciously. Do we have a deal? We draw him and help you and you let us go?"

All three cops looked as if they were in deep thought and Officer Timulty, probably to regain his honor, said, "Don't worry, detectives, I'm on this beat. I've seen them before. I'll check all the schools. They lie to you, I'll find them."

And Paulie pulled out some drawing paper he had just bought at the woodworking shop before meeting his friends. Before he could start, Beauregard asked, "Paulie, what were you guys going to do over here? It's clearly your meeting place."

In a whisper to the Captain, Paulie said, "You can't let this old man know anything. He's a lookout and they'll hurt us. I'll tell you but throw him off the porch, and don't let him know I told you to do it."

Beauregard signaled Mason to come closer, and explained the problem. Mason looked at Officer Timulty, winking at him, and said, "What the hell is this guy doing here, Timulty, when we're trying to find out where these kids live? Does he live here?"

Timulty said, "No, this is the guy who says he's security. He sits here five hours a day, right, Alfie? You want him out of here, Captain; he's gone. Move on, Alfie."

Alfie took a long time to get off the porch as if he were infirm, but once off, he practically ran to a house near the end of the street, prompting Mason to signal to some uniforms to keep an eye on him. One of the community police uniforms told him the old man lived with his son and to the best of his memory the son drove Alfie around in a big new SUV.

Beauregard continued with his conversation with Paulie. "Look Paulie, what gives here?"

"Detective, do you know the school officer at Hoffington School, Officer Simeon. I don't know his last name. It might be Harrington. Anyway, he swore some of us in as neighborhood watchers. We're supposed to watch our neighborhood for any trouble, not tell anyone, but call or text his cell phone. Here it is." And he showed Beauregard the number on his iPhone, which was an upgrade on Beauregard's phone.

"So, what does that have to do with this situation where all three of you were meeting over here on Spruce Street?"

"My friends are both from Camelia Street. Nothing goes on there; that, I can tell you. We meet over here regularly in the woods and draw. Last week we realized there's a lot of drug action on number eight. We decided we'd draw what we saw. They normally close up shop at this time of day, and the kingpins walk out; all three of them. We were going to draw their faces, one face for each of us and give the drawings to Officer Simeon, but all the shooting started and I had trouble sneaking in from the woods. I've seen the guy running out of the back of the house before and Jackson and Wayne see him every day because that's the way they come to meet me in the woods."

Beauregard said he might take them seriously and asked the kids to draw the guy. Scrambling quickly, the boys each went to different corners of the porch and started drawing; separately from each other. While they were busy working, the captain asked Mason if they were able to get into the first and second floors in their search of the house.

Mason said, "Yup, exigent circumstances, Captain. They're mixing product on the second floor and selling on the first. The third floor is completely empty except for two hard chairs and a folding table. Not a rendezvous for sure; maybe a meeting for transfer of info or connected to the operations downstairs, but the neighbors say no."

Not even ten minutes later, all three boys had made a drawing of the man who had run out the back and although separately done, it was obvious the three had drawn the same man. Jackson said, "That's him, Detective. I promise. Now can we get out of here and go home before I get killed by my mom?"

Beauregard laid down his conditions: names and addresses and no baloney. The kids gave in and left as fast as they could; all certain he would break his word and show up at their homes later.

Beauregard thought, *won't hurt for them to worry a little, but I'll keep my word.*

2

Ash Fights for his Life

Detective Petra Aylewood-Locke was a wreck. Normally composed, she found herself in tears waiting for the doctor performing surgery on Ash. She thought, *he's my partner, my friend, my music tutor; he just can't die. And Ted; what about him? I gave him a hard time when he first came on. The Mayor shoves him down our throats and I was pissed. Then what happens, he turns out to be stable and a different kind of detective. He ignores all the snide remarks, and within a week we all thought he was always with us. He's insightful in giving the Captain what he most wants in these cases, a look at the facts through a new lens. God, please make us whole again.* She cried and was mumbling when she answered her husband Jim's call.

He said, "What's the matter, Pet? I just now saw what happened on TV. I've been following someone today on a corporate theft case. How is Ash? Will he make it?"

And she broke down, letting Jim with his calming voice help her deescalate; knowing he was the only one who knew how to help her. He finally said, "I'm worried about you. You don't cry like this. Are you okay?"

Dr. Azbouf, Ash's surgeon interrupted the conversation. He brought her into a quiet room and said, "Detective, I've just talked with the families. Ashton and Theodore are both doing well. Ashton suffered a great deal of blood loss from his femoral artery that put him in shock. The surgery was always within our scope for recovery, but whether his body can retain its balance and not give up is the question. He has much going for him. His age helps, but just as importantly, he is in very good shape. It is not absolutely certain he will be able to continue maintaining his progress but I give it a ninety percent. He will need a lot of therapy, as the use of his right leg and nerves take even longer to mend than muscle and bone for recovery. It will be painful. Theodore will be leaving the hospital in two days, but will also require therapy for use of his shoulder. He is lefthanded, actually both detectives are lefthanded, but Ted had the injured shoulder on the right side. It's a good day when I can deliver good recovery news. I think they'll be fine, Detective."

And she cried and cried in relief. Martina McKay, Ash's lady friend walked over to her and hugged her saying, "I just knew God couldn't take him away from me; I just couldn't take the loss of Ash after searching for so many years for his love."

A woman approached them who looked vaguely familiar before Petra realized she was the mayor's sister and Ted's wife. She introduced herself. "You must be Petra and Martina. I'm Charlotte Toddington, and I believe we are some of the luckiest ladies in western Massachusetts today. I thought I married an engineer and would have this safe and secure life. He so didn't look like an adventurer to me when I married him. And he sprung it on me, 'I want to be a cop. I've always wanted to be a cop.' I have never been able to say 'no' to Ted, nor would I want to. And he's happy; shot in the shoulder but happy. In fact, he's just angry with himself he didn't see it coming. He must be on happy pills because he's all gushy in there. Can you imagine Ted being all gushy? And the kids are going to be so impressed. Hell of a world we live in, isn't it, when their father has to be shot to impress them?"

Petra and Martina laughed; both in relief and definitely surprised Charlotte was normal and funny, despite her being Mayor Fitshler's sister.

Captain Beauregard was invited right into recovery where Ted was in the process of being removed to intensive care. He learned that this detective was fighting to get out of the hospital although just having surgery and still drugged; he was certainly forceful. The staff left the two detectives to converse. Ted's story brought nothing new to the table. Ted said they were just following up with interviews of neighbors on a house invasion near Spruce Street, because a neighbor said there was a fishy tenant on the third floor of number eight. When they approached the building, they did it from the rear entrance based on information the tenant only used that door. There was an old iron exterior staircase. As they got past the second floor and were apparently visible to the occupants of the third floor, someone shot them both through the dirty glass door and a man exited the third-floor door.

Ted went down from two shots and had to hold Ash when he was shot to keep him from going over the iron handrail that certainly wouldn't meet building code standards today. The man did a flying jump over them and was quite agile missing Ash who tried to grab his leg. Ted was able to see him run through the landscape and houses to the next street but then lost sight.

Beauregard called the Captain in Vice and told him Detective Tagliano was being moved to MCU. The Captain said, "No problem, she always has ideas of her own and frankly doesn't want to be used as a shill despite the fact she's one looker. She questions everything. I'll send her over to you in an hour, but I expect the paperwork to be signed by you. I don't want problems with her thinking it was my idea. These women's issues have me crazy. Believe me, Rudy, Tagliano can be a handful. Good luck."

Next, he called the captain in the uniform division and said he was authorized to move Officer Flores to MCU. The captain said, "He's not a detective, Rudy; do they know that moving him over means moving him up and it will kill their budget. He has to be detective to be in your unit. Shit, there is a current detective opening, but Vice is after it. This is going to be another shit-show and you know that. Not fair, just because you have the big-ticket almost murder show."

Beauregard told him to stop the pity act. He needed help and told the captain, saying, "Two of my detectives are out. I need help now."

He emailed the Mayor and Chief's office with his selections so they could get out in front of the movement of personnel. He knew that at no other time could he get away with this. After all, he had no authority to create a detective; and perhaps it wouldn't work. His chief might decide to put a uniform in the division. It had never happened before. The fact that Officer Flores is Mexican maybe would help his cause; although that's not why Beauregard chose him. He'd seen Flores in action several times deescalate situations that few cops would have been capable of doing. And while he waited for the fire storm, Rudy mourned his wounded detectives thinking, *how can I protect them? We think it's the uniforms that are the targets, but it's anybody in policing.*

It was about an hour later he received paperwork from Officer Flores who as he entered his office looked like a 'deer in the headlights.' Flores said, "Captain Beauregard, this paperwork from the chief and my captain says I'm to report to you and that I'm elevated to detective. I know there is an opening and I passed the exam with high grades, but you know I was not on the list. What happened here? I need to know to answer all the questions that will be thrown at me. Is this just because I'm Mexican?"

The captain hunched his shoulders and glared at Officer Flores, but only said, "Juan Flores, I'll say this once and only once, I don't give a rat's ass about race, gender, and ethnicity. You're here because I asked for you. You don't want the move; go back where you came from. Clear?"

Juan Flores smiled broadly responding, "That's all I needed to hear, Captain. I'm thrilled to be here now I know you chose me."

"Don't get too high off this, Detective Flores, my detectives work hard here and I expect that. Now there's an empty desk over there. Go occupy it and familiarize yourself with all the open files unassigned on the table, while I wait for another new addition to the squad."

As Beauregard was finishing his sentence, a woman walked in carrying a large plastic bin and said, "Hi, Captain. I can't thank you enough for getting me out of Vice. I don't have to wear skirts and heels and make-up to work anymore. Show me where to drop this stuff; it's heavy."

Flores could not believe it was Lilly Tagliano from Vice. *This is going to be a hell of an experience. The captain looks tough and Lilly's known for running her own show within a show. Her boss was dying to get rid of her. I wonder if the captain knows what he's in for.*

Beauregard pointed to the last desk next to Juan. She dumped her stuff, looked around and said, "Hi, Juan, how'd you get over here? You got the open detective position. There'll be hell to pay for that. Don't worry, you're one of the good guys. Glad to work with you."

The captain said, "Detective Tagliano, a word please" and he pointed to his office.

Lilly rolled her eyes looking at Juan, whispering, "Here I go again; another bad start because I say the obvious. Probably okay, because they're down two detectives and need me."

In his office the captain addressed what he thought was an important issue. "Detective Tagliano or Lilly, whichever you prefer, MCU is a successful operating unit because we respect each other, back up each other, and don't rap about police gossip. You're here today because I asked for you. Now, I found no hesitation in getting Captain Chilicot from Vice to recommend you. That's never happened before. Can you tell me why he was so easily convinced he could lose a detective before assuring himself he had a new detective in line?"

Lilly was surprised. She saw the Captain was throwing the ball in her court; not assuming what he heard about her was true, instead asking her to spell out her problems. *Christmas, I can't get mad at him. He's waiting for me to tell him all. Is it possible he's not judgmental? Maybe he's just a smart manager. I tell him all. It's in my file. Later, when there are problems he pulls the file out and has a reason to get rid of me. What to do here; I'm screwed either way; may as well tell the truth.*

"Captain, I sometimes have trouble working with people who don't work, don't think things through, put us in danger, and especially anyone who tries to do the 'Little lady, let me help you with this.' Now I know Petra and I know she would not put up with any of that stuff, so maybe my history won't be in the way here."

"Lilly, this unit's detectives work together; don't compete for number one; help each other out; and always have each other's backs. Those are plain basic law enforcement rules. I have an additional rule; well maybe two rules. They're simple, do what I tell you and do nothing behind my back. You'll be gone in a flash however if I have to get rid of you; if you do not abide by my rules. Now I'm going to the hospital to see my detectives. You work with Juan. Show him how to be a detective. Work on the home invasion case that started this mess and have Juan talk to the uniform community police officers in that section, one by one. Why would detectives be shot just for asking questions? I don't think from what I've heard the home invasion has anything to do with the perp who shot Ash and Ted, but I need it ruled out as a possibility. Get the forensics reports ASAP and look at the kids' drawings. It's the same guy in left, straight and right profiles. These were kids who saw the guy. They did the drawings in front of me so there was no collaborating; unless they are drawing some other guy they know. My gut says they're telling the truth."

Lilly got up to leave, saying, "I'm sorry about the detectives. Will they be okay?"

Beauregard nodded and let Detective Tagliano leave without another word; she could not believe she and Juan were given orders so quickly with a goal, a purpose. She thought, n*ew day on the force for me.*

Millie called into the room, "Captain, there's a report of a dead girl over near the Holyoke line by the river, still on our side. Maybe it's a drug overdose. The uniforms on scene have a lot of questions; one is whether the body was moved there."

The captain said, "Mason will go. Damn if it's a moved body, for sure it's drug related. What the hell is going on?"

He motioned Mason to his office reminding him to look carefully at the scene. "Mason, if the officers at the scene think the body was moved; then for sure it was. Look for every detail; maybe they missed something."

Detective Aylewood-Locke was shaken by the afternoon events, but thankful to God her friends were spared. She left the hospital and drove over to the scene of her colleagues' shootings and did what she always did; she walked the streets and the woods and talked to any neighbors who were around. She was one street over in the rear of the shooting site and noticed two orange road barrier cones on one parking space but one was tipped over and dented. Looking around she saw two older Latinas sitting on a big oversized porch with an amazing array of furniture stuffed in the porch and a big magnolia tree shading them. It was getting warmer now because the sweet breeze had died down. It was supper time and she could smell the rice and pork cooking. She realized the two women were watching her and that the average walker-by couldn't easily notice them. She thought, *that one gorgeous magnolia tree may not be a tree, maybe it's a bush the way it's shading them. I bet no one's interviewed them.*

She introduced herself with an 'Hola' and was hopeful they spoke English and not just Spanish. Her high school Spanish had been reinforced mostly by her years of beat work on Boston's police force, but was still nowhere near perfect. "Senoras, do you speak English?"

Both ladies laughed and said, "Yes, Detective, we were born here and went to high school here. We were wondering when the police would see behind the magnolia." And they both laughed and were clearly not the least bit intimidated by her.

She wondered, *how do they know I'm a detective?* So, she asked them.

Senora one in the gorgeous flowing silk blue dress said, "You'd never be walking alone on this street unless you were a hooker, a user, or police and you're not in uniform, so you're a detective."

Petra climbed the porch steps and entered what looked to her like the soft environment of old Savannah, and so she told them.

The other lady who said her name was Sara was wearing a similar dress to the first lady, although this dress was in a vivid jade green color. She said, "Well we did our job didn't we, because that's what we designed. It is pretty, terribly comfortable, and provides ambience for about five months of the year. Then we go inside and have holiday themes. We're not millionaires but we live like them. You should come to our Thanksgiving, Christmas, New Year's, Armistice Day, Valentine's Days and other open houses. Everyone does; now you're invited. The community police team officers always show up. Just tell them about Sara and Miriam. Would you like a gin and tonic?"

Much as Petra would have liked one, she refused thinking, *on the job – must deny having fun.*

Instead she sat down in the midst of layers of pillows that came close to completely swallowing her in soft cushion. Miriam said, "Don't worry about dampness. We take all the pillows in every night and tumble them to get rid of anything floating in the air. It takes a lot of work for us to feel like 'Southern Ladies'."

Petra couldn't resist and said, "I just have to ask, why if you are looking for a Southern look, why not do a design with fans and stuff like in Puerto Rico?"

Both ladies giggled and Sara said, "You assume too much, Detective. We both are a mix, Puerto Rican, Cuban, Caucasian, and other islanders. Like you, we steal ideas from every culture. Italians can be Anglophiles, English can be Francophiles; you know the world is open to us too."

To cover her embarrassment, Petra laughed and said, "Sorry, I should know better. Nothing in life is as it seems, is it?" And she got to the point of her visit, "Sara and Miriam, there are two broken cones over there, well at least one is smashed. I assume they're there to hold a parking space. Are they being held for a tenant in one of those buildings?"

Miriam was quite clear. "No, none of the tenants would ever do that. The space is a private handicapped space for Mrs. Rojas who lives alone, although her son is often there, at number 23. She never goes out but has the space designated. Her son took down the handicapped sign but we all know we can't park there. Instead he rents it out. For the last year it's been rented out to a nice-looking corporate type man who parks there and goes through the houses to Spruce Street. Today he got in his car and didn't even bother moving the cones; he was in such a hurry to leave. He is what my daughter calls a cool dude, and a dude like that really doesn't fit in this neighborhood."

Knowing the captain had drawings of the perp, Petra asked, "If I come back with a drawing of this guy, would you be willing to identify if it's him?"

Sara said, "Absolutely. He's not a druggie, but we'll look at your drawings. You can find us here every day socializing. We're both retired and life is good. Our families visit and bring us dinners. Life is good."

Petra stood and was about to say good-bye, but remembered the three boys who the captain had mentionexad. "Ladies, do you remember seeing three boys riding around on their bikes here: two white and one Latino?"

Miriam spoke first. "You mean Jackson, Wayne, and Paulie. They do nothing wrong. They try to come to our open houses but don't tell their moms, except for Paulie who tells his mom. Talk to them; they know everything going on in the neighborhood. Jackson and Wayne say nothing interesting goes on where they live over on Camelia and they come around and ask for iced tea with mint in it. We love those boys. In another year they'll be in their next stage of life and won't be around us anymore. We'll miss them, I can tell you that."

Petra left for the stationhouse and while driving called Jim, her husband, to report she would be late. It was no problem because he was being delayed. At the station, Petra met the two new detectives and was momentarily startled at the thought, *I'm no longer the only woman detective and Lilly is famous for playing outside the rulebook. Maybe she'll make me look like a good doobie. Ha, that could never happen. I like Juan. He actually helped me last year on a case when no other uniform could be bothered. How the hell did the captain get this to happen; two detectives? Lilly was high on the list passing the detectives' exam; but I don't know if Juan ever took the exam. I suppose he could be a temporary until he passes the exam, or maybe the powers that be will let the exam requirement slide.*

Petra informed the two about her meeting with the faux 'Southern Ladies.' They all had a laugh while Juan commented, "Taught you a lesson, Petra, about making assumptions."

"Yup, I got called. Nice ladies and I'm going to their holiday parties. I'll get to see what different kinds of people are in our town that I normally wouldn't meet. Maybe I'll meet a few criminals."

Juan laughed. "You're on the mark, Petra! They'll be criminals there. There's not such a separation between the slightly bad and the good in that part of town. Actually, I've got it wrong. That's true everywhere, but the slightly bad in the suburbs don't have police records normally. By the way, did you know that suburb is really a Spanish word coming from the Latin and my gurus say Spanish is the modern Latin?"

Petra and Lilly had not seen this side of Juan and both said, "No shit, Juan."

After they all laughed, they discussed who would bring the picture to the ladies the next day. Juan offered, "I can't wait to meet them. My patrols have always been in the upscale sections of the city except when I was back-up for drug raids or juvenile support. I'll probably get them to tell me more."

"OOPS! Who's making assumptions now, Juan?"

Mason looked at the young girl's body, thinking, *sometimes I hate this fucking job. Those guys had better get well quick; this is not what I do best. Where the hell is Petra when I need her? This girl is no more than*

seventeen, if that, and I don't know if she's Italian or French or Puerto Rican or maybe has a good tan. Hell, her hair is streaked all shades of blonde, but you can't go by that. All the sisters have blonde streaks and they're not white. Those needle marks on her arm are all new. She's a newbie unless they find her injecting elsewhere. She's not wearing the teenager uniform of tights or jeans. She's wearing a short skirt and no panties. I don't like this. Maybe it's a sex crime and a drug murder. There's no cell phone. No kid this age is without a cell phone, but there's a pocket on the skirt with tissue hanging out of it.

Mason pulled the tissue and it was wrapped around a bracelet engraved with, "My Baby Candace 10-12-02." Mason had the evidence retrieved. He was overwhelmed by the heaviness of the weight of unseemly death on his psyche and left for the station as soon as he could.

3

Undercover Informers!

The next day brought the three boys, after much negotiation, to the game store. However, Wayne in calling the other boys, had said, "We got a different kind of gaming today and I've only got about two and a half hours before I have to be home."

Jackson said, "I have a problem anyway. My mom says you're trouble and she's going to put the kibosh on our relationship; whatever that means; so, I can't be late. I gotta be home by 4:45."

Wayne retorted, "The old people say the word kibosh all the time. It means she's gonna break us up. My mom said they both agree we should go to different high schools. Don't want that. West Side High is where I want to go. Paulie, where are you going? Is your mother going to pull that stuff about you being a minority and put you into the exchange program for Longmeadow?"

Paulie laughed. "None of that. She says whether I'm good or bad, doesn't change her job which is that she has to keep track of me. If I get out of line, and if she can't control me, my stepfather will do it. He's a good guy, but he's former military and doesn't let me get away with much. Any kid from the district he doesn't like, he just confronts. They go away. My mom thinks you guys are okay; just have too many material things that interfere with what is important. That's what she says."

Jackson laughed now too. "Your mom trusts you. Our moms are certain we're born troublemakers. They're kind of girlie, so they don't appreciate our jokes. They think we'll end up in juvenile detention. I think the counselor in school told them about that one time, when we used that radio to interfere with all the cell phones in the school. They blamed us but couldn't prove it. It was just a joke. My father says we'll mature in a few years and have a better sense of humor. My mother was wild; told my father he was guilty of problem avoidance, that he was just plain chicken when it comes to solving family problems. Big fight! But what do you think about going undercover?"

Paulie was the first to embrace the thought and said, "Sure, but we have to understand our mark. He looks like a white businessman, seems important, you know the type that's at the country club and has a second home at the Cape or at the Connecticut shore; that type. So, it's opening day at MGM Casinos in Springfield. He'll go in there around lunch if not today, tomorrow. All the businessmen will be there sometime tomorrow. This casino opening is big for Springfield. Everybody wants to be part of it. I think if we watch today we'll figure out how we can hang around without being bothered by the cops. After today, we can each go when we're able to. That way Wayne can be there while Jackson is home and the same when Jackson's in Springfield. They won't get suspicious. My mom just needs me sometimes to take care of my little sister Rosie. I can even take her with me although my mom doesn't like me around the circle and bridge; says it's dangerous. Rosie won't talk. She's pretty smart for a little kid. We'll go now."

The boys, Him, Me and Paulie, spent the next morning viewing the entrances to the casino. Jackson had said earlier they would only be able to view from a distance on this day. The crowds were enormous and they had this parade with two girls painted like zebras or something doing acrobatics. They all watched that, Wayne saying, "How'd they do that? I'm good at gymnastics, but I can't do that."

The boys watched the Clydesdale horses and then separated to watch people's faces for an hour. Paulie and Jackson were moved twice by the cops with, "Get out of here, kids. Not a place for you."

Paulie told Jackson they probably thought, as we are kids, we were going to grab a pocketbook or something, but the cops weren't really being mean to them.

After two hours the boys rode back over the bridge and congregated outside the game store. Jackson said, "This is gonna be hard. It won't be crowded like this after this weekend and more of the locals will going there. But school starts in a week, so we'll miss the lunch crowd and that's when you'd see a local businessman."

Wayne was certain there were problems in the plan and said, "We're doing it wrong here. I know he's local. He's a businessman or a lawyer or a politician. I think one of us should go to City Hall. We don't know all the politicians and players. Every politician according to my dad has a camp of followers. We can pretend we're doing a civics paper; get pictures of all the bigwigs. The guy's not the mayor, I've seen him; but maybe he's one of the mayor's honchos. One of us can do reconnaissance, like Special Forces or CIA or FBI, by the courts in case he's a lawyer; but maybe he doesn't go to court. My dad says practically no one goes to court anymore. Whoever this guy is, he's over here, because he's not in West Side. I would have seen him if he were from West Side. I think he's from over the bridge in Springfield; it makes the most sense. We have a week at lunch to spot him."

Jackson was frustrated and responded, "This is not going to work. I'll do lunch hour for us all down by the casino next week. That means I'll hit Red Rose and AC Produce and Mom & Rico restaurants at the same time. One of you has to go by the Fort Restaurant and one of you down by the entrance to the casino and the Starbucks on Columbus Ave. He's going to be a walker, not a driver."

Wayne interrupted, bringing Paulie and Jackson up to date and furthering his thoughts. After fifteen minutes of vigorous discussion, they reassessed their plans deciding that the type of guy they were looking for was either a victim of habit who went to the same restaurant most days, or a jumper hitting different ones. So, Paulie figured, "No need to be the same place every day. Jackson should stay by the casino because he's the least suspicious looking one of us. He can hit those restaurants. Wayne should hit City Hall and see what he can do. I'll hit all the downtown lawyers' offices selling candy; give them the ole 'help me play soccer this year routine.' Should work."

And the boys went about their business.

Rudy was in the operations room reviewing the home invasion file. Murmuring, but loud enough to be heard, he said, "It smells like the Russians are looking for drug suppliers, but I believe that here is a little production section of Puerto Rico, not a Russian section."

He heard Juan's voice behind him retort, "Captain, there has been underground chat that Petro Gavel and Hector Ramirez have been seen together and they are not natural partners. It's got to be a supply chain problem for them to work together. Spruce Street is in Hector's arena, but Puerto Ricans generally don't do invasions like that here in West Side. So, I agree, but it's got to be a pretty big problem for those two to join ranks."

Beauregard actually raised his voice, reciting, "Drugs, drugs, drugs! I'm sick of this shit poisoning our citizens. Hector was always behind the cocaine coming in from the islands and Mexico. Is he still mainly cocaine? And this kid, they found, is it related to this?"

Lilly, who had been silent but listening, answered, "I know nothing about the girl, Captain; that's Mason's shtick, but no to your other question. Every purveyor on the street is into everything; from OxyContin to heroin to marijuana. There are many sources of Oxy, or O.C. available. The street buys from patients who are on prescriptions and don't need them, gets them from thefts from pharmacies, hospitals, doctors, and even from federal hospitals. That's the easy route, and you have to remember the manufacturer is in Connecticut. The deal is if there is an authorized buy from the manufacturer, the feds don't follow up that carefully about what happens. I read one clinic doctor prescribed over 11,000 OxyContin pills in 2016, worth a street value of six million dollars.

"If I get a prescription for ten pills sold by the pharmacy for four dollars each, I can resell them for forty dollars each giving a profit for my little prescription of three hundred and sixty dollars. Half a week's pay and nobody will ever know; enough to keep me in chronic pain and tied to my doctor for a long time. That's a supplemental salary for anyone and most of these patients see nothing wrong with it. They don't realize Oxy killed 53,000 people in the US in 2016. That's a lot of killing."

"Lilly, I thought you were in Vice, not Narcotics."

"Before I was on the force, I was a pharmaceutical rep. Learned a lot out there. Never wanted to be in Narcotics, Captain; you see the living dead there. Here in MCU, they're dead already. Somehow I handle it better than dealing with people knowingly killing themselves or others."

Juan said, "Lilly, you left pharmaceutical sales for the department? What were you thinking? Lot of money's made in drug sales."

She laughed. "Juan, I did well dollar wise, but believe it or not I'm a people person. In sales you're always at a conference making the best connection; you're always wearing three to four-inch heels trying to look better than the competition; you have to wait in clinics, hospitals and doctors' offices at their available times; and you can't give out the perks that used to be given. Often you invite people out on your own tab, so it doesn't go through the firm, just your own tax return. The company reimburses those expenses if you get a sale. I was a born entrepreneur and did very well because I'd risk my own money, but I saved and got out of the industry. It's even harder now to do well in sales with all the controls being put in place. Actually, the industry needs more controls on truth in advertising their drugs. My history with my grandfather as a cop in New York City was important to me; and, well, I think policing is an honorable profession despite what the press says."

The captain said, "So, back to who shot my detectives and how do we get them? And is this dead girl case related to what's going on? I hate coincidence. Do we have the ME report yet on her, Mason? Who is she? Do we know that yet?"

Mason answered, "Not yet, Captain. There is a lead. A bracelet was found at the scene."

Juan said, "Call Narcotics Captain Chilicot; there's a CI there who'll know who could have done it." Lilly agreed.

The captain said, "Is his code name 'Putin'?"

The two detectives were amazed the captain was connected enough to know about 'Putin'.

Juan said, "Yeah, Captain, but how did you know? I thought it was a state secret."

Beauregard said, "And you two are in on state secrets and I'm not; how do you compute that?"

Not waiting for an answer Beauregard said, "I'm to meet with him today in a rather strange place for a meeting at a little restaurant called 'EATS' in East Springfield. He called me. Until then I never heard of him. He said we could go out through the kitchen to a little back area to talk and have lunch."

Petra knew the place and agreed Putin had made a good choice. She said, "That's interesting, Captain, that he would call you. A CI would not have a discussion with another cop without his handler's permission."

"If it's our own Chilicot who is his handler, I wonder why he didn't call me." Beauregard continued, saying, "This thing is bigger, I just know it's bigger. It's outside of our department; otherwise, Chilicot would have called."

An hour later found Beauregard entering this small but busy restaurant. It had taken him less than ten minutes to drive there for the meet with the criminal informant 'Putin'. He was completely thrown off his stride when he recognized Putin. Enough to make him blurt out, "You were fuckin' there, and you didn't report it. What the hell were you thinking?"

Putin was shocked Beauregard knew him. Without answering he moved them through the kitchen into the back outside patio where Beauregard pushed him against the wall. "You better have a fuckin' great story. You were there and left my guys bleeding on the back stairway. CI or not, you're a punk. Spit it out."

Putin did not lose his cool. He remarked, "It's difficult to explain when you're choking me, Captain Beauregard."

Beauregard let go of Putin's neck but still provided a major block of any escape action, thinking, *this is why I didn't get his name from Narcotics. They were sitting on it until I cooled down. No wonder the police aren't trusted. My guys could have been my family who were just in the wrong place in a narcotics set-up.* He nodded for Putin to spill his guts and he did.

"Captain Beauregard, I called it in as I was running to my car. I couldn't help them anymore than that. I saw they would live. I've been out there in the wilderness for three years; I'll not blow it. The guys who shot your detectives are both Dominicans, not Puerto Ricans. That's why not one of the people living on Spruce Street will give you information. These Dominicans are new to the area and they are members of an assassination for hire group from the island; they just kill to instill fear. The Russian and Puerto Rican factions in the business are now using some Dominicans to get product through Mexico and into the States and not just overland, but through fishing and entering offbeat ports through a Caribbean route. The Mexicans are working with them in Mexico; not here. I believe they think the Caribbean route will work to access Europe as well as the U.S. I have most of the routes identified; just looking for two other shippers. We generally know all the locals in the trade, except that in the last few years Mexicans have moved into Springfield. On the whole they are really good family people and workers; but now that they are ensconced in the city, the Dominicans are grabbing their personal info and bringing some bad dudes in as relatives. No one says no to this group of Dominicans in town. They're part of this new business model with lots of low-level managers and no easy path to the guys running the business. No one squeals because there is always a relative in Mexico who will suffer if anyone here talks. Normally the Mexicans only kill people in Mexico, but the Dominicans have no trouble in killing *Norte Americanos in the U.S.*"

Beauregard demanded, "So who are the bastards who shot my detectives? And will you testify?"

"It's a problem, Captain. I'll tell you who they are. I'll even tell you how to catch them in another situation, but if I testify, all my work will be for nothing. I can't do that. You have got to understand, I can't throw away all of this; besides, the FBI won't let me testify. They'll be contacting you on this. Loughman, the head of the FBI Drug Task Force for this whole area, says to tell you that you had better keep this under your hat or else. His words, Captain, not mine; and he doesn't want to talk to you about it, which means he doesn't want to be included in people who denied help in a police shooting investigation. You get it!"

Beauregard blustered before saying in a hoarse whisper, "So my guys don't count; the blue line has disappeared. If it were FBI agents, he wouldn't say this. Fuck you all; you're not on my side; I don't even recognize you as good guys; I can tell you that. Together we could have figured out a way to protect you and prosecute these assholes who are so stupid they shoot two detectives in daylight, when they weren't even after them."

"Wrong there, Captain! The detectives were on their trail; these punks who shot your detectives did the home invasion. You made assumptions the Russians did the home invasion; well this group of Dominicans does whatever is necessary. The Mexicans don't like to kill over here; they murder family members in Mexico for retaliation. The Russians only do home invasions as a collection device. These are Dominicans in the drug business. They are just now hitting your city. I'm not surprised you didn't know; probably your Narcotics Division is just now getting some hints about the Dominican action and influence."

"Wrong, Putin, my detectives already are aware the Dominicans are in town."

Beauregard continued. "I want these guys, and I don't care who says or does what; I'm going after them. You help me or your cover's blown. I don't give a fuck about drugs; I care for my detectives. Help me or you are blown; get it? I mean it."

"Look, Captain, I get it and I agree. I am way up in the business side of this empire and it is a distribution empire. I am considered an ordinary businessman by other businessmen in the city. I'm just a guru on transportation. I serve on several non-profit boards. I'm on the City Council's task force on gambling in Springfield. I'm so clean I squeak; except I'm a CI. Why do I do it? I'll tell you.

"I'm one of seven kids of Irish immigrants. Three of my siblings are dead from drugs. I have eighteen nieces and nephews who could be next. That's why I'm doing it; not for the thrill. As far as your detectives are concerned, their shooters will be dead by six a.m. tomorrow. I'll give you their names, but I promise you will not get to them before a Dominican team will get them. They are Bruno Polanco and Jimmy Jimenez. I raised hell with the Mexicans; told them they had to control the Dominicans they used. They can't do it and nobody can do it but the Dominicans. My meet at Spruce Street was supposed to be with two higher level guys. Instead I was sent Polanco and Jimenez, supposedly to give them hell for the home invasion. They could also have been there as bodyguards for the big guys and that's why they acted out. The big guys never came because the shooting stopped them. Your detectives climbed the back stairs and all hell broke loose. All the Dominicans would have had to do was leave by the front door, but they apparently thought the place was surrounded. They're dead by tomorrow; not to worry, Captain."

A very red-faced Captain Beauregard snarled, "That's not going to serve for justice in my book. I'll take care of this. Now get out of my sight." And with a fist he added, "Not another word, Putin."

Beauregard returned to the restaurant, while Putin left with his take-out salad; a weekly ritual for him. There were several other patrol officers chatting up the waitress while Beauregard waited for his order. He texted Petra and Mason requesting they use every resource to find Polanco and Jimenez. He would wait for info and meet them. Next, he called Springfield MCU Detective Joe Stellato and said they soon would have the address of the shooters and would text it to him, saying, "Meet us there with some uniforms in an unmarked car."

Fifteen minutes later he had an address. It was less than ten minutes when three unmarked cars approached a rehabbed four family apartment building near the Water Shops section of the city. Mason walked over to the captain and said, "I've got this, Captain. You and Petra just stick out here," as he removed his sports jacket, pulled his tight afro loose, and walked the walk.

Neither Petra nor Beauregard ever saw the actor in Mason before. Stellato said, "Christ, the college boy looks like a ghetto drunk. Did he do undercover for you, Rudy?"

"Nah, not Mason, he doesn't like field work; likes his computers."

Mason headed for the package store, bought a bottle of wine in a bag, and slowly, very slowly circled the specified destination building. He thought, *no security, no guys sitting outside – therefore no production or sales going on. We got this address too easily if it's where they live. Supposedly the second floor is their home. Too much stuff on the roof; HVAC and birdcages but no drop-down ladders and no fire escape; however, there are three exits from every unit including one from each back porch. I think I'll just settle back here on this tree stump and watch.* He texted the Captain with 'All is quiet.' The other cars had parked in the nearby old school parking lot behind trees.

The wait took about thirty minutes, at which time a large Black Durango SRT, all showy, pulled into the apartment parking lot. Two men with long leather jackets got out to enter the building. The weather was too warm for long leather jackets. The men did not match the description of Polanco and Jimenez. Mason texted the Captain, Stellato, and the others and informed them about the potential home invasion. The captain decided Petra should stand alone by the side door with a view of the Durango while Stellato and his uniforms led the captain and Mason into the building following behind the two invaders. Springfield Lieutenant Stellato knew they were headed for more than an arrest and made a call for back-up.

By the time the Springfield contingency with Beauregard and Mason following them reached the second floor, the two home invaders had forced an apartment door open and were opening fire. Stellato shot the last man entering, hitting him in the chest as he turned when he heard the detectives behind him. There was more firing in the apartment, when Beauregard stepped over the second intruder's body. He shot the first intruder who was aiming at Stellato who had moved trying to get by the body. In ducking, the first intruder received the shot in his shoulder. He turned to shoot the captain, when one of the residents, who was wounded, fired the final shot that killed him. One resident was dead and the other severely wounded, but still was trying to shoot his weapon; a Sturm Ruger 9 MM. The captain stomped on his hand and removed the gun.

Petra entered the apartment and said, "Well we'd better have a story. Polanco, Jimenez and one of the assassins are dead with the other assassin barely alive; lots of bodies to explain. Why are there so many of us here questioning a suspect in our detectives' shooting; and just who are all these shooters? Best of all, is the question: how did we know where to find the perps who shot our detectives?"

Stellato said, "We did everything by the book. As to how you knew where to find the perps, inform me. I should have asked you. I thought we were just here for an arrest. But it's clear to me the two intruders were carrying their weapons by their side and meant to create chaos. We followed them in and the crime was in progress. We never expected this; else why did we leave Petra outside?"

"Yeah, Captain, just why did you all leave me outside?"

"Cause, I got the news, Petra, 'cause I got the news. There are two of you now. No more dangerous situations for you for the next eight months, and don't argue."

No one had ever seen Detective Petra Aylewood-Locke blush a bright pink before as she muttered, "Damn department, there are no secrets and no personal life. How did you know? Did my husband Jim tell you; if he did, I'll kill him!"

Before Beauregard could answer, the Springfield Police had five squad cars and a couple of detective cars screaming outside with Loughman, head of the local FBI drug task force riding shotgun in one of them.

In questioning later, detectives from the Narcotics Divisions of both West Side and Springfield told Stellato they had seen the two perps, the detectives' shooters before, but could never get them on anything.

What was a revelation to the West Side detectives was the sight of FBI Task Force Head Loughman congratulating Captain Beauregard on his quick action in catching the home invaders who shot his detectives. Accompanying him was a member of the press who was speaking with the Springfield Chief of Police. That chief supported Loughman's claim and confirmed this was a two-city collaboration to capture the West Side detectives' assaulters. He proudly stated, "It just shows how successful this collaboration was in that two known hit men from out of town were caught and one of the original shooters was left. This attack was to stop the pair who brought too much attention to the region's drug trade and inadvertently shot the two West Side detectives in a mishap."

After due time, the West Side detectives left the building. Mason Smith verbalized their feelings with, "I'm an actor in an FBI stage play. What the fuck, we were set up to do this, Captain, but we don't know any more now than before. Good thing we brought Stellato and his men in and didn't do a loner. Yeah, we've killed some bad guys, but they won't let us near the wounded shooter, who could have told us more. It's not right, Captain. I know we could have been in bigger trouble, but we chose that. This is not right and we don't have answers."

4

Revelations

The dinner talk at Wayne Dion's house was from his perspective, 'boring'. His dad had received a report from his mom. Mrs. Loyal complained about him; that he was teasing their dog and Jackson and Wayne should take a break in their friendship. Wayne thought, *thank God, it's only the three of us tonight; Jocko and Phillip are at some computer workshop for geniuses. Dad's looking at me for a good answer. He knows the moms here are nuts. Mrs. Loyal wants to separate me from both of my two best friends.*

"Dad, Mrs. Loyal thinks I hurt the dog on purpose. I tripped over him and he cried and Jackson socked me for being careless and we got into a little fight and Mrs. Loyal is used to Chelsea who never got in a fist fight. Jackson and Paulie are my best friends."

Wayne realized very quickly that mentioning Paulie was a mistake. His mom broke in with, "I'm sure Paulie is a very nice friend, Wayne, but he lives in a side of town that makes me nervous."

"Ma, he's half Puerto-Rican and that makes you nervous. You can't be racist."

To stop this discussion in which Wayne knew his father would defend him making his mom start a war, he said, "Look, all me and

Jackson and Paulie did was draw this guy we saw. I think my drawing's the best. We love our art class and go over to the strip mall to get our supplies and draw faces. We don't get into trouble; we draw. This is pretty good, don't you think?"

Warren Dion pulled the picture away from Wayne and said, "Where'd you see this man, Wayne? I know him. It could only be him; if, as you say, this looks like him."

Wayne retorted in the quickest lie he could think of, "He was getting gas at the mall station. We decided to have a contest on who could draw him better. We each took a different view of his face like our art teacher told us; you know to learn to notice parts and not just the whole. Who is he, Dad?"

"That's John McKinney, a kid I grew up with in Springfield. He came from a big family. He's done well, but some of his brothers and sisters had problems. He owns a big transportation outfit up near the Chicopee line, but lives in West Side nearer Westfield. He's a good guy; just look at his face and you can tell."

Everything quieted down as Mrs. Dion purred at her son's talent. She thought, *I'll call Teresa and explain that the kids are really okay together; if all they're doing is art maybe even that Paulie is okay. I'll ask Teri to 'cool it.'*

After Wayne cleared the dishes he closeted his body in the shower so no one could hear him, knowing Jackson would also take the call in his bathroom, or not take the call, thinking, *what is it about these mothers today? They listen in, they watch, they call, and check on us with other mothers and our teachers about everything we do. No privacy for us. That must be why Dad has his man-cave, so Mom won't know everything going on in his world.*

Wayne filled Jackson in on his lie and laughed when Jackson said he had made up the exact same lie with a little bit more embellishment.

They both agreed Jackson was the better storyteller. He needed to be, with his mom. She was a truth finder, if ever there was one, was Wayne's conclusion. They ended their conversation with Wayne's plan. "You call Paulie and we'll all meet at the police station. I'm going to walk over to Captain Beauregard's house and get his eye. I hear him mowing his lawn. Normally his kids mow but tonight they're all gone. Jackson, you can't do it. Your mom is too friendly with Mrs. Beauregard and she'll want to know what you talked with him about. I think the captain can handle her, but you never know what's up with husbands and wives."

Wayne decided to ride his bike over and just stop by, chatting to be friendly. The captain looked twice at him and said, "Wayne, I didn't connect you that day until later when I saw your address. What's on your mind?"

"Can't talk now, Captain, but we'll be at your office at nine in the morning with our story. You'll be there, right?"

Beauregard decided this was serious business for the boys and it would not hurt to honor Wayne's professionalism and so he nodded his head in the affirmative and watched Wayne ride off. Not a person on the street noticed the interchange.

Captain Beauregard didn't have to wait a moment the next day upon entering the station before he found the boys waiting inside the door. The desk officer on duty said, "The boys say they have business with you, Captain. If not, I'll run them out of here."

The captain nodded to the boys who followed him inside MCU to the captain's private office. The kids noticed the other detectives' surprised looks. But the captain motioned him and his friends to get down to business and they told their story. Beauregard was taken back. He did not want this information out and now the three boys and Wayne's parents knew the man was John McKinney. He questioned them and breathed a sigh of relief at Wayne's lie. Finally, after thinking carefully and allowing silence to drag on in order to signal the kids this was a serious moment in time, the captain said, "You guys have worked undercover for Officer Simeon, but even he can't know about this operation. Mr. McKinney is not who you think and we have to protect him. I can't tell you why. You cannot tell anyone about his whereabouts on that day. That's an order from me; I'm your handler. Now you are not a CI, commonly called a confidential informant. You are an SOI, a source of information."

The captain saw the disappointment on the boys' faces and so he explained, "If you boys were CI's I'd have to register you with paperwork and all, and you're minors. You see my dilemma. You have done a good job, but the job is over. The shooters have been apprehended. So, for now just keep your eyes open for Officer Simeon and thanks; good job identifying this man. Please, however, get rid of any copies you have of Mr. McKinney' drawing; okay?"

The boys left feeling somewhat happy, but the captain did not tell them the connection Mr. McKinney had. Paulie could not resist. "He doesn't want us to know about Mr. McKinney. I'll bet he's a CI from Springfield. We could still follow him now that we know who he is and maybe find out what he's doing for the police. He shouldn't be in our town if he's a Springfield CI, so this must be a big drug case for a bunch of towns."

Wayne said, "My dad says he lives in West Side; that he was originally from Springfield. We could be wrong, but we have nothing else to do but this. There's only one more week before school starts, after which we will have Monday and Wednesday afternoons from three to five available after that. We can find out more about Mr. McKinney. Jackson, get on your computer and find out the name of the transportation company he owns. Chances are McKinney will do his dirty work at coffee break and lunch like the spies do on television. Find out where he lives since he supposedly lives in our city. We have to get to know him. Maybe people are following him."

The junior G-men, as they thought of themselves, and modeled themselves on the 'Half-Life' game's character of the powerful government bureaucrat, agreed.

Petra Aylewood was acting as if she had lost her best friend forcing Mason Smith, her colleague, to speak out. "Okay, Petra, so you're pregnant. Get used to a fat belly and a slower life. It's not the end of the world. I'll bring in pastry and you can eat till your heart's content. I like chunky women."

She yelled, "Sexual harassment, Mason, I'll get you on it yet!"

This remark left the two new detectives a little uncomfortable with Lilly loudly commenting, "I heard nothing. I'm a witness to nothing."

Mason said, "Not to worry, Lisa, she harasses me more than I ever harass her. Poor Petra has to pay the price for love - poor baby. Yeah, the poor baby, how you going to take care of a kid, Petra? You'll be jogging with the baby throwing up on your backside. I can't wait for this payback."

Petra threw a box of staples at him, which landed with a thump next to him. Juan decided they should get back to business and said, "So, our job is to figure out what's going on in the West Side drug trade that's new. I talked with the community police officers in the Spruce Street district and they confirmed an influx of what looked like commodity movers who were not Puerto Rican; some Dominican and some Russian and a few bikers. What have you seen, Mason; what noise on the computer have you got that may point to new hoods on the block?"

"I've seen some FB stuff from the Russians and it appears they're talking 'dark connections' which, they think they're so smart, means color connections. Nothing but family stuff from the Puerto Ricans and I can't decipher if it's truly family stuff or a doctored language for business. Juan, you should look at it. You'd know better."

"I'm Mexican, maybe I don't know the local code of Puerto Rican writing meant to hide meaning."

Mason laughed saying, "Yeah, but I don't speak Spanish; well a little maybe. You're it, Juan, pull your weight."

The two looked over some computer FB stuff Mason had saved, while Lilly called a Russian friend who worked in one of the stores in the strip mall, was a smoker, and therefore was outside her store three or four times a day for a smoke. Lilly thought, *she might know if there were unusual activities by the Russians in the area.*

Juan said to Mason while they were working the FB entries, "What about the Dominicans, Mason? You're originally from Springfield; what do you know about them?"

Mason said, "Sorry, Juan, they don't identify with the brothers; they're islanders. I don't know any of them personally but my cousin Latoya used to dance at one of the clubs and the manager threw a bunch of Dominican clients out because they were trying to hustle the dancers onto the street. She had a friend who married one and it's a closed shop when it comes to gossip; but I'll contact her, if she's still speaking to me, and see what I can do."

Mason and Juan, after an hour's work, came up with some chatter that did not make sense. When Juan translated the chatter, it referred to trucking loads into Springfield camouflaged as women's lingerie. They worked the material some more and it seemed there was a trucking to biker connection for moving goods. Bikers were from Northampton and Chicopee and were called 'Chicokers' and the trucking company was located in Springfield, but they found no reference to a name. They googled 'Chicokers' and found a biker group who'd rode in support of raising funds for kids who have cancer. That info made them unsure of their assumptions.

Petra listened to the discussions around her and was most interested in the one-way conversation she heard Lilly carrying on. She motioned to Lilly, who agreed to let her listen in. It was a revelation. Svetlana's observations were stunningly on point. She said, "Lilly, I know people from my old world who haunt the area about a hundred yards away. I do not care how well or poorly dressed or how Americanized the outfit, I know them. I can tell you there is some big money in town. In the last month I saw someone I know who now lives in Somers, Connecticut and for some reason is in and out of the coffee shop near here. It is not a Russian coffee shop and he is not always alone. The kind of money he is known to have has no source I know of; therefore, it is some criminal activity. Since he is not with women, it must be drugs."

Lilly asked, "Do you think you could identify him or take a picture? I don't want you to take any chances, Svetlana, so don't do it if it's chancy."

Svetlana not only had a deep throaty voice, but her laugh was hearty and pleasant when she said, "You think I am stupid, Lilly. In Russia a pretty girl is always taking selfies. Can I help it if I have selfies with all these men?" And she truly laughed for what seemed inordinately long.

Lilly asked if she could send the photos to her and the arrangements were made.

After the end of the conversation, Petra told Lilly, "Welcome, Detective, you've done good work here; nice to have you in MCU. The captain will love this. Now let's try to get a match of the big time Russians from Svetlana, who is sending pictures. Send them right over to Mason and he'll do his magic; for sure there should be one or two matches if these guys are legal."

Juan responded to an earlier question, saying, "Lieutenant, I'm Mexican and believe it or not there are more Dominicans here in western Massachusetts than Mexicans and of course many more Puerto Ricans. Mexicans up here are not as important lately in the drug trade as the Dominicans. In fact, it used to be that the Colombians would funnel drugs through Venezuela through Mexico, then that stopped, and now drugs are being pushed by and through the Caribbean by the Dominicans or coming through there from China. Finally, I'm not Russian. No different from you, Lieutenant, a Russian name is Greek to me, but I'll try."

Petra grimaced at her thoughts and said, "I'll ignore that remark, Detective, but I do remember back in 2010 when I was on the Boston force and there was this enormous drug bust of thirty-three pounds of fentanyl; enough to kill everyone in the city. That was when they were funneling drugs in by Mexico's Sinaloa Cartel."

Juan said, "You know in the last census, Springfield had only 1.7% Dominicans. But we know the Dominican portion of Hispaniola makes it the second largest country next to Cuba in the Caribbean, and the country's murder rate as of 2009 has risen to twenty-three out of every hundred thousand people. That rate implies big money and big drugs and big business over there. Just how the Russians mix, I don't know, except when we consider the European market stats I read. They listed the number of Blow users in Europe is about thirty-four billion dollars almost as big as the thirty-seven billion dollars in the North American market. Europe and Cuba need to join in the fight against drugs over here but they haven't so far; at least as far as I've heard."

The captain walked into the squad room or 'office hell' as some called it and motioned to the detectives saying, "All but Mason, we're going to visit our fallen. Lilly and Juan, you get to meet two great detectives.

Mason was there early this morning, so he can hold the fort here for an hour. Anything new you can fill me in on the way. We'll take one car.

"Mason, can you get a report on that dead girl please? We'll talk about it when I return."

5

Stake-outs

Jackson was able to get out earlier in the morning than either Wayne or Paulie. Wayne had to mow the lawn, whereas Jackson's mother thought the fancy lawnmower they had was too dangerous for Jackson. What Teri Loyal didn't know was that Jackson would mow other folks' lawns for money with the fancy lawnmower, which he would hide from his mom. Paulie had to mind Rosie until noon this day, so Jackson rode the seven miles to the Springfield-Chicopee Trucking Depot over by the Chicopee/Springfield line.

Jackson rode the old road rather than the highway so it took longer. He figured once he was over the bridge to Springfield, taking Chestnut Street to Carew to St. James Avenue to Page Boulevard was the best route for biking; but he was really tired as he approached his destination. He thought, *I must have gone seven miles and what is this mess on the left?*

Jackson noticed an old rundown shack with a sign saying, "Lunch" on the dirty window. There was a row of really nice motorcycles in front; Harley-Davidsons and some newer styles that looked more like a bike. He thought maybe a Suzuki and a Honda, but what really made an impression were four men in front of the building drinking beers. He mused, *they are rough looking and they're drinking beer at only quarter to ten in the morning. The Trucking Depot is next door. Are they lookouts for the Trucking Depot? Nah, probably just my imagination Mom's always complaining about. But I don't want to get on their wrong side; better I just wave at them.*

Jackson yelled, "Boy, I wish I had one of those beauties. My dad says they cost a lot."

A big massive guy with a crazy red beard yelled back, "Go to work, kid, and make some money. These bikes are expensive."

Jackson nodded and kept going. He thought again, *it's a good thing I look skinny and young. Don't want them to think I know anything.*

Jackson passed the dirty wooded barrier between the bikers' parking area and the Trucking Depot just as a trailer truck passed him. Jackson slowed down and cut into the Depot parking lot where there was a lot of foliage hanging over the fence. He found a spot hidden from view, moved a big spider web away and ate his morning snack he'd grabbed from the house before leaving. He was now ready to stakeout the goings on at Mr. McKinney's place hoping to get a clue as to McKinney's schedule. He quickly realized the movement of the many massive trucks often hid the employee entrance from view. He could not see any other entrances other than all the truck bays. He looked for a fancy car thinking Mr. McKinney would own one, but only saw the usual Hondas, Toyotas, Fords, and a few small pick-up trucks.

He sat back and waited hoping the seven miles he rode were not ridden in vain. He'd nodded off a bit, when he heard some men come through the bushes behind him to the left. He saw two of the bikers. He scrunched up as small as he could thankful for having carefully hidden his bike earlier. The two bikers were entering the back of what appeared to be a closed in trailer that earlier Jackson noticed and could not see anything in it. He was wrong. The men came out of the trailer with large green garbage bags and walked back through the woods.

They returned three times and brought more bags out until they did not return. Jackson was quite proud of himself thinking, *I got a good picture of them, although mostly a three-quarter side view, and of what they were doing. For sure it's drugs. Captain Beauregard will now see we are good at this.*

Paulie met Wayne down by the casino entrance. They walked over to the South Market in the casino which both speculated would be a place where Mr. McKinney might have lunch. The boys were disappointed Jackson got to see the drug operation and sent them pictures; although both agreed the bikers, if they caught on to the kids, might present a serious problem for them. Wayne said, "If we get in trouble with bikers, our mothers will keep us in home jail forever."

After an hour waiting until, with frustration, finally agreeing they could only stay another twenty minutes, a limo pulled up and several men dressed like businessmen got out with Mr. McKinney the last one. One looked Dominican to Paulie and he got a picture of all their faces by looking like he was holding his hoodie up to inspect for some damage to it as if he'd ever care. There were four men in all and one of the four, although dressed well, looked uncomfortable in his threads. Wayne remembered his art teacher talking about modelling, "A good model looks like he or she belongs in what is being worn. You shouldn't see the dress before the model, despite what designers want you to see. If the model doesn't look like she or he belongs in the outfit, then design goes out the window." One of these guys does not belong in his clothes was the thought on which both boys agreed.

Later, Him, Me and Paulie met in West Side at McDonald's getting dollar deals; their parents would be aghast seeing them indulge in such questionable eating habits, if they were ever in the know. The trio summed up what they just witnessed. They agreed there was still some time to go see Captain Beauregard before they had to be home, but thought they should call him first. Wayne volunteered to call the cell number he had been given. Captain Beauregard answered with, "Beauregard here." And there was silence until Wayne said, "This is Wayne and we have good information for you. Where can we meet? Should we go to the station?"

Wayne and the other two boys presented a dilemma for Beauregard. He had told them to report to Community Police Officer Simeon, but realized maybe this was something more; something that could not be shared with community policing if it was about McKinney. His gut instinct said it was about McKinney. He said, "I'll be riding by Hoffington Park in five minutes. Can you get there?" They assured him they would be there in seven minutes.

At the park the captain addressed them in a very serious tone, "I thought I told you I didn't want you doing any investigations; just to watch out for anything unusual. What's going on?"

Paulie was adamant about their work saying, "We got a lot for you, Captain Beauregard. We didn't take any chances. Don't worry." And the boys showed him the pictures and told him their stories.

The captain had them forward their pictures and sat back saying, "Your work is of the highest caliber, but underage witnesses are useless in court. I applaud you, but Jackson what you did is dangerous. I can't have it happen again. This matter is dangerous for adults, let alone kids your age. Promise me you won't do any more investigation into this matter. I'm telling you if you do – well, then, I'll have to have a talk with your parents and we don't want that. Not as a punishment, but as a protection. You guys are good guys and we need all the good guys alive. Promise?"

All the air went out of the boys' balloon of self-importance, but not one of them wanted their parents involved, and so they promised.

After Captain Beauregard drove away, Paulie said, "He forgot to erase our pictures. We still have them. Captain Beauregard is fifty if he's a day; dudes that age don't always think about this stuff; any kid would know enough to erase our photos. Let's go over to the print shop on the strip and print these out. I've got five bucks that will cover it. We can ask around about these guys. One is Dominican for sure, one is Russian I think, and is the other really business looking guy, other than Mr. McKinney, I've seen around in West Side. Let's find them before the captain I.D.s them. What say? I've seen on tv that undercover guys work the field and find things out 'Control' can't find out. In the spy stories, 'Control' is there for protection. Also, we'll find these guys and maybe follow them. That's called following the 'Rabbit'."

An agreement was reached amongst the boys; all hoped their parents would never know what they were up to.

The next day, Captain Beauregard sent the pictures to Mason for identification. He called Lieutenant Stellato in Springfield Major Crimes and asked if the casino folks shared photos when there was a police investigation in need. Stellato said, "That's a problem, Beauregard. They're not going to report a big roller, and unless it's a current murder, I don't think I have the connections to make them give up photos. Give me a hook to work with. Is it related to your detectives again? You know we're off that. It's the Feds you have to talk with."

"Nope, it's related to some drug problems here in West Side, but if you can't help, you can't help." Rudy clicked off the phone and thought, *this is not going to be easy. I should never have called him. Shit, first I have junior investigators getting me answers and now I realize any questions I ask about anything will be deemed connected to the shootings of my detectives. Something is going on in West Side and that something is going to blow up big; I can just feel it.*

Beauregard headed to the station comfortable that in his visit earlier to the hospital both his detectives were on their way to recovery. He was also pleased there were two new additions to the MCU team, although he felt some guilt that the shooting of his detectives enabled the additions. At the hospital Ash Lent had said, "Hell, Captain, we have to get shot for the chief to give us more manpower."

Ash spent much of his time, blaming his slow recovery, which wasn't slow, on the pain medication, and his intrinsic need to harass Petra. He kept stating, "Petra, will you look like a pear or an apple in six months? Just can't wait to see the beautiful Petra slow down and give kisses and hugs to us all. That poor slob, your husband Jim! Well, we should all thank God he's a psychologist. He'll survive, ha, ha, ah!"

The ah! was after Petra threw his rubber exercise ball at him. Beauregard mused, *it's all good. Let Lilly and Juan see that this is a close unit, totally loyal to each other; like a family; just the way I like it.*

A signal 7 was sounded calling all cars to 27 Fir Street for a shooting in progress. He turned his car and headed to the address noting it was only four blocks away from Spruce Street. He wondered, *awful close. Could it be connected?*

Petra and the new detectives beat him to the punch. They greeted him with, "One guy looks like the Dominican you asked Mason to identify. The other is a low-level wannabe. He's white. I don't know what he was doing with the Dominican. Both are dead, Captain, and there's a woman who's also shot on the sidewalk. She could have been running when she heard the shots or she's connected. She doesn't have a pocketbook with her which makes me think she may have been with the guy in the car and just ran. She's pretty seriously wounded. There is no car near here that appears to be the victims' car, but we're searching the lot across the street in the mall for a vehicle. Mason is working on IDs."

Beauregard's reaction was instant. "Fucking drugs bringing lowlifes and violence here as they bring to wherever the trade is. We're in trouble. I think the Dominican's dead because he ordered the two guys to Spruce Street for a conference, who in fear, shot our cops. We had no info on who put the order in; and we never got the chance to interrogate the guy left alive in the apartment building. The Feds and Loughman took care of that. Don't know if these other two are just dead because they saw the shooter. Are there any bystanders who may have seen something?"

Lilly answered, "Yeah, Captain, there are three kids over in the parking lot outside of the print shop who said they'll only talk to you. They must have seen something. How do they know you?"

Captain Beauregard muttered a low but agonizing groan without answering Detective Tagliano, and carefully found his way across the busy street to the strip mall parking lot thinking, *we're damn lucky the Big E exposition hasn't started yet. I wouldn't be able to get across the street then. I'm going to kill those kids; why didn't they go home after our talk? If they're witnesses to this, I have a lot of explaining to do.*

The boys were not nervous to see the captain; they were excited. Wayne said, "We saw the get-away car, Captain. It was right in front of the lot. The girl was running towards it when the Dominican, who we thought was dead, shot her. The other guy, who shot the Dominican and the white guy with the Dominican, had jeans and a black windbreaker on. We thought when the guy got out of the car with the girl, that it was strange. It's ninety-two degrees out; why wear a windbreaker. Then the guy from the car pulled a gun out of his jacket; that's when we knew there was a reason for his wearing the windbreaker. He shot the other two and he and the girl headed back to the car. The shooter was opening the driver's door when the Dominican who was not dead shot the girl. We all saw it and we all agree on the facts. We can draw the shooter; maybe."

The captain asked the boys, "How do you know the dead guy's Dominican?"

Paulie answered, "I saw him good, Captain, and he's Dominican just the way he walked and acted in the lot. If you want we can just say he's black or dark skinned. I know about this politically correct stuff; that we can't just say anything. Besides, he looks like one of the guys in the photo from the casino, Captain."

The captain wanted to kill his witnesses but just sighed, thinking, *the stars, as my Mona would say, are aligned against me. Time to accept my destiny!*

He told the boys to give a full report on this afternoon's events omitting their worry over politically correct thoughts. He said, "The rest of the report has been taken by me. Was the shooter white or Dominican or Puerto Rican, do you think?"

All three boys said, "White, Captain; golf club type of white."

The Captain thought, *A new description for white. Is there also a black golf club type given Tiger Woods' success?*

Detective Aylewood took the boys' report and despite her many questions asked, she received consistent answers from all three. From her experience, three different people rarely agree on all the facts on an incident. She told the boys that and Jackson answered, "That's because we're artists and have good visual memories. Our art teacher has taught us to look for details and we do."

Petra was just about to let it go when she saw attorney Norberto Cull approach the kids and her. He seemed to know the kids so she said, "Well, Attorney Cull, how can I help you today?"

He bowed slightly and said, "I know Jackson's mom through Mona Beauregard. When I saw you talking to Jackson and his friends and all the police cars over there at what I have been told by my police scanner is a triple homicide, well I came over to see if they need help."

Jackson said, "It's okay, Mr. Cull. We just saw the shooting. We were over here across the street from the lot. Our mothers will kill us. We were in the print store and had just come out when it happened. Detective, we don't have to be taken home by you, do we?"

Before she could answer, Attorney Cull said, "Nah, I'll take you home. Put your bikes on the rack on my car. Better you get a ride home with me rather than the police. You've done nothing wrong. I'll explain it to your parents. Will that be okay with you, Detective?"

Detective Aylewood-Locke considered the reports she would have to make and the time it would take to talk with three sets of parents and decided the kids were in good hands with Attorney Cull. She nodded her okay.

In Cull's car, Jackson begged him not to tell their mothers, "Mr. Cull, they'll have us under house arrest for just going to the copy store. Do you think that's right? Please don't tell them."

Norbie Cull pulled his car over and faced the three boys. "Look, guys, in case you don't know, I am a criminal defense attorney. Do you know what that means?" Before they could answer, he continued, "It means I have a lot of experience with murderers and robbers and home invaders. It means I know you may be able to identify the shooter. It means your parents have a right to keep you under house arrest for a while until the police can sort this out and find another person from that parking lot who can identify this shooter. Do you get me? This is serious."

All three boys nodded, but Paulie was not to be prevented from saying, "I know the woman who was killed. She lives on Spruce Street, four houses down from where the detectives were shot. Mr. Cull, she was not the kind of woman to be with the shooter. She's just a low life hooker type; not a golf club type. We think the Dominican shot her because she was only with the shooter to identify the Dominican."

Norbie looked sternly at Paulie and said, "Paulie, Jackson and Wayne, am I right on your names?" With their nod, he said, "Get me when I say… do you understand… this is very serious. Keep your thoughts to yourself. I'll check in on you every night. There had better be no more investigating or I'll get involved. One thing would be good, if as I understand you draw people well, is that you would draw the white guy you said was the shooter. Other than that, if you see anything you don't like going on around you, call the captain or me. Here is my card with my cell number on it. Text if I don't answer. Do you have Captain Beauregard's number?"

When they answered yes, Norbie thought, *since when does an MCU Captain give his cell phone out to a bunch of kids. There's more going on here.*"

Norbie spent the next three hours reassuring parents about their children but also insisting they keep an eye on them for a few weeks. He repeated over and over, "Sometimes we're just inadvertent witnesses." Although he did not believe this was the case in this situation.

After leaving Paulie's parents and assessing they were a lot smarter about this issue than the other parents, Norbie called Rudy and had a discussion. Norbie shared the identity of the woman killed, but did not say the info was from the kids; just said one of the on-lookers in the parking lot said he thought she lived on Spruce Street. He felt that would be enough for the cops to find her. He noticed Rudy was antsy about the kids and thought, *there is definitely more I don't understand. I went to high school with Teresa Loyal and I feel a duty to protect these kids.*

On his way home, Norbie stopped by the grocery store. He had been instructed by his wife Sheri to stop and pickup one-half gallon of unsweetened thirty calorie almond milk and cold-pressed cocoa. He knew, *I'll never find the second item but I have to try. She'll want to be sure I completely searched the hot beverage aisle.* And then he was saved from his quandary, he thought, but in the end not saved at all.

Angela Monroe, one of his not so near but near enough neighbors, was calling and she had a crisis. "Norbie, Candace is missing. I called the police early this morning and they said to wait a little while to be sure she isn't just with friends. If I report it, they'll put it on NCIC, the National Crime Information Center. Barry doesn't think that's a good idea. We need you to go to the police station for us. See what can be done, please, Norbie. You know our Candace, Norbie. She's a good girl. She doesn't even have a special boyfriend. She's a serious soccer player."

Norbie said, "Slow down, Angela, I'll take a ride over to the station and have a talk with them. Can you text me a picture and the names of some of her friends with contact info? Do it right now. I'll call you in an hour."

Angela agreed still crying and whispering, "I have a bad feeling about this, Norbie, a bad feeling."

Norbie was at the station and parked in eight minutes; *a record,* he thought. Millie met him and said the captain would be in shortly. Norbie asked how Ash and Ted were doing and Millie appeared to be appreciative of his concern. They were interrupted by Petra Aylewood-Locke who had just returned from the murder site. "Attorney Cull, kind of suspicious seeing you, a defense attorney, twice in an hour. I hope you're not defending the perp in this case. I have nothing to tell you and I doubt the captain will have anything to say."

Norbie was miffed with Petra and confused. His annoyance showed as he said, "Detective, I know the rules and don't need to be reminded; further you know that. I have to believe you're still upset about Ash's and Ted's shootings. I get that. I'm here because a good friend and neighbor reported their daughter's disappearance today. I'd like some help. I know it's not likely to be an MCU's case, but I think she's not the kind of kid to get in trouble. Before it goes on NCIC, I thought we could see if you've heard anything about missing kids. Maybe she's not the only one. I have her picture here and the names of some friends. This is important, Detective; she's only about fifteen years old."

Petra felt rebuffed and further thought Cull was right, thinking, *I'm being bitchy. My mom says it goes along with pregnancy. I can't be this way. I should know better; Cull would never take a shortcut with staff.*

She asked Millie, "Anything going on with missing juveniles in the station, Millie?"

Millie said, "Mason's out at the river where a young girl was found in suspicious circumstances. They estimated she was about sixteen years old or thereabout."

Norbie said, "Does Mason have a picture he can send or can you send this picture of Candace and see if it matches. What's your cell; I'll text it. I hope like hell this picture doesn't match, but I have to know. Just send this picture to him."

Millie told Petra, "May I speak with you about another pressing issue now?" And they both moved into the captain's office to talk.

Millie had received some info about the scene from Mason; one item described was a bracelet that said, 'Candace 10-12-02'. "Petra, it may be the girl he's looking for. She'll be sixteen and Candace is not a name you see every day."

Petra called Mason because he had not sent any pictures, just sent a rough description stating this death was a potential homicide with some of the details. She forwarded the request to Mason by text and called him to tell him to pay attention to the text. He checked her texted picture and immediately called her, "It's probably the same girl, Petra."

Captain Beauregard had returned and was speaking with Norbie in Millie's office. Updated on Norbie's mission, he was about to escort Norbie to his office when Petra and Millie entered the room. He knew as did Norbie, just by looking at them, they had bad news.

The captain said, "We'll contact the family later when we confirm identification. You don't have to tell them, Norbie; we should do it and will have to when we know for certain."

Norbie shook his head and said, "No, I'm doing it now, Rudy. They're my friends and this shouldn't happen to any family. I feel certain it's Candace and they should know sooner than later. I'll tell them to expect your call and that I hope I'm wrong. Candace was a great kid. I won't get in your way with this, Rudy, but I'll need to know more, if you're not able to quickly discover what happened to her. It would be helpful if you tell me what you know now. The family needs to have some info."

Rudy said, "We don't know much now. We'll know more after the medical examiner does her work. She's good, Norbie."

Norbie left the station, sat in his car and ruminated on the little girl who always had a lemonade stand with her brother when she was eight. That whole summer cost him a buck a day to keep her happy as he drove by her house on the way home from work. She did drive-time in the afternoon, setting up her stand from four to six every afternoon. The girl became a soccer nut and he saw less of her. One of his sons was her friend. He had trouble holding back his tears as he said to no one in particular out there, *fucking life. This will destroy them. She was a rising star. She sold Girl Scout cookies and was a great salesgirl. Later she ran car washes for soccer and candy sales for her church. It's suspicious, this death. Candace would not be at the river by herself. She was healthy. Rudy is not telling me anything, and I know from Petra's reaction this is at least a suspicious death. Who the hell is on that detail in that district; community police would have been called right away? After I see Angela and Barry, I'll hit Moriarty's, the West Side cops' bar.*

Better yet, I'll call Jim Locke. Most cops forget he's not still a detective and is now a PI. He's the best choice and he would go the distance for a dead little girl.

6

Beautiful Girl Dead

Angela and Barry opened the door before Norbie could knock. Although he thought he presented a demeanor lacking in emotion, they knew. He thought, *I've given it away. They know. Their faces have practically collapsed. Gareth, Candace's brother, is behind his dad and even he knows I have the worst news. How do I get in off this stoop? This is not the place to talk.*

Angela without addressing the issue had the presence to say, "Come in, Norbie." Crying softly, she moved Barry, Gareth, and herself aside enough to let him find his way into the big room, the name they had for their family room. He'd been here many times before for family parties; they were that close. He was thinking, *I haven't told Sheri yet. She'll be devastated. This kind of loss of a beautiful child has reverberations far outside the family. I'm devastated. I'd rather be anywhere but here. I hate this part of what I do; give bad news. Who ever thought that bad news would be delivered here?*

Before Norbie could even sit, Gareth said, "She's dead, isn't she? Candace is dead."

Gareth's verbalization resulted in Angela wailing loudly and falling into Barry's arms. Barry and Gareth cried but very quietly. After what

62

seemed to Norbie a long time, but actually allowed him a moment to recover from witnessing their pain, Norbie told them Candace, and it was Candace, was found by the river. They found her identification bracelet in her pocket. Norbie said, "I believe the death is suspicious. Right now, the police will not tell me or anyone anything. You will be called to identify the body, and will be questioned; all of you. Do not talk to anyone without me there. The press may try to interpret lack of information into a horrible scene, but I think unfortunately there is a not so nice story here. You will have to say I represent you. To do that you will have to sign one of my forms. Barry, there is no charge for my services. I want to help you. I am going to try to do some investigating on my own to see just what the police are thinking. They will tell us later, but we need to know now what's up. I have to prepare you for the public's analyzing this in the news.

"Do not talk with your neighbors. You are in mourning. You do not have to explain. Only answer the phone for family. I'll come by in the morning at ten and tell you what I have learned. If the police come by and ask any of you to come into the station, tell them to call me and I will make arrangements."

Barry took the paper Norbie had taken from his jacket and without reading it, signed it and had Angela sign it. He must have watched television shows because he gave Norbie five dollars. The grasping of legal and business logic by Barry despite his loss brought tears to Norbie's eyes.

Norbie asked them what they knew of Candace's plans for that day and when they had last seen her.

Angela explained Candace left for school, which was not in session yet, but some of the clubs were meeting to plan for the semester. She left at 7:15, and that inspired her to question her daughter. Candace said, "I have something to take care of for school and it's really important.

I won't be there all morning." Angela said she assumed Candace was going to school to do some big project.

"Look, Norbie, she was second in her class in school. We never had any idea about her schoolwork. She was way ahead of us. Then she didn't come home for lunch and wouldn't answer our calls. I had Gareth call all her friends, even what he called the 'Geeky' ones who would be working on projects before school started. Frustrated and worried, I called the principal and he said that yesterday, not today, was the only day the school was open for students working on projects for clubs. That's when I knew there was something wrong. I called Barry and we called the police. They insisted she was probably off with a boyfriend, but that's not our Candace."

"Tell me what she was wearing, and can you give me a better picture of her please?"

Gareth said, "She had on jeans with holes in them and a T-shirt that said, 'Women have five letters making them bigger than men.' She was nuts on the women's rights movement and the 'ME TOO' business and any group that was active in making change. She's not a drinker or druggie. Mr. Cull, Candace has been secretive lately. Did they find her cell phone? She's been talking to someone and when I come in the room, she hangs up. That's been going on for the last two months."

Norbie as gently as he could said, "Is there a guy she's involved with, Gareth?"

Gareth looked edgy and actually blushed saying, "I saw her talking with a guy outside of school a couple of times. He was in a convertible and looked older; you know, a good-looking stud in his twenties. I asked her about him and she said he spoke to the class, but she can't lie, Mr. Cull; she's no good at it and she was lying."

Gareth could not remember the make of the convertible but thought he might recognize the guy if he saw him again. Norbie left Angela and

Barry questioning Gareth who was bereft with guilt over not telling his parents about the guy.

Jim Locke was already at the cop bar with a beer in hand when Norbie entered the bar, Moriarty's. The long bar was lined with cops, detectives, and police wannabes; fortunately, no one from Major Crimes was present. Norbie sat at a table, signaled Jim, who ordered another beer for Norbie and joined him as if it were an accidental meeting. Norbie explained what info he needed and that he needed it soon.

To his surprise, Jim had already ferreted out some facts about the girl found by the river and already knew her name was Candace. Norbie wanted to know: who found the body, in what condition was the body, the estimated time of death, was the scene preserved, and what were the details about and around the scene. Jim said, "Get on your cell phone as if you have a big client calling. That'll give me a reason to leave you and pump the boys over there on what they know. I'll get two more beers. If you don't want to drink them, dump them in the potted plant behind you. This might take a good twenty minutes, so step outside and get some air pretending you need privacy."

Norbie thought, *A good plan, and I certainly need privacy to tell Sheri what happened to Candace. She will have to break it to Brady. He's in Candace's class. Our other kids all knew her and liked her. She used our pool all the time. Kids just don't know the impact they have on us; they just don't know.*

He called Sheri and before he could say anything, Sheri said, "Norbie, Candace Monroe is dead and it sounds fishy. Angela called for your cell and wouldn't tell me why. I thought Barry must have a legal problem, but Brady said Gareth told him she was dead. I'm heartsick. I didn't know she was even sick."

And Norbie told her about his afternoon and his plans for the evening. Sheri stopped crying and told him, "However long it takes is okay with me. Do good work, Norbie. They are suffering. I don't know how you can help them, but do what you can. I'll talk to the kids."

As he clicked off about ready to return to the bar, Jim exited the bar and said, "Let's meet over at Friendly's, where you can get a coffee and I can get some ice cream. We'll be able to talk there without anyone noticing us."

When the two men settled in at the restaurant, Norbie with a coffee and Jim with a strawberry ice cream sundae, his choice of food when under stress, Jim relayed what he had heard. "The girl was moved, Norbie, and her clothes were new. The family tried to file a missing person's report and the officer took a description of what she was last seen wearing, and it was not what she was wearing when they found her. She had no underwear on; no bra and panties, and she had no shoes. There were needle marks in her arm but only a couple and they were new; maybe even that day. The cops on scene did not think she was a user. They found her identification bracelet wrapped in a tissue in the pocket of her skirt. They think she was a drug overdose victim and the body movers didn't want her to go unidentified. There were no witnesses that have showed up yet. The guess, for time of death, is maybe seven to nine in the morning. The body was found in early afternoon by some kids who were going fishing or up to something else. They have alibis for earlier and they're pretty young. The body was in rigor but still had some heat. She was not in the water, just near the water. The blood pooling intimates she died sitting up and was later brought to the site and laid slightly bent on her side. That's all I could get. They took tire tread impressions on three sets from different cars, but it was dry at the site and the officers didn't think the imprints were complete.

"That's it, Norbie. By the way, any work for this girl, anything you want, is on the house. Petra's pregnant and I guess I can't help being more sensitive to the parents' loss of this girl. I'm all in as I guess you are. Let me know what else I can do."

Norbie asked Jim to attempt to pin down Candace's journey that morning if he could. He'd inform the Monroe's if any of their neighbors call to question why Jim was at their door, that they had authorized him. "Wait until tomorrow, Jim; okay."

They said their good-byes and both left for home. Norbie did not think tonight was a good time to revisit the Monroe's. He thought, *Tomorrow is another day and my family has need of me now, if just for reassurance that together we can face this.*

At the MCU morning meeting the next day, the captain informed the detectives, "Candace Monroe, the young girl found by the river yesterday, is our case now. Mason and I explained to the chief that it is, at the very least, a movement of a body to hide cause of death and must be investigated. I also impressed upon the chief that we don't think Candace was a regular drug user. We'll get confirmation on that from the ME this afternoon. Right now, I think we should explore just why anyone would go to this much trouble to either attempt at confusing authorities on the place of her death or maybe actually try to hide a murder. This is a potential murder, even if the drug overdose was given by accident. Why do Mason and I think it's a murder? Cause there is no reason for her to be moved here.

"If someone was trying to hide her overdose, why not just dump her anywhere in her original state. Her clothes were changed, but she was neatly dressed and laid out where she could be found. Maybe it was a necessary but regretful kill; we just don't know, but this death needs answers. A beautiful young girl with what appears to be no drug history is now dead on our turf, and she is from our turf. We have to know what happened."

None of the detectives argued with the captain. At that point, Detective Toddington entered the conference room which caused quite an uproar. The detectives noticed the sling and bulky wraps on his shoulder and the captain reacted immediately. "What the hell are you doing in here, Ted? You're on paid leave and need to stay home and recover."

"Captain, the doctor at the hospital said I could return to work to do paperwork until the shoulder heals. I don't even have to have more surgery and I'm off the happy pills. I'll go crazy sitting at home."

"It's got to be our doctor who decides if you're ready, Ted; not the doctor at the hospital. Make an appointment with him, but I'm telling you not until at least a week from now. Do you understand there are repercussions from a hit like this? Now maybe those repercussions are a ripple in your case, but I don't know; now, get the hell out of here and take care of your recovery business."

Lilly and Petra both tried to hug Ted without hitting his shoulder, while Juan and Mason just shook their heads in admiration. Juan said, "Ted, go fishing for a few days. Make the time work for you. You need rest. You just don't know it yet."

Mason said, "Captain, can I take his time off?"

There was laughter until Ted said, "Ash is in there for a while and he's getting bored. He's got all his musician friends out in the hood asking questions. He might know more about drug trafficking in West Side than we do. Captain, maybe you could talk to him and calm him down. That long skinny frame works well when he can move it. He's not so good at sitting down; just in case you haven't noticed. By the way, what happened to the Monroe girl? Charlotte knows her and her family and is really upset about this."

The captain couldn't act fast enough to prevent his detectives from telling Ted what little they knew. Ted was then kicked out of the station.

Within an hour a preliminary medical report was received, most notable for its quick turn-around.

Beauregard summarized the findings. "The pooling of the blood, the placement of the body is estimated at two hours after death, the fact the body had been bathed and hair washed before dressing her in new clothes with labels torn out, confirmed the detectives' observations made at the crime scene. There were no shoes at or around the site. The identification bracelet had been cleaned of fingerprints. Candace was not a regular drug user and there were two injections made in her arm, estimated to be made within ten minutes of each other. She was injected with the first shot of methamphetamine which at this time discussion guessed it may have caused a stroke. The ME did not think the dosages were an accident; they were meant to do harm or kill. The report states she couldn't have administered both injections herself; that the first injection would have left her unable to focus enough to do the second injection. Further, she is righthanded and the injections are on the right arm which is not normal. We'll chase her new clothes to see if their purchasing history, probably on that same day, is available. I'd like to know just where are the clothes she wore before leaving her house."

The detectives came to agreement on how to proceed and a team of two headed for a meet and greet at each house along the street to the bus stop. Petra mused aloud, "It's over a mile to the school and there is a bus on that route. The driver will remember her if she took the bus."

Lilly and Petra were headed for Candace's neighborhood. Petra said, "We'll be less conspicuous than the guys."

Mason and Juan broke up the calls to retailers between them, but hoped the local department store was the purchase site. Juan said, "That store has cameras. It would be great if the clothes were purchased there."

Rudy wondered how her old clothes could be found, thinking, "They're probably in a dumpster; maybe in a commercial building near her home or near the site she was found." He followed up with a call to the uniform squad to check dumpsters in that part of town.

The next morning, as Norbie had suggested, found Jim Locke doing his survey of the Monroe's neighbors. As instructed, he identified himself as an investigator for the Monroe family. He started north on the relatively short street, Mountain Laurel Place, heading toward Pearce Road, the major bus route road. Not one neighbor saw Candace go by that morning. He visited ten houses and five of the neighbors were out that morning; two were gardening early before the heat came. Yet not one person saw Candace. Jim returned to the Monroe house and went in the other direction where the street turned south and became Evergreen Road. After a visit to the sixth home, he hit pay dirt. Mrs. Florence Bender talked with Candace that morning. She inferred Candace was in a great hurry and was not her usual talkative self. He asked if she was headed to one of the houses on the street. Mrs. Bender said, "I lost sight of her after she passed Abernale's house not far from the new neighbors. The new neighbors are in the really rather too contemporary house a few doors down from Abernale's house. Ask at Abernale's; Liz is awfully nice and keeps an eye on things. I'll bet if Candace walked down that way, Liz would have seen her. I don't know if Liz knows about Candace being missing yet. She'd be concerned."

Jim felt guilty about not telling the neighbors Candace was dead.

He knew it would be on tonight's six o'clock news. He also knew that the Monroe's immediate neighbors knew about Candace's death, but had been told by the Monroe's to keep it quiet until it was announced by the press. He skipped up to Abernale's and Liz, at least he thought it was her, was trimming some flowers by her front door. Jim introduced himself and explained his mission. Liz was clearly upset and said, "Mr. Locke, I saw Candace yesterday morning. She was practically running up the street which is a bit of a hill, and no one normally runs on it. Even the joggers slow down. She just waved. I lost sight of her at the Losocala's house. Mrs. Losocala may be home. I don't know her first name; they're new here, from Las Vegas."

Liz relayed what her husband had said about his conversation with Raymond Losocala.

Jim thanked her and headed up the street, finding the incline a bit tiring, thinking, *this is challenging or I'm not getting enough exercise. I hope I won't get fat along with Petra. All my friends gained twenty pounds when their wives were pregnant. Lots of changes, but nothing like what the Monroe's are facing. Mine are happy changes; theirs are disastrous. Damn, these houses are really separated. I'll bet every lot is two acres; all reaching back to lovely woods. The Losocala house is sited way back from the street and the shrubs are all the way forward on the drive. Maybe I should ask at the house two doors before Losocala's because their home has nothing for shrubs and those shrubs abutted the foundation. There's a greater chance someone could see a passerby; especially since the home's kitchen is on the front of the house. I can see the cabinets. When did that become a design specialty? When I was a kid, the kitchens were all at the back of the homes.*

As he approached the front door of the house, an elderly woman emerged; and she was stunningly dressed. He had seen similar apparel when he shopped with Petra at Bergdof's and he was certain he could not afford the outfit, despite his now earning more than he had ever in his life. She had silver hair, wonderful skin totally untanned, and waved at him with grace saying, "Nobody walks up this hill. Clearly, you're not Jehovah's Witnesses; they always come in pairs. And you look normal and probably not a vagrant, so how can I help you? I'm Grace Gordon, call me Grace, please; how are you doing? Come in and we'll have some iced tea. It is warm and my husband is late, so I have nothing on my agenda now. You have all my attention." And Jim introduced himself.

Jim told her he was looking for the Monroe girl who was missing and thought, *wow, I'm impressed. This lady is charming and sure of herself. How does she know I'm not one of Captain Beauregard's sociopaths? She didn't before I identified myself; maybe she's just a risk taker.*

He followed her into the home as beautifully dressed as its owner and said, "Grace, this is quite a designer's home."

Her answer surprised him. "Yes, it is, Jim, but I don't take credit for it. I am a decision maker par excellence, but not a designer. I go to the best designers, architects, builders, educators, and after they present their plans, I make decisions about what I want. I'm a really great decision maker, but the talent lies elsewhere. I was smart enough to choose the right husband and lucky enough to have a few beaus to choose from. I know people, Jim; I know people. Now let's get down to business. What do you need from me?"

Jim explained the time frame he was focusing on and showed her a picture of Candace. Grace studied the picture and thoughtfully said, "I've seen this young lady several times in the last two weeks and yes she went by my house yesterday very early. I'm outside putting around early in the morning, every morning. She always waves when she does come by. I hope nothing bad has happened to her."

"Where, Grace, did she go after she passed your home? Did she go into a neighbor's home or up to the left near that small park?

"She passed the next house and maybe went into the new neighbor's yard; for sure she didn't head up to the park. I would have seen her go that way. It is actually over to the left and is clearly visible from my front yard."

Jim pushed, saying, "Do the new neighbors have children her age?"

"Jim, I sincerely doubt it. I'm certain they will not be long living here. They don't have the New England perspective; if you know what I mean? Look, I overdress for West Side, even for this section. Instead of wearing jeans and a good sweater, I wear designer labels. I just love them, but I have area values. Those folks are all sparkle; you know the types who think, 'We have the best of everything', kind of people. They are not at all interested in children. Maybe Candace went into the house before or after. Check with them. I doubt her destination would be the Losocala home. They only have time for people who can do something for them."

Jim soon left Grace and tried the next home but there was no answer when he rang the ring doorbell. No one was at the Losocala home either. He tried the house after it and a dignified man of about sixty answered the door and was only too happy to speak with Jim. He looked at the picture and was pretty certain she had never gone by his house. He said, "I have a camera on at all times and I check it every night. I may not remember faces from a month ago, but I can guarantee she didn't come by yesterday."

7

Drugs and Murder

The MCU detectives were meeting or more importantly arguing, debating, and forming conclusions about drug trafficking in West Side. Ted was back with a note from the police doctor saying he could not be in the field if it meant he was in danger, but could do office work. Despite his natural inclination to move away from desk work now that he was in policing, Ted was happy to be back, even if it meant just sitting at a desk. The captain reviewed the doctor's letter and asked if it was legitimate saying, "In all my years, Ted, Doc Martin has never turned in one of these letters in less than ten days. We had our talk, what, yesterday or the day before, and today I have a letter. What kind of pull do you have?"

With a smirk Ted replied, "I'm negotiating with IRS for a 2016 underreporting for the doc. He forgot something and understands he has to pay but wants the big penalty removed. Anyone can probably do that for him if there's a good reporting history with the service, but I am happy to put my knowledge to work to help the little guy."

Lilly wondered aloud, "Is that graft or just a slight nonmonetary favor?"

Juan and Petra both smiled and repeated the unit's familiar phrase,

"Can't help it if the public wants to help the police because we always help them."

Beauregard was ticked off at himself for bringing the subject up at the meeting, thinking, *Of course Ted had some pull; the doc normally doesn't move fast. I didn't know what it was, but knew it was there. I had to open my mouth. Now the others will push the envelope on another day even further.*

Petra brought them back to house business with an observation. "Fentanyl is the biggie now, not amphetamines. Opioids and heroin and fentanyl are big. Look at the drug busts recently in Massachusetts. The northern route busted this year going from Lawrence, Mass to New Hampshire and Maine was fentanyl from China. All those kids in New Hampshire dying really brought the house down."

Juan said, "The Feds seized eleven kilos of heroin and fentanyl and five thousand pills at an industrial warehouse. The trouble is even my mother had a fentanyl patch after her neck surgery. She doesn't know it's fifty times stronger than heroin. She thinks because it's made in a lab and is given by prescription by her doctor, that it's safe. I read in one of the papers ninety percent of people who died from overdoses in our state had fentanyl in their systems."

Petra, not to be out done, commented on a report she had read after the Lubbock, Texas raid in 2016. "Fentanyl patches are highly concentrated. If one broke open and got on your skin, you'd probably die. Let's say you sleep on an electric blanket or a heating pad; well the heat would increase your circulatory system and you are dead."

Lilly couldn't believe they had this info and said so. "Druggies are always looking for more. If what you say is true then I don't know how we don't have all the users ending up dead. I was in the pharmaceutical business and never thought about electric blankets and patches and possible synergy there. I guess the pros know how to protect themselves."

Beauregard asked the important question. "Candace died of an overdose of an injection of amphetamines and it traced as street made. Is there a connection to the lab in the house where Ash and Ted were shot? What reports do we have on it, Mason?"

Petra answered the question. "Captain, there is no lab for meth there. There is evidence of processing; crushing of pills, mixing drugs, and bagging. Samples of dust and powder from the apartment showed heroin, fentanyl, and some other substances, but no meth. It's probably not directly connected with Candace's death."

Mason cut in with, "Don't be so sure, Petra. You might have a mixing process here and a meth lab on the next street. The Puerto Ricans and the Russians have shown absolutely no history of discrimination when it comes to product. The Dominicans don't either."

Beauregard asked about the ME's report on the shootings across from the strip mall.

Lilly had the report. "Look, Captain, it fits with the three boys' interviews. The car driver and the woman in the car walked toward the lot. The driver shot both of the men in the lot in succession. He and the woman were getting back in the car and the woman was on the sidewalk opening the car door when the Dominican or person of color who was still alive shot the woman and was shot again by the driver. The ME says it looks good that way. If the woman was with the other two, why would they kill her and the kids say she was with the driver shooter."

Beauregard pushed with, "Do we have the victims' vehicle yet and if not, how the hell did they get to the lot, walk? Also, if it's a professional kill, why didn't the shooter give a final shot to the head? That's standard if there's time."

Juan said, "That's just it, Captain, it was a busy street and no time. The community police found a stolen car, not in the mall parking lot, but on the side street next to the vacant lot. They're processing it now for prints."

Ted, nursing his arm carefully, asked about the dead woman's address on Spruce Street.

Petra quipped, "You've been reading the file, Ted? You just got here. How'd that happen?"

"I have a computer and access to my email at the station and our kids were gone with my wife; they couldn't stop me from working. So, what about this woman? Does the old man Alfie know her?"

Juan said, "He not only knows her; she's his girlfriend. He's in mourning. Her name is Marisol Garcia. I think Alfie lives with his son called AJ; the son's only about thirty. I'd guess Alfie's in his late sixties or older. The ME says she was higher than a kite and totally drugged up on heroin and fentanyl when she was killed. The old man told me and believe me it was difficult to understand him, 'I told my Mariii not to go with the mother-fuckin Dominican; fuckin hookers, they go with the money. The guy told her he had some good stash. There's no easy way to get drugs on this street since the police shooting. I'm out of my security job. She knew I got nothing for her. She took good care of me.' And Alfie started bawling. It's the way it is with these guys and their skanks. Although Alfie is probably forty to fifty years older than her, he had a house; for some of them, that's enough. The son AJ looked disgusted when his dad started crying."

Beauregard shook his head. "Fentanyl and heroin again around the corner practically from the shootings of Ash and you, Ted. I've got a problem with this. I spoke with the federal drug task force earlier. No, actually, they called me. They want me to downplay these shootings. Now I know why. I asked what was new in the supply chain; were the Dominicans, Puerto Ricans, and Russians collaborating? Got a strong reaction like, 'Where the hell did you hear that, Rudy?' I know we're in the midst of a drug war, but I have three murders on my watch and two cop shootings that are connected to this. And maybe Candace is a fourth murder connected. I could be wrong about Candace; she was shot up on meth, but we have to figure this mess out."

Ted agreed and said, "I've read all the latest printouts on national activity. The heroin coming in from China is laced with Fentanyl unknown to the users. This makes the heroin incredibly potent and dangerous. Now if we have local mixers involved, there is the additional danger that more of one drug is added on another using any drug available, and the potential effect on the user is unknown.

"This is a fuckin chef of the day special kind of thing that kills. Drug activity like this is not what's involved with Candace, Captain. In fact, we haven't seen this stuff on our streets yet; we've only seen it on the North Shore and New Hampshire, but that's not the NY, Springfield, Vermont route that we are supposed to be settled right in the middle of. The Feds think it's coming our way."

Lilly showed some emotion when a small tear fell from her eye, continuing with, "My former boyfriend died of an overdose. He was a great guy but got depressed easily. He was also raised in a home where if two aspirins cured your headache, then four would cure it twice as fast. That kind of thinking leaves you vulnerable to drug overuse. I wasn't dating him when he died, but it didn't make any difference. When you really know someone you like, the loss does hurt deeply."

Beauregard noticed Millie standing at the doorway. He didn't have to acknowledge her for she quickly said, "Captain, I've got good news and bad news. Ash has left the hospital and is doing really well. He walked out and called an Uber without telling Martina. She called and said he walked in like nothing was wrong. She knows he must be hurting, but he's acting like he was never shot. Now the bad news, another body was found near the river, half a mile away from where

Candace's body was discovered. It's a young man. The uniforms called Narcotics Unit first. Lieutenant Brown is there on site and says it's suspicious. The kid is Ollie Rapusca, eighteen years old. He has been noticed before, by community policing, buying drugs, but mostly pot. He has needle marks in his arm; two of them like the girl. They want you there before this information gets out."

Beauregard and Toddington stood by the boy's body. Laying there was a young and handsome youth in jeans and a tee shirt that said '#metoo' on it. He did not have shoes or sandals or socks and when Ted looked, no underwear. The captain concluded after discussion with the uniforms and Ted that the body had been moved; just like with Candace. "Do we have another serial murder? Not the same gender but around the same age. Certainly, he looks like he was redressed. No kid as good looking as he is would willingly wear the kind of jeans I wear. See, Ted, they're all baggy; can't catch a girl or a guy like that. He has the same two injections sites. The uniforms on the scene say he was noted for buying a lot of weed; but was never caught for anything else. So, if he's not a big-time connector, what the hell is he doing dead here? What's his address? Is he out of high school? Did he ever know Candace?"

Officer Timulty who was at the Spruce Street shooting of Beauregard's detectives motioned Rudy aside. "Captain, those three kids were just here and before anyone could shoo them away, that Santiago kid ran up on the rocks and took a picture of the body. Before we saw him, he started running and got on his bike. They left in a hurry, when they realized we saw them. Want me to go hustle them back here, Captain."

"No, Officer Timulty, I'll take care of the situation." Rudy was thinking, *damnit, my potential juvenile detention informants are everywhere. I don't need a focus on them. I'll find out what they think they can do with that picture and how they were here so soon.*

Beauregard told Ted to hop a ride back to the station with one of the uniforms saying, "I forgot to do something, Ted, and it will take some time."

To say that Beauregard was on a mission, to Ted's mind, was an understatement as he watched his boss's car almost jump from the compressed dirt section to the road. Ted turned to ask Timulty for a ride and the officer's smile with a retort that answered all of Ted's questions. "Left you in the lurch, didn't he? The captain is on the warpath after those kids who were here. I think he's afraid for them. He'll find them even if he has to wait at one of their homes."

Beauregard wasn't waiting at their homes. He knew better than that. He was in the strip mall parking lot parked between two large trucks thinking, *those kids have really good vision. They will probably run if they see me before I see them; but these trucks are perfect camouflage.*

And he waited, not even for half an hour, before the undercover trio showed and entered the game store; which was crowded. He waited for them to get comfortable, entered the store, and walked over behind the boys. He put his hand on Jackson's shoulder fearing he was the most agile and reactive. He could easily run as could Paulie. Wayne generally was slower in making decisions. Instead of running, Jackson said, "Captain Beauregard, we were just going to the station after we checked some things. Ya see, we saw the dead kid by the river, took a picture, and checked with the kids here at the game store. He was a regular. His name is Ollie Rapusca. The kids said he had stopped doping and was working with some other kids on some secret stuff. We heard Ollie belongs to some anti-drug club now. Does that help you,

Captain?"

Beauregard stood very still and thanked God he was by nature slow to react thinking, *I was about to kill these kids and they have saved some shoe leather for my detectives. How do I give them credit for their work when they shouldn't be involved in this at all? They are good kids, but they don't listen; just like my own kids.*

"Okay. You did good today. Now tell me why I'm not angry. Tell me why I shouldn't talk to your parents about you three investigating police business. Tell me why you thought it was okay to investigate this boy. Did you know him; sounds like you didn't. Why were you at the river? Tell me why I should trust you in the future? Remember I have to trust you and you are kids. You don't have an adult's experience to know when to stop. So, tell me why."

Him, Me and Paulie, as they would refer to themselves; looked very seriously at the captain. Paulie was the first to speak. "We listened to you, Captain. Honestly. we did and you don't have to worry about our knowing when to stop. My dad, I told you he's former military; well he's taught me about authority and our duty to listen. We know that, right, guys?"

Jackson, said, "Yeah, we didn't even ask some of the other kids that we heard were part of this 'no doping club' anything. We thought if we showed too much interest, they'd be on to us and look at us suspiciously."

Wayne finished Jackson's thoughts with, "We think the girl who died, Candace; well that Ollie died the same way. We think, Captain, you have another serial murderer on your hands. You'd better really look into this. We promise not to do anything further; but if we see something unusual, we'll call you first. Okay?"

Paulie added, "To answer your other questions, we don't know Ollie but we heard about Candace through Jackson's mother who knows Candace's mother. We knew Candace three years ago when she was at

Hoffington School. She was really nice and pretty. We heard all about how they found her body by the river too and she had needle marks in her arm. Candace never did drugs."

The boy investigators all nodded their heads in agreement. Captain Beauregard said, "All right, you get a pass this time as well as a thank you; but remember it wouldn't be good for you guys to be on my bad side."

Beauregard left thinking about his exchange with the boys. *I was resourceful as a boy, but I never put myself out that much; not like these boys are doing. They are good kids. I'll tell Mona about them soon. She has such great trust in young people. She's said in the past that given this crazy world we live in, these kids do really well just surviving.*

Lieutenant Stellato called Rudy. He was ready to enter his car when he heard more negative news. "Rudy, I just heard about the body by the river you guys found; well this morning a body of a young man around twenty was found in a similar situation over near the bridge not far from the Basketball Hall of Fame and the casino. Funny thing that's different is his convertible is nearby, but the rest is similar in that his clothes have been changed and he has two needle marks in his arm."

Rudy was silent which triggered Stellato to say, "Are you still there? Did you hear what I said? We have a fucking serial murderer out there and two of the victims were found in your town. You better get the DA involved, Rudy."

"Not to worry, Joe, I'll contact the DA and have a meeting set up later today or tomorrow with him and his task force. You or one of your guys should be there. I guess maybe I'll be lead, but I'm also guessing you and I are probably going to see more of this. Something's up. Three young people dead from meth injection; it was meth injection on your body, right?"

"Yeah, we're trying to find out more about this guy. His name is

Herbert Brent, Jr. He's from West Side over by the park not far from Westfield. We don't have a sheet on him. You better get one of your detectives on him. Local police will learn more. Have you done profiles on your victims yet?"

Rudy was feeling pressure and answered, "Two bodies in a day and another one not long before; not a lot of time, Joe. Send me a photo of the guy; text to my cell? I'm out and about doing some surveillance and I know a photo of Brent will help."

A text with the photo appeared on his phone. He did not enter his car which had not been moved since his first conversation on Ollie Rapusca a bit earlier. Entering the store again, he found his boys and asked them to meet him outside. They immediately looked concerned and Wayne said, "You're not going to tell us you're talking to our parents. Even Attorney Cull covered up for us."

Feeling his face reddened, the Captain said, "What do you mean Attorney Cull covered for you? What does he have to do with this?"

Wondering why this was a problem, Jackson said, "He's a good friend of Candace and her family. He's out there trying to figure things out. My mom says he's taking her death personally and that means as Mom said, 'He'll leave no stone unturned.'"

Cooling down, the captain showed them a picture of the dead young man and asked the boys if they had ever seen him. They studied the picture and Paulie yelled excitedly, "It's the guy we saw Candace with. It's the guy in the red convertible." Jackson and Wayne shouted in agreement.

Jackson said, "You have a connection, Captain; just like on television, you have a connection."

Wayne jumped in saying, "All three are probably related, Captain. Candace knew Ollie, I'm certain of that."

Beauregard asked Wayne, "Why do you think Candace knew Ollie,

Wayne?"

"Don't you remember, Captain, we told you the kids in there said Ollie went to West Side High. There's not much difference in age. He just graduated and she's going to be a senior. They have to know each other."

Captain Beauregard sighed and responded, "Look, guys, thanks for your help. Please, as I've said before, do not talk about any of this. I'm certain this information on identity is important and I thank you. We would have discovered it soon but this info is helpful and you got it for us early." All the while he was thinking, *I would not have known this victim knew Candace without some investigating and maybe wouldn't have learned it at all.* He cautioned the three boys, "Look, what's the cardinal rule in policing? You all know that it's to take care of yourself; to not put yourself at risk. Talking about what you know is not what cops or lawyers or any professional does. If you guys consider yourself professionals, then shut up."

The boys nodded and promised that they understood the captain's worries about them. Beauregard left them still concerned, thinking, *it's time now that I talk with their parents. They know the boys saw the assassinations of the Dominican and the woman. That's a basis to lay on some protection. I don't know how they've insinuated themselves into two investigations. Getting rid of them is like trying to get rid of lice. And maybe it's time I talk to Attorney Cull.*

8

Motives on Hold

Captain Beauregard had tasked the new MCU detective Juan Flores to mix with the kids and adults at the strip mall game store saying, "Infiltrate. In ripped jeans and t-shirt, you'd look years younger. There's supposed to be an anti-drug group of kids who meet at the store, and from what I understand, are casting a net for new members. It's a good place to fish. Find out who belongs and how they're holding up. Also look at who is pretending to belong and really is working for the killer or is the killer of these three young people."

Juan responded, "It's too bad I'm Mexican. The Puerto Ricans will spot that immediately; the others won't care. But maybe it can work in my favor. Not too many Mexicans here in West Side, so the group might think I'm lonely; or the perp might approach me to make me work the group for his benefit. I'll get right on it, Captain."

Now that Juan was directed on his undercover mission as a juvenile, Beauregard met with his MCU detectives: first to finish required paperwork, second to assign small cases to each detective.

For the third time the detectives reviewed info on the drug case. The captain rebuffed the detectives' complaints on how the Federal Drug Task Force and its FBI leader Loughman were controlling without informing. He said, "I don't want to hear your complaints. And let me answer this way. Yes, I am a member of the task force, and yes, my two detectives were hurt, and yes, I should be informed; but I wasn't. From the Task Force members' perspective, the shooters have been found; both dead and one of the shooters is struggling for his life. It is now a drug case. The shooting cases will never hit the courts. We don't deal in drug cases, but I do think that, we, despite what we have been told, can quietly still look into the home invasion. No one on the force specifically told me to stop investigating the home invasion; only Putin told us it was connected. The Task Force doesn't know we've connected the dots; of that I'm sure. Putin would not have relayed what he told me."

Petra was now excited, saying, "God, Captain, I thought you were going to let it go. Look at Juan's report on the old guy Alfie, who was the lookout at the drug house on Spruce Street. A lowly lookout normally gets paid in drugs and some money. Juan reports he's driven around by his son in a new big priced SUV. Isn't Alfie an old man, and his kid is only about thirty? Juan, how old is Alfie and does his house look like every other house on the street? You know what I mean. Is it better kept than the other houses? Maybe the kid is involved in the drug activity on the street."

Juan answered, "It could be, Petra. The house looks like the others; it's a large two-family home; but for sure on the exterior it's in much better shape. Most houses on the street have been sided over, but this one looks like those big old mansions in Springfield. I go on the Springfield Preservation Trust's home tours every year, and the paint jobs on these homes are beautiful. Alfie's house is in perfect repair, has a great paint job; but you know it's all kind of subtle for down there. You don't notice at first, it's different. He's got it all fenced in; all the way around back and even along the walkway to the house. Without jumping the fence, you can't get in the backyard. There are small high-end model cameras on the front porch, but some of the other houses on the street have cameras. I went to the street behind and couldn't get through the house behind Alfie's because it's got all new fencing."

Beauregard said, "Find out who owns both houses and check on activity in the back house. Mason, I want a background check on both Alfie and his son AJ. Alfie looked old to me but when he got off the porch that day, he ran pretty good! He may be a bigger player here than we thought."

Beauregard finally brought the issue forward on possible motives for the three serial murders. He had no problem calling them serial murders despite knowing they didn't fit criteria for a serial murder perfectly. He explained, "I know there are three dead kids, but one is certainly a juvenile, so National Center for Analysis of Violent Crimes will have to choose between Behavioral Analysis Unit BAU 3 for children or the BAU 4 for adults. Also, all the victims fit in a relatively consistent age pattern, but two are males and one is a female. All three have the same injection marks in one arm, were redressed, were moved from the killing site to a site near the river, although one was found on the Springfield side of the river; the girl had intercourse before dying and the boys had anal intercourse before dying; there is no evidence the intercourse was forced; the clothes, they were found dressed in, are new with tags cut out; the third victim's car has no fingerprints on it; it has been wiped and probably was the vehicle in which the body was moved. There was no deliberate attempt to hide the identities of the bodies. I'm waiting for tests on stomach contents and fibers, etc."

Lilly responded first. "I think it's highly unlikely these kids all had consensual sex. What does the ME say about the boys, Captain? Did the bodies show hard anal sex? Why does he think it was consensual? Could he tell if it was a first time for both boys? Was the girl a virgin?

She's supposed to be a scholar and a good girl with no particular boyfriend. If it's a first time, there should be more trauma effect on the body."

Beauregard answered, saying, "We just have a preliminary report and the ME saw evidence of sexual activity without trauma; whatever that means. We should be getting a detailed report later today on Candace; who knows when on the other victims."

The captain continued asking, "Mason and Juan, how'd you do on the search for Candace's clothes? Did you find any retailers who could tie them down and describe a purchaser?"

Mason said, "There are two stores that carry the girl's clothes as we described them over the phone. We haven't yet gone over there to follow up. We both think we should take all the victims' clothes to these two stores. Maybe if the perp came back two or three times, a clerk will remember. Maybe several people bought the clothes and the perp used other innocent purchasers. I don't think I can be sure about motive for redressing them, Captain."

Ted reacted saying, "Look at the common details. They are all dumped by the same river although one on the other side from West Side. Maybe it just got too hot here to do the third dumping, since community police have doubled their tours on this side. All the victims are young and all have been sexually attacked indiscriminately for the perp's sexual fantasy. Two were found on the same day. To me, and I'm not a psychologist, but my wife is, it speaks not of sexual implications, but instead maybe is a put down of these kids. The victims are all upper middle-class white kids. Maybe that's the motive. Clearly the perp has a killing site he does not want us to know about. So, we have to chase who saw each of those victims and who they were seen with on the day they died. The red convertible is important, because the perp must have driven it from the killing site, or maybe a second site, to get it to the Springfield side of the river. It's a pretty showy vehicle; it's very noticeable. Also important is how did the perp leave the drop site? Did he walk away? Was there an assistant who was in another car?"

Beauregard said, "That's a good summary but the method of killing these victims says everything about the perp having knowledge about drugs; he or she is either in the trade or is a user. That's a lead we and Stellato can follow. There's lot of planning here that, from my way of thinking, disallows a heavy druggie as the perp. I don't think we can ignore the potential fentanyl/heroin increase in traffic here, just because the perp used meth. I'm thinking, and it's a bit farfetched, that the perp could be killing the kids with meth, not a drug high school kids use, as a warning to other kids. This no-drug activist activity could be a serious problem for all drug dealers in the area, if the kids are effective in reporting information to some of our community police. Lilly, go talk to all the first and second shift community police officers for info about what's going on in their districts. I mean all; don't just limit your investigation to the drug region. These kids are not from that area. Petra, check with the middle and high schools' psychologists and social workers. They often hear through the grapevine what's going on. I don't understand the murder weapon. These kids would not have allowed the first injection unless they were asleep or somehow confused."

Mason said, "If these kids were fighting drug activity, maybe they got some classes on drugs; like at Bay State Hospital or the courts' classes for kids who are caught first-time using, or at the YMCA, or the schools. I'm certain if they're out there and proselytizing, they have to know something about drugs. On my Facebook yesterday, someone posted a picture of four meth users before and three years after use of meth. Well before they looked like clean-cut twenty-year old's and after, they aged to seventy years old with missing teeth and really skaggy looking. I was repulsed, and frankly, I was frightened when I thought about the future of this city."

"When was the last time we had a meth lab arrest?" asked the Captain. "I can't remember when. Maybe up in the hill towns, they crashed one."

Petra said, "Captain, what about the one in your hometown Holyoke and there was one out in Monson?"

Lilly added, "Springfield has had two in the last year and a half. One was a big lab and the Feds were involved. Most of these lab crashes have been accidentally found by local police based on the condition of the building or smells emanating or trash outside."

Beauregard pushed on, asking, "What about in West Side? The Spruce Street lab was not a meth lab. It was a mixing lab for fentanyl, heroin, etc. Why kill these kids with meth? It's not the easiest drug to get. Heroin is a lot easier. Could this be misdirection by someone in power? Cannot be a meth user! They can't plan like this; consistently redressing bodies with new clothes. Despite that, my gut tells me the murders are somehow involved with this mess with drug suppliers."

Rudy was thinking as he was talking, *could the victims, if these activist kids had the chutzpah of my undercover thirteen-year old's, cause enough trouble to make themselves a target? Hell, they're old enough and could be aggressive in achieving their goals. How far would they go; would they enter the lion's den?*

Beauregard realized he had a call after noticing his iWatch throbbing. Although he ignored the call, he saw the other party was his brother Liam.

The team of detectives divvied up the workload, and with the meeting ended, the captain retreated to his office. First thing he did was call Liam, who said he would be there soon with a friend. Liam assured Rudy the friend was Rudy's from Holyoke High School. He refused to give Rudy the guy's name, but promised to be there in a jiffy.

Rudy brooded, wondering if this friend was someone he liked back in the day or just a low life, but then thought, *no, Liam would not put up with a lowlife, and how in hell did Liam know my friend from high school?*

As he waited for Liam and the supposedly old-time friend to come, Rudy mused on his inability to easily feel close to those who were not family, thinking, *well that's not really completely true. My detectives are like family too. Actually, anyone who needs me is important to me and I often develop a feeling of closeness. What I think, is, that I'm fearful of being sniggered into a relationship on any level until I'm certain I can trust the other person. Is it a New England thing; is it a French thing from Lizette and Roland; is it from the memories of my childhood; is it a result of my experiences in my chosen professions? Nah, it's just me being me. I'm a cynic and I question motives in all situations without sometimes realizing what I'm doing. I don't question motives when I see victims suffering. I feel for them, sometimes too much.*

Although not planned, Rudy's reverie prepared him for Liam's visit. His brother walked into the minimalist governmental office appearing to take over the room, if for no other reason, then from his larger than Rudy size. He was accompanied by a man Rudy immediately remembered from over thirty years ago as Jake McGourley from Holyoke High School. What captured Rudy was the mournful look on Jake's face. It was not the face of yesterday; and not because the face had aged badly. This face now was not reminiscent of the happy-go-lucky jokester he remembered.

Rudy shook Jake's hand, which was not enough for Jake. He pulled Rudy in for a bear hug and said, "Am I fucking glad to see you, old friend. I need your help. I need someone to help me. I thought moving away from the city was the answer; and it was, for a while. Now I realize there's no fucking single answer. We're never safe. Thank God I know Liam; I didn't know he was your brother until today. He never told me before."

Rudy sat with his old friend and listened to his story; one Liam had already heard. It was a story too familiar to Beauregard; Jake's beautiful daughter was found dead from a drug overdose in the Shelburne Falls area, not far from the beautiful Bridge of Flowers. The police told him her body had been moved to the site. Jake cried as he insisted his daughter was a good girl. She was never involved in drugs. In fact, she was active in the anti-drug club at her high school.

Rudy reacted, saying, "What drug did they find in her, Jake? Was it ingested or by needle?"

Jake now completely engulfed in tears and while rubbing tears from his eyes said, "Meth, Rudy, they said it was meth. Stella would never take meth; maybe smoke a joint, but now she was so active against drugs, she wouldn't even take an aspirin unless the doctor insisted. It's bogus; I'm telling you it's bogus. Someone killed my Stella, Rudy, and you gotta find him. The police at home, I live in a town near to Shelburne Falls, told me it's a drug death. They said it's unfortunate but kids just don't know how much to take of this stuff. They told me it was injected. Hell, I'd fight Stella tooth and nail to get her to take a flu shot. She would not inject herself!

"I want to see the autopsy and, like on television; I want to know what's in her stomach contents and if they can tell if she used drugs regularly. I know the answer to that, but I need facts to make them look into this case. Someone's got to pay, Rudy. My wife Alice is a basket case and I have two sons who are swearing vengeance. They're eighteen and twenty and I'm afraid they'll do something. Help me, Rudy. I know you'll discover who killed my Stella. Look, you're famous for catching serial killers; you can help with one plain murder. Help me."

And Jake leaned over in his uncomfortable chair in Rudy's austere office and sobbed. Liam looked at Rudy and said, "Bro, you have to help. I'll do anything to assist you. Just direct me. I've money for investigators."

"Liam, you know I can't investigate another city's case, and you stay out of it. I will call one chief I know up there to see what police force is on the case. This chief, who I have met before, is a really good guy. He'll help me learn what there is to learn. I will do that for you, Jake and if there's even a hint, or an inkling the police are not taking this seriously, well you could hire an investigator. It's your family and it's your right, but let's hold on a bit before you act."

It took an hour of further questions before Jake and Liam left leaving a distraught Rudy musing over his history with Jake, Jake's loss, and Liam's involvement. Talking aloud, Rudy, heard by Millie as she entered the office unannounced, was saying, "Fuck it, new family complicates my life. I don't need to put my nose in an investigation in the Shelburne Falls area; I have enough to do right here. Besides, the police up there will not love my trying to investigate a local death."

Millie, who could inject her Southern roots in language when needed, and said, "Captain, family is there for us in the easy and hard times. Liam, your newly found brother, knows that sugah is needed. Your parents Lizette and Roland know when sugah is needed. Sugah in this case is for you to use your skills and find out what's going on. That's your sugah. You never avoid problems, Captain, stop struggling just because Liam brought you to the situation."

Millie had further instructions for him. She said the medical examiner had sent in the final report on Candace. She left him to review the report. Candace had Flunitrazepam, commonly known as Rohypnol or roofies, in her urine and in addition she was injected with meth with two injections. The information gave Rudy a new understanding of the logic trail of the murder as he thought, *the roofie made Candace out of it which allowed the perp to make the first meth injection keeping the victim alive for the rape and then the second injection after the rape. It all makes sense. The perp bathes the body, redresses it, moves it to a vehicle and brings it to the discovery site. It has to be a male perp unless there are two perps. A normal woman could not easily move the concentrated weight of a dead body. What's perverse is this male is raping the woman vaginally and the men anally. I don't think the perp is in a sexual frenzy. I think he resents his victims and wants to put them down. Can't wait to see what the BAU profiler will say about this. And the report just shows some roughing in the vaginal and anal areas. Can't tell if she was a virgin. Doesn't matter anyway.*

Rudy's cell rang. He noted it was his wife and answered. Mona had much to say. "Rudy, I overheard students in my biology class discussing a club. Most of them are members and apparently the club is very active in this anti-opioid issue. One of my students, when I questioned her, told me Candace was very aggressive in pursuing information related to those selling opioids in this city. She told the other members there will be a big dumping of fentanyl on the streets soon. I thought you should know. My student's name is Betsy Printer and she lives near Spruce Street. I can't access her records."

They talked a bit longer and then signed off leaving Rudy thumping his right hand on his desk thinking, *kids investigating; first thirteen-year old's and now high school clubs looking to clean up the streets and then dying. I better step up our game before babies solve the cases and die while doing it.*

The captain was reviewing reports the next morning when Petra, without knocking, walked right in. In her usual speedy fashion, she dumped bits of info out in record time, "Captain, I checked with all the arresting officers of drug sellers in those hill towns like you asked last night. They all got a lead in each arrest case from what they call, 'The

Phantom Collar'. You like that. They make a collar based on a note to them. In every case, specific info, on who had the drugs and the amount and when they were delivered, was right on target. So, I got this idea to call our guys about any drug arrests in the last year and a half in West Side, and other than one big one made by the task force, all the others were based on a note to the right person in drug enforcement. I'd call Stellato, but I don't think he'd go there given we're forbidden to follow the drug cases on our own and certainly not in their territory. Someone was in the know? How did you get this lead to follow, Captain?"

"Not important now, Petra, did you check out that student of Mona's I asked about last night?"

"You mean the second of three things you asked for after 8:30 pm when I was watching a great Netflix TV series called, 'Intelligence.' I think they might have killed off Jimmy Regan, the star last night. He's a hood but totally cool."

"Bolt, I don't need television reviews. Did you call Betsy Printer and ask her about Candace and the other students' activities in anti-drugs?"

"Yeah, Captain, I'm meeting her in the West Side Library. She's calling me on a date that works with her schedule. That's where all the kids' meetings would take place. They all were told drug dealers don't go to libraries. Smart, I thought. I'll follow up if I don't hear from her."

"Okay. Petra, I am particularly curious about this Herbert Brent, Jr. with the red convertible. See what she knows about him. After all, he's from West Side, just the other part of town. And as to the high school psychologist, what did you hear from him?"

"Sexist of you, Captain, it's a she and she's sharp. She identified five students who appeared to be sticking together and talking anti-drugs. They would leave notes in her office listing lockers that would have drugs. Our schools' principals have the right to search student lockers without a search warrant. Don't know how that got through our city government; it's not true in most towns around here. The searches were all productive; but the parents of the kids made a lot of noise. They should have been grateful because the high school just gave the kids a week off. Our narcotics unit agreed that if there were small amounts they would just collect the drugs. It did give them a heads up on the kids who were buying. Lots of stuff goes on in the schools we don't know about, Captain."

9

Faces and Friends

Paulie's mom had him babysitting his little sister Rosie the whole of Saturday morning. When she returned home with groceries and a few items from T. J. Maxx, she insisted he help her make lunch for the family. Paulie was chomping at the bit and tried to rush the eating process for them all. Finally, Maria put her foot down inferring, that if he continued acting this way, he could stay home all day and help her. She said, "Paulo, what's so important you have to get out of here so quickly? Just what are you up to?"

Paulie made up a story that he and Jackson and Wayne had artwork due on Monday and they needed to talk about it together. Maria suggested the boys could work at their house while Rosie took a nap, it would be quiet. Paulie rejected the suggestion with news that they needed some art supplies. Maria responded with an offer to buy them for him if the amount was modest, saying, "I could have picked them up for you if you had told me, Paulo."

Paulie put his mother's offer off, because he felt some guilt about lying to his mom when all he was going to do was meet up with his friends. They had planned to visit the 'Southern Ladies' on Silvain Street near Spruce Street. He called his friends and suddenly felt better.

Both Jackson and Wayne were compelled to do household chores and were also ticked off explaining, "We think our parents talked to each other and are trying to keep us separated." Wayne insisted he had to have the afternoon free for an art project the three were doing.

His mother, who didn't believe him, called Jackson's mother and when the mothers realized both boys had the same story, they let them go. The three met and hustled over to the 'Southern Ladies' on their bikes arriving within ten minutes. It was Saturday, always a good day to visit the ladies. Visitors always brought a lot of food and with what the ladies had cooked, the offerings to the boys made up for all the stress in getting there. Their plan, involving all three of them, consisted of watching the visitors to see if they spotted anyone of interest. They knew it was important to get a view of the faces of the guys who ran the drug operation on Spruce Street that was now interrupted. Paulie had said many times, "Old habits die slowly. That's what my mama says. These guys are probably setting up a new base for selling drugs; but meanwhile they'll want to keep their connections with their customers in the old location." So, it was important to be at Sara and Miriam's house.

There were cars parked on both sides of the street except for the house with two orange cones situated directly across from the 'Southern Ladies' porch style home. Foot traffic was heavy, but the laughter embellished the house with an aura of welcoming goodwill. The boys jumped on the porch and Miss Sara who was leaning against the high table setting out some refreshments came over and hugged them. She and Miriam were dressed in matching printed dresses in orange and gold for the fall. They thought the ladies looked and smelled great. Sara said, "Now Him Me and Paulie, what do my three artists want today, lemonade or pink lemonade?"

Sara and Miriam both got a chuckle when they had heard how

Jackson referred to himself and his friends. "You absolutely can't have soda; don't want your mamas dressing me down because you're on any artificial sugar high when you go home. We have some nice desserts for your sugar: peach upside-down cake, or bourbon pecan pie or some nice cranberry sugar cookies or my favorite lemon Lucy cake from my own grandmother's recipe. For dinner, today we have ribs and beans and homemade coleslaw and cornbread and potato salad. It's a feast and we have lots of it, but act fast. As you can see, once all these adults finish their gin and tonics, they'll eat it all in one swoop; like locusts."

The boys, before piling their plates, asked Miriam what the occasion was. Sara overheard them as she delivered their drinks and said, "This is the fifth anniversary of our purchase of this lovely home and we are celebrating like it's a holiday."

The boys chose a long bench at one end of the big circular porch from which their view of the guests entering and leaving was certain. Paulie quietly gave a monologue of the local low-lifes versus the more typical residents and the boys tried diligently, as they ate, to commit to memory any face that seemed to their brains to be potential trouble. A woman exited the house across the street that had the two orange cones in front. She was maybe Spanish according to Paulie, but Wayne thought she looked like his aunt from Canada. They agreed after a chat that she was really pretty. None of whom Paulie had described as low-lifes tried to cozy up to her. They thought the lack of interest in her, when the men gave a lot of attention to all the other pretty ladies, was strange. Paulie whispered, "She must be very important. They're careful to show respect. Have either of you ever seen her before?"

Both answered no. Jackson said, "I thought only the old lady in a wheelchair lives in that house. I've only seen her once and she sure didn't look like this lady. She got picked up the day I saw her by a guy in a big car. He had trouble getting her up into the front seat. Let's draw her. Our art teacher will be impressed we're drawing a woman for a change."

As the boys were busy drawing the pretty lady whose name was Carmen, Detective Juan Flores climbed the porch stairs. The boys knew he was with MCU and hoped he wouldn't try to get too friendly with them. Wayne whispered, "If these people think we're cozy with the police, some of them won't let us hang around." They had nothing to worry about. The detective practically ignored them, which made them feel like real informants for the police.

Wayne noticed the party brought in lots of people from the streets, some of the ladies' friends, the detective, and two community police officers (both officers were unknown to him), and a couple of suits. He went for another plate of ribs before all the adults got to finish the buffet. Other than a little girl, who insisted on twirling around until she got dizzy, there were no other kids. He walked towards his bench, when three big guys climbed the stairs. He was face to face with the first of the three and it took all his effort to ignore him as if he'd never seen him before. He pretended just as he would when he was at home, avoiding his mother's eyes, when he knew she'd want him to do some work. Wayne slowly walked back to the bench and whispered to Paulie about the men. Paulie had already noticed them and when he got a punch in the ribs from Jackson, he knew Jackson was also aware of the visitors and their identities. Paulie said, "Now we get to draw their faces. Captain Beauregard will love this; pictures of the three drug dealers from Spruce Street. I'll do the middle one, Wayne, you do the first one, and Jackson, you draw the third one. One of them is Dominican and the other two are Puerto Rican. Don't let them see you drawing them. Keep that picture of the pretty lady Carmen in front to hide what you're working on."

The boys had no worries; the three men were interested in Carmen and the hostesses and never even looked in their direction. Paulie thought he saw Carmen give a big envelope to Miriam. He told his friends. The effect was immediate. All three informants looked crestfallen. Finally, Jackson said, "If it's money, maybe it's a donation to some good cause. Sara and Miriam can't be crooked; they just can't be. When we're finished eating, let's get out of here." There was no disagreement and shortly the boys were giving the ladies a hug and left on their bikes.

Within minutes Jackson called Captain Beauregard. The captain did not answer so he left a cryptic message saying, "Captain, we have important information and some drawings for you."

Mason was at the station having his own problems with faces. It was Saturday and he was working. Well he was actually avoiding work. The ladies in his family were having a big to-do on Sunday at church. His wife, daughters, sisters and sisters-in-laws, and blood, female cousins, and mom and mom-in-law were all in his mom's big kitchen cooking. He thought, *any halfway intelligent man in the family knew enough to get out. I'd rather work any day than be the stoop-and-fetch guy for the ladies.*

Faces were bothering him. He was looking at the drawing of Putin. *Damn if I can remember him from the hood. He doesn't have that kind of background, but I think I've seen him somewhere. Maybe when we were investigating the dead dancers and went to all those Irish bars; maybe that's where I saw him.*

Mason examined the crime scene photos from the three murders of the young anti-drug activists. There was something wrong with them. He felt there was more staging of the bodies than just washing the bodies and changing their clothes to prevent identifying the perp. No, he thought, *the bodies were deliberately splayed; I think he is dehumanizing them. I think he hates them. They are not placed to be sexually provocative. They are laid out to look like they're not important. This guy hates them; so why sexually assault them? It's an assault. No matter how hard I try to see what kind of man would do this. The answer is, someone who feels nothing; one of Beauregard's sociopaths. He insists evil sociopaths are the most difficult to discover because they look and walk like one of us and feel no fuckin guilt. What kind of face could ignore the suffering of young people; young and innocent people, and then make them look less than human?*

Mason worked on some of the details of the three murders having just received some reports from the Springfield police on the third murder. His inbox contained the Medical Examiner's report on the second murder in his city. The report showed the same evidence as in Candace's murder. Flunitrazepam, commonly known as Rohypnol or roofies, was also found in his urine along with the two injections of meth. The body's orifices had been wiped clean showing evidence of multiple rubbings. It was as if the two bodies were processed by a manufacturer in an extremely hygienic manner. Mason was annoyed. Who could be that careful two times? He did not have the final report from Springfield and he hoped it showed more than what he had on these two bodies. He posted some data on the murder boards and planned to set off to visit his relatives for dinner at his mom's home in Springfield.

Before leaving, Mason reviewed reports in his inbox; they were background reports from community police and Ted Torrington on the two victims. Many were interviews of their friends and also included school information, but nothing about the anti-drug club. It would take a couple of hours for him to read and synthesize the info from the reports. Sighing, he said aloud, "That's what tomorrow's for."

Mason had just started the trek over the bridge to Springfield, when he heard sirens. Up ahead there was a maze of Springfield and state police cars, two ambulances, two fire trucks, and passing him were two West Side police vehicles. He pulled over in the Avocado Street section. A uniform tried to wave him away, but let him through when he showed his badge. The officer said, "It's a shit show, Lieutenant; there's blood and torn flesh everywhere. Probably there are two or three shooters. No evidence of assault weapons. I saw a Glock 40 lying by one of the victims' vehicle."

Mason moved forward and saw three cars with doors open not far from the gas tanks, an area now roped off. Although the police were not near the tanks, the firemen had set sand bars around the tanks because one seemed to be leaking, and a wide swath of space had been wetted down. He saw an environmental truck with tanks and hoses attached approaching. He did not think there was danger, mainly because the site's protection was limited, and that would not be true if the environmental cops thought there was a big problem.

Mason approached one of the West Side officers for information. He'd seen him talking to Springfield MCU Lieutenant Joe Stellato who West Side detectives had worked with in two major serial murder cases. Joe asked what he was doing there; but still was agreeable to talk to him when he realized Mason was just going to Mama's house for dinner. Stellato said, "I won't be grabbing anything for dinner tonight but one of those ham sandwiches from the convenience store. Shit, it was a quiet day until this mess. Bunch of drug trafficking cowboys let loose; they must be fighting over turf, or one group trying to consolidate; used to be better when we had the Italian Mafia. At least we knew what was going on and generally on my watch civilians were not hurt."

Mason pushed Joe for more info, asking, "Joe, how many are dead and of those, how many civilians?"

He chided himself as he was questioning the lieutenant thinking, *I can see. What was I thinking when I asked him about what's right in front of me. There's a woman and a kid being covered with a sheet and a little girl, yelling, "Mama and John are dead. I want Daddy." I can't see how many others are dead other than some legs showing at least two others sticking out from one car.*

Stellato quickly informed him, saying, "Four men are dead. Three are known to us. One is Freddie Morales from the North End; another is his brother Jorge from the South End; a third is Mercure Diaz from Indian Orchard; and the fourth is a guy named Victor Sokolov who's not a citizen. He's from Uzbekistan and all we have on him is just a domestic assault charge. The other three are drug dealer kings in their own territories. There's not much on Sokolov."

Mason wanted to know if they caught the shooters, and if not, did they get descriptions. Joe sighed, shook his head, saying, "No description, but probably Dominicans from what the cashier inside the convenience store said. She won't testify. Said, 'I am a Dominican, and I know a Dominican when I see one. These were bad Dominicans. They don't live here; they're drug dealers. I know who to stay away from and I'm not dying; public service is one thing but it doesn't mean I have to die.'"

Stellato continued summing up. "She knows what she's talking about and she gave a description of the car as a Cadillac SUV."

The cashier had reported, "The car looks like the owner of the meat wholesale company's car. It has the same big soccer sticker on the back."

Stellato commented, "She was right. It was stolen off his company lot right in the middle of the day, and he didn't know about it. He went ballistic. We've put a BOLO out. It's probably parked less than a mile away. The prints will be wiped, but we'll diligently process it hoping for some trace evidence. Probably get nothing for our efforts. You know how it is, Mason, one in ten processing gives us a heads up."

Mason knew if Joe was talking, that his role was to agree with him to keep the information flowing, and so he agreed although he thought Joe's statistic was a bit light. He questioned, "What about the civilians, Joe? The little girl says her mother and brother are dead. I can't really see if the sheets are all the way up."

Joe replied, "The mother is Mrs. Sally Randall from West Side. She was making a delivery of vegetables to the wholesaler in back of the station. She's badly off, but not dead yet; don't know if she'll make it. She tried to protect the boy whose name is John. He was in the front seat of the car. He's eleven years old; he's not dead, but he may never play ball again. The girl was in a car seat in the back. She's six years old but small for her age. Her name is Mandy and all she can tell us is her address and mother's phone number and the next-door neighbor's telephone number. She wants her daddy, but we don't know how to reach him."

Mason whispered, "What's the surname again, Joe, maybe I know something."

"She's Sally Randall. Do you know her?"

Mason's answer was, "I do and this is not good. I think she's Beauregard's sister-in-law. I'll call JR, her husband, and Beauregard. Beauregard will want to be here. Okay?"

Joe groaned at this complication, but grieved for Beauregard thinking, *Christ, how come it happens to the good families. Her husband had her make a delivery for him. He'll blame himself forever.*

Mason made the calls and waited for Beauregard. He told JR to go directly to Baystate Medical Center where the two had been brought. As he waited for Beauregard, he called his Mom, and explained his delay. She said, "I'll wait an hour or two, Mason, and then your wife and sisters can bring some dinner to the family. Suffering families don't think about those things. Keep me in the loop. Don't worry, Mason, the ladies won't go up there if you think they shouldn't."

Mason thought, *they talk about Italian mothers and the 'Mangia' concept. My mama thinks that eating will help us bear all the vicissitudes of life. Not this kind of trouble, Mama.*

10

Innocent Victims and Faces

Beauregard called his wife Mona from the hospital to update her on the shootings. His normally logical wife dissolved into tears and spewed a particularly vicious comment on the region's criminal justice offenders; and she cried and cried before finally collecting herself. She went into Mona auto mode, as their kids would describe her normal helping behavior. She said, "Can Mason bring Mandy to the hospital? I'll wait in the emergency room. It's best I take care of her. JR will be out of his mind, but will still need to see his little girl. Rudy, catch these bastards. I thought if our kids weren't into drugs we would be safe; but we're never safe with these vicious purveyors of sickness. Pray, Rudy, please pray. Sally, JR, and the kids are our family. Please pray and get involved in solving these shootings. JR will be a basket case. I'm going to the hospital. Call the kids and check on them. Call Roland at college before the other boys call him and scare the hell out of them. I love you, Rudy -- take care of yourself for me. I need you."

A bit later, Rudy talked to Mandy, kissing her and hugging her, telling her that her mother and brother were both hurt, but they might get better. Like her Aunt Mona, Beauregard's wife, Mandy repeated the same thought, "Get them, Uncle Rudy. They're very bad. Mama and John did no bad things, and the other big men are dead. I don't know if they were bad."

After a few minutes and based on the emotional resiliency of Mandy, Rudy was able to bring the child to her Aunt Mona in the emergency room. He left for the site.

Beauregard walked the scene with Joe Stellato at his side. There were gulls flying high above; something he never understood, thinking, *How the hell do gulls get ninety miles inland? I see them around every large mall that has restaurants and food markets. Mona says they're a different species of gulls than the ones found near the ocean; but most gulls follow the food source. This development is loaded with wholesale meat and vegetable marts. The area looks like a movie set with the gulls flying low like vultures following the scent of blood.*

They looked at the bodies in place. The medical examiners were doing their job, but it was clear to both of them there were many bullets. Joe said, "Automatic weapons and Glocks. This was a planned shooting. The girl inside saw the new car as it arrived at the pump behind the four guys in the other car. She thought they were waiting for the pump, but two guys got out and opened fire. She said the guy lying outside the driver's door opened the door, got out, maybe said something, tried to duck and was shot by one of the other perps. That perp was moving closer to the victims' vehicle to get a better shot; to make sure they were dead. She thought the driver side victim got a couple of shots in before he died.

"We think maybe one of the victims wounded one of the perps because there's blood near where the shooters' car was parked; about where we estimate the front passenger side of the perp's vehicle was. We have a lot of blood and bullets. The Russian was in the front passenger side and he was just about out of the car and talking to the perps when he was shot; maybe right after he fired his gun. The two in the back seat were shot like clay pigeons practically still sitting in place. It's a fucking miserable site to process. The medical examiners and detectives will be here for hours documenting this mess."

Rudy observed something that brought some interest from Stellato. "Joe, when did you ever see Puerto Ricans put a Russian in the front seat when there's four in a car; just when?"

"I never have, unless the Russian is the boss and the Ricans are looking for something like hosting their new money man, or drug source, or market."

Rudy was about to remind Stellato about the 'noise' coming down on big changes in drug distribution in the western Massachusetts channel from NYC to Springfield to Vermont to Canada when members of the task force arrived; he bit his lip.

The district Attorney joined the scene to assist the Springfield police. A state police car with the troopers attached to the D. A.'s office pulled up. One of the occupants was Loughman, FBI Director of the drug Task Force. A trooper from the car approached Rudy immediately quietly stating the party line Rudy had heard before, "This isn't even your town, Captain. What are you doing here?"

Controlling his burning anger as well as he could, Rudy said, "My sister-in-law and nephew have just been gunned down by drug enforcers you told me you were going to take care of. Now get out of my face. This is family: first my cops are shot and now my family. You're not controlling anything. You won't let us keep this mess under everyday control. That's what we do. You're supposed to be looking for the big guys, but meanwhile you're stopping us from working the streets.

"You don't care about innocent civilians or kids dying with needles in their arms. No, you want a halo for when you do your job; when you get the big pusher. Not good enough for me. I don't want to hear another word from you." And Rudy walked away.

Loughman's aide rushed over to Rudy and said, "Beauregard, you don't want trouble. Loughman's under the gun and he's really doing a good job." In Rudy's mind, there was what was called, 'a stare down;' and Rudy walked away.

Rudy drove to the hospital again mainly to keep himself sane and to find out before forensics could process, what bullets were taken out of Sally and John. He also wanted to give solace to his brother-in-law JR. He hoped his presence would tell God how important these recoveries were to him. He prayed.

The hospital scene from Beauregard's eyes was different from past scenes. This time he had relatives as victims; this time he had enormous personal risk. He found little Mandy sitting between her dad, JR, and Mona in a private waiting room, which he knew from past experience was set aside for families of seriously and dangerously sick loved ones or in this case for criminal justice victims. Both JR and Mona had hold of one of Mandy's hands and were talking casually to the child hoping to ward off fear. But he could hear Mandy wasn't having any of it. Although only six years old, she expressed her world view saying to Mona, "But, Auntie, I saw Mama and John. They didn't look good. When the bodies look like that on CSI, they're always dead. I don't want Mama and John dead, but I think they must be almost dead. Where are the doctors to tell us, they are not dead?"

The child pulled her father's hand and crying said, "Where are the doctors, Daddy?"

At that moment Mason's sister and wife wheeled in a cart loaded with food; the smell of which filled the room. Little Mandy perked up and said, "Is that fried chicken? Is it for us?"

Despite the gravity of the situation, Rudy noticed that the prospect of food distribution and the ladies' insistence that everyone needed sustenance took some of the emotional heaviness away. The ladies explained they all had to remain healthy in order to care for Sally and John. Mandy drew some conclusions from this saying, "You mean Mama and John are coming home; and they will need us?"

The adults looked stupefied at the child's conclusions and felt responsible for perhaps implying too much hope that may in the future be taken away. Fortunately, Dr. Francisco, one of the surgeons, entered the room and called JR aside. JR, as a matter of course, dragged Rudy and Mona with him. Rudy noticed JR's normally rosy tinted face was devoid of any color at all. Dr. Francisco said Sally was in serious condition, but he hoped she would pull through commenting, "Your wife is super strong and healthy, Mr. Reynolds. If she weren't she would not have survived. She's lost a lot of blood. The bullets bypassed her organs but there are muscles and nerves hit that will take a long recovery period. As to young John, he's got some shoulder involvement which may require future surgery but he's already rallied. I can't tell you everything is fine yet, but it's looking a lot better than when they were admitted. Sally coded then, as I know you know from what the nurses have told me. I'm very hopeful, but although we have hope now, nothing in this business is for certain."

Rudy, Mona, and JR asked many questions, but the doctor did not deviate from his statement. Rudy thought, *just like with the police, the doctors have a public rhetoric which promises nothing. They just say they'll know better tomorrow.*

After the surgeon left, Mona prepared to leave taking Mandy home with her, leaving JR to holding vigil. He hoped if he waited and prayed that his family's life would continue for the future. He kissed Mandy and assured her he would do his best to help Mama and John. Rudy noticed JR kept his voice steady; probably hoping to make Mandy certain that things would be okay.

Rudy decided he would stay at the hospital thinking his brother-in-law would need to talk to someone who cared. While JR went over to talk to the nurses to see if he could get their take on his wife and son's condition and to question when he would be able to look in on them, Rudy checked his voice mail. He listened to several calls before receiving one from an unknown number. When he answered, he heard Jackson's voice detailing the info about the drug dealers. He called Jackson back, listened to his story, and asked when he could pick up the drawings. Jackson said he would give them to Officer Simeon, who he saw every morning near his school. Beauregard okayed the plan despite his nagging problem about letting anyone know he had kids giving the police information. He cautioned Jackson about being careful and he could not argue with Jackson's response. "Captain, we were just doing what we do. We can't help it if the ladies had unexpected guests at their unexpected party and that we recognized them, can we?"

Petra and Lilly were sitting in the office with Juan on the day after the shooting attempting to get their heads around Sally's and John's suffering. Petra, who had done eight years as a street cop in Boston and seen women and children shot in ancillary damage before, believed this was different. Now pregnant, she thought, *I have all these hopes for this babe of mine and look at what could happen; shot by mistake. I hate those drug dealers, I hate them.*

She started to cry and Juan said before Lilly could offer, "I'll get you some tea. You'll feel better."

His kindness just helped her waterfall of tears increase until she was almost wailing. Officer Simeon walked into the squad room, and apologized for entering unannounced saying, "Millie's not there yet. I'm sorry for interfering." His apology was apparently not important but the vision in front of him would stay with him. He remarked, "Tough Mexican Juan is bringing Lieutenant Petra a cup of tea. You never did that for me, Juan, and she's married. Wait till this gets into our cop harassing gossip line."

Petra shouted at him, "Keep your mouth shut, Officer, I'm pregnant and I understand I'll probably be crying for the duration; but laughing at me would be a mistake. I can laugh at me, but you, nope, you can't."

Officer Simeon's face reddened deeply and he apologized profusely; so much so that Petra laughed and told him to forget about it, that it was just a bad moment in her day. She asked, "What is it that you need the captain for, Simeon. He's home with family this morning or at the hospital. I don't know which, but I'm sure you've heard through the vine what happened to his sister-in-law and his nephew."

Simeon answered, "That's why I'm here. I was told by three kids that the captain needs to see these drawings. They have them so taped up I couldn't open them, but they said it's important and the captain would want to see them immediately. They're good kids and often tell me what's going on in the district but they think they're 007s and all info must be a secret."

Lilly opened the taped-up mess and was able to get out intact three sketches of some tough men who from her experience were probably Dominicans or South Americans or Puerto Ricans. She did not think their facial structure looked Mexican or Caucasian. She showed the drawings to Juan, Petra, and Simeon and asked if they had seen any of them before. The answer was negative. She said, "Well we'll have to wait for the captain to see what he wants to do with them. Maybe when Mason comes in he'll play with them and do a search. He'll know if the drawing is good enough for the computer to search. Actually, it looks a hell of a lot better than what our in-house artist does on victims' sketches."

Simeon left, grateful to be out of there. He thought, *too much stress in there today for me.*

Petra noticed the turnstile of people entering and leaving the squad room, as Simeon left and Mason arrived. Juan greeted him happily, shoving the sketches of the three men in his face saying, "Mason, you ever see these guys? The kids the captain's been working with, sent these to him; what do you think?"

Mason putting down his briefcase and looking annoyed stopped to review the drawings, saying, "At least let me breathe a moment. I got stuck behind an accident for twenty minutes before the cops came. One guy thought he was a cop and tried to direct traffic, one car each way one at a time. I was too tired from being at the hospital and entertaining my family last night to bother assisting him. Alright, what do we have here?"

Mason stared at the three pieces of paper for at least a minute before answering and finally said, "I've seen the guy in sketch number one but not the other two. He used to hang around near a market over by St. James Avenue in Springfield that was later raided for drugs. None were found despite the fact that an undercover agent bought some the day before. I know for a fact the Springfield narcotics guys saw a New York registered SUV delivering to them the day before. They took an extra day before they went in to cover for their undercover guy. The cops later figured something or somebody wised the dealers up and maybe they took the delivery away in the same SUV without ever delivering. The dogs found a small stash but nothing substantial. I can tell you the drug team's tail was between their legs. Why they didn't have a watch overnight, I don't know."

Petra, still annoyed with herself for her previous explosion of emotion, impatiently said, "Get with it, Mason. Who is he?"

Mason shook his head and said, "I don't know but I know he's Dominican and he's connected to drugs and I'm certain he's in the system for something. Even if he isn't, Springfield Police know him. Have the captain call Stellato. He's Springfield Major Crimes, normally outside of Narcotics Division or the drug taskforce. He won't be as protective of info as the taskforce."

Petra asked, "Why can't we look for him first? I guess I'll answer my own question; now that I remember Stellato and the FBI drug task force head told Beauregard to stay out of all of this. They're not going to help us identify someone, especially if they've had their eye on him before. The kids told Simeon these guys were conductors of the drug business on Spruce Street where Ash and Ted were shot. And then last night the fireworks over by Avocado Street may be connected -- better wait for the captain before we do anything."

Petra heard a voice behind her say, "Why do you have to wait for me before you do something. Since when have any of you worried about that?"

Nobody laughed which indicated to Beauregard there must be a situation that needed to be put right and by him.

The detectives alternated among themselves in telling the story of the kids' drawings, Mason's recognition of one of the faces, and the fact that the one face Mason recognized connected to a non-successful drug raid in Springfield.

Beauregard responded, "Nexus, nexus, you may have found the nexus. We had someone in our own backyard carrying on business and we fell for the Feds when they told us to disappear. What's interesting is this one is Dominican, not Puerto Rican. That's not Dominican territory; or it wasn't. They didn't want us to know how important that business was in the scheme of things. Even Putin pooh-poohed it as a minimal operation. I'm not sure we can utilize the drawing in the system without being shut down.

"I'm certain the right people could canvass the St. James neighborhoods and find someone who knows him. We have to have a story for them; a story that is not connected to drug wrongdoing."

Lilly said, "Captain, he's probably got a lady. Most do; in fact, many have more than one. You could use the ruse his girlfriend is being sought by the wife. I've used it before. Either the wife's friends lead you right to his domicile or the girlfriend finds him."

Petra mused aloud, "But it's Springfield and we can't do it."

Mason supplied an answer with a question saying, "Who could we ask? Do we have any funds for Hunt and Find Detectives; Jim Locke would be great?"

The captain said, "We have funds and we're moving on this. These punks aren't shutting us down just because Loughman doesn't want us to investigate. First, I'm going to see that clerk at the convenience store near Avocado Street. She knows my family got hurt. What do you think, Mason, maybe she'll recognize these guys as the shooters yesterday; as long as she doesn't have to testify?"

Mason replied, "Captain, why don't you let me do this. You're on the hook with the FBI task force and if anyone sees you over there, you know it won't be good. I'll question her. She'll be much more forthcoming with me and Jim Locke is not our cop anymore; he's an outsider. He can use whatever will work to snoop over on Saint James Avenue. You shouldn't be involved in this investigation."

A clearly annoyed Beauregard reluctantly agreed but tried to put himself into the hiring of Jim Locke saying, "Petra can't do it. He's her husband. Lilly and Juan don't know him, and besides I should do the hire."

Mason disagreed but followed with a suggestion. "Ash should do it. He and Jim are good friends, especially after the dancing ladies' murders. He's also pretty creative and between him and Jim, we'll get a good result. Also, he's not off sick call yet."

The captain said, "I thought I just saw a release for him to return to duty soon; at least that's what he told me."

Mason laughed, jokingly saying, "He said that, but it was a referral to desk duty not field duty, Captain."

A grumbling captain, after authorizing their suggestions, left the room saying, "JR insisted I need not come to the hospital; that I need to find the sons of bitches who shot his family. He wants me to make sure they get big time. He's frantic and my presence just reminds him of what happened. I want to be there, but not today."

Petra quietly answered the captain, "I'll go to the hospital, Captain. I'll keep you informed. It's good you're not going. The Springfield police will be waiting for Sally to feel good enough to give a witness statement and they won't let you near her when they do."

Lilly showed her distrust in police procedures with witnesses, saying, "Captain, your family will need a lawyer. First reason is to keep the little boy John's description out of the paper and the second is to get any information about the crime for you. That Springfield MCU detective may be your friend, but the FBI would have really scared him about sharing by now, at least from what I've heard."

Beauregard knew what he had to do and he made the call. In fact, when he looked at his messages, there were fifty of them, with one call that interested him. He thought, *Serendipitous!*

11

Two Problems Chased

Beauregard headed over to the Slainte Restaurant, an Irish Pub in Holyoke, for lunch with Attorney Norbie Cull. Norbie greeted him with a big bear hug that brought tears to Rudy's eyes. He thought, *Hell, Norbie's half my weight and two to three inches shorter, but still he got his arms around me.*

"How are you doing, Rudy? I called this morning when I heard Sally's name. I wasn't here yesterday. I was in East Sandwich with Sheri trying to recover after a difficult and nasty trial. It's what I do. One or two days by the shore, smelling that sea smell, eating fresh lobster, and I'm a new man. Look, whatever you want I will do. No charge, no worry, I'll do anything to help your family."

Rudy could not hold back the sarcasm; mostly he thought, because, *I don't know how to accept gifts. That's what Mona and Lizette say.*

He said, "Christ, Norbie, they'll take away your shark's badge if you start helping people for free."

Instantly regretting his wise-ass remark, he continued, "I'm sorry. It just felt normal being a punk. Thank you, Norbie, I need your help. I can't be seen active in this investigation. The FBI is really after me to stay clear of all drug investigations. First my detectives were shot and now my family. I love my sister-in-law and nephew. Mona and the kids are devastated. JR's little six-year-old daughter is living with me because frankly, JR is not able to do the parenting that's needed; but that's okay. Mona is there. The Springfield Police will be looking to interview the two victims and little Wanda, who is supposed to tell them what she saw happen. They won't let me there to hear what's said or to support the family. I called JR on my way here, told him you are his family lawyer and threatened him. He will listen to whatever you say. That's what I need, Norbie."

The two were interrupted by an energetic and particularly hospitable waitress. She sang out the specials in a melodic voice and pointed out her personal favorites listing: Shephard's Pie, Guinness Beef Stew, and the Corned-beef Reuben. Hoping she would leave them alone they ordered quickly; the Reuben for Norbie and the Stew for Rudy.

Norbie got back to business quickly. "Rudy, certainly I'll represent your family and make certain Sally, John, and Mandy are protected from the police. As their attorney, I have the right to be there. I'll clear my schedule for the next couple of days. Let Stellato know I'm on the job, and nobody gets interviewed unless I'm there. Don't worry; I'll put my ear to the ground for info on these killers. I heard they might be hardcore big-time drug dealers; but killing Russian and Puerto Rican dealers who have their own solid defined area says the goal may be territorial – you know -- to take over. I'll talk to some people in the know for you, Rudy. Hurting innocent bystanders is a major sin and a big mistake. Sounds like the shooters don't understand this turf."

They finished their meal with each having a second coffee, and a scuffle for the check with Norbie ensued with Norbie moving faster in the grab. Rudy complained he was asking for the favor and therefore he should pay, to no avail.

Norbie then left for the hospital with his earpiece on and called his office.

It was at this moment that Rudy, struggling with what he could do this day when so many investigative avenues had been closed off to him, had an insight, thinking, *today is a good day to visit Shelburne Falls and Buckland and take a look at this Stella's death; find out what's going on down there. Could there be a connection to the other three bodies; meth was the drug, her body was moved, and her dad mentioned she was really anti-drug now. On top of that the police in her town have not yet sent me a report. How long does that take? Even investigating Candace's death with nada to show for it; it's now almost two months since Ash and Ted were shot. I've not made any progress in discovering the underlying platform for these killings and this drug activity.*

Beauregard headed towards Shelburne Falls, a town whose importance he thought is its representation of nostalgia. The Bridge of Flower is its centerpiece. He considered, *the bridge town has less than four thousand full-time residents and it connects two towns on either side of the Deerfield River. How the hell could this town have a drug problem, for a kid attending Mohawk Trail Regional High School, that wouldn't be noticed? Stella lived in Buckland. Buckland has a chief of police, two patrolmen, and eight part-time officers; while nearby Shelburne Falls has a chief, a sergeant, a patrol officer, and six reservists. Shelburne Falls is a village. If Stella was found on the bridge, I wouldn't know which town would own the incident. I suppose it would depend on which part of the bridge where she was found. I hate even the thought of dealing with two police bureaucracies; if anyone could even think that these small departments could have bureaucracies. I thank the Almighty she was found in Buckland and not on the Bridge.*

Understanding police protocol, Beauregard called the chief's office and learned the chief was at a tourist planning conference. Using his friendliest manner, he explained after introducing himself to the officer, who answered the phone, what he hoped was a polite inquiry, "Officer

Tynan, I had a break in my schedule for a ride to your town. It's simply a beautiful autumn day, but I hope my ride will be productive. I sent a request for info relative to the death from drugs of a teenager and I haven't received any response yet. I thought maybe there was a lot of detail that was difficult to describe and it might be best for me to come in person."

He was informed they were in charge of the investigation and had received his request earlier. Officer Tynan said, "I apologize for taking so long to get back to you, Captain, but my chief has been busy. I am just now ready to respond to your request about the Stella McGourley death. The family thinks it's more than an accidental overdose. The chief looked into the death. Although the body was moved not far from the bridge, the medical examiner said that she had sex recently; and the conclusion was she over partied. Now maybe she was partying with a boyfriend and they were injecting each other, but the chief doesn't believe we'll ever know."

Beauregard's tone in his answer was guarded. He said, "I'll be there in forty-five minutes. Would the report be available then? Perhaps I could speak with an officer who was on scene that day. I don't know which police department was first called, but I'm certain that an officer who was present at the scene saw the big picture better than any report written up. Officers see everything."

Officer Tynan laughed and seconded Beauregard's remark with, "Right on, Captain Beauregard. We get lazy or just filter so we don't look nuts in filing reports. Come on up, I'll be here and show you everything. I'll think on it because I was the officer who found her. The family insists she didn't do drugs, but there's a lot of junk up here. We have a new center in Greenfield for substance abuse recovery and that's not far from us. Pristine environment does not mean everyone living here is pristine. The other thing, Captain, is that the junk is everywhere, in small towns and big cities. It's this century's scourge."

On arrival Beauregard immediately liked Officer Tynan, who without any hesitation presented the chief with a file on the death along with a hot cup of freshly made coffee. The officer cleared a desk and told the chief he could take as long as he wanted to examine the file. He said he was available all afternoon if further information was needed. Beauregard appreciated the young officer's efforts and realized quickly Officer Tynan hadn't an obstructive bone in his body. The file was almost identical to the West Side teen death files. Stella had been moved to the dumping site and was splayed out. The medical examiner said the victim had sex within three hours of finding her. There was evidence of Flunitrazepam or Rohypnal, two injections of meth with the estimate that the first one made didn't kill her but a second one did. Her clothes were not her own, but there was no inquiry in the file related to the new clothes; all were without labels and brand new. There were very good pictures of the body and he could see there was no evidence of footprints near the body. The estimated time the body had been deposited on site was around four a.m. and it was found about seven a.m. by a jogger. The jogger saw her amongst some leaves where her bare feet showed. The jogger thought she was sleeping and tried to wake her. When she couldn't revive her, she called the police and practically collapsed when Officer Tynan, the first to respond, got there.

Beauregard questioned Tynan about what he concluded from the site or from any other info or report he had received. "You have to understand, Captain, there is not a lot to do up here except during the tourist season. We're part of a group of rural towns surrounding the city of Greenfield which itself has only a little over seventeen thousand residents, but at last count had thirty registered sex offenders; that's about 1.8% of the population. The kids go to Greenfield or maybe Deerfield for entertainment. Deerfield has a little over five thousand residents. Those are the locations for their opportunity to participate in eating at more diverse restaurants and night life.

"Drug activity is rampart up here. When there's nothing to do, well why not try to numb yourself with alcohol or drugs. The kids need more entertainment. But why this kid, Stella? I knew her. She did not hang around with the 'idgits;' no she did not! She was an activist against drugs. Who knows, maybe she just got sick of being out of the loop."

Beauregard asked, "How do they get access to drugs? I mean these towns are small and wouldn't you know where the drugs are coming from? Don't you know when someone is hanging around who doesn't, you know, belong here? Maybe during tourist-time, I could anticipate some confusion, but I don't understand why there's so much drug activity going on in these hill towns."

"Captain, you're busy trying to stop the major drug highways from Trenton and the eastern ports that come up through New York to Springfield and Holyoke to supply the west and northern areas. One highway goes through Providence and heads to Boston and Cape Cod; it also hits your area as well. Those are big time distributors. Our deliveries are by auto and truck delivering some other goods. We can't stop every car going through our towns. Greenfield gets hold of some stuff that is occasionally found when some kid gets frightened by a parent who's caught him or her high; but that's rare. Kids up here don't squeal except those who have missionary zeal about drugs. Stella lost a childhood friend who overdosed last year. Don't know what that means."

"Have you seen anyone suspicious who you haven't been able to feel comfortable with, maybe someone driving a fancy car? Maybe you've seen someone who stays one or two nights even in the non-tourist time?"

"Several come to mind, Captain. There's this New Yorker who

comes in his Land Rover and spends money wildly, but he doesn't talk to the kids, just the waitress at the local restaurant. They've hit it off and now he visits her. He's harmless. There's another guy in his early thirties who comes around fairly often and is not from these parts. He looks okay, almost good looking, but with a sneery edge to him. That's what my mom would say about guys like him. His drive is a new, not a particularly showy SUV; maybe it is American made. It's not a Mercedes or Infiniti or BMW. I don't like him because he looks at you like you're nothing; you know what I mean. Even the gas station attendant says he treats him like dirt. I've seen him talking to some young kids, but he doesn't go after the girls; at least from what I've seen."

"So, did you ever see him talking to Stella?"

"Yeah, a couple of times, but she was with a couple of other good kids, so it seemed harmless to me. One of those kids is seasonal and he went back to New York in September for school. The other is Barney Lester. He lives a mile from Stella. Talk to Stella's family. They'll arrange a conversation with him quicker than I could."

"Thanks, Officer Tynan, I will."

"Good luck, Captain. I really mean it. I think something's fishy here, and anything you can accomplish that casts some attention on our drug problem, I'm all for."

Rudy, anticipating a difficult conversation with Stella's family, walked over to a place called "Hearty Foods" on Bridge Street. He was not impressed when he discovered it was a vegetarian restaurant. However, when he went in he noticed some amazing looking desserts. Settling in quickly, he ordered a dark roast Colombian coffee and a sweet looking pastry loaded with nuts and fruits and coconut. He mused how Mona would kill him if she knew; but he absolved himself of guilt knowing he was facing a call that would be heart wrenching. He sat in a corner that afforded him some privacy; particularly because it was later in the afternoon and there were only two other occupied tables.

Rudy made the call to his friend Jake McGourley, Stella's father. Jake answered with a gruff hello. When he heard Rudy was in town investigating, Rudy noticed a big change in Jake's his voice. He said, "You didn't forget me, Rudy. Come on over to the house and tell me what you've learned. I'm not crazy, am I?"

Rudy explained, "I probably won't be up here again, Jake; and I'm hoping you can get one of Stella's friends over to your house for an interview. I'm told he's a good kid. His name is Barney Lester and he lives near you. It's pretty late in the day so unless he's working after school, he may be home. I'll go to where he's working if that's necessary. See what you can do while I drive over to your house. What's the address and do you need me to pick anything up on the way?"

"Nah, we have all we need except our Stella is gone from us, Rudy; but I'll get Barney over here. He's a good friend of the whole family. He'll come right away."

Rudy chose a box of pastries for his friend and decided it was no wonder they tasted so great, they were expensive. His brain examined the issue. *these earthy crunchy places have to charge a lot. Mona says they have all organic ingredients. Hell, I can't tell the difference. I just know the stuff tastes great. Then again, I eat devil dogs; what do I know?*

Jake's house was situated on about four acres of land and had lots of attachments ending in an enormous barn. He took in the New England landscape and the big porch surrounding two sides of the home and mumbled, "This is gorgeous, what we all dream about. Living well, but still he loses a daughter to drugs. No fucking way this should happen to anyone."

Rudy trudged up with his bakery box of goodies and before he could knock, the door opened. Jake stepped onto the porch and hugged him in a bear hug. A strong looking but spare woman, behind Jake, said, "Let the poor man in, Jake. I'll make some coffee. He's brought dessert from Hearty Foods. Set him down by the fire."

Jake smiled at his wife and said, "That's my Alice always trying to comfort."

The warmth of the room with its old-fashioned fieldstone fireplace helped mitigate the aura of sorrow that overwhelmed these two nice people. At least that's how Rudy felt about the room. He explained what he had heard from Officer Tynan, but only in the most limited way. The McGourleys were not police. They were victims. Jake may be a friend, but still Rudy thought, *I have to be careful about what I share with them.*

"Don't be too hard on Officer Tynan, Jake. He was most helpful and thought there may be room for more investigation, despite the fact that on its face, it looks like an overdose and movement of the body to hide other users who were with her. I am looking seriously at this death, but I cannot investigate here. It's not my town. I think if Barney can tell me more about Stella and her friends, it could be helpful. How often did Stella go into Greenfield or Deerfield for entertainment? And if she did go to either place, who went with her?"

Before Jake could answer either question, two young men ballooned through the door, one pushing the other. Jake yelled, "This is still a home, guys, and we have a guest. Captain Beauregard, this is our son MJ and our friend and Stella's friend Barney Lester. Sit down, guys, please. The captain has some questions for you."

Never was there a more intent audience listening to the captain's questions. Both boys quickly responded which was helpful in preventing

Jake from putting a negative spin on all answers. Finally, his son MJ said, "Dad, you're actually not at all helpful. Captain Beauregard is your friend and he's smart. He doesn't need a history lesson about every person we talk about. And he's looking for stuff that we know, but he doesn't. He's the investigator. He knows what's important."

The resulting conversation was smoother. Barney spoke about the group in which Stella and he belonged, whose purpose was to act against kids selling and using drugs. It included their identifying pushers and silently reporting them into a secret system that filtered the information to authorities without the kids being identified. They'd been active for about a year and a half. He said, "There's been a lot of oxy, meth, and heroin on the scene lately. We don't even look at marijuana anymore. We connect with groups from Greenfield and Deerfield, but the guy who inspired us is a guy from Springfield. His name is Herbie and he's young and full of fire and energy. I'm telling you he could inspire anyone. Practically every drug arrest in our area during the last year and a half is based on the secret system."

Beauregard asked for info to whom they secretly reported. MJ said, "Stella would drive to Greenfield with her girlfriends and go to dinner. While her friends were eating dessert, she would leave for a short while to hide an envelope under this crevice on a rock by the City Hall steps. She never knew who it would go to. One night, Barney went with her and he and Stella waited in a car a block away; although it was dark, she saw an older guy, maybe in his fifties, pull out the envelope. On another night, they watched and it was a younger guy who picked up the envelope. That was a month ago and all drug arrests, except for DUIs, stopped, then."

Barney continued, "We, Stella and me, told the others we needed to change the system, but we haven't seen Herbie to tell him. We think someone told the wrong person about the system, 'cause there have been very few drug arrests in Deerfield and Greenfield for the past month. We keep track. Stella said she had an idea that the last guy, the younger one was probably the bad guy and she was going to follow him. She promised not to go without me, but I work Saturday nights, and those are the nights we'd bring envelopes with info. Not every Saturday night, but every other one. I think she went without me, 'cause Stella would never use drugs."

"Why in hell didn't you guys tell me what was going on? What the hell's the matter with you? You had information and you didn't tell me."

Beauregard spoke up in a very loud voice. "Cut it out, Jake. Stella, like all of us who try to do good, thought she could do it on her own. Just like you and me have always done and we thought it okay to risk a lot. No one, from what I have learned about your beautiful Stella, would have been able to stop her. She was on a mission. She thought she was doing important work and she was going to do it. The problem is Stella was young and inexperienced, and I am absolutely certain she could not see that a person would want to murder her to shut her up."

Alice spoke out, "I just heard Swiss scientists have confirmed that all humans come from one woman and one man. If that's true and they're saying it is and furthermore, that there is no great evolutionary process involved; I don't understand how there can be so many who do evil deeds compared to those doing good." And she continued to cry until her son spoke.

MJ reminded his mom, "Mom, you teach geometry and know all about tangents, like Grandma used to say, 'As the twig is bent, so grows the tree.' Stella died doing good and left us with her memory. She was Stella; always looking to do good. We can cry, but we can be proud. She stood up when others ignored the drug problem around us. Captain, please find who murdered her; she did not kill herself doing drugs."

Beauregard was moved by MJ and reminded himself of how much

wisdom each person has, even a teenager. He asked about the leader called Herbie, and about the make and color car he drove. He thought, *how many young kids today are called Herbie, unless they're a junior? Could this Herbie be the Springfield victim?*

Barney told them Herbie had a cool red convertible. He said that, "Druggies would never think he was a good guy. He looked like a cool dude into himself, but he wasn't. He would never tell us his last name. He said we should be careful. Just do the drops when no one was around and there'd be no problem. He said he worked with people near each drop site who would forward the info to the right people."

Beauregard asked if Barney knew how many drops there were in the whole area. His question, on whether there was only the one drop site near the Greenfield Town Hall, was answered affirmatively. He pursued the idea with, "Barney, do you have a list? I need the people who were responsible for the drop."

Barney said he knew only Stella was one, because she told him and she normally didn't like to go alone to Greenfield. "We often met in groups; we all heard Herbie talk at a speak-out against drugs at a small church in Greenfield. That's when our group of kids all connected with him and gave him our cell numbers. When he would come to town occasionally he would meet with us over coffee and talk about what was going on in all the towns. We'd tell him things we'd never tell our parents or the police. There was never any trouble in telling Herbie anything. That is, until now."

It took Beauregard another hour of discussion before he was able to leave the very sad group. Jake McGourley hugged him as he was leaving and said, "You did what I asked. It doesn't heal our pain, but as MJ says, it was who Stella was! Catch the bastard, Rudy." And he wiped his eyes.

12

Herbie and His History

On the following day, Captain Beauregard found himself gazing out his office door window at the everyday squad room view and mumbling, "Mandy sits with my son Lucas who tells her all these tales about when he was in grade school. She asks him about her mother and brother and he's able to soothe her better than Mona. He says things like 'Bad things happen to good people' and there's even a bumper sticker about it. She then asks him will bad things happen all the time and, in his innocence, he says, 'No way, Mandy. Only so many per family, I think'. She's comforted by him. It's all a lie. Some families only have bad things happening."

Petra rushed in and as her nickname Bolt intimated, she explained in less than two minutes she had all the info he had asked her to get on the previous evening. "Captain, calling me at quarter to nine at night; well, you're lucky I was awake. I went to sleep two seconds after I ate my dinner. This is the second time you've called me late in two weeks. But, not to worry, I've got most of your answers."

Rudy asked, "Did you speak with Mona's student Betsy Printer about the anti-drug crusade and Candace?"

"I'm meeting with her after school today at the West Side library.

Did I tell you that's where they always met? Their mentor told them drug dealers never go to libraries and it was a safe place."

"Yeah, Petra, you did. Who the hell is this mentor? Is it Herbert Brent, Jr. the Springfield victim?"

"Yup, I think so. The mentor drove a red convertible and is named Herbie. How'd you know?"

"I have my ways, Lieutenant. I have my ways."

"Remember Captain, he lived in West Side, over by Westfield; he's one of ours and he's not that old. I've called the father and asked if I could speak with him about his son. He said the Springfield Police had already been there, and he told them everything he knew. I reminded him his son was very well thought of and his anti-drug efforts with young people could have put him in the spotlight that resulted in his death. He wants to meet with you, Captain. I said you would go there around noon, because it was the only time his wife wouldn't be there. He says she's not ready to talk about Herbie Jr. yet. He also said, 'No way would Herbie use drugs and that he was murdered;' and he told the police they better not cover it up."

"I'll go. It means cancelling my appointment with the Chief. Good job, Petra. Did you also check with the West Side High School psychologist about Candace, Ollie, and maybe Herbie?"

"She has time in an hour. So, I'll have my notes on your desk when you come back from seeing Mr. Brent."

As Petra left, Lilly entered. Unlike Petra, Lilly quietly walked in and sat down with a loud sigh. "Captain, the West Side community police know all about these students operating their anti-drug campaign. The students in our city are mostly high school and first year college students. They've had three meetings in the last eight months at several churches talking to youth groups. Our officers never attended the meetings; they just heard about them so they don't know all who attended. The officers know Candace and Ollie, but don't know Herbie Brent. They have seen a good-looking guy in a red convertible talking to Candace. Candace, according to them, was a take charge kind of girl and a major force in this movement. They never saw any danger. They said someone would occasionally send information in an envelope directed to the Narcotics Division. They opened the first letter and it was a list of drug transactions and location of drugs in the city. They never opened another one after Captain Chillicot gave them hell. They would then just forward the envelopes to him."

Beauregard requested Lilly interview the students known by the police. He wanted to know how the group started, who in the group were the most vocal, areas of the city where the groups would meet, sections of the city where each student lived, and any other info she could get out of them about the red convertible and Herbie Brent, Jr.

Beauregard left the office stopping at Friendly's for a grilled cheese sandwich, an ice cream sundae with hot fudge and whipped cream, and hi-test coffee. Seeing a third set of grieving parents in a few weeks was for him a crisis. He'd developed his very bad practice, years ago, of treating stress with food, at least that's what both Mona and Lizette told him. He knew they were right, but today, he considered it a necessity to get him into the difficult role of questioning a father about the son he lost to murder.

Not feeling a bit guilty but instead feeling quite robust, Beauregard headed toward Westfield. The Brent's lived in an enormous nineteenth century updated yellow farmhouse at the first major left off the route to towns west of the city. The home had ample land; but the modern architectural designed homes on either side of the Brent's home interrupted his reverie into a simpler past. He parked his car and waited to settle down to the job before him.

Lifting his bulk, slowly as usual, Beauregard approached the archway porch, meeting as he climbed the three stairs, a handsome man around fifty years old. He immediately greeted him. "Thank you for coming, Captain Beauregard. Your fame precedes your visit and you look like your photos in the news."

They entered the home and settled in a warm sitting room to the left of the large center hallway. The home was remarkable in its attention in décor which stayed true to the home's historic era. Despite the lit wood fireplace and the comfy tall back chairs Beauregard thought, *the chill of loss is here. I feel the same as when I went to Stella's home. Different sites and backgrounds but I feel the hell of their suffering; and actually, what can I do to help them? I'm powerless, other than perhaps catching the perp. What good does that really do for those suffering? I used to feel reassured when I found the perp; one more perp off the streets. What good does that do for the victims and their families? What good is it going to do for my brother-in-law's family; although he says it's important to him!*

Herbert Brent asked Rudy to call him Herbert. He said he took that name when Herbert Junior was born to differentiate him from his son, saying, "Maybe I'll go back to Herbie so when my wife calls me 'Herbie,' I can think of him, my son."

Beauregard felt a glitch in his throat at Herbert's statement. Stuttering at first, he asked about Herbie's work with drugs and whether Herbert knew about it. Herbert did and explained what had happened. Junior's best friend died two and a half years before from chronic use of oxy. He'd had a serious neck vertebra injury and several surgeries and rehabilitation stays where he was regularly given prescriptions for pain meds. When he tried to wean himself off, he had terrible pain. Finally, the doctors would not give him further medication beyond normal analgesics. His parents thought he was being a baby and to be honest he didn't share his serious pain with them. He hit the streets. He'd work after classes and all his money went to drugs. Kids would steal oxy from their parents to help him out. Nobody at that time understood what was happening, and then he drove his car over the side of the road near the woods in Westfield and hit a tree. The Medical Examiner found he was under the influence of oxy and heroin. Nothing was said about it in the papers because it was a single car accident and nobody was hurt. "I'm telling you, Captain, for my son, it was a call to arms. Herbie did everything in overdrive. He was an A student, an excellent athlete, helped everyone at our church functions, took the neighbor's daughter who was handicapped to her senior prom when no one else would ask her, and never needed to be prodded to do anything for us around the house. I should have known when he first started with this anti-drug campaign. He called it 'OIEO' or 'Our Investment in Each Other'. They pronounced it as OH-I-OH, almost like Ohio. It was a year before I understood what the OIEO meant. He was a sophomore at the University and insisted on commuting. We should have known that was not the norm. Most kids today want to board if their parents can afford it. We could afford it."

"Herbert, how did he get other young people involved and do you know any of them?"

"Herbie spoke at churches, on drug panel discussions at schools all over, at youth panels on drugs at hospitals, had an anti-drug exhibition booth at the Expo in West Springfield; he did everything he could to highlight the problem. He went on the march to the State House in Boston. I couldn't go anywhere with him that people didn't come up to him to discuss what was going on."

"Herbert, would you let me look at his computer and records in his room? I'm going to ask for access to his computer. You know, it's always in the details that we find connections to places and people who lead us to evidence that works to solve cases. I think there are other deaths, well murders, connected to your son's."

Herbert said, "I told the Springfield Police it was murder, but they would not confirm it. I thank you for that."

Beauregard said, "It's important you not say anything about murder. I told you because you should know, but early public knowledge will interfere with the investigation. The public does not want to share information in a murder. Generally, they are afraid. They will share information in what is considered by them an accidental death. So please help me out with this."

Herbert agreed. Beauregard told him he was calling Mason Smith, the MCU IT guru, who would bring an additional officer; that it would take a few minutes before they would arrive. He asked if it would be too much for Herbert to join him in his initial search of Herbie's room saying, "Normally two detectives would do a search, but with you with me, we will certainly be able to preview what may be important outside of the computer. It's not normal, but doable. We will take the computer with us, but will also connect with the Springfield Police. I don't want to wait for them if there is information that could be immediately helpful. I'll call them before we leave if we find anything of importance."

Beauregard made his call to Detective Mason Smith, and he and the suffering father climbed the stairs to start their search. Herbie's room was quite large with low dormers and windows on two sides. It had a queen-sized bed and what Beauregard would call a French reclining couch except it looked too masculine to be like the French divans his wife was always looking at in *Architectural Digest*. Herbert sat on the divan while Beauregard started the search in the first of three closets. The first two held clothes, shoes, and a selection of baseball caps that would have been the envy of his three sons. The third closet was built into the eaves and had inside cabinets. Herbert said, "I've never been in there, Captain; not sure my wife has either."

Beauregard sat his ample body on the floor and slid into the main portion of the closet thanking the Brent's for putting lights in the closet, thinking, *certainly lights in a closet weren't a code requirement in the eighteen-hundreds. Love that they rehabbed some of this.*

The doorbell rang and Herbert went to let Mason Smith in, while Beauregard searched the alcove cabinets and the search was astounding. One cabinet contained over one hundred pictures which after he looked at the first few, he was certain, were photos of drug transactions. The second cabinet contained a portfolio with a page for each name, organized alphabetically within each town, also listed alphabetically. Two names caught his eye for West Side: Candace Monroe and Oliver Rapusca. He checked for Shelburne Falls, but there was only a Greenfield sheet and one of the names on it was Stella McGourley. He thought, *three is not a coincidence. Three is evidence. Hell – what Herbie and these kids were doing to fight drugs got them killed. Were they so successful that their interference with drug business caused their deaths? Why the hell kill them in the way they were killed with obvious deviant sexual overtones?*

The third cabinet had a red legal brick filled with newspaper clippings of drug busts and obituaries from western Massachusetts cities and towns.

Detective Smith laughed when he saw his boss on the floor with papers and photos surrounding him. "Got something, Captain?"

"Yeah, it's not what I expected, and far more than I could ever have dreamed."

Herbert said, "Captain, I know you won't tell me what you've found, but does it redeem my son? Does it clear the air that he's not a druggie? It's so important to my wife."

The captain tried to stand up quickly and almost fell over as his knee gave way. Fortunately, Officer Landers grabbed him before he fell on his head. Embarrassed, Beauregard groaned, "My wife tells me to get this weight off. I don't listen, but I will now. I need my knees."

Beauregard, when he was finally upright, put his hand on Herbert's shoulder and stated, "Herbie was an exceptional young man with a missionary zeal to help. It is clear he devoted himself to dealing with a drug problem that is a societal problem. In a vacuum of leadership, your son took the lead and to top it all off, he knew it was dangerous. He kept meticulous records of what he knew and saw and hid them in these inner closets behind boxes. No one, I mean, no one would suspect they were here. He knew enough to protect his work. Mason, have a look at his computer while I rest a minute."

Herbert now was sitting on Herbie's bed and cried a little while Beauregard rested on the divan watching Mason do his magic and Officer Landers bag the papers. What seemed like an eternity to Beauregard, and in his estimation was only about twenty minutes of silence with the exception of Herbert's weeping, with Officer Landers trying to stand at attention, and Mason typing away on the computer. Mason finally ended by asking Herbert several questions.

"Mr. Brent, did Bernie have a special girlfriend?" After a negative answer, Mason asked, "Did he have an Uncle Sam he was close to?" Again, Brent gave a negative response, and he further explained Bernie had no uncles, only aunts on both sides of the family.

Mason announced he needed much more time to work on the password and he'd like to take the computer back to the station. He explained he would return it later; the date dependent on what would be found for evidence, if any.

Herbert said, addressing Beauregard and Smith, "I have no idea what password Herbie would use, but I can tell you it will be complicated. That's who my Herbie was, complicated. The very least you can do, Detectives, is tell me what you think you've found and who Uncle Sam and the girlfriend are. You may take the computer. I know you could get a warrant if I said no. I want the culprit, so I would not say no; but tell me what you think you've found. I need something. I have to tell my wife something. She sits on his bed. She'll know what's missing. She may not know what's in the closet, but she'll know the computer's missing for certain."

Beauregard spoke. "Mr. Brent, try to explain to Mrs. Brent that Herbie died from trying to do good work. He did not die from drug use and we're trying to do everything we can to find out who killed him. Tell her Herbie left a valuable trail for us; almost as if he expected there was a need to leave the trail. I think he knew the danger he was facing. Tell her she raised a wonderful socially conscious young man. I know it's not enough, but it's all I can say."

13

Synthesizing Somewhat

The West Side MCU detectives were busily poring through files and data as they sat waiting for the captain to join them in the conference room. Juan, although new to the unit, showed a love of methodology and searching for unasked questions. He had handwritten sticky notes attached to every file to remind the others about what he thought may be missing. Lilly Tagliano remarked, "Juan, you must be practicing to be captain. Haven't you heard of computers? There's WORD and EXCEL. You're too young to be in the paper category with the captain."

Lilly noticed the other detectives smirking and just knew before the captain spoke that he must be behind her.

"Detective, just what is wrong with paper? Juan is saving us time by communicating in one step. He's done some analyses, jotted down what he thought was needed, and left it for all of you when you pick up a file to examine it; if you ever pick up a file to examine it!"

Chastened, and hoping to show good will, Lilly responded, "Yup, Captain, you may be on to something I hadn't thought about; my apologies, Juan."

The captain, with a sharp look, silenced the snickering going on at the table. He insisted they go through the files of info and look at all the stickies and answer the questions saying, "I have a list of questions myself; maybe answering Juan's stickies will also answer them and we can be done."

The captain started his questions by going back to the shootings of Ash and Ted, which resulted in the mess of shootings in the Springfield apartment, and was followed by the shootings of the young woman, Dominican, and another in the field across from the strip mall.

He said, "I see here that Juan has a few stickies:

1. Was the shooting of the detectives truly accidental? If so, what was so important going on in the second-floor apartment that enticed the Dominicans to think they needed to shoot their way out? And then one of them gets killed and the other wounded and their shooters were killed. So, why was it so important to shoot the two Dominicans on Fir Street? Were they responsible for the detectives' shooting fiasco and were therefore fingered to go for their stupidity, or was it just that they could name who hired them to arrange the original meeting that went awry?

"2. Why was the young druggie gal shot after she fled towards the car? Was she the person who arranged the meeting for the assassinations? If so, did the victim know who she was and was shocked she fingered him. She's a two-bit hooker living with an old man on Spruce Street. So how does she have the juice to be with, according to those kids' interviews, a white golf club type? The ME report says she's a user and not in good shape. She ran to the car. Was she duped by someone in the know, given that I don't think she could plan anything on her own. And what self-respecting triggerman brings a druggie with him when he assassinates someone? Contract killers are normally brought in from outside. So, is he not a contract killer? Maybe he's not a pro because he didn't give a shot to the head for finality. He may be a local guy with a reason to kill, but not be a contract killer. There are lots of unanswered but reasonable questions here to ask.

"3. Juan checked Alfie's house and it's in impeccable condition. Where's his money coming from for the repairs and what about the house behind it? Does the son AJ really live there with Alfie? The neighbors say he just comes there sometimes, but not often.

"4. The nice ladies living the good life on the street behind Spruce Street know everything about everything. One of the nice ladies, according to a note Juan just found in the bottom of that taped package Officer Simeon brought in from the kids, received an envelope from a pretty lady named Carmen who lives in the house across the street from the 'Southern Ladies'; the house with the crippled old lady who lives there with her son. It's the one with the orange cones saving the parking space in front. So, who is the lady Carmen and what was in the envelope and who lives in the house with the orange cones in front? Does Carmen live there and if not, why did she come over to the porch party from there? Is she a regular visitor, maybe the old lady's daughter? Juan has a report on the houses, one on Spruce and this one. I'll let him tell you about it."

Juan said, "Something smells here, Captain. Each house is owned by a different limited liability corporation (LLC). Each of those LLCs is owned by a common regular corporation, the owners of which are three registered normal income individuals owning around 10% each which total 30%, and a law firm owning another 40%, and a pharmacist owning the remaining 30%. I checked the law firm and it's one of the biggest in Springfield and deals with real estate. The pharmacist is a woman married to a local politician; and she has no record. The normal income individuals include a long-distance trucker, a beautician, and an insurance disability claims adjuster. I've run all the names through our database and other than parking tickets, nada. Still smells to me. I think we need to investigate these people."

The captain looking at his notes asked, "Alfie lives with a son who drives him around in an SUV, right?"

Receiving vertical head nods from all but Juan, he questioned Juan, "Does he or does he not, Juan? Wasn't it in your report?"

"Captain, I don't know. When I interviewed Alfie about his girlfriend Marisol's death, his son seemed totally appalled at his father's crying. I don't think those two could live together. Maybe I'm wrong."

Digesting this information with what looked to the detectives as distaste, the captain continued with, "Their house borders the common ownership house on the next street where the lovely 'Southern Ladies' live, right?"

Again, there were vertical head nods with no dissent. "The house that borders back to back to Alfie's supposedly has an old lady living there and is owned by her son. Now we hear that a beautiful lady named Carmen visits there and brings an envelope to one of the 'Southern Ladies.' Who is this Carmen and where does she live? Do we have a description of the old lady and the son? Who are they? Juan, you and Petra continue with this. Visit both houses and see if you can get past the front door. Think of some excuse. Complaints from neighbors or something but don't get too aggressive. I'm going to visit the 'Southern Ladies' when I'm free on a weekend. When is their next big deal on the porch?"

Juan said, "It's starting to get colder, but they're having their 'Autumn Blaze' Saturday and that's pretty decent. Tell them you want them involved in Community Policing, Captain; maybe you can deputize them. They'd like that."

Juan got the 'look' from the captain and stopped with the wise guy remarks. Discussion continued on the next three files for the murdered teens and according to the Captain's report, were really four murders.

Ash commented on the similarities in the murders and made a statement to which nobody disagreed. "Same perp, Captain, same MO, different genders maybe but they were all on the same big anti-drug campaign. Victims are close in age and pretty much innocents and non-drug users. Perp violates them after giving roofies and maybe one dose of meth to them. Enjoys the sex with a helpless witness and then kills them. Washes them up and dresses them, moves them to another site, and splays them like they're unimportant. Perp is a loose cannon and angry. When will we have a profile done? Has the District Attorney been notified yet there is a serial murderer out there? I guess there'd be two District Attorneys involved because Greenfield is in Franklin County and the other three murders are in Hampden County."

Beauregard looking tired raised his hand saying, "Stop, enough of this. I have a tiger on my tail I have to deal with. Our District Attorney has planned a meet twice, but it's been cancelled twice. I'm starting to wonder if we have a pervert serial murderer working within the drug business who is unknown to his bosses.

"I do have a meeting today with both district attorneys and the task force. Since two of the murder victims were found in West Side, the third victim was found in Springfield but lived in West Side, and the fourth was from Buckland near the city of Greenfield, our department will hopefully lead the investigation. That could be good if we solve these murders of the kids, but given that drugs are involved, I hope the Feds don't think it's connected to their big drug case. I will emphasize the different drugs used and perhaps they won't make a connection."

Petra replied, "Wouldn't look connected by most law enforcement, Captain. Why do you think there's a connection?"

"I don't like coincidences, Petra. Anti-drug crusaders dead while we're expecting a big influx of drugs is too much of a coincidence. It makes me nervous. Now let's consider the two guys who shot my family.

Do we know yet who they are? Mason, you were going to speak with the convenience store clerk. Is anything new on that front?"

"She's a nice but antsy lady. Not for a minute did she want to help me, but I have powers of persuasion, even if I do say so myself."

Midst groans from the other detectives, Mason continued, "I told her I would personally protect her name from being used. She's got kids, you know. She has a right to be frightened. I showed her the pictures. She was uncertain but thought one of the men was in drawing number two. If that's so, then it's connected to the Spruce Street drug operation which consisted mainly of mixing of drugs. It could mean that Spruce Street was some sort of a center for this stuff and those guys are trying to take over other territory. Where are they operating from now? Captain, if the clerk is correct, then the three guys were operating on the first and second floor of Spruce Street and are connected to your sister-in-law and nephew's shootings, and may be trying to take over distribution in two Springfield sectors. One other guy in the drawings has been seen in another distribution section of Springfield and the next thing we'll find out is that they're all connected to the kids' deaths, and like you just said, too coincidental."

The captain sighed commenting quietly, "My gut is telling me they're all connected and if we start to solve any one of these cases, the whole drug case will blow up on the FBI. That possibility is not going to stop us; we've got skin in this game.

"Get out and investigate. Mason, go through Herbie's computer and put two and two together about 'Uncle Sam and the girlfriend.' Ash, hire Jim to check your guy from St. James Ave and then check on his progress. You are off the clock, so if you want to help Jim, it's none of my business. Just stay in the car so you're not seen by Springfield cops who know you. Leave the questioning to Jim."

Mona Beauregard, after a long hiatus raising her children, had returned to work in September as a science teacher at West Side High School. She was checking some books out from the city library before going home to plan the family's supper, when her eye caught Betsy Printer and two other students from the high school talking with Petra Aylewood-Locke. She was pleased, thinking, *Rudy took my conversation with Betsy seriously. When I told him about it, he seemed not to be interested. It's his way; he's always slow to jump but still mulls over everything he hears.*

She was about to leave when Lieutenant Aylewood-Locke spied her. She waved her over to one of the carrels away from the students, saying, "Talk about dumb luck, Mona, I want you to sit with me with Betsy, Amber, and Joely; if you will. I think your presence would be helpful. I know these gals have perspectives on this case. I think you will be able to coax them into sharing. They're a little cautious about saying anything to the police. Will you help me, please? It will just take a minute."

Mona joined Petra and the girls, who seemed surprised Mrs. Beauregard knew the detective. Mona explained to them her husband was the Major Crimes Unit Captain investigating Candace Monroe's death. The girls seemed impressed. Mona talked with them about the loss of their friend causing the girls to cry. They insisted Candace would never take drugs. They said they had heard through the underground, meaning social media news, that there were three drug related deaths of young people in the area. They knew Candace must have been murdered and they knew why. Each girl had a different story related to their speaking with Candace before her death. Candace was on to someone over near Spruce Street, who was a major player in what would be a big new drug distribution network. She thought she could find out more and leave the info in a note at her drop sight. She said she had contacted Herbie and he was also going to work with her.

Mona asked just why the girls didn't come forward. Betsy started crying, "Mrs. Beauregard, we just wanted to help stop this stuff from coming into our city. We don't want to die. Candace didn't want to die either. If the police identify us as witnesses, we'll be dead too. Our parents are going to go ballistic if they learn we've been involved with Candace and Herbie and Ollie. I don't live that far from Spruce Street, although in a much better neighborhood. If Candace was right, the big dealers can easily find me. I walk by the Spruce Street area practically every day to go to one of the shops in the strip. Please don't expose us."

Mona and Petra spent a quarter hour reassuring the girls that under no circumstances will anyone know about their involvement. Petra insisted however they stop all their anti-drug action for the time being, saying, "Do not think I don't admire your good intentions here, but, and I'm very serious about this, this is a police matter. Interfering with a police investigation is a crime. So, go home and do your best to forget about them. You see Mrs. Beauregard at school; she is someone you can talk with if you think of something you may have forgotten today. We are going to find Candace, Ollie, and Herbie's killer; don't you worry. Remember, it is best you don't talk about any of this with your friends or on social media. Were you three the closest friends to Candace?" The girls nodded yes, and per instructions, practically ran from the library.

Petra asked Mona, "Do you think they'll be all right?"

"I don't know Petra; teens are difficult to convince not to act out as they emotionally feel at any moment. It's helpful they're frightened. I will seek them out in a few days to confirm for myself that they are in a good state. I'm uncomfortable not talking with their parents. It is my duty to inform parents if their children are in danger and these girls, if they speak loosely, could be in danger."

"I've talked with the school psychologist at the high school, Mona, and she has already spoken to the parents. Apparently, it's all over the school Candace is dead due to her anti-drug activity. We think we've kept it quiet. Well, kids have their own smoke signals and instant knowledge. This is police business, Mona. I don't have to remind you, you can't interfere and there is no reason for you to in this case. Their parents already know. The psychologist met with every known student in the anti-drug group."

"What about Betsy Printer? She lives somewhere within a mile near Spruce Street. Candace has told us Spruce Street was the locus of the major drug players. Although, if I were a drug distributor and had funds, I certainly wouldn't live over there, I can tell you that. I want her safe, Petra. She lives too close for my comfort."

"If a big-time guy lived over there, Mona, there has to be a good business reason. Can't imagine why but we'll follow up. Probably he isn't normally looking at schoolgirls; but I get that you think the serial murderer may have different motives than just drugs. Thanks, Mona, for your help with the girls. They surely didn't trust me. I absolutely love these fortuitous moments when God moves players over to help me. It seems to me like it happens often, at least for me!"

Mona spent a few minutes chatting about the expected baby and saw a side to the quick moving Petra she had never seen before. She and Petra discussed how exceptional was the town's expanded new addition to the library. They looked around, surprised to find there were only a few people, mostly retired types walking around with the exception of a nice-looking man who seemed to be moving quickly towards the door. Mona thought, *He must work here as an administrator. He has no books with him.*

Mason had cracked the password, but not due to his computer expertise. Instead he figured Herbie would use something personal. On the outside of his case was a heart with the names "Uncle Sam loves Claire." It only took Mason a quarter-hour before he noticed it as something of importance, remembering Herbie's father said his son never did anything without a motive or goal; he further explained to the detectives that he knew of no current girlfriend of Herbie's. The kid left a trail. Mason felt an ache, when he realized Herbie knew he was in danger; so much so that he left the trail, thinking, *damn it, the kid was foolish to take this on, but he was brave and smart. No wonder the captain is on the warpath. All these innocents murdered and their murders reduced in importance to a drug investigation. That's what history is all about. There are innocent victims everywhere who are cannon fodder for bigger societal goals.*

Mason shook his head and started his computer investigation. He concluded his work in two hours and typed a report as quickly as he could, attaching printouts from Herbie's computer. He did not leave the report with Millie; instead he went directly to the captain's office. His disappointment at the empty desk was noticeable when he groaned loudly, saying, "Where the hell are you, Captain, this is important."

Ted heard Mason, and said, "What's so important, Mason? The captain had a meeting with two District Attorneys in Springfield. He'd put it off for a week, but they wanted a command performance. He had to be there, but it won't take more than a couple of hours. He's coming right back."

Beauregard spent over two hours with the Hampden and Franklin County District Attorneys. The meeting became heated when

Loughman interrupted. Both DAs had invited Loughman into the room. His sole role in attending this supposed conference on a potential serial murderer was to remind everyone, that any murder investigation could not put his work in jeopardy. Thinking about his own reaction and its consequences made Beauregard cringe. *I can't believe they let Loughman in. The whole meeting today was not to put our heads together to investigate four murders of young people, young good people. No, it was to let me know all my investigative pursuits will be limited by their needs. So, in answer, I got up to leave, the only thing I could really do when I wanted to wring Loughman's neck. What happened? I was told to sit down and Loughman was excused. Mixed signals are what happened. The meeting continued. What did we accomplish? I must have been told five times to tread carefully with the Feds and not to talk with the press and to stay out of Louckman. Hell, Louckman is the site of one of the murders. I was not told to stay out of Springfield, another site for one of the murders. I was the only cop in this meeting. It was not about the investigation. It was my warning. My chief wasn't there. A FUCKING SETUP is what it was.*

A truly pissed-off Beauregard stopped at the Palazzo Café at One Financial Plaza in Springfield. The owner took his order for a cappuccino to which she added a perfect Italian cookie. He thanked her and settled on a small chair and slowly lowered his blood pressure while drinking some caffeine to raise it. It seemed logical to him; whatever caffeine did to add energy could not be harmful. He didn't believe everything his doctor and Mona told him. They couldn't be right, when now he was feeling much better. He glanced around and noticed a face that looked vaguely familiar. The man was dressed in a two-thousand-dollar business suit. He thought, *that suit really is too showy for this city. How do I know that face? I don't travel in the high-class suit group; except for when I'm with Attorney Norberto Cull. But Cull is not full of himself like this guy. This guy is an old glad hand type, but I still I recognize him. Must be a lawyer or in real estate. He has that Boston or NYC kind of arrogance.*

Beauregard left to get his car, parked for free with his police placard in the windshield, and left for the station. Where did he see this suit before? Well, he'd put the face in the back of his mind for now thinking, *too bad those kids weren't with me today. They could have drawn him and I'd have a picture to send out for identification.*

The captain shook his head in wonder, saying aloud, "Just the mention of those kids and their drawings or pictures and it's the hook that tickled my memory. This guy is in the photo of the four guys they saw at the casino. This is only two blocks from the casino. It must be where he works or hangs out. I'll get Jim to take the kids' photo to the nice gal in the café and see if she can connect the face with a name."

14

More Undercover Trouble

While Captain Beauregard was glimpsing a sliver of light in the investigations, Jackson and Paulie had biked over to the casino looking for the fourth man in the picture they had taken a while back. The boys had planned many times to renew their search, but school and family obligations always got in the way. Wayne was not available today. His mom was bringing him to the orthodontist, much against his will. Paulie said, "Wayne doesn't want braces. He says they're for girls who want to be pretty and his teeth have only one tiny overlap. He says lots of guys don't have perfect teeth."

Jackson told Paulie moms would win in that kind of fight; and Wayne ought to give it up and go along. Looking very sage like to Paulie, Jackson said, "We shouldn't sweat the small stuff; that's what my dad says." He asked if he could have a copy of the picture so they could split up when they got down by the city green.

Paulie had a surprise for Jackson. He said, "I photocopied the photo and enlarged it. I did a drawing that is even better than the photo. I am the greatest for visual memory for detail, even if I do say so myself. I made a copy of the drawing for you. What do you think?"

Jackson was impressed and told Paulie. He thought maybe the

drawing was more accurate than the photo if that was possible. As the boys walked their bikes up and down Main Street looking at well-dressed men's faces, Jackson spotted a guy talking with two guys and he thought, *one guy looks like an ad for Ralph Lauren and the other two are dressed like hoods like on TV, with gold chains and open shirts. They look all girly like except they must be weightlifters too.*

Jackson nudged Paulie who glanced at the three men and whispered, "That's the guy in the picture and the other two are like bodyguards or hoods. Let's follow them. I'll take the guy; you follow the bodyguards if they split."

The group of men moved away towards a large black Mercedes SUV and all got in. A driver, who the boys had not noticed before, had been waiting for them. Paulie got a picture of the plate number and the boys decided to follow the SUV while it was in traffic hoping they were not going far. Their hopes were dashed when after the casino, the traffic lightened up and the SUV sped away.

Not completely frustrated, given they had the plate number if not the name of the man they were looking for, the boys decided they should contact the captain directly with the car plate number info. Jackson excitedly whispered, "Paulie, the cops can follow that plate. Even if it's a rental SUV, they can find out who rented it. I think we should call Captain Beauregard right now. If he doesn't answer, I can bring it by his house when I go home. It's too late to go to the police station before we go home, but I can check into my house with my mom and then go for a walk. She won't question that and she won't know I'm going to the captain's house. I don't think his wife will tell my mom. If we don't get him by phone we'll leave a message I'm bringing an envelope for him. Let's get a hotel envelope from the Hampton Inn. They let me use the bathroom even though I'm a kid. I'll tell them I have to leave a note for one of the guests. I just won't leave a note."

Jackson made the call. The captain didn't answer, so he left their agreed upon message. An hour later, Jackson rang Captain Beauregard's doorbell. Mona answered just as the captain pulled in the driveway. Captain Beauregard yelled out, "Hey, Jackson, do you have that envelope from the school I asked you to bring?"

"Yeah, Captain, I have it right here." He said goodbye to Mrs. Beauregard rather quickly and ran over to the captain as he exited his car slowly.

Jackson thought, *He moves slowly but he sure thinks fast.*

"Captain, we saw the guy in the photo," and he gave Beauregard the drawing Paulie had done as well as the license plate number and how they saw the man in Springfield.

Beauregard commented, "Jackson, who did this drawing? If it's from memory, you boys have great memories."

He looked at the drawing again, frowned, and said, "You guys kept the picture. No one has that great a memory. I told you to stop investigating. You took advantage of me and I'm disappointed you would do that."

Jackson was surprised the captain figured out they had a copy of the picture just from looking at the drawing. The captain kept the drawing.

Mostly, Jackson was upset Captain Beauregard was mad at him and his friends. He tried to explain that they accidently kept it on their phones; and that Paulie drew the face just because they had the picture. He knew as he told this story the captain wasn't buying it, when Beauregard said, "Jackson, just what were you doing in Springfield on a school day down by City Hall and the green? Don't lie to me, Jackson, don't lie to me."

A contrite Jackson tried to apologize, but the captain brushed his words aside. Beauregard mumbled, "Go home. I thank you for the information. It's good, but Jackson, stop investigating."

Beauregard got back in his car, called Mona from the car, told her he would be late and not to mention to Teri Loyal that Jackson had been there. He returned to the station.

Beauregard expected to find only Ted covering, but instead, found Lilly and Petra having a girl fest with catalogs on baby furniture and clothing. Since neither was on duty he couldn't complain, but found he was annoyed, thinking, *kids do my investigating for me while my detectives are planning a baby shower. Hell, my world is always upside down.*

Closeted in his office, Beauregard, through deep breathing exercises his kids had taught him, slowly lowered his blood pressure. He thought, *if I were honest I'd admit I had wanted the kids to do a drawing of the guy from the picture. They do it and I give them hell. I want them safe; yet I've put them at risk by rewarding them with my thank you for their work. They forget I've warned them, that I've yelled at them.*

He called Mason and gave him the plate number. While waiting, he looked at Paulie's drawing. It was more specific than the photo. He decided Paulie had one hell of a visual memory and thinking he'd make a great witness, he expressed out loud, "Like I'll ever let that happen. And hell, I know this guy. I've seen him around; maybe I've seen him in West Side. Logical since I spend most of my time in this town."

Mason said the SUV was registered to a Nevada LLC called "G-Supply, LLC." He went on, saying, the manager of the LLC was a Raymond Losocala. I checked him out because the SUV has Mass plates and the address is over on Evergreen, the street next to Candace Monroe's street. It's a hell of a coincidence, Captain, don't you think; it's a hell of a coincidence?"

Beauregard did say he thought it was quite unlikely to be by chance. He pulled Petra and Lilly's report of their canvass of Candace's family street. The detectives checked with some neighbors. They walked both north and south on Mountain Laurel Place by a number of houses all widely separated from each other. The report stated the frontage on all the houses was well over two hundred feet. Not one neighbor they questioned had seen Candace that day. They also spoke with the bus driver on the Pearce bus route. He also had not seen Candace that day; and he said he did know her. They assumed she was picked up by a car since Mountain Laurel Place is a short street, and if she wasn't seen by a few neighbors then perhaps she had a planned ride. Beauregard thought, *I've never liked assumptions. Why in hell do they put assumptions in the report? Lilly must have written the report because Petra knows how I feel about assuming anything.*

"Mason, get everything out there on this guy Raymond Losocala. I want his history in Vegas and here and wherever else he's lived. If he's connected to the casinos I want to know in what capacity. He's living over there on the next street to Mountain Laurel Place. I know that section; it's a high rent district. He has to have a history. Does he have kids who knew Candace; all that personal stuff I need and I need it now."

Before Mason left to make his calls, he told the captain they needed a sit down on what he found on Herbie's computer. At that point, Millie buzzed Beauregard with a call from Attorney Cull.

"Hi, Norbie, and before you ask, no, I don't have any further news on the Monroe girl. How are you doing with my family and their questioning by the Springfield Police?"

"I sat in on the interviews, Rudy. I have to say they didn't push Sally, who is now doing well as you know. But I think Sally saw more than she told them; I think she's decided she doesn't want to be a witness. I could be wrong, but I'm pretty certain Sally's holding back. I told them to leave the kids alone and they have. They already had a statement from Mandy at the scene. They're not killing themselves solving this.

"But on another note, I want to tell you I authorized Jim Locke do some checking on the Candace Monroe route taken when she left home on the day she was murdered. Her last sighting was on Evergreen near the Losocala home, number seventy-three. Two neighbors saw her and waved or talked with her that morning. She was last seen walking near the Losocala home. Jim says Losocala is a big supply vendor to the casino and just recently moved into the house. He has a wife and no children. I don't want to interfere with your investigation, Rudy, but you should look into this. Jim says that, other than one additional home beyond Losocala's, there's nothing but woods up past the Losocala home. He couldn't figure out just why she'd go up that way if she wasn't going to his house."

"Have you ever met him, Norbie?"

"I don't think so, but I'll make it my business to do so if you think I should."

"We'll go forward, Norbie, and see what this is all about if anything. I thank you for doing this for us."

When Cull hung up, Rudy mused, *I get info from him on the same day we see the picture of this Losocala. It's got to be divine providence giving me a heads up. Whatever it is, I'm thankful. This guy, if he's a major player, can't be stupid enough to kill these kids in such a perverted setting. If he were the one doing that, there has to be a history of activity in the cities he's previously lived in; if he's connected to this drug business. Yet there seems to be a connection to Candace on that morning. He's seen with McKinney outside the casino with two others, one who is the Dominican who shot my detectives and then was killed along with two others. Connected, connected, connected!*

Ten minutes later Beauregard was grilling Mason on Losocala's history. "Mason, what have you got? I want to know every location where he's ever lived."

"Hold on, Captain, he is a legitimate supplier/vendor for the casino, but only for security. He's lived in Las Vegas, Atlantic City, and Palm

Springs. His company, G-Supply, LLC, has a stellar reputation. He's on his third wife and has no children; at least as far as we know. Since he's been here and I'm not certain how long, he and his wife have been out and about with all the important pols. He only purchased the house he has in West Side recently. Probably stayed in a hotel or rented a condo before he bought his home. I googled him and he's been at lots of city hearings on the casino and has attended many charitable balls including hospital balls. Saw some pictures of Mr. and Mrs. Losocala at a big charity auction for a mental health organization. No, he's been around. What are you looking for, Captain? Shall I check the other cities he's lived in? You want houses, other marriages, problems with the law, etc.?"

"Not just that, Mason. Ask about any suspicious drug deaths of young and innocent kids in any of those cities during the times he's lived in each location."

Mason appeared to be excited as he moved over to his computer mumbling, *could this be the guy? Why would a guy with all this money and position kill these kids and display them in such a perverted way? No fucking way, that I will ever understand these kinds of sick acts. I understand greed, and acting out in the moment, and all kinds of crimes; these I don't get. I suppose if I did get their reasoning, then it wouldn't be a good sign; unless I were a shrink. How do shrinks deal with listening to this shit all the time? It'd make me crazy quietly absorbing and taking him or her seriously; someone who would do this stuff. Sociopath, psychopath, I don't care what the captain says, if I see one, I'll run. I don't want to get in their brains wondering why they do the stuff they do. That's why I like IT; it's safer for me mentally.*

The captain left the station to attend to family matters. Certain Norbie was on to something, he was comfortable enough to head for the hospital. Sally was to leave for home the next day. He had determined the matter needed clarification.

Twenty minutes later, he parked his unmarked car with a police placard on the dash near the emergency room. He walked quickly, in contrast to his normal more leisurely pace, to get to the elevators. Sally was on the seventh floor. Entering her room, he saw a composed woman. She appeared altered. He said "Hi" to her, but she didn't respond in her usual bubbly manner.

Sally said, "Rudy, don't think I'm going to be a witness; I'm not going to be one. I could see Norbie understood why I couldn't remember. He's too smart. I knew he'd get to you. He's supposed to be my lawyer and therefore shouldn't be telling you anything. What's happened with the confidentiality business? Isn't he my lawyer? Shouldn't he accept what I say?"

A stunned Rudy took a moment to consider how to respond. Finally, he replied, "What are you talking about, Sally? Norbie told me everything went well with the police. Do you know something you didn't tell the police or Norbie? If so, you'd better tell me. I certainly intend to solve this case and you don't have to be a witness. We have a witness for one of the perps who got away."

Sally started crying and sputtered, "I want to be brave, Rudy, but I can't be. I almost died. I would never have seen my children grow up. My little John may never play baseball again. It's not fair. I'm not putting us at risk, and don't give me that moral outrage about citizens doing their job. I'm a victim now. John's a victim. Mandy's a victim; she thought we'd died. Do you think that's right? Why can't you police get these people off the streets? Why can't you protect us? That's your job."

And Sally cried as she grabbed tissues and rubbed her already reddened eyes vigorously.

Rudy waited quietly for ten minutes until a calmer Sally faced him saying, "You're not going away, are you, Rudy? Mona says you never give up. She says you're like an ant, you just keep moving along; slow but moving, always moving. I have always respected your work, Rudy, and I'm sorry for my outburst; but I am so frightened. Can you understand that? Please tell me you understand."

Annoyed to be compared to an ant by his wife, Rudy suppressed his feelings and went on to talk with Sally. After ten minutes Sally again said, "You're not going away, are you? I'll tell you what I know if you promise on your goddaughter's life you won't make me testify and no one will know I said anything."

Rudy promised knowing he would never have let her testify. Sally's first recollection of the incident seemed to match with all the police reports. That was until she discussed what she saw before the attack. Sally reviewed the time right before the shooting started. She was there to fill-up her gas tank, but was digging in her bag for the company credit card which she only used for business. Since she was delivering foods for JR, it was business. Her eyes looked to her left and she saw the two Dominicans talking with one of the Puerto Ricans who was killed. The Puerto Rican man was standing at the driver's side of his car and the two Dominicans were standing by at their respective seats outside their car. The group of men did not seem to be angry until the Russian man exited the victims' car and said something. It was in Spanish and she thought it was maybe full of swear words. Despite his use of Spanish, she was certain he was Russian. The shooting started. She thought she could recognize the Spanish words if she heard them again. She wanted JR's worker who is Spanish to say Spanish swears to her, but JR nixed it saying, "I don't know if he knows any of these people. Keep quiet, Sally. Stay safe for all of us. Mandy and John want their mother and I want my wife."

Rudy assured her there was nothing special in what she had heard; that it had no consequences for the investigation. However, if it made her feel better, he'd have Juan from MCU visit her and together they could see if he recognized the Spanish words she heard. She liked that and asked if he could do it today. He visited for a while longer and left.

Driving back to the station, Rudy called Juan and told him about Sally's memory and the related problem. Juan agreed to leave for the hospital immediately, and promised not to talk to her about anything else related to the case. Rudy thought, *what was so powerful, that was said in a few words, to make the Dominicans start shooting? Normally, if it were a planned kill, then they would not have talked to the marks before shooting. Maybe it was a planned warning, but the shooters were pushed by what was said. The shooters were equipped with enough firepower for a hit. What am I not getting here?*

15

More Undercover Trouble

While Captain Beauregard was glimpsing a sliver of light in the investigations, Jackson and Paulie had biked over to the casino looking for the fourth man in the picture they had taken a while back. The boys had planned many times to renew their search, but school and family obligations always got in the way. Wayne was not available today. His mom was bringing him to the orthodontist, much against his will. Paulie said, "Wayne doesn't want braces. He says they're for girls who want to be pretty and his teeth have only one tiny overlap. He says lots of guys don't have perfect teeth."

Jackson told Paulie moms would win in that kind of fight; and Wayne ought to give it up and go along. Looking very sage like to Paulie, Jackson said, "We shouldn't sweat the small stuff; that's what my dad says." He asked if he could have a copy of the picture so they could split up when they got down by the city green.

Paulie had a surprise for Jackson. He said, "I photocopied the photo and enlarged it. I did a drawing that is even better than the photo. I am the greatest for visual memory for detail, even if I do say so myself. I made a copy of the drawing for you. What do you think?"

Jackson was impressed and told Paulie. He thought maybe the

drawing was more accurate than the photo if that was possible. As the boys walked their bikes up and down Main Street looking at well-dressed men's faces, Jackson spotted a guy talking with two guys and he thought, *one guy looks like an ad for Ralph Lauren and the other two are dressed like hoods like on TV, with gold chains and open shirts. They look all girly like except they must be weightlifters too.*

Jackson nudged Paulie who glanced at the three men and whispered, "That's the guy in the picture and the other two are like bodyguards or hoods. Let's follow them. I'll take the guy; you follow the bodyguards if they split."

The group of men moved away towards a large black Mercedes SUV and all got in. A driver, who the boys had not noticed before, had been waiting for them. Paulie got a picture of the plate number and the boys decided to follow the SUV while it was in traffic hoping they were not going far. Their hopes were dashed when after the casino, the traffic lightened up and the SUV sped away.

Not completely frustrated, given they had the plate number if not the name of the man they were looking for, the boys decided they should contact the captain directly with the car plate number info. Jackson excitedly whispered, "Paulie, the cops can follow that plate. Even if it's a rental SUV, they can find out who rented it. I think we should call Captain Beauregard right now. If he doesn't answer, I can bring it by his house when I go home. It's too late to go to the police station before we go home, but I can check into my house with my mom and then go for a walk. She won't question that and she won't know I'm going to the captain's house. I don't think his wife will tell my mom. If we don't get him by phone we'll leave a message I'm bringing an envelope for him. Let's get a hotel envelope from the Hampton Inn. They let me use the bathroom even though I'm a kid. I'll tell them I have to leave a note for one of the guests. I just won't leave a note."

Jackson made the call. The captain didn't answer, so he left their agreed upon message. An hour later, Jackson rang Captain Beauregard's doorbell. Mona answered just as the captain pulled in the driveway. Captain Beauregard yelled out, "Hey, Jackson, do you have that envelope from the school I asked you to bring?"

"Yeah, Captain, I have it right here." He said goodbye to Mrs. Beauregard rather quickly and ran over to the captain as he exited his car slowly.

Jackson thought, *He moves slowly but he sure thinks fast.*

"Captain, we saw the guy in the photo," and he gave Beauregard the drawing Paulie had done as well as the license plate number and how they saw the man in Springfield.

Beauregard commented, "Jackson, who did this drawing? If it's from memory, you boys have great memories."

He looked at the drawing again, frowned, and said, "You guys kept the picture. No one has that great a memory. I told you to stop investigating. You took advantage of me and I'm disappointed you would do that."

Jackson was surprised the captain figured out they had a copy of the picture just from looking at the drawing. The captain kept the drawing.

Mostly, Jackson was upset Captain Beauregard was mad at him and his friends. He tried to explain that they accidently kept it on their phones; and that Paulie drew the face just because they had the picture. He knew as he told this story the captain wasn't buying it, when Beauregard said, "Jackson, just what were you doing in Springfield on a school day down by City Hall and the green? Don't lie to me, Jackson, don't lie to me."

A contrite Jackson tried to apologize, but the captain brushed his words aside. Beauregard mumbled, "Go home. I thank you for the information. It's good, but Jackson, stop investigating."

Beauregard got back in his car, called Mona from the car, told her he would be late and not to mention to Teri Loyal that Jackson had been there. He returned to the station.

Beauregard expected to find only Ted covering, but instead, found Lilly and Petra having a girl fest with catalogs on baby furniture and clothing. Since neither was on duty he couldn't complain, but found he was annoyed, thinking, *kids do my investigating for me while my detectives are planning a baby shower. Hell, my world is always upside down.*

Closeted in his office, Beauregard, through deep breathing exercises his kids had taught him, slowly lowered his blood pressure. He thought, *if I were honest I'd admit I had wanted the kids to do a drawing of the guy from the picture. They do it and I give them hell. I want them safe; yet I've put them at risk by rewarding them with my thank you for their work. They forget I've warned them, that I've yelled at them.*

He called Mason and gave him the plate number. While waiting, he looked at Paulie's drawing. It was more specific than the photo. He decided Paulie had one hell of a visual memory and thinking he'd make a great witness, he expressed out loud, "Like I'll ever let that happen. And hell, I know this guy. I've seen him around; maybe I've seen him in West Side. Logical since I spend most of my time in this town."

Mason said the SUV was registered to a Nevada LLC called "G-Supply, LLC." He went on, saying, the manager of the LLC was a Raymond Losocala. I checked him out because the SUV has Mass plates and the address is over on Evergreen, the street next to Candace Monroe's street. It's a hell of a coincidence, Captain, don't you think; it's a hell of a coincidence?"

Beauregard did say he thought it was quite unlikely to be by chance. He pulled Petra and Lilly's report of their canvass of Candace's family street. The detectives checked with some neighbors. They walked both north and south on Mountain Laurel Place by a number of houses all widely separated from each other. The report stated the frontage on all the houses was well over two hundred feet. Not one neighbor they questioned had seen Candace that day. They also spoke with the bus driver on the Pearce bus route. He also had not seen Candace that day; and he said he did know her. They assumed she was picked up by a car since Mountain Laurel Place is a short street, and if she wasn't seen by a few neighbors then perhaps she had a planned ride. Beauregard thought, *I've never liked assumptions. Why in hell do they put assumptions in the report? Lilly must have written the report because Petra knows how I feel about assuming anything.*

"Mason, get everything out there on this guy Raymond Losocala. I want his history in Vegas and here and wherever else he's lived. If he's connected to the casinos I want to know in what capacity. He's living over there on the next street to Mountain Laurel Place. I know that section; it's a high rent district. He has to have a history. Does he have kids who knew Candace; all that personal stuff I need and I need it now."

Before Mason left to make his calls, he told the captain they needed a sit down on what he found on Herbie's computer. At that point, Millie buzzed Beauregard with a call from Attorney Cull.

"Hi, Norbie, and before you ask, no, I don't have any further news on the Monroe girl. How are you doing with my family and their questioning by the Springfield Police?"

"I sat in on the interviews, Rudy. I have to say they didn't push Sally, who is now doing well as you know. But I think Sally saw more than she told them; I think she's decided she doesn't want to be a witness. I could be wrong, but I'm pretty certain Sally's holding back. I told them to leave the kids alone and they have. They already had a statement from Mandy at the scene. They're not killing themselves solving this.

"But on another note, I want to tell you I authorized Jim Locke do some checking on the Candace Monroe route taken when she left home on the day she was murdered. Her last sighting was on Evergreen near the Losocala home, number seventy-three. Two neighbors saw her and waved or talked with her that morning. She was last seen walking near the Losocala home. Jim says Losocala is a big supply vendor to the casino and just recently moved into the house. He has a wife and no children. I don't want to interfere with your investigation, Rudy, but you should look into this. Jim says that, other than one additional home beyond Losocala's, there's nothing but woods up past the Losocala home. He couldn't figure out just why she'd go up that way if she wasn't going to his house."

"Have you ever met him, Norbie?"

"I don't think so, but I'll make it my business to do so if you think I should."

"We'll go forward, Norbie, and see what this is all about if anything. I thank you for doing this for us."

When Cull hung up, Rudy mused, *I get info from him on the same day we see the picture of this Losocala. It's got to be divine providence giving me a heads up. Whatever it is, I'm thankful. This guy, if he's a major player, can't be stupid enough to kill these kids in such a perverted setting. If he were the one doing that, there has to be a history of activity in the cities he's previously lived in; if he's connected to this drug business. Yet there seems to be a connection to Candace on that morning. He's seen with McKinney outside the casino with two others, one who is the Dominican who shot my detectives and then was killed along with two others. Connected, connected, connected!*

Ten minutes later Beauregard was grilling Mason on Losocala's history. "Mason, what have you got? I want to know every location where he's ever lived."

"Hold on, Captain, he is a legitimate supplier/vendor for the casino, but only for security. He's lived in Las Vegas, Atlantic City, and Palm

Springs. His company, G-Supply, LLC, has a stellar reputation. He's on his third wife and has no children; at least as far as we know. Since he's been here and I'm not certain how long, he and his wife have been out and about with all the important pols. He only purchased the house he has in West Side recently. Probably stayed in a hotel or rented a condo before he bought his home. I googled him and he's been at lots of city hearings on the casino and has attended many charitable balls including hospital balls. Saw some pictures of Mr. and Mrs. Losocala at a big charity auction for a mental health organization. No, he's been around. What are you looking for, Captain? Shall I check the other cities he's lived in? You want houses, other marriages, problems with the law, etc.?"

"Not just that, Mason. Ask about any suspicious drug deaths of young and innocent kids in any of those cities during the times he's lived in each location."

Mason appeared to be excited as he moved over to his computer mumbling, *could this be the guy? Why would a guy with all this money and position kill these kids and display them in such a perverted way? No fucking way, that I will ever understand these kinds of sick acts. I understand greed, and acting out in the moment, and all kinds of crimes; these I don't get. I suppose if I did get their reasoning, then it wouldn't be a good sign; unless I were a shrink. How do shrinks deal with listening to this shit all the time? It'd make me crazy quietly absorbing and taking him or her seriously; someone who would do this stuff. Sociopath, psychopath, I don't care what the captain says, if I see one, I'll run. I don't want to get in their brains wondering why they do the stuff they do. That's why I like IT; it's safer for me mentally.*

The captain left the station to attend to family matters. Certain Norbie was on to something, he was comfortable enough to head for the hospital. Sally was to leave for home the next day. He had determined the matter needed clarification.

Twenty minutes later, he parked his unmarked car with a police placard on the dash near the emergency room. He walked quickly, in contrast to his normal more leisurely pace, to get to the elevators. Sally was on the seventh floor. Entering her room, he saw a composed woman. She appeared altered. He said "Hi" to her, but she didn't respond in her usual bubbly manner.

Sally said, "Rudy, don't think I'm going to be a witness; I'm not going to be one. I could see Norbie understood why I couldn't remember. He's too smart. I knew he'd get to you. He's supposed to be my lawyer and therefore shouldn't be telling you anything. What's happened with the confidentiality business? Isn't he my lawyer? Shouldn't he accept what I say?"

A stunned Rudy took a moment to consider how to respond. Finally, he replied, "What are you talking about, Sally? Norbie told me everything went well with the police. Do you know something you didn't tell the police or Norbie? If so, you'd better tell me. I certainly intend to solve this case and you don't have to be a witness. We have a witness for one of the perps who got away."

Sally started crying and sputtered, "I want to be brave, Rudy, but I can't be. I almost died. I would never have seen my children grow up. My little John may never play baseball again. It's not fair. I'm not putting us at risk, and don't give me that moral outrage about citizens doing their job. I'm a victim now. John's a victim. Mandy's a victim; she thought we'd died. Do you think that's right? Why can't you police get these people off the streets? Why can't you protect us? That's your job."

And Sally cried as she grabbed tissues and rubbed her already reddened eyes vigorously.

Rudy waited quietly for ten minutes until a calmer Sally faced him saying, "You're not going away, are you, Rudy? Mona says you never give up. She says you're like an ant, you just keep moving along; slow but moving, always moving. I have always respected your work, Rudy, and I'm sorry for my outburst; but I am so frightened. Can you understand that? Please tell me you understand."

Annoyed to be compared to an ant by his wife, Rudy suppressed his feelings and went on to talk with Sally. After ten minutes Sally again said, "You're not going away, are you? I'll tell you what I know if you promise on your goddaughter's life you won't make me testify and no one will know I said anything."

Rudy promised knowing he would never have let her testify. Sally's first recollection of the incident seemed to match with all the police reports. That was until she discussed what she saw before the attack. Sally reviewed the time right before the shooting started. She was there to fill-up her gas tank, but was digging in her bag for the company credit card which she only used for business. Since she was delivering foods for JR, it was business. Her eyes looked to her left and she saw the two Dominicans talking with one of the Puerto Ricans who was killed. The Puerto Rican man was standing at the driver's side of his car and the two Dominicans were standing by at their respective seats outside their car. The group of men did not seem to be angry until the Russian man exited the victims' car and said something. It was in Spanish and she thought it was maybe full of swear words. Despite his use of Spanish, she was certain he was Russian. The shooting started. She thought she could recognize the Spanish words if she heard them again. She wanted JR's worker who is Spanish to say Spanish swears to her, but JR nixed it saying, "I don't know if he knows any of these people. Keep quiet, Sally. Stay safe for all of us. Mandy and John want their mother and I want my wife."

Rudy assured her there was nothing special in what she had heard; that it had no consequences for the investigation. However, if it made her feel better, he'd have Juan from MCU visit her and together they could see if he recognized the Spanish words she heard. She liked that and asked if he could do it today. He visited for a while longer and left.

Driving back to the station, Rudy called Juan and told him about Sally's memory and the related problem. Juan agreed to leave for the hospital immediately, and promised not to talk to her about anything else related to the case. Rudy thought, *what was so powerful, that was said in a few words, to make the Dominicans start shooting? Normally, if it were a planned kill, then they would not have talked to the marks before shooting. Maybe it was a planned warning, but the shooters were pushed by what was said. The shooters were equipped with enough firepower for a hit. What am I not getting here?*

16

Serendipity

Beauregard had not yet visited the 'Southern Ladies' as he had promised to do. Knowing he had already asked Juan for info, he felt embarrassed to call Juan to his office again; but he did. He asked if the ladies were entertaining visitors this weekend, reminding him it was now November. Juan assured him the ladies were having their Armistice Day celebration on this Saturday the tenth, even though the holiday is on the twelfth. The ladies go to a small parade each year on the twelfth to witness a military service dedication for veterans who are buried in the military cemetery in Agawam.

Juan said, "I'm told the ladies wear 1918 French style dresses and decorate the house with artificial poppies. It'll be indoors not on the porch, but Captain, it should be a really good time. If I know them, they'll have some sort of famous food from the World War I era. You know these ladies are doing a service with this celebration. Most Americans can't tell you Armistice Day is about the end of WWI. They think it is just poppy day, or about WWII. Want me to go with you, Captain? Why didn't you go on 'Autumn Blaze Day'; it was on the porch then?"

"No, Juan, I don't need a chaperone and I didn't go before because

171

that Saturday was filled with family cares and woes. I'll just tell them Juan and Petra said I have to get to know them. I couldn't possibly go undercover because as I understand these ladies, they read the newspapers and watch television. That's what Petra told me. They'll recognize me. I think I'm looking forward to this visit with these ladies."

Recovering from the vision of visiting two ladies dressed in WWI French costumes, Beauregard settled down to review for the umpteenth time the murder boards for the young victims. He wondered, now that there was evidence of six more deaths, whether his detectives would be able to link them to Losocala. He also wondered if there were more victims out there. If there were and Losocala was not in those areas, then they'd be better off to look at his associates. He called Mason and said, "Get our murders into the FBI's VICAP database, Mason. Maybe the perp has been elsewhere. The program filters info so not everything can be discovered. I have a hunch here, Mason; I have a hunch."

Seemingly satisfied as if he was certain he was moving in the right direction, Beauregard initiated a new map of the people and places involved in his detectives' shootings, his sister-in-law and nephew's shootings, the four drug-dealers' murders, the murders on the lot across from the strip mall, and the drug activity over on St. James in Springfield. Beauregard was miffed because Springfield MCU had not identified the Russian who died at the gas station. Talking to himself, he said, "It certainly wasn't Petro Gavel. Even the FBI wouldn't be able to cover that one up; he was too well known in the community. Was this a local Russian drug dealer or was he from out of town? Who was he and how do I find out?"

Beauregard called a friend in the Russian community. Well maybe he wasn't a friend, but he remembered, *Sergei Rozovsky expressed his thanks to Beauregard many times. Rudy forced Sergei to make one of the most difficult decisions of his life; when he had to choose between his wife and his daughter in the Sunnyside Road serial murders. Still, he knew that Sergei felt grateful to him.* He placed the call and Sergei agreed to come to the station to assist the police which as Beauregard later told his detectives, "Is no small feat. He was raised to be suspicious of all those in power in government; and he had every right not to want to help me; but he came anyway to be of service."

Sergei entered the station and the desk sergeant brought him right away to Beauregard's office. Other cops stared as Sergei followed him. The captain and Sergei greeted each other, if not exactly with camaraderie, but with respect. At least that's what the desk sergeant told the cops in the front room when he returned.

Beauregard thought, *West Side is not big enough to swallow the identity of a child serial murderer's father, moreover, one who actually helped to make my case. I could never have done what Rozovsky did; or maybe I could. I'd never let Mona take a fall, not even for my boys.*

Beauregard explained that because he was not a part of the Springfield Police Force and the District Attorney was in involved in the investigation of the murders and assaults at the gas station, that he could not go forward with the investigation; and that it was his family who was also assaulted. He told Sergei a little bit more about the facts and what help he needed. It was not until then that Sergei realized it was the Captain's family members who were assaulted including his young nephew. Appearing to be thinking, the Russian finally responded. "Captain Beauregard, we have to protect the children. I don't want anything to do with drugs or drug kings. People who talk about them get hurt. My family needs me. Your sister-in-law and nephew were almost killed; then that's different. I know the man who was killed. He has many names, but the one most known is Vladimir Sokolov. He is big and important. He is a killer, not a nice man, Captain. Killing him is no loss."

"Exactly what was he in charge of; what sections in Springfield or our city were under his control?"

"Captain, I only know what my workers say. I listen to them. Sokolov has been running around with a big drug dealer in the area who is Russian, not Puerto Rican, which makes sense. He is called 'Chavos', which is a junk Spanish word meaning money or moola. He's called that because whatever Chavos does, there's money in the deal for him; he never misses pay dirt. My guys say Sokolov was partnering with the devil and the devil's spawn; that Chavos would never have let him takeover. They say Sokolov was stupid and greedy. Sokolov is dead now, which means Chavos wanted him out. Sokolov is known for having a big mouth and one of my workers said it got him killed."

"It doesn't make sense to me, Sergei, because the Dominican killers took out three Puerto Ricans who headed well defined distribution areas. I think I can see why this Chavos would want to kill three big time Puerto Rican dealers? I can't see why he might want to get rid of Sokolov, but if he killed his own kind, that could create serious ramification with the Puerto Rican drug soldiers. It would mean from their point of view they couldn't trust this big one, Chavos."

"Captain, I'm Russian, which means I don't trust easily. It's true I'm closer to Russians than to non-Russians. What does that mean if I'm greedy and evil and am what they call my Anya? They call her a sociopath. I read about that and the internet says lots of things about sociopaths and yes, also, psychopaths. They don't feel bad when they do bad. Sociopaths don't have horrible dreams. They don't apologize. They get what they want and don't care who they hurt. Chavos is named Chavos for a reason. Money and power are his gods. It looks to me like Chavos wants the City of Springfield and the surrounding drug trade for himself. The soldiers and the other drug chiefs will either go along with him or die. That's what this attack at the gas station was about. He wouldn't do this unless he saw an opportunity for bigger profits. I don't know enough about the drug trade, Captain, but I know business. There must be a new product or a new market for him to create such a shit storm."

Beauregard responded, "Who is Chavos, Sergei and, where does he live? What has been his role in the Russian drug trade? When did he come here or is he native to this area? I need information on him.

"Captain, I only know he is from Georgia, Russia. I first heard the guys talking about him when I hired a Puerto Rican tile setter. Mostly my tile setters are Russian, but this guy is fast and has a great talent for design. I'm often hired because they know of Ramon's work. He said Chavos married a Puerto Rican girl and used the relationship to move into the drug business. She had a son and she was killed in a strange car accident. Her car went into the river. There was nothing in the paper about the cause of the accident. Chavos raised the son. No one knows his name or if they do, it's never mentioned. It's just Chavos."

"Do you have an idea, Sergei, about what date his wife had the accident? It would help if you could give me a time range. Also, in what city did the accident happen?"

"1997 to 2002 is my best guess and the car went over the river on the Springfield side in the North End. There's a space where you can go through the fence. Ramon said he thought it wasn't an accident because to go over in that spot there's about a hundred yards of grass and rubble. He figured even if she were high, the bumpy feel of the road would have stopped her. He thinks it was suicide or murder."

"Who would want to murder her? Was she an addict? What was her name?"

"Captain, her name was Maria Alonzo and her family returned to Puerto Rico right after she was buried. It's still talked about according to Ramon by the local Puerto Rican community."

The two talked some more, but it was clear to Beauregard, that Sergei could offer no additional information. Sergei did ask Beauregard not to talk to Ramon. He needed his skills and thought if he were questioned by the police he would run. Beauregard agreed.

After Sergei left, Ash knocked on Beauregard's door saying, "Captain, I've some reports for the chief you requested. I just finished them and they're late, so could you sign them, so I don't look so tardy?"

"Sure, Ash, but I need a favor from you. Mason is busy. Normally, he'd do it, but I need info on a Maria Alonzo whose car was found in the river with her, dead, inside. It was called an accident, but there may be more to it. She had a son. I need his name and location. Most of her family left for Puerto Rico right after that accident. The date is unknown; somewhere between 1997 and 2002. Start with the newspapers and with the Springfield police. She had a Russian husband, although probably not a formal marriage. It's important, Ash. Find what you can. Also let me know if you've ever heard of a drug dealer named 'Chavos'."

Ash agreed and told Beauregard, "I see a glint in your eyes, Captain, we on to something, maybe?"

"A big maybe, Ash."

Beauregard's office quieted down after Ash left allowing the captain to catch up on some paperwork. On the top of the in-basket was a letter addressed to him with no return address and labeled private. Observing it had no postmark, he assumed It had been hand delivered, but by whom? Before opening it, he called Millie and questioned her. She said, "The desk duty sergeant didn't know. He thought someone slipped in when he was dealing with several lawyers."

The captain opened the letter and found words from a magazine cut and pasted with a message, "Stop this drug deal stuff, please before my daughter is next. She knows too much and is going where it's dangerous. I've tried talking to her but she denies everything. I found stuff she doesn't know I know about. She thinks she's doing good but her friend died. Now she feels guilty. Help us."

Rudy thought, *it's written in decent English and if I am to believe it, the daughter is a friend of one of the victims. Time to pull the reports on the victims' acquaintances and I hope it's not Herbie that's the friend because everyone on the righteous anti-drug teams knew him.*

The captain pulled Petra in, who was on desk duty filling out department reports, and asked her for assistance. Petra appeared to be thrilled with the change in her day when he told her about the letter. "Captain, this person has gone to a lot of trouble in cutting and pasting. It's probably legitimate, but I'll get the camera feed on the desk sergeant and see who did it. That's a start. I'll pull the files. We all did interviewing of the victims' friends we knew about, and their families, so we're all in on identifying the person. She, probably a she, was pretty cool getting this by the desk sergeant. What I don't understand is why she wouldn't call us. Are these mothers today so afraid of their children's reactions? Hell, it's for the kid's safety. I don't get it."

Beauregard nodded in agreement and told the detective to work on this identification as quickly as possible, reminding her a girl's life was in jeopardy.

A few days later the captain grabbed a report from Juan regarding Losocala's history on the McAllen police force. The Chief of Police had done some asking around and discovered that Losocala, when he was on the force, was often seen on the Mexican side in the city of Reynosa. There were rumors that for a gringo cop, he was too familiar with some not so well thought of Mexicans. Rudy thought this info may add some fuel to the fiery hypothesis Losocala had unknown resources who financed his security business.

The report stated also Losocala was Italian on his father's side and Czech on his mother's side, but the name was often thought to be Spanish. Rudy wondered, *maybe that's his entre into the Mexican community. Maybe it just happened that the Mexicans assumed he was some sort of Spanish-American. Enough of this, I'd better get to the bottom of this administrative paper stuff.*

As Rudy worked his way through his backlog of work, he picked up the drawing of Losocala and after giving a definite nod of his head, he decided. He headed out to Evergreen and the Losocala home. As he drove he called Lilly and asked if she had scanned the reports on Losocala. She had. He directed she should meet him near Evergreen before the street turned to go uphill saying, "I'm putting some pressure on Losocala. I'm going to interview Mrs. Losocala. I want you with me."

Lilly quickly reached the planned meeting space and parked. Clearly happy to join the captain, she smiled as she scanned the community policing reports for the Evergreen address that she had compiled the day before for her report to the captain. The report was due later today. Unbelievably, the policing team reported only four cars in seven days that turned in the subject's driveway. One car was regularly parked in front on an almost daily basis. She had translated the plate numbers for all the cars noted to their owners. The cleaning lady, named Luisa Garcia, who parked on the street, lives over on Spruce Street. Lilly knew Spruce Street was where her two colleagues were shot and she noticed the number, but it was not number eight. The name Garcia struck a chord, but she knew Garcia was a pretty popular name. She'd ask the captain. The other cars were registered to Latino sounding names. There was not much activity at all. Hearing a noise, she saw the captain had pulled up next to her. Jumping quickly out of her car, she joined him. As she opened the door to his vehicle, he said, "Thank you for joining me, Lilly. Your job today is as a witness to my conversation. Normally, Detective Aylewood-Locke would attend this type of interview. I hesitate to say this but I must. No matter what you think I am missing or that the interviewee is not being forthright, say nothing. My interview today is to evaluate the subject and to perhaps plant some thoughts; that is all. Do you understand?"

"Sure, Captain, I'll contain my tendency to take over. Everyone in the department knows it's my strength and my downfall. I can be a silent witness; Petra says I'll learn from you and won't know it until later. Before we go there, I have the community policing report. The Losocala's do not have many visitors. They have a cleaning lady who visits daily and lives on sixteen Spruce Street. Her name is Luisa Garcia. The name sounds familiar to me, and I know she lives on the street where Ted and Ash were shot."

Beauregard took the reports from Lilly and called Mason, instructing him to get any information on a Luisa Garcia on sixteen Spruce Street and her relationship with Marisol Garcia who lived with that old man on Spruce Street saying, "Mason, is it the same house? I can't remember the number of that house. Juan investigated the street and all the comings and goings. Ask him if he ever saw this car, a 2008 cream colored Chevrolet Impala."

After giving Mason the plate number while driving, Lilly and the captain pulled into Losocala's drive. Both Lilly and Beauregard valuated the misfit of the home in the neighborhood. It was not that it was too modern in comparison to the other homes, which all were built in the McMansion American style, but it was more 'out there'. Most of the homes had detail that drew you to the New England sensitivity. You knew where you were without asking; but this home's finishing was in trending contemporary. Beauregard said, "Losocala is from Vegas and he'd go for this house. Locals probably wouldn't. I wonder how long it sat on the market before he came along. It is well-kept, Lilly."

"Well, Captain, the owners of homes like these have outside labor for repairs and maintenance. They don't do their own lawns."

As they walked toward the front oversized door painted in a neon shiny green, the door opened and a stunning woman greeted them as if she expected them, saying, "Hi, I'm Janine. I've been feeling oh so left out. You've been to all my neighbors asking about that teenaged girl who's missing and you didn't come to me. Welcome. Please come in."

Neither of the two detectives expected this reception, requiring Beauregard to reassess his focus. Janine brought them to what Beauregard thought was the family room, which was situated adjacent to the living room. She told him she called the two connected spaces the 'great room,' because of its size and that's what they had in Las Vegas. She commented she and Raymond had been married in their great room in Las Vegas shortly before they moved here. Further she said, "I'm not sure I would have so quickly agreed to marriage if I knew I'd have to move to New England. Nothing against your city, Captain Beauregard, but it's just different out here. You folks don't like a lot of splash and every person I've met is careful with their money. And let me tell you, I don't look forward to the winter. I've already ordered parkas and boots."

Lilly in order to maintain what she thought was just girl talk, broke her silence and said, "It's difficult to make these changes, Mrs. Losocala. I fully understand, but you'll find that West Side folks are really quite hospitable. The women in this town are great shoppers. They'll love to give you info on shopping; they'll send you off to New York City, West Hartford, Boston, and all of our discount plazas."

To Beauregard's mind, Lilly's simple welcome to Janine seemed to throw her off balance and he quickly learned he was right, when Janine said, "It's been lonely for me, Detective. I have no children and that's the easy way for a woman to get to know people in a new place. I don't work. I am a bit of an artist, but not really arty. Thank you, I'll try to make more of an effort to get to know my neighbors. Raymond is perfectly happy wrapping himself in his work and going to balls and dinners with businessmen and their wives that he's never met before. It's more difficult for me."

Beauregard said, "Mrs. Losocala…."

Before he could continue, Janine said, "Detectives, please call me Janine. I'm still not used to being called Mrs. Losocala and besides I'm the third Mrs. Losocala. Call me Janine, please."

Continuing his conversation Beauregard said, "Janine, we are here to ask you about that young woman called Candace Monroe. I have a photo here I'd like to show you."

Beauregard handed the photo to Janine who looked at the teen and very quickly said, "I've seen her. She stopped by one morning. I only noticed her because she was talking to my cleaning lady Luisa. Luisa asked permission to leave for an hour to drive the girl to the high school. Luisa said the girl was quite upset about some problem and asked for a ride. She thought she was doing a good deed, Captain. You should talk to her about this Candace."

"Janine, do you remember what she was wearing?"

Janine described pretty clearly the outfit Candace was wearing that day. In fact, Beauregard thought she had one hell of a memory. He explained to Janine Candace was the victim of sexual assault. This was not what the police would normally share with a witness in an interview, but Beauregard appeared to be interested in her reaction. It was not what he expected. "Captain, that's not what the papers said. They said she died using drugs. That is horrible." Janine started weeping while continuing to talk. "Luisa said she was upset. Was the assault a result of family abuse? This is a lovely town, and I can't believe that a pretty girl like Candace would be abused by family here."

"Janine, it was not family. Clearly, it was someone she had met; someone she hoped to influence for the good. That someone was not to be influenced. What did Luisa say after she came back to work?"

"Actually, Captain, I don't remember. She did not seem at all upset; not like her sister Marisol, who used to work for me. She was always late and emotional, and not a very good cleaning lady. I think she was on pills or something. Anyway, when she didn't show up one day, I told Raymond I needed help. He must have talked to someone; probably the person who gave him Marisol's name in the first place. When Luisa came, I could see right away she would work out fine."

The two detectives left shortly after this interview against Janine's insistence they stay for coffee. Lilly was the first to speak, saying, "Captain, she is either the greatest liar I have met or she knows nothing. Her tears appeared to me to be from true emotion. I know a great liar is one who tells partial truths, but she puts the victim at her home on the day the victim dies. She doesn't even give a story as to why the victim walked around the corner up to her house when the high school is the other way. It's a story with big holes in it. So maybe it's the truth. What do you think?"

"I think, although it sounds improbable, that Candace and the other murders may be connected to the attacks on our guys on Spruce Street. I think Marisol's attack stems from the Spruce Street assaults. I think McKinnon's undercover work is related to Spruce Street. I think the killings at the gas station and the assault on Sally and John are related to Spruce Street, somehow. I have thought about this for a long time and Janine just added the frosting on the cake. She is not stupid. If she thought for a minute her husband was involved, she's intelligent enough to say nothing. There is always the outside possibility that she hates Raymond and wants him gone. I don't think she's that smart to play that game. I want Janine's history investigated."

17

Armistice Day Celebration

Beauregard could not find a parking place on Silvain Street today. He went down and back and down again. He mouthed a swear, got out of his vehicle, moved the orange cones across from the ladies, and parked in the saved space; placing his police placard in his car's windshield. He thought, *Maybe I'll see some resident of this house come over and complain giving me an opportunity for an interview.*

The captain was dressed in what he would call his Saturday at home outfit of khakis, golf shirt, and windbreaker. He climbed the front stairs of Miriam and Sarah's home. The weather was chilly for that early in November and he was grateful his jacket had a fleece lining. He checked his iWatch which clocked the temperature at forty-three degrees and he shivered. The double-wide old-fashioned doors opened wide in the center and a handsome looking woman in perhaps her late sixties greeted him with, "Rudy Beauregard, the famous catcher of serial murderers, and the young man who used to look like he was dozing in my class at Holyoke High School," and she opened her arms to hug him.

Taken back by this abrupt show of affection, Beauregard blushed a bright red. Miriam's hug was not to be prevented as she quipped, "Oh,

Captain, don't you remember me? And I know you were never really sleeping in class; you were too good a student, but you were quiet, quiet, oh so quiet."

Beauregard remembered her and said, "Mrs. Brown, you're one of the 'Southern Ladies?' And you remember me?"

"Of course, I remember you and your mama Lizette, who secretly checked in with me on a regular basis explaining you were shy and I was to ignore your slow movements; that you were very smart. I'm telling you, Lizette was one smart mama. She knew it was her job to let me know you were special, but I figured it out on my own. Sarah and I have been watching your career and I told her I knew way back then you'd do well."

Miriam dragged him over to meet Sarah who was pouring 'Soixante Quinze' into tall champagne glasses from a shaker filled with ice and a liquid. There was a standing sign labeling the drink. Miriam introduced Beauregard and again he was roundly hugged as if he was a child. Sarah laughed and pinched his cheek to his great embarrassment, saying, "I can't help it. Miriam and I read everything in the papers about you, and Miriam brags about her early prediction that you were a quiet mouse waiting to become the fox. I think it was a fox or a cat; I can't remember which. Probably it was a cat. Miriam thinks they are thoughtful but instinctive creatures who think before they pounce. Yes, it's cats not foxes."

Despite his head spinning, Beauregard recovered enough to ask what was in 75 she was pouring. The ladies giggled and Miriam responded, "Sarah, he was raised by Lizette Beauregard, and of course he knows 'Soixante Quinze' translates to 75. The French 75 Cocktail was one of the most popular drinks during World War I. It has champagne, gin, sugar and lemon juice shaken with ice and poured into champagne flutes. We had to rent enough flutes for today, but the rental agency charged next to nothing because we let their staff attend. We often do trade. Captain, don't tell the IRS."

Hoping to ingratiate himself further, Beauregard said, "I'd like to try one, Ladies, and it's my day off, so why not?"

"Why not, indeed," the ladies said in unison as if scripted.

It was generally known by his colleagues that the captain was not the king of small talk, but today he outdid himself. The ladies let their other guests know he was one of Miriam's former students and he was a special guest today. Beauregard noticed they did not tell their guests he was a captain on the police force. He thought that was a good thing, since he saw a few there, who had previously been guests of the state. The ladies found him a seat near the buffet table. He wondered if his twenty or maybe thirty extra pounds hinted to them, that he would want easy access to the piled-up goodies. Sarah explained the repast and said they tried to include recipes from the wartime experience which mostly replaced sugar with molasses or the British equivalent called treacle. Many recipes replaced wheat flour with potato or rye or some other flour and of course they would use vegetables for their cutlets. Pea soup was a basic because it used a dried vegetable as its base, and an apricot buckle using whatever bread was available with the cooked dried apricots was another favorite of the time. This dessert was also made using any dried fruit. Miriam had made a prune-buckle; however, she did use sugar. Friends brought in all the meats which were often unavailable in 1918. The ladies did make the traditional war-time stew, bonza bog stew with minced leftover meat. Beauregard tried most everything, but was partial to pea soup, a dish his mother Lizette made monthly. He decided, evidenced by his finishing two cups of the soup, that the soup was on a par with Lizette's.

The captain, looking up as he was finishing his feast, thought this was a great way to spend a Saturday afternoon. His focus diverted to a handsome brunette woman who entered the room. She was given a great deal of attention. When he heard Sarah greet her as Carmen, he also gave her his attention. Sarah seemed pleased to invite her in with, "Carmen, you're looking well. How is Mrs. Rojas? Is she still holding her own; the poor dear is always so closed in except when visiting her doctors. I don't know why you can't bring her to one of our little parties. The men here would happily help her."

Carmen handed Sarah an envelope and said, "You do enough, you and Miriam, watching the house for me. She insists nobody live with her. She has been alone for over twenty-five years, and insists, after her experience with her abusive husband, being alone is a welcome respite. She's relatively healthy for such a frail looking woman. She is tall but looks so small in her wheelchair and she's always bundled up. She gets so cold. I keep the thermostat at seventy-four degrees and it's stifling in there but suits her. I feel so obligated to her that I gladly help her out. She was so good to me when I was a little girl."

Beauregard heard Sarah say, "I hate to take this money, Carmen. All we do is watch the house to make sure there are no intruders. Is her son helpful? We see him take her to the doctor's office for a visit occasionally."

"He's a good man, but he's a man. He can only do small things like bring her some groceries. I do the rest when I visit. I know what she likes and prepare little dishes for her, put them in the freezer, and she takes them out and heats them for two meals a day. She gets around in her kitchen. Fortunately, it's a good old-fashioned sized kitchen which allows her wheelchair to move around easily. Her bedroom is on the same floor as well as her sitting room. It is a perfect setup and she's happy. She watches Spanish television and writes letters to her sisters in San Juan. I deliver them. She gets her mail at a post office box, because I don't want anyone we don't know bothering her; and that includes a mailman."

Sarah practically cooed, "Carmen, you're a good woman and Mrs. Rojas is lucky to have you."

Beauregard watched Carmen interact with others on the porch and greet Miriam with hugs. He thought, *this lady is pretty cool. Her English has no trace of an accent and despite the name and the black hair, she looks neither Puerto Rican nor Mexican. Maybe she's from Spanish or Italian or some other southern European background; she has pretty light skin, but I'm probably wrong. Anyway, who can tell ethnicity today with all the mixes of nationalities? Look at me, I'm a mongrel. I think the population is getting, in my mind, better looking for it. Unless It has to do with better healthcare, or as Petra and Lilly would say, better beauty products and plastic surgery; although I don't believe that.*

More adults crowded into the room. He noticed they mostly appeared to be old friends and neighbors. The group seemed harmless and then, Him, Me and Paulie walked in. They were startled to see Captain Beauregard, big as life, at the Armistice Gala as the ladies called it. They ignored him until Jackson moved to the buffet and whispered, "Nice to see you, Captain. We have no information for you today. See, we're doing what you asked."

Beauregard did not move a muscle pretending he hadn't heard and hoped Jackson would take the hint; and he did. Paulie was the next to hit the buffet, but he just winked at the Captain which only encouraged Beauregard to decide it was time to exit the gala. Leaving was not easy. Both Sarah and Miriam insisted he be introduced to the crowd as Rudy, one of Miriam's stellar ex-students. He thought, *it's damn embarrassing to be treated as her kiss-up student at my age. Carmen is very interested in me. I'd better get out of here.*

With unusual alacrity for Beauregard, he extricated himself from the ladies and attempted to leave, a journey which forced him to walk by his confidential informants or sources of information. He said 'Hi' to the boys, ruffled Wayne's hair, and practically fled from the house. On making the six steps down to the walkway, he saw a lace curtain move and a face looking out as he approached his car. The orange cones had been moved to the side of his car forcing him to move them in order to drive away. He realized Carmen knew who he was and thought, *how stupid of me to use my police placard. Still it wouldn't make any difference if I hadn't, even thirteen-year old kids recognize an unmarked police car. I wonder if Carmen parked her car on this street.*

He looked around and spotted a car parked in an open garage behind the house. Barely able to see the car, he pretended while he was moving the cones, to look in the window where the face had appeared, knowing that the person would look away. It gave him time to look more carefully at the black or navy, blue car. Rudy always had on hand in his vehicle a 5X magnifier loupe used by roofers. It was convenient today as he used the loupe and was able to pick up five of the car's six plate numbers; the last one was not visible at this distance. The car was registered in Massachusetts.

Rudy headed home and while driving he reviewed the image of the face in the curtained window. Then the revelation snapped his brain into focus. *The face in the window could not have been sitting in a wheelchair. It was too high up in the window frame. Carmen wasn't there, and it wasn't the old lady Mrs. Rojas. It probably was the son. Is his name Rojas?*

Beauregard called Detective Tagliano who was on Saturday duty. She was quick to respond. He asked her to search for anyone named Rojas living in or near Spruce Street; maybe an older woman between sixty and ninety living with a son. He gave her the address of the house and told her to check medical records. He also gave her the partial license plate of the car telling her that it might be in the name of someone with a first name of Carmen. Beauregard was proud of his afternoon's work and continued on home.

It wasn't ten minutes after Beauregard left the Armistice Gala that Him, Me and Paulie agreed with each other they should follow Carmen after she would leave the house. Carmen stayed and partied for a long time, stressing the boys out, who were scheduled to be home by 5:30 this day. Finally, the lady left and the boys said their goodbyes. Outside, they pretended to be fixing Jackson's bike while stalling for time. The visibility was good and they watched as Carmen went to the garage across the street and left. The boys memorized the plate number on her black SUV and made a call to the captain. He did not answer so they left a message. Paulie cut through the wooded section and was by the mall before Carmen's car was on the same street. Paulie was pretty certain she would go over the bridge and so he started over there himself expecting her to cross over and she did. She headed straight after going by Monarch Place to Boland Way to Harrison Avenue. She stopped at the light and Paulie caught up to Carmen's car. This allowed him the ability to see her turn left on Chestnut Street and shortly thereafter turn right at the Apremont Triangle.

He knew, just knew, she was hitting the city's Mattoon Street section from the back. He hustled up Mattoon Street which was one way toward Chestnut and waited. After ten minutes he decided he was wrong, was about to leave, but instead rode up to the end of Mattoon, and parked. On his left, on the side street, he saw Carmen's car. He took all the numbers of the houses on this street called Elliott Street and called the captain with this new information. He was disappointed Beauregard did not answer, but still was pleased with his new information. Next, he called Him and Me. They were exhilarated with

Jackson, saying, "Paulie, a real cop couldn't have done it better." Wayne asked him if he wanted to be a cop or an artist since he was really great at both. He did not give an answer.

Rudy was reading his newspaper on Sunday morning after returning from church services. He checked his phone and saw the two calls. The information was helpful, but Rudy's blood pressure immediately rose enough so he noticed it. Mona also saw the change and said, "Rudy, what is the matter? Please don't read about politics early in the morning. I don't need you fuming for the day."

Beauregard assured her it wasn't politics and explained his problem, expecting her to agree with him that the situation with the kids was untenable and dangerous. Her reaction surprised him. She questioned his anger saying, "Rudy, these boys are doing what your kids would have done or what I would have done. Imagine, if you are able, that you were a kid that age and you had the chance to help the police catch what we all know are the bad guys.

"The whole thing is what the lawyers would call an 'attractive nuisance.' A kid just couldn't refrain from getting involved. These boys know they have done police work and they feel good about it. Now I understand your concern for their safety, but right now they've only reported what they have seen. As to Paulie riding his bike around, no adult will be suspicious except maybe that he might steal something. Do caution them, but please don't suppress their wonderful exuberance, their desire to be of service."

Practically sputtering, Rudy retorted, "Safety, Mona, they are playing with fire and I can't allow it."

Dinner today was to be special because Roland, Jr. was bringing a girl home from college. Mona told Rudy to call the boy detectives, talk to them nicely, and lose the attitude. She reminded her husband that this is the first time Roland, Jr. had ever entertained a girl in their home. Mona said, "I'll not countenance any negativity today, Rudy. Roland would think it meant we didn't like the young lady. Maybe we won't, but he's entitled to family support."

Beauregard made a call to Jackson and asked if the boys could meet him at Hoffington Playground in an hour. Jackson thought it would work for them all, but if not, he would be there.

Beauregard was there five minutes early only to find the boys already waiting. He had a long conversation with them, but he modified it in respect to Mona's earlier input. Later, Beauregard would congratulate himself on the political and sensitive aspects of his conversation considering, *Mona understands kids. I really laid into the safety aspects of their work, but told them also how valuable their discovered info was to me. They were so happy, but I don't know if that was the right course to take. They'll continue to play detective, although they promised not to. Dear God, make sure they don't come to harm.*

Beauregard arrived at the station remembering Juan was covering the unit. He apprised Juan on the situation. Juan loved it, calling the kids 'Junior G-men' and applauded their work saying, "Captain, this saves us some work." He grabbed Lilly's file from yesterday. The RMV listed just two cars with the first five numbers with that make and color. Neither one was owned by someone named Carmen. However, the kids had the complete plate number and that one was owned by a thirty-five-year-old woman named Carolina Contreau who lives on Elliot Street, and who is the chief administrative assistant for a human resource company called, "Assistants-Now, LLC."

Beauregard told Juan to research her and the company she worked for. He left for home satisfied, that there was a potential trail of information on the goings on at the Silvain Street house. It was now time to meet Roland's new friend. He thought, *God, how I hate change.*

18

Working Past Reports

Juan was busy looking up Carmen or Carolina's company on the Massachusetts Secretary of State Corporations Division website. The company was there. Carolina was listed as manager in the LLC, but after reviewing he found that ownership was in a financial investment firm called FSB, LLC. He sourced the financial investment firm, and its home which was located on lower Main Street in Springfield with a local attorney as the contact. He googled Carolina Contreau and discovered she was Canadian and her Facebook was active connecting to several Canadian sites. He reviewed some activity on her Facebook; it looked harmless enough. He'd wait until tomorrow to see if she had a green card or was a naturalized US citizen.

Juan pulled his unfinished report on his several undercover visits to the game store. He had gone for an hour or two on several different days. Writing the report was difficult; mostly because there were only a few facts, just his assumptions and conclusions formed after viewing the game kids' behaviors. He knew at first the kids ignored him, but on his second visit when he outscored the leading guy on 'Black Ops,' he was noticed. He let them brag about their abilities gaming, but in listening, he learned they mostly loved playing 'Fortnite' on the internet. He had not played all the games they played, but for the one he did play he was a winner, which definitely opened them up to conversation.

Part of his work with them was to convince them he was a non-druggie, a good guy, who was having trouble being welcomed in town, given he was Mexican. By his third visit, he was approached by a girl who asked him if he had heard of the anti-drug activity at the high school. He explained his family had just moved to West Side, and he was still at Commerce High School in Springfield until graduation. She asked him to meet her at the West Side library; that she had a friendly group of people like her she'd like him to meet.

On the day of the fourth meeting, he entered the library and saw two girls and three guys waiting for him. He was certain the meeting was only about him because they weren't even talking until he sat at the table. They assessed him as 'reliable' almost instantly and initiated a call to action. They couldn't shut up. Amber, the girl who had approached him, said two of her friends were dead because the team had been successful in getting some of the drugs off the street; that what they were doing was dangerous. She said, "Jose (his undercover alias), what we're doing is worthwhile. The police just don't know how to integrate into teenagers' community. Herbie was our mentor and he was killed. He was really street smart, but he was out there. You know, 'known in the community.' He actually put us at risk. We think keeping quiet is most important for our safety. Keeping quiet is not the same as giving up."

Juan listened as the group discussed the new system they were putting in place. He had been careful about asking their names; but like kids everywhere they had notebooks with their names scribbled in script. At least the girls did. He only saw the guys' first names.

The kids had the name of Detective Aylewood-Locke. They figured she was okay because she knew Mrs. Beauregard, who had been at a meeting at the library with the detective. Amber said, "I met with Mrs. Beauregard and the detective and I just know they will keep our secret."

Now Juan was in a tough position. His report had to include the captain's wife and from his frame of reference, that would be a no-no. He couldn't fudge the report because the system the kids described had already been implemented, and it included some new kids which one of the guys said worried him. He implied they weren't properly vetted and had big mouths. Juan decided he should give an oral report to the captain. He could ask Petra who had interviewed some of the kids at the library. She however never said the captain's wife was there. He thought better of it, thinking, *I'll just wait for the captain*. Juan looked at Captain Beauregard's calendar which he knew kept a lot of planned appointments, but not all his appointments. It was one of those see in one view monthly paper calendars; he thought it was evidence the captain didn't trust technology that much. Unfortunately, the calendar appeared to have the captain out of the office on the next day. He thought, *this can wait until Tuesday.*

Monday morning found all of the detectives at work. There would be no Unit meeting today. The captain was out of the office for that day. Juan busied himself writing the summation of his interview with the captain's sister-in-law Sally. He had spent an hour trying to figure out what Sally had heard. He thought at the time, she surely murdered the Spanish language, but she was vehement about the sounds she heard. He finally wrote the sounds and spaced them in the manner she insisted she heard them. Then as if he was struck by lightning, he knew what had been said, *Eres una mosca. La arana es tu duena.* When translated it said, "You are a fly. The spider owns you." It was the only phrase that made sense from Sally's "e-ris- oo-na-mo-sca-la-ran-ya-e-too-do-anya. *But just who was the spider who owned this guy, the fly?* Further, Sally insisted the man who said it, said it very slowly as if to emphasize every word. It was the Russian, speaking Spanish, who spoke the words. He was with the three Puerto Ricans yelling this to two Dominicans. Juan's knowledge of the Dominicans he had met was, that they were very family oriented. He thought, however, they would not take being put down as a fly well. What was said alienated the shooter, but again, *if my translation is correct*, he wondered, *just who is the spider?*

He asked the other detectives what reports each was working on and if they'd ever heard of a drug king called "The Spider." They hadn't, but Lilly said she'd call a detective in the Narcotics Unit she once had a date with saying, "He'd do anything for me and I don't mind calling. I was pretty brutal with him. He thought my work in Vice might spill over into the evenings. Instead of just educating him, I dumped my martini on him and left. This was in front of several other cops; you know we were at Moriarty's. He was called the 'stalker' after that, but I think he still likes me."

Mason said, "Sister Lilly, you have to stop taking advantage of a poor guy who just wants to get to know you really well!!!!"

"Mason, I'm not your sister and he's not a poor guy and the way he wants to know me skips about twenty dates. I won't hold it against you. You're just a male hyena with a stupid sense of humor."

Juan replied, "Sounds like you're a misogynist, Mason; you know the lady is sensitive to such issues."

Petra screamed, "Shut-up. Lilly, I'm dying to see if the guy even talks to you, let alone does your detective work. Are you talking about Detective Danny Abdoul? He's the only guy who's single over there."

"That's him."

Lilly made the call, and after about five minutes of reassuring him that she may have misunderstood his intentions, she laid out her interest in 'The Spider' and his identity. He responded quickly with, "What's MCU doing dealing with 'The Spider.' He's of interest to us, Lilly."

After Lilly explained that one of their witnesses in the shooting of the detectives mentioned that 'The Spider' would be angry with the interruption of business, Danny insisted on knowing the witness's name.

Lilly said it was just in the general notes of that day made by one of the officers who were interviewing on Spruce Street. She reminded him she wasn't appointed to MCU until later that day. Also, she told Danny the witness wasn't even identified. She clarified, "Danny, I'm new here and I'm just going over all notes on all our murders to see if I can add something. I thought, in the back of my brain, that I may have heard 'The Spider' name in some other context before; maybe in Vice. Who is he, Danny? Is he a drug dealer in Springfield or Holyoke or where?"

Lilly thought, *if he thinks I'm just asking out of general interest, he'll be more likely to tell me what he knows; but if Danny thinks I have a live investigation into a drug lord, he'll go quiet. He will have heard that Beauregard has been told not to investigate anything having to do with drug deals.*

Danny seemed to have bought her story. He detailed for her, "'The Spider'. Lilly, the Spider is everywhere but nowhere. I'm not sure if he's real or not, but drug users think that he is a scary guy. There are stories that when he runs he leans forward and because he has long arms hanging down, he looked like a spider and was so named. I don't know if it's fiction, but the street shows fear when that word is mentioned. We arrested a dealer who was working the town's youngsters. He was all set to accept a plea for a reduced sentence from the assistant district attorney, when his lawyer gave him a piece of mail with a spider on the outside. We had no idea if it was important, but he wouldn't deal afterwards. The case is still ongoing and will go to trial soon. We thought at the time it was from one of his friends attempting to scare him. If so, it worked. Whether there really is 'The Spider', we don't know."

"Is he Latino, Danny or not? If he were Latino, wouldn't they use the Spanish for spider?"

"If they're Latino, they often say 'La Arana' but also say 'The Spider'. Don't know what that means. So, Lilly, how about a coffee date? I can show you I am not the guy you think I am. Maybe we can do lunch this coming weekend or even dinner if you dare."

"I dare, Danny. Dinner will be fine, but not at a cop's bar. Okay?"

Lilly was ragged incessantly after she clicked off. She realized her colleagues could put the whole conversation together since she was in the habit of repeating phrases aloud after hearing them. It was a comprehension technique she learned in a reading class she took in college. The professor called it "ear to brain to mouth to ear" practice for memory and retention. Despite her knowledge of her own habit, she was still surprised at Petra when she said, "Good job, Lilly, and you didn't have to give him your body, just dinner."

Before Lilly could answer Petra, the other detectives present started singing, *Danny Boy*. With a disgusted look, Lilly said, "Idiots, he's not even Irish."

Juan finished his report after inserting Lilly's input.

Petra was sitting with Mason as they analyzed pictures of the woman who had delivered the cut and paste letter about her daughter. She had been pretty careful in hiding her face. Petra shared, "Mason, for a novice, this lady has her hand over the side of the face to block the camera, which she's doing so well in most of these pictures, I wonder if she's been here before."

Mason agreed with her analysis, but pointed to three stills they had cut out of the video and enlarged. Although they weren't perfect, she was identifiable. They printed the photos and passed them around the room. Ash said he had seen her somewhere. This did not surprise the other detectives as Ash played violin in so many venues. He said to give him some time. Ted looked closely at the photo and said, "I've seen her at some of the mayor's shindigs. She's either some public relations type or she's just politically active. Let me ask Charlotte if she can make her. She has a good eye."

Ash asked, "Do we have access to the Massachusetts Department of Transportation facial recognition program? Maybe that program could do it. I know we're one of forty-three states that have it. Although before I go there, give me a day before we try that. Either my or Charlotte's memory will prevail, and we won't have to explain what we're doing; especially if the lady in question is notable."

Petra laughed. "Uh-uh, Ash, would need a warrant for that. We don't have enough for one."

They all heard Ash groan and mutter, "Another barrier access against the good guys."

Ted said, speaking to Juan, "While we're all in a group, I heard you and Mason were doing a retail source find for the new clothes found on the bodies. Did you guys ever get anything helpful?"

Juan and Mason both sighed with Juan saying, "Well, the clerk at checkout remembered a guy in his early thirties who came through the register with a whole bunch of clothes of different sizes. He said he remembered him; it was a slow day and he didn't look like the kind of guy to make this type of purchase. All the clothes were unexceptional, while he was dressed to the 'nines.' They were all purchased before the first murder. We've got the video for that day but he had a hat pulled low. You can only see a corner of his chin. We can estimate he's over six feet tall and well built. We think he might be the perp, but nada. We told the captain but I forgot to put it on the board."

All their phones throbbed as Millie walked into Operations and said, "There's another body over by the river near Agawam. Narcotics called and it looks like the same as the other murders."

Ted and Ash attended the scene along with Petra. There was a young woman, girl actually, lying splayed out, just like the other bodies. Her school I.D. was in her hand, which was the only change that was thought to be significantly different from the other murders. Petra, however, did not need the I.D. She knew the young girl as one of the students who had been at the library, when she interviewed those active in the anti-drug activity in town. The girl was Joely Peters, and Petra felt sick. She did not think it was her pregnancy that caused her to run away from the scene to vomit; it was her increased sensitivity to seeing someone she knew as a victim. In all the years on the force Petra realized, *I've never seen a murder victim on site I had met personally. Why didn't she listen to what I said?*

When she picked her head up after vomiting, she saw not even a foot away, a silver Kennedy dollar coin. She pulled a glove out of her purse and put the coin in an evidence bag thinking, *just, who, walks around with Kennedy silver dollars? It's right on top of the clutch of flattened grass. It's not wet and we had rain last night. I'll bet it's the perp's, just bet it's his and he'll miss it.*

She heard Captain Beauregard's voice behind her saying, "Found something, Lieutenant?"

She showed him the silver dollar and pointed to where she found it. He took and put it back in place and told her to photograph it and recollect it. Petra was sorely embarrassed to have been told about a basic police procedure she had ignored.

The captain whispered apparently to prevent others from hearing him, "You're seeing Dr. Ford, Petra, and today. Do you understand?"

"It's just normal hormones that come with pregnancy, Captain. It's not fair for you to punish me because I'm pregnant."

"I'm not and you know better. You had a difficult time when we witnessed Candace at the first murder site. I let that go, despite the fact I never saw any serious reaction from you before when you were confronted with horror. It is time for you to talk about your feelings and if you can't do it, then I see limitations on your service to MCU. Petra, you had difficulty closing the door on the debacle of your first marriage. It took Jim, and his sensitivity, to assist you. What makes you think therapy is a punishment? In fact, I'll make the call now to see if he'll see you today. Don't tell me no, Petra; I'll put it in as a normal service appointment based on the shootings of Ash and Ted. No promotion board will hold that against you."

As the captain made the call to Dr. Ford, Petra with tears in her eyes thought, *he wouldn't do this to a guy. I could sue him for sexual discrimination. What am I talking about? I know I need help and I'd never get it if it were up to me. He's always been in my corner. I love my job; it's just the memory of these girls lying, dead, splayed out like a frog in a high school biology class, keeps running through my brain. I can't stop the visuals.*

The captain informed Petra she had an appointment in an hour saying, "I made it at his Longmeadow private office. That way you won't have to explain you're visiting the 'Shrink Room', near the Chief's office. Don't hold it against me, Petra. It's the right thing for you to do now for yourself and that baby."

Petra nodded, but couldn't find it in her heart to say, Thank You.

At that moment, Chief Coyne arrived on the scene accompanied by some Staties attached to the district attorney's office. She could see the captain was embroiled in a serious discussion about the investigation. She heard Beauregard say quite adamantly to Chief Coyne, "First I had to convince you these were murders. Now you want the FBI task force to take over the investigation when our work is finally productive. Give me some help here and we'll solve this. Have an FBI profiler in on this. I asked for one three weeks ago, and no action was taken because you were still denying that these deaths are murders."

In an aside, Coyne said, "Rudy, you told me you identified some similar murders through VICAP. Do you think they won't notice? I can't be seen to be obstructive. I've got to notify them. You have four murders here."

Beauregard replied, "Five in western Massachusetts, Chief, there are five. One is out further in Buckland."

"Are you certain, Rudy?"

"Unfortunately, I am very certain and VICAP identified a bunch more. Give me some time, Chief? That's all I ask."

The two walked away towards their cars preventing Petra from hearing the final word.

Mason, who happily stayed in office hell as he called the squad room, was busy looking at photos that Svetlana, Lilly's Russian friend, had taken of what she said were wealthy Russians who must be in the drug business. And Mason agreed when he was able to recognize Petro Gavel in one photo. He thought, *what the hell is going on here? What is the most important Russian king of drugs doing in a strip mall near Spruce Street? He's supposed to be located in Holyoke or Westfield or Springfield.*

He looked at the other photos but didn't recognize them. One was of a tall slim man in his late fifties or early sixties, another was of a man whose build was tall and broad with even features, and the third and fourth were surely bodyguards; one was certainly Russian and the other Latino. He could not give ethnicity to the tall slim man or to the bigger well-built guy, because their features were in shadow and blurred. He yelled over to Lilly who was busy pulling data on Janine Locosala, "Have you ever seen these dudes before, Lilly?"

She groaned saying, "Bring them over here, lazy. They're pictures, not video."

When she saw the pictures, she was certain about three of them; she said she'd never seen them before. The picture of the good-looking well-built guy caused her to pause. She looked at him carefully and asked Mason if he could pull up a whole body shot and not just a head shot. Mason did, but commented, "Lilly, we have to recognize the face."

"I know that, but the guy, I remember, had a pinkie ring with a twisted metal design; it had a distinctive look. He wore it on his left hand. I remember that."

Mason pulled up a whole-body picture and looked for a pinky ring. It was there in the photo. He now realized the guy's physical presentation was of one who was in control. "Lilly, how tall is he; do you remember?"

"Well, I was working Vice in the park area in my six-inch red spangled shoes when he stopped his car. The street was really busy because there was a damn festival. He scrolled his window down and asked how I was doing; but try as I might I couldn't get him to say anything incriminating. I had a deal with my partner that unless the john said something that showed illegal sexual intent that I wouldn't get too near the car. You know later-on, the john could say I entrapped him. Most of the johns are dumb and ask how much for an hour or a night. Not this guy. He acted like it was a romance. I didn't like him and unlike some of the johns, I didn't feel sorry for him. He was sitting down, but the seat was pushed way back, so he's at least six feet tall. He had his left hand on the steering wheel, and when he talked, he moved his right hand."

"Do you think he's Italian or Spanish?"

"Well, Mason, my dad's Italian and if you cut his arms off he'd be a mute; so maybe his waving his right arm meant that. He didn't look Italian. He had a nice light olive complexion, but had smaller more even facial features. You can see that from your picture. He is handsome but my sex deviant radar went off enough that I wouldn't get near the car. Also, my partner at that time was notoriously slow, and I didn't take chances when he was the main cover for me."

Mason looked at the pictures again and said, "Lilly, is the tall guy wearing the same ring, but it's on his right hand?"

The two detectives enlarged the photo on the screen and although it was a blurred view, the two rings were much alike. Whether it meant anything at all, they were unsure. Lilly said, "Maybe they're gay or related or the ring means some common club membership."

Mason enlarged the two rings and sent it over to the department's police artist and asked him to sketch it better so they could look for a source of the ring.

They got a return email almost instantaneously. The artist wrote that the ring is a 'Russian Tattoo Signet'. Mason called him and was told, "Mason, you can see almost perfectly this is a tattoo ring with a heart stabbed by an arrow from the upper left diagonally and a sword from the upper right diagonally; both crossing each other inside the heart. It's called the 'hard love tattoo'. Russian criminals love to wear tattoo signets, but wearing the 'hard love tattoo' ring is different."

"What about the fact that two men who are somehow involved in drugs would both wear that ring?"

"I would assume they are related, maybe have a thing about women or are in the sex trade, or were in jail in Russia together, or belong to the same group of criminals who choose to wear that ring as a symbol, or maybe it has no meaning at all."

Mason thanked the artist and turned to ask what Lilly had to say. She pointed to the pictures of the other men noting that not one of them had the 'hard love tattoo' ring and said, "The ones with the rings could be related or in the sex trade; just those two. I say that because the young one rang my deviant buzzer, Mason. Look at the older one. He's much leaner and the same height as the younger one, but the younger one has dark hair and darker skin. Maybe they aren't related; the builds are different, but they seem to stand in the same way. You know, they look like they're in charge; I mean like I think they're arrogant. Both of them are arrogant."

"Could be a little of both, Lilly, I wonder if our sketch artist added thirty pounds to the older one; if that would improve their similarity in facial features."

Mason called the department's sketch artist back and asked him if he would be willing to work on the picture. He was and said that his program was great and he'd get back to him in a jiffy.

Back at her desk, Lilly was reading Janine Locosala's biography pieces. She appeared, from the reports, to have had a normal California history: from winning the junior miss pageant to her high school graduation in Santa Monica. She graduated with honors from Santa Monica College. There was a two-year marriage when her surname of Brunder was changed to Russell. After the divorce, she took back her maiden name and moved to Las Vegas showing various employment gigs at the casinos. Lilly thought, *she must have done great work, because she went from assistant planner at one of the smaller casinos to chief event planner at one of the top three casinos. It was in that position that Raymond Losocala must have noticed her. She would have seemed special to him with her daunting looks and professional expertise.*

Nothing jumped out in Janine's background as suspicious except she thought, *why would such an accomplished woman want to be a third wife. Could it be that being a third wife is not so unusual out there?*

Lilly's thoughts were interrupted by a phone call from Petra, who summed up the new murder case and asked a question. "Did you and Ash get anything watching Losocala's office downtown? These murders are really getting to me. I won't be back there for a couple of hours. I forgot, I have a dentist appointment. Hold the fort for me."

"Not to worry, Petra, the report on Losocala's holdings has not been too fruitful. I'm just now pulling up the pictures. We have quite few. There are many photos of businessmen, Las Vegas types not in suits, local politicians, and lots of muscle going in and out of his offices. I'll put examining the photos aside until you and Ash are here."

"I'd appreciate that, Lilly."

19

Partying in Evergreen

Liz Abernale inspected the dining room table and console with a sigh of satisfaction. She had dressed the table with material; not just a beautiful linen tablecloth, but with colorful cloths hiding the various metal stands scattered on the table at different heights. Presentation was everything to Liz. Good tasting food was of course essential, but Liz was aware that even more important was the ambiance of serving it. She'd planned the table and console design weeks before. She thought, *the party tonight will be a little different. Not just the neighborhood is invited. No, I've gone out of the neighborhood. Normally, I do include Teresa Loyal, my friend who doesn't live in our Evergreen area, but tonight she pressured me to ask the Dions and the Beauregards. The Dions are invited only to allow Teresa to get to know them better, because she's not sure their son Wayne is a good influence on Jackson. Teresa is such a control freak.*

I invited the Beauregards for both Teresa and me. Maybe I can get some information from Rudy about what is going on with drug activity in West Side. I also think Rudy should meet our new neighbors, Janine and Ray Losocala. Wesley thinks they may not be what they appear to be. It's just like Wesley to listen to every word someone says and make judgments, but then, again, he's almost always on point. I really want to get into that house they bought. They had contractors coming in and out during the first week after they purchased it. The previous owners were not house people.

Liz, hearing the ringing of their new ring doorbell system, yelled for Wesley to answer. The first to arrive were the Benders followed by the Gordons along with Craig Spencer. Liz couldn't help thinking, *of course they're here first, they'll all over sixty and six o'clock means just that. They waited until five after six. They know guests can't be early but they shouldn't be late either. Some of my neighbors will arrive an hour late, after my perfected table setting will be a mess. Oh well, after two wines everybody will love my efforts. I bet my lobster sauce on linguini will be a big hit. I won't brag that I found the recipe from Wesley's aunt in Italy, when I was visiting. Wesley won't care if I pretend it's my recipe.*

The ringing at their door was now incessant and finally the Beauregards accompanied by the Loyals and the Dions followed by the Losocalas presented themselves. Liz started with the introductions and she appeared to be surprised that Janine Losocala and Rudy Beauregard already knew each other. It was also obvious to those nearby that Ray Losocala was confused at Janine's knowing Rudy when he said, "Rudy, aren't you the famous serial murder closer? How the hell do you know Janine?"

Rudy took his time answering which allowed Janine to say, "Ray, the Captain, Rudy now I hope, and his detectives went door to door trying to find the route that our neighbor Candace Monroe traveled the day she died. She came by our house. Our cleaning lady drove her to her destination and returned immediately. I haven't seen Luisa since you visited. I called her to tell her you wanted to speak with her. I didn't get her, but left a message. I didn't tell you, dear, because you've come home late every night this week."

If Ray Losocala was discombobulated, he sure didn't show it. Instead, he turned to Rudy and said, "I hope you discover who this serial murderer is, Rudy. That girl lived near us. I don't like this at all. It's too close for comfort. And her family, are they here tonight?"

There was what appeared to all present, a pregnant moment, before Liz's husband Wes answered. "The Monroe's are probably not ready for partying; if they're ever going to be able to be ready. I can't even imagine how anyone recovers from such a monstrosity as the murder of one's child. I told Liz I have anxiety attacks from the realization that being a murder victim could happen to our family, friends, or acquaintances. I never even thought about such things before. Liz has always been the kinder of us, but she's doing better with recovery than me. I can't get Candace's death out of my mind."

Surprising to all, Rudy said, "Wes, it's normal what you're feeling. My detectives face these types of atrocities every day. It takes a piece out of them. You are the norm. This stuff hurts us all. It hurts all of society because we lose trust. Who could do this resonates and we find ourselves becoming even more cynical. For those of us living in the Northeast, well we don't need to be more cynical."

Mona Beauregard regarded her Rudy with an admiring look and changed the climate by stating, "Janine and Ray, I think it's helpful Liz has planned a get together for your neighborhood and we are thankful we've also been included. Let's have a wine and some food. It's just about the only way forward to recovery from this horror; we must continue living while the police move forward. Catching this monster won't help Candace, but will prevent another murder of an innocent. Let's enjoy the moment, shall we?"

The group moved toward another larger room that connected to the dining room. Their spirits appeared to be lifted by the music and the sumptuous offerings displayed so beautifully on the dining table.

As predicted by Liz, all their guests were happily imbibing, eating, and discussing politics within an hour. She seemed pleased with the conversation focusing on jobs, Trump, Democrats, the city's schools, and clubs, until one neighbor cornered Rudy and asked him just what he was going to do about drugs in town and the murder of three West Side teens. The neighbor in question was a businessman who worked at home half time and in New York City for the rest of his week. His favorite topic was comparing hokey West Side with the big city where big things were happening. Liz thought, *Jordan is such a troublemaker; he needs the spotlight all the time.*

"So, Captain, you have drugs and murders all over the damn city, but you find time to come to this party. I hope it's to give us information about how to protect our kids."

If it wasn't for Mona pulling at Rudy's sleeve, the captain might have said more. Instead, he responded in a loud whisper, "What makes you think I'm not here at this party investigating you?" Rudy handed Jordan another beer and walked away.

Jordan's wife snapped at her husband, "When will you ever learn, Jordan?"

Meanwhile, Ray Losocala asked Rudy, "Look, I don't want information from you, Rudy, but for an area noted for its many colleges and universities; this current crime wave is jarring. And as I understand it, you've been the architect for solving serial murders in the past; but just what brings such a need for your services in our pristine small town?"

Rudy made an instant decision to go on the offensive with, "Come now, Ray, I understand you've lived in Las Vegas and so you think that serial murders should only happen in places like Las Vegas and Palm Springs."

"I didn't mean that, Rudy. How did you know I once lived in Palm Springs? I've never told you that."

"I have murders to solve; one was a murder of Candace Monroe, a neighbor who lived around the corner from you. She was last seen alive by your wife getting into your cleaning lady's car. Of course, I know about you and would particularly like to know about your cleaning lady and how to reach her."

Ray Losocala's face whitened slightly but he quickly recovered enough to answer Rudy, "Listen, I'm sorry if you think I wasn't sensitive to your efforts to solve these crimes or if you think I was putting western Massachusetts down, but the statistics on these killings; well they're pretty high. And as far as Luisa our cleaning lady, I'd like to know where she is too."

"Ray, perhaps you can help me. How did you get to hire Luisa Garcia as well as her sister Marisol Garcia? Did you know Marisol was murdered in a multiple shooting near the strip malls?"

Rudy saw the surprised look on Ray's face and doubted he could have faked it, thinking, *could he be involved in drugs and not know that drug related shooters were killed with Marisol? He didn't know Marisol was murdered; but he should be able to tell me how he hooked up with these two cleaning ladies. I'm sure he's also just realized that Luisa may be missing for, maybe more than just a lack of energy for working.*

"Ray, did you go through an agency to hire the Garcia ladies? I mean how did you get to know them? You're new to western Massachusetts and my wife says finding a person to help with cleaning is not an easy task."

Ray answered quickly. "Rudy, you're right. I asked one of the guys who works for me. He knows the community well. He's Russian and knows technology. I'd say he's one of my most valuable employees. When I followed the casino opening here and got the contract, I needed local talent. Getting IT and security types to come to Springfield from Vegas and Palm Springs was not a go. His name is Vladimir Grant. Grant, as he tells it, is an Americanization of a long Azerbaijani name.

Anyway, I was surprised he sent both ladies as maids and that they were Puerto Rican. I did not expect that, but what do I know about the area. He said I could be assured that they could be trusted and I believe that. I'm shocked to hear what happened to Marisol."

The front door opened and Norbie and Sheri Cull entered carrying a large basket of wines while apologizing to Wes and Liz for their tardiness. Norbie announced, "It's not my business made us late; it's our daughter Sydney who just won a creative writing prize. Naturally, we had to be there and wallow in her majesty."

Settling in, Norbie headed to the bar where he greeted Rudy. Introductions were made to Ray, and after some small talk, Norbie asked him how he liked the neighborhood. Ray responded that it seemed great so far except that Rudy just told him his former cleaning lady had been murdered. Norbie raised an eyebrow and encouraged Ray to tell him all about it; mostly about where this woman was murdered. Rudy was compelled to give the newspaper version of the murders on the empty lot across from the double strip malls. Norbie insisted on knowing, by softly asking Ray, how he met this woman and hired her. Rudy was uncomfortable that Marisol's story was being repeated. Ray continued with the fact that Marisol's sister Luisa was the replacement for Marisol for the cleaning job at his home, and she had now walked away from the job without explanation. Norbie asked Ray for the sisters' last name and where they lived. Before Ray could answer, Mona and Janine came over to the bar. Mona introduced Janine to Norbie.

Norbie thought, *I can't gracefully go after more information now. I'll invite him to a golf match and also invite Rudy so he doesn't think I'm trying to out sleuth him. Rudy was having apoplexy over my questioning; could be he already has all the answers.*

"Well, Ray, as a form of welcome, I'd like to get a golf foursome going for tomorrow if you and Rudy and Wes are available. It's time for you to see ordinary life in our city and meet some non-casino personnel."

Ray immediately accepted the invitation as well as did Rudy, but it turned out Wes would not be able to attend explaining, "Liz will kill me if I don't do my duty tomorrow in cleaning up after this get-together."

"No problem, Wes, I'll invite Jim Locke. Sound good to you, Rudy?"

Rudy answered in the affirmative, but couldn't say more because the Monroe's just entered the family room. After an uncomfortable moment of silence, there was almost a rush to approach them. Only Rudy, Norbie, and Ray did not move forward. In a few minutes after the deluge of empathy, Angela and Barry Monroe moved over to the bar with the obvious purpose of seeing Rudy and Norbie. They hugged them both leaving Ray out of the circle. He did not move. Instead, without waiting to be introduced and having caught their names he said, "Angela and Barry, I'm new in the neighborhood, but I am very sorry you have suffered such a loss. My name is Ray Losocala and my wife Janine is over there. If there is anything I can do please let me do it."

It took a few minutes before Angela and Barry could pull Rudy and Norbie away. They were hungry for information, but all Norbie and Rudy could do included stating the obvious; that the investigation was moving. It was not enough. Angela almost cried in frustration, but held back the tears saying to the two men, "My trust is with you both. Please don't let me down. It won't help Candace, but I just need to know this pervert is off the streets of my city. It's important to me. I need something!"

The party was now over as far as Rudy was concerned; but it wasn't over for his Mona or for Norbie. He thought, *What the hell is wrong with me? I don't enjoy nor do I make small talk. Just watching the Monroe's hurts me in my gut. Norbie and Sheri and Mona, well they seem to know what to say. It's not my being a cop, because every detective in my department knows how to enjoy a party. I'm always thinking about something else I think is more substantive; yet I love my life.*

Norbie walked towards him and said, "Let's cut out of here, Rudy. I asked Sheri to take Mona home and they both agreed. They know we are both bored. What do you say? I'll tell Liz there's a problem with a client who's at the station. Okay?"

Rudy started driving to the destination Norbie had chosen. He'd previously called Jim Locke and asked that he meet them at Jim's favorite place, Coldstone's, in Springfield telling Norbie, "I can always get Jim to come out at any time if there's an ice cream sundae in the offering; Besides, Petra is already asleep; he says she's asleep by nine every night. He's happy for company. We need him to play in our foursome tomorrow and we need him to get Ray to talk. I have to say Ray's not what I expected. He may not be involved in this stuff. Not that I think he's an angel. More likely he is in the business side of this mess, if at all. Rudy, I don't see him involved in murder."

"Neither do I, but wherever he has lived before, and this is QT, Norbie, there have been similar murders to Candace Monroe's murder. Ray may not be involved, but he knows someone who is. He would not want to be involved; at least that's what I think. Jim has to discover who is in his wide entourage. You don't move a business to western Massachusetts so quickly without having some connections. So, our job is to lay out for Jim what he needs to fish for tomorrow at our golf match."

Jim had called before Rudy and Norbie hit Springfield and made a change telling Norbie, "There's no way we'll be able to talk at Coldstone's. There are two busloads with travelers lining up to get their ice cream. Alternate plans are required. I'll head over to Friendly's. I love their ice cream."

Rudy thought about the call, *used to be that Jim Locke would call me with messages. Now he's a PI, not a cop. Life goes on. We're all connections to each other always; it's just that the connections evolve over time.*

Jim practically slurped, not ate, his strawberry sundae with pistachio ice cream, as he absorbed the information request from his former boss. Norbie, his new client, then said, "You're on the clock for this one, Jim. It's no longer a volunteer effort. Capisce?"

20

Therapy and Other Answers

Petra settled into work on Monday but thought about her visit to the psychotherapist the previous week. Her memory of events resulted in a wave of shame and embarrassment. She thought, *I'm supposed to be a professional. Not that day, no I wasn't.* And she reviewed those events.

She had reluctantly sat on the comfy chair as directed by Dr. Ford. His reception room had been welcoming and she immediately noticed its handsome furniture which embellished the warmth of the shrink's office. It did not resemble the meeting space he occasionally used if he saw a cop for a required conference at the police station. Petra had read in a police-related journal a few years back, something to the effect, that the psychological impact of police-work inherently led to the need for therapy. Although still annoyed by Beauregard's pushing her to therapy, she did remember the challenges listed in that publication about what police encounter regularly which included: facing toxic situations daily whose effect on the psyche eventually become a burden that must be dealt with, but often is not. Why, the article asked and the answer given, intimated that police don't and sometimes won't recognize their need for help until they are almost broken as evidenced by alcoholism, drug abuse, anxiety, depression, domestic problems; and sometimes they never recognize their problems resulting in suicide. Police mental health problem stats are higher than average. Petra thought, *I know that. I read all the stuff on it, but still I struggle. I don't want to be here. I think it's a sign of weakness.*

His therapy room reminded Petra of a man's den. It didn't have walnut paneling, but it did have a carved mahogany table desk with a massive computer screen on top accompanied by a small laptop, printer, and skinny scanner aligned next to it. The chairs were all dark brown leather, slightly worn, but terrifically comfortable. There was a huge canvass hanging on the wall behind the Doc's desk of some interpretive design. She thought it was an enormous Rorschach painted in shades of blue and violet and certainly appropriate for a shrink's office.

Her reverie was stopped when Dr. Ford smiled at her and asked her how her pregnancy was going. Controlling the sudden fury, she felt, that she knew was inappropriate, she responded, "Dr. Ford, does everyone and their mother know I'm pregnant? I'm not really showing, so the captain must have said I'm responding differently because of my condition; is that right? I mean I'm an object now and subject to comments by everyone."

Dr. Ford did not reply. He waited. Petra waited. Finally, she broke the silence and she knew that talking first was giving in. It was letting him control, thinking, *what the fuck, I may as well get into all of this.*

"I'm sick of the jokes. How will tough detective Petra handle being a Mommy? She's going to hate to lose her figure. What pregnant woman wants to get fat; it's just a necessity of wanting a baby. Not fair; the daddies don't have to be drowned in hormonal flushes. Who told you I was pregnant?"

"Well, unfortunately, Petra, the whole department knows, but it's not really, gossip. Everyone is pleased you and Jim found each other and are starting a family. Now let's talk about how you feel about having a baby. What are your fears? How is your job impacting your personal life? I don't have any information. Only you do, and I hope you'll share some of it with me. Talking through your experiences in a trusted setting with a trusted counselor often helps with having insights into problems currently being confronted. You will become the problem solver; not me. Let's start, Petra. Just tell me about your history and we'll roll with this psycho-babble as you once told me was the true meaning of therapy, when we were both at a department Christmas party."

"I didn't say that, did I? And if I did, Dr. Ford, I apologize. It's because of the post traumatic event therapy my partner and I were forced to attend, when I was a cop in Boston. We were first on an accident scene with one child dead, another in rough shape, and the mother who was very aware she was dying still pleading with us to wake her dead child. The mother died on the scene. The therapist was all hugs and assurances that this terrible happening was rare. Not for a second did we believe her; but if we spoke our minds, we'd have been on desk duty and extended therapy for months."

"Well, Petra, you just had a lot to say when all I did was to remind you of your remark about the efficacy of psychotherapy. You are entitled to your opinions, and yes, even your opinion about my work, renaming it psycho-babble.

"However, you have been directed here today, and I do want to help you. I think I would be able to help you; that's if you let me. So, clearly, you've been on scene and have personally witnessed horrible atrocities. You have a great record on this force. Occasionally, you've been described as assertive and overly dedicated in pursuit of the bad guys. I want to use general terms like bad guys rather than rapists or murderers or drug dealers, because I don't want you to get caught up in describing evidence, or gruesome details. I want you to talk about your real, emotional feelings and I think that is difficult for you to do, Petra."

And Petra started to cry and couldn't stop herself. She blurted, "I can't stop crying. I want to blame it on my pregnancy, but I get really pissed off if someone else says the same thing; that it's because I'm pregnant. I know my reaction is not normal. Hell, it's not even logical, and yet I react this way in spite of all my training. I'm also aware, as the captain reminded me, that I took a long time to recover from a six-month marriage when I was only nineteen. I don't forget things. My memory makes me a great cop, but it's screwing me up now. Those teenagers, treated like dirt by the perp and posed in such a flagrant manner, are parked in my memory, Doc. I can't sleep."

Petra continued her conversation with Dr. Ford for well over an hour; long enough for her to ask the Doc just how was he going to bill this to the Department? He said, "My worries are not yours; but for a while your worries are mine. Let me help you with them."

Petra did not go back to work after leaving the therapist's office. She drove to a parking area by the river in Longmeadow. At first, she cried. As she looked at the beautiful, grey-blue water and its stillness on this day, she herself felt still; the overwhelming sense of stillness seemed magical to her. She no longer felt the anxiety of the last few months. Smiling, she started her car and she sang aloud, "I'm seeing a shrink - a doc who will link - all my dreams and cares - til I have no fears - and won't blink at the horrors we share."

She repeated her long self-composed mantra over and over, while congratulating herself for taking her meditation exercises to new lows.

Rudy and Norbie were in one cart driving to the fifth hole, while Jim and Ray drove more slowly. The first two golfers didn't mind the

other two were lagging behind. They did become concerned, when the twosome, after their foursome, signaled them on the previous hole. They requested to play through. Norbie said, "Cripes, having Jim with his lengthy interviewing techniques could mean we'll have twelve twosomes asking to play through."

Jim had just ignored the request; they thought he was probably not even aware of it. There was no problem now. One of the women in the twosome lost her ball and was in discovery mode. Norbie said, "You and I, Rudy, will never get home for dinner at this rate."

"I have to tell you, Norbie, I don't mind if we spend an extra hour on the course. It's a cool almost chilly day, my kind of day, and I have nothing better to do than rake the last of the leaves at my home. They're talking about snow next week. Enjoy this time unless you and Sheri have bigger happenings on your calendar."

"Nope, but Sheri will remind me I need to be more present; that the younger two should not be gypped out of my attention. I'm actually safe today because all four kids have activities that won't allow my attendance. Normally, I'm on the sidelines cheering them on. My daughter Sydney will require me to attend all her performances in a play next weekend. It will be a must for this burgeoning thespian. She's been acting since she was two years old. I blame Sheri and Sheri blames me. So, I guess I'm agreeing with you that having no need to rush is really nice for a change. Besides, as you know, Jim Locke does his best work slowly, very slowly."

At the end of the match when Norbie suggested drinks at the nineteenth hole, Ray Losocala regretted he could not stay, telling the other three Janine had plans for dinner with a couple she met at the party last night. "Janine's been slow to make friends here and I have to support this effort on her part."

Norbie brought the drinks over to his favorite table by the bar when he was not sitting at the bar, which he normally would have preferred. Today was different. Today was not an opportunity to reacquaint with current goings-on, which was what would have been his practice. Today, Jim would report some new information; at least he hoped Jim had derived some additional helpful history from Losocala.

Jim was eager to tell them Ray was a schmoozer and public relations kind of guy who could, in his estimation, keep secrets. He did not think Ray was the type to do any dirty work, believing that murder was not in his bag of tricks. "Look, Ray Losocala had two divorces, all nice and quiet, and three marriages. So, unless you tell me his previous wives were murdered or were paid an extravagant amount to shut up, I don't think his purview includes hiring muscle and certainly not doing any dirty work himself.

"That does not mean he doesn't cut corners for money. When it comes to business, Ray would consort with the devil. I don't rule out him being connected with drugs; just not in planning murders or clean ups or sex trafficking, etc. Money washing, maybe it's possible; also, he would supply internet and other security for anyone without researching their legitimacy. That's what I got.

"Losocala also said the he was referred by one of his associates to a woman who works for Assistants-Now, LLC. She gave him Marisol and Luisa Garcia's names. He got her name from Vladimir Grant, one of his associates, who said that Carolina, the admin assistant at the firm, Assistants-Now, knew all the local people who could be trusted. Marisol and Luisa did their jobs although he thought Marisol looked strung out. I'll check on this Carolina and Vladimir for you if you like."

"We have someone working on Carolina, but Vladimir Grant, if that's his real name, we don't know," replied Rudy. "I'd like to know who Vladimir's associates are; who he hangs with. I can't go into Springfield, but if you find out he's West Side, then I'll want to follow that trail then."

Rudy asked about the famous unknown Chavos. "Norbie and Jim, has anyone ever seen him? I hate these nicknames, not real names. He's supposedly Russian. Aren't their names distinctive enough; they still get nicknames and one of them has a Spanish nickname, supposedly. I guess there are a million Vladimir's, Dmitri's, Sergei's, and Petro's; so maybe after all a nickname like Chavos is necessary. Just find what you can, Jim, on Vladimir. Maybe it will lead to Chavos."

On Monday morning, Detective Ash Lent was reviewing the Maria Alonzo newspaper accident report from April 19, 1999. There was no mention of her spouse in the newspaper article. The reporter had excerpts of an interview with Maria's sister Teresita, accompanied by a photo of Teresita and Maria's son Aldalberto. He didn't think he could easily get the police accident report from Springfield. Ash was thinking, *there has to be a birth certificate. The paper says she lived in the North End of Springfield but didn't give an address. Not much info. It was a one car accident. Adalberto was around ten years old at that time. I'll check out births in the Springfield City Clerk's office. I'm guessing she wasn't married to the father. Even if she wasn't, I can still get the father's name if it's listed and not an unknown father.*

Ted interrupted Ash's musings with, "I can't fuckin believe it and the Captain won't believe it either. You didn't call him about it yet, did you, Ash?"

"No, he'll be here later to do the interview. I docked it on his calendar."

"Pretty sad when you think about how we discovered the woman's identity; the one who dropped the note at the station. Good work, but

I probably wouldn't have done it. I mean, Ash, we were there to tell the family their teenaged daughter had been murdered. I was talking to the husband, and out of the corner of my eye I saw you pull out the photo. I think I cringed, but didn't show it. How'd you know enough to show her the picture, Ash?"

"Long story, Ted, it was in the moment, you know, in the moment when you feel the timing is right. The impulse to move this investigation along overcame me; I thought I was Petra for a moment. You know Petra's called Bolt', because she moves so quickly; you can't stop her. Well, I was Petra, for the moment. I'll never do it again. I had such guilt afterwards.

"Pay-dirt, I hit pay-dirt, when Mrs. Peters told me all about Mrs. Printer, mother of Joely's friend, Betsy. As you heard, Mrs. Printer had been talking to mothers of the other girls who Petra interviewed at the library. She thought the girls were in danger. Mrs. Peters dissolved into tears when she looked at the picture saying, 'Jeanette Printer insisted our girls were in trouble. We didn't listen to her. We thought she was exaggerating and now I have to live with this. I should have listened. I should have watched my daughter more closely. The three girls were always sneaking out together to the library. I say 'sneaking' now; then I thought they were being studious. Joely so fooled me. Now she's dead.'"

The captain walked in during Ash's recounting his conversation with Mrs. Peters. He asked, "Ash, so this Jeanette Printer I'm scheduled to meet with today, is the lady who surreptitiously sent the warning letter, and will be crying her eyes out over her guilty conscience when I see her?"

"Yup, look, Captain, I'm feeling some guilt myself over showing her the picture so soon. I know how this Printer lady must feel."

"Ash, you know what I think about guilt. Lizette tells me all the time that the only time guilt is a good attribute is when the thought of it prevents you from doing something wrong. After that, she says, it's not so important. Showing guilt maybe helps you if you're being charged with something and you want to convince those in charge that you're really sorry. Heck, most of the time, it's bullshit. I think Lizette has something there. After you've hurt someone, apologize and then forget it. I often think shrinks live off people feeling guilty. It could be more complicated than that; what do I know?"

Ted stated, "Captain, my wife Charlotte also identified the woman. I'd brought the photo home with me, but forgot to show it to her. Then after Ash got her identity on Friday, I questioned Charlotte. She's seen Jeanette Printer in a lot of places. Mostly, Mrs. Printer is politically active and a real do-gooder. I think we'll be hearing a lot from the mayor on this death. I'm just warning you; expect trouble."

"You think we don't have trouble already? This is a mess and now we know the perp or pervert, whatever, is chomping at the bit. He likes these sweet little do-gooders. Those other two girls in that group need protection. I'll talk to Jeanette Printer and ask her to fill me in on the third girl from the library. They must have done something to activate the perp. Their actions apparently caught his attention. I'm left thinking the other two girls may know something. We have to bring both girls in and now."

Ash said, "I'll contact the other mother, after your interview, Captain. She may actually help you with this."

Before Beauregard could agree, Millie interrupted their conversation with her presence announcing, "Mrs. Printer is here with her daughter Betsy and the daughter's friend, Amber."

Beauregard sighed. "It's possible you won't need to contact the other mother, Ash."

The captain and Detective Toddington met a composed woman dressed in a navy-blue suit and heels. She sat with two teenage girls. They could not help but be hit by the contrast between the teens. It was obvious that the one sitting closest to Mrs. Printer was her daughter Betsy, who had golden braids, deep dimples, and a stubborn look on her face; while the other girl, Amber, was a dark haired, brown-eyed beauty.

The captain conducted introductions. Jeanette Printer quickly took control, which seemed to be important to her; at least that's the assumptions the detectives had, which they supported by allowing her to direct the conversation. Jeanette said, "Detectives, I'm certain you have been informed I am the woman who brought in that letter. I have explained to Betsy that I am loaded with guilt because I did not stop their antics, and now as a result, her friend Joely is dead; murdered."

Betsy stopped her mother saying, "Not antics; we were not playing like children. We were doing what every citizen should do to stop drugs. I won't stop. My friend is dead. Am I scared? Yeah, both Amber and I are; but until the police stop these drugs, we're going to work to stop them."

Jeanette Printer lost all composure. "See, Captain, I can't stop her. You have to help me. She doesn't understand she could be the next victim."

Beauregard now felt they might be ready to listen, saying, "You are here, as I believe you understand, to help us with our investigation. Let's switch over to our need for and your ability to supply information. Betsy, let's start with you and Amber. What did Candace do or see that made Joely so energized that she thought she could be effective? Did she have a trail she was following? Did she see some character that looked suspicious to her?"

While Betsy looked to her mom before answering, Amber spoke, "Captain, if I say anything, you can't talk to my parents. I'll tell you everything. I'm more frightened than Betsy. She's really brave. I play it safe, but Betsy is my friend and so were Candace and Joely. You don't have to worry about me being active in investigating again. I promise everywhere I go I won't be alone. Just don't tell my parents, please."

The captain had heard these words before from his thirteen-year-old informants and true to his nature, he ignored her request and pushed on. "Amber, tell me what you remember. It's not just about you, Amber, or Betsy here, there are many more young teens involved in this anti-drug campaign. Herbie Brent ran a professional organization. You know that! I know that! And I'm afraid that the killer knows that. If so, to protect you, I need to know just what you know."

Amber again was the first to speak. "Joely said she saw him. We asked her where and she said she didn't actually see his face, but he was present too often where we were."

Betsy excitedly added, "Captain, she said he was at the library one day. Amber asked her why she didn't point him out to us. Joely insisted that it wasn't until she went home that she realized he had the same way of walking and moving as a guy she saw at Hoffington Park. We were at the park one day to pin down a man who was supposedly selling drugs, because the kids in school told us someone was dealing there. The dealer was nobody we knew, but I followed him home at a safe distance and reported him that day. Joely and Amber stayed at the field. It was in the paper he was arrested two days later.

"It wasn't until after the library incident, when we spoke with your wife Mrs. Beauregard and Detective Petra, that Joely saw the man again. She said that he was there in the library that day, and she thought she could recognize him if she saw him again."

Amber jumped in saying, "I know Joely. She must have gone after him and found him; and he killed her."

Mrs. Printer could no longer control herself, chastising Betsy for following a drug dealer home. Beauregard had all he could do to deescalate the situation, while Ted resumed the interview with, "Amber and Betsy, who is your COI?"

There was a sudden silence in the room. Neither girl spoke. Beauregard was about to read the riot act to the girls when Mrs. Printer, apparently experiencing a new but calm demeanor, spoke strongly to both girls, "What is a COI, and just who is your COI? And don't tell me you can't divulge a confidence? Two of your friends are dead; dead, do you hear me? It's time to come clean not for me, but for your friends."

Amber gave in, not Betsy, who set her jaw sharply as she grimaced at her mother. Amber replied, "Mrs. Printer, COI means 'Couriers of Information'. We only know about one COI, but Herbie said he had several COI's. There was only one we used as our contact. Candace was the one who would bring the info to the drop. We always went with her; although we hid in bushes."

Betsy said, "We can't give his name. He'll get in trouble. It's not his fault, and we were not supposed to know who he was. You can't tell him, Amber."

The captain banged his fist on the table. The women and even Ted jumped. His serious expression was not lost on the occupants of the conference room. In fact, his deep and low voice made his words particularly impressionable when he stated, "I want his name. You don't understand what this man did to your friends. He didn't just kill them. What will it take for you to realize this is not a movie? This stalling will stop now. You're withholding essential information about a suspected serial murderer and that is a crime, a serious crime. Do I have to say more? Now talk to me."

Surprisingly, Betsy spoke first. "What did he do to Candace and

Joely, Captain? I want to know."

Her mother took her hand, saying, "I don't know the answer to that, Betsy, but I do know it must be bad for the police to keep it out of the news. They need to keep it from the public, so that they will know if someone does confess, that it's a real and true confession. You know that from television. Betsy, this is not a place for gossip. Now tell the detectives about this COI man and tell him now!"

Before the contest between mother and daughter could be decided, Amber said, "Mrs. Printer, Detectives, it's the crossing guard at the Burrell Smith Grade School. He's really nice. We call him Hank. We don't know his real name, but he's the one who picked up our info and I think brought it to the station. That's all we know, just about Hank. Don't be mad at him. I heard his nephew overdosed two years ago. Don't hurt him, please."

The captain excused himself saying, "I need to confirm this information."

Before he left the room, Betsy said, "You knew about this COI stuff, Captain. How did you find out?"

Surprising himself, Beauregard said, "Herbie left notes, Betsy. He wanted to leave a trail in case anything happened to him. He was smart. Telling us today is the smart thing, and his leaving the information, that you were holding back, tells up about what he wanted. That information will assist in our stopping this travesty."

Beauregard said he would return shortly and left the Printers and Amber with Ted. He approached Mason at his desk and asked him to pull up the initials of the COI's. Sure enough, one set of initials said HP. He explained Hank's job and told Mason to get him in to the station for an interview immediately saying, "Have one of the community police who run school crossings bring him in. He should be there now. I mean now. I don't care who it inconveniences. Call the school department and tell them his presence is necessary as a witness in an important police case.

"Mason, I also want you to get the date Petra met with the three girls at the library. Where is that report? I want Petra in here now. When you get the date, call the library and ask what kind of cameras they have on the entrances and the main lobby meeting tables; is it video and how long do they save it? They give you any fuss; then get me. I know all the trustees to help hurry the process. You may mention Norbie's wife Sheri's name. She's the president of the Board of Trustees. She'll make a call if we need.

"Also, Mason, get that sketch artist up here from Vice. I need him now."

While Mason moved to get Juan to help him with the three requests, the captain rejoined Ted in the interview conference room to await Petra and the sketch artist. He began quizzing the two girls about the man they thought Joely might have followed. Had they ever really seen him? Their answer was they couldn't clearly remember seeing him. Betsy did say, since they only really met at the library or school when they were talking about what they learned from their friends about drug activity, then she must have seen him there or possibly over near Spruce Street.

They told the Captain they all went to the mall for nail polish, makeup, shoes. There was a great fashion shoe shop there. He asked if they ever saw a man around thirty, tall and with a good build and dark hair, and dressed well, in the area. Amber said the man they saw, as she remembered him by just glancing at him, had pretty regular features.

At this point the sketch artist entered the room. Beauregard instructed the girls to give the artist their ideas on the man saying, "Help him with descriptions of height, mannerisms, the way he walked, his arm length, his weight, his attitude; anything that strikes your memory. He'll make several drawings. Ted, please stay here. I'll be back shortly. Ask Millie if she's able to bring in some drinks and food. We've been here a long time."

Mrs. Printer said, "It's okay. The girls barely eat during the day. I don't either. Water or coffee will be fine and thank you, Captain. You've handled them well."

Rudy exited the room looking for Petra. When he found her, Petra was more than willing to help. Beauregard summed up the girls' statements, and asked Petra, "Did you see a man, on the day you were at the library, lurking around? Who besides you, the girls, and my wife did you see? And finally, why do I just find out from witnesses that my wife was involved in an interview of these girls? And, why in hell, was she involved?"

"Captain, I thought Juan already gave you the report on that day. Remember, I was forced out of the office on Friday by you. I know Juan was reviewing it along with some other stuff and was to get to you on Monday. I remember now; you weren't in on Monday."

"Detective, that may be the answer to the delay, but that does not answer why Mona was there in the first place? Why would you involve a civilian in an interview?"

To Lilly who was there, Petra's response sounded defensive. "She was there in the library checking out some books. It wasn't planned, Captain. I didn't plan to involve her, but the girls were so suspicious, and I knew Betsy Printer trusted Mona. It seemed like a good idea at the time to establish trust. The girls promised they would stay out of any further investigating activity; they would only talk to Mona if they passively heard stuff from other students."

"You know better, Petra. If we need a witness from that day, then how do I explain the presence of the wife of Captain of the Major Crimes Unit's presence? Mona would then be a witness."

Juan had walked into the room and heard part of the conversation. He tried to explain, "I had this report, but didn't want to leave it on Millie's desk for you, Captain. I called you but you weren't available."

Beauregard sighed with disgust thinking, *not only is this a messy situation, but now I have to ask Petra if she saw anyone hanging around the library that day; and I'll have to do the same with Mona. Mona has eyes like hawks. She doesn't miss anything. Hell, she might be the only one able to recall a strange man there, if there was one. Fortune just loves to knock me down pretty regularly.*

The other three detectives watched their captain as he grimaced. They were thrilled to have Mason walk in saying aloud to the captain, "Got it on my computer, Captain. Want to see it? They save all their video. When the library built the new addition, they built in all kinds of bells and whistles. Apparently, book theft in a library is big."

Running through the day's video took longer than the detectives expected. It was Petra, familiar with the library's layout, who pointed to what at first appeared to be a shadow near the main entrance. There were several cameras' videos that required checking to see a person going from one room to another. Petra insisted, "I thought at the time that this guy worked in the library. He wore a suit. No other person there wore a suit. I figured he must be in administration."

They followed the man from the entry room to the stacks and out to the room where Petra interviewed the teens. Lilly spotted the man in one short section where a sliver of his face showed. She said, "Hell, this guy's walk doesn't make sense. He's practically hugging the walls. Didn't you see his behavior, Petra? Look, when you went to get Mona, he tried to see what you were doing without turning his face to the camera. That's when the camera got that sliver of face.

"Every other photo shows him in the room with you except for one time when he looks like he's going upstairs to the study carrels. He's not gone long enough to go up there, look at a book, and come down. I think he just turned the corner so he wouldn't look suspicious. He did that when the librarian came into the room. He didn't want her looking at him. I say it's certainly suspicious behavior."

Petra appeared distraught for a moment. She stated, "I can't believe I didn't notice him. But I think I did notice his movement. I was so concentrating on the teens and getting Mona to help me build trust that I didn't see him. We were all talking in a low voice, because the girls were acting very secretive and it seemed normal. He was there and I can't even give you a description."

The captain asked Mason if he could get a final close-up on the man's clothes and whether some assumptions could be drawn from their style and materials. The resulting enlarged photos showed a very expensive and well fitted suit, but there was no way to see a shirt and tie. The detectives concluded that if he were the perp, it was strange he was dressed like an executive. Although Mason said, "Maybe he's some weird executive type but dresses down later. He has a really great build. You can see by the shaping of the suit in back and on one side. He moves like a cat burglar in the video; seems to have some grace in his movements. Dark hair and well groomed. I can't get a good one on the shoes. Men's shoes tell you a lot."

Mason received a call from Jan the sketch artist. He'd sent a file with the tall skinny guy enhanced by thirty pounds. The detectives thought it just made him look fat; that his body was built too narrow to properly hold that extra weight. They didn't think he looked like a relative to the other very well-built man.

21

What People Know

That evening, Rudy, in a most solicitous manner, asked his wife about her day at the library with Petra and the teenagers. He thought, *I had best be careful and not criticize her for speaking with teens. That'll get me nowhere. Mona's nothing if not consistently kind and supportive to students. I know that it would never occur to her not to help Petra with the girls, but what the hell was she thinking? She's smart enough to stay away from a police interview. Didn't she think into the future enough to realize she could be a court witness later on; and the defense would use our relationship to debunk the police assertions?*

Mona looked quizzically at Rudy, answering, "Why are you just asking me about that now. It's been awhile since I met with the girls. You looked so tired when you came home the night you discovered Joely's body, I didn't dare assault you with questions about her over the weekend. I found out most of the details of her death from the news and from school. You never once asked me about my library meeting for what four days; and now you want to know. You just found out, didn't you, Rudy, and you're angry with me? How come it took so long for you to know what takes place in your own unit? It seems to me, that your management skills need honing." And with that Mona walked out of the room.

Rudy was disturbed and angrily spoke, but in a whisper, "Good, Mona, go ahead and use offense as a good defense. You know you should have told me about it that day. Now you make me think I'm a bad manager for not knowing what you should have told me. I knew she'd be sensitive about this. Damn, I've never won an important argument with her. Damn that woman."

It wasn't five minutes later that Rudy went to make peace with Mona. She was waiting and was very upset saying, "Rudy, I should have told you about it but we were so busy it slipped my mind and then, well then when Joely was killed, the guilt I felt was overwhelming. I wondered if I had told you right away, whether she might still be alive."

"Mona, I'm not that smart. I wouldn't have been able to solve this case that quickly, even if you had told me. I have the information now and I haven't a clue about a solution."

Mona left her chair in their very big bedroom where she had been crying and moved to hug Rudy. For once in his life he met her far more than halfway and comforted her whispering, "I never want you dragged into this stuff, Mona. I need you to think happy thoughts. There's only room in this family for one person seeing ghosts. You did not do wrong. Petra should not have brought you into an interview with witnesses without some serious formalities and recordkeeping. But Mona, as long as you were there, maybe you can help me. Are you willing?"

Her answer was as expected. Mona suggested they sit with a cup of coffee for him and herbal tea for her, while they talked. He questioned her about the man in the library. Well, first he asked her if she saw anyone unexpected in the library that day. She said she did. Without leading her, Rudy asked what made the person unexpected. Her answer was on target with the library video. Mona related, "Rudy, the man I saw was a well-dressed man in a suit; and not just any suit, but, you know, he was wearing a designer suit. When I noticed him, he was headed toward the exit moving rather swiftly. He had a lovely small print tie in burgundy and yellow and navy detail that matched his navy suit. He was quite nice looking as I recall Rudy. He moved gracefully for a big man. He must be an administrator, or a member of the library board of trustees. Nobody else would dress like that to go to the library."

"Do you think you could help the department's sketch artist in developing a drawing of him?"

Mona was willing to try but gave no guarantees. Rudy's response was short as he stated, "Honey, there are just no guarantees in life. We just try and sometimes we accomplish something."

Mona told Rudy she had promised Petra that she would check with the three girls after the meeting, saying, "I tried, Rudy, and I was successful in talking to Betsy and Amber. Amber was far more forthcoming than Betsy. I remember thinking Betsy was acting strangely and very secretive. I never saw Joely. I think I heard she was home sick for a few days. You might want to check on that, Rudy.

"At the Abernale's party, Liz chatted with me about a 100-year birthday party held for Nigel, who is Liz's gardener. She's worried about his safety. She said he lives over near Spruce Street and is a member of that club down there, near where Ash and Ted were shot. Liz says Nigel isn't worried about his own safety and accepts the drug activity down in that district as normal. I wondered if a man like that may be thoughtful. He's lived a long time and my experience with older working people is that they see what's going on, but would never call the police. Maybe you could talk with him; you know, Rudy, in a nice way. Make sure he's safe."

Rudy did not respond.

◀━❀━▶

The next day brought busy work to the unit. Mason said it was like house cleaning with his wife. "You start off cleaning one closet, and then she has you in the basement, and then back upstairs sorting my clothes for Goodwill; mind you all against my will, just like this.

"You know these teenagers did really good work. I've pulled information from six police departments in towns in Hampden County and the information they secretly received led to lots of arrests. One captain said he waited for the letters which were delivered to them, sometimes by mail, about every two weeks. He'd get a call and find an envelope in the mail or on some cop's desk. Not one of them could figure out who was doing the delivery. Some amateur detectives out there!"

Juan laughingly jested about MCU's problem in finding the identity of a prominent woman who left an envelope for them, saying, "Don't be too harsh."

Juan was making lists. Amused, Petra said, "You're the most like the captain, Juan, always making lists. Can't you just freestyle?"

"Nada, Petra, Mexicans are family people. We always have chore lists if not on paper then in our minds. My brain shuts off at ten items. We have more than that with these cases, so a list it is."

"Give me your list, Juan. I don't want to do the same list. It'd be redundant and therefore a waste," said a smiling Lilly.

The captain responded to Lilly as he entered the open office area saying, "What list? Let me see it. Lilly, you have a list?"

Sighing with defeat, she said, "No, Captain, Juan has a list. I'm not a written list person. Lists are in my head."

Juan gave up his list insisting it wasn't complete. His protests were ignored. The captain went ahead and chalked on the board a few items. The first was a question about Carolina's history before she came to

Springfield. Number two indicated there was a need for additional evidence, if available beyond the photo, that showed McKinney and Losocala were together. The third item, suggested by the captain earlier in the day, was to question Liz Abernale concerning her gardener Nigel's knowledge about drug activity and people near where he lives in the Spruce Street area. Number four indicated the need for a review of all the photos from Las Vegas on friends of Losocala; while number five questioned more information on Vladimir Grant.

The captain viewed Juan's items and said, "There's more to look at than this. You should compare the videos from the retail store, where you have a tall man as the purchaser of the outfits used to dress the victims, with the library video. I have a sketch artist working with Mona to see if she's able to pin down a face from her memory. She thinks she saw the man at the library. I'd feel a whole lot better if we can confirm the man is the same man in both videos. Also, who interviewed the crossing guard potential COI? Where's that on the list?

"Mason, I haven't seen a report on the COI aka crossing guard named Hank P. Where is it?"

"Captain, he lawyered up and his counsel wasn't available to come in immediately. Try guessing who his counsel is; you're going to be surprised."

Petra spoke before Beauregard and said, "Not Cull; it's not Cull, is it?"

"Yup! The infamous defense attorney falls back into our laps."

The captain did not seem amused at the banter, but he also did not appear upset. Instead he thoughtfully replied, "May not be the worst thing to happen. How can this crossing guard afford Norbie as a lawyer?"

Mason had an answer, saying, "He's retired from a big management position. His acting as a courier of information, that the kids call a

COI, is simply his doing social work along with his volunteering as a crossing guard. He donates his salary from being a crossing guard to the food pantry. He's a well-to-do and humble do-gooder, Captain."

"Do we have a scheduled date with Hank what's his last name, and Norbie?"

"It's Henry (Hank) Pimental and they are coming in this afternoon at four."

Beauregard was surprised and replied, "I know Hank Pimental. He was an investment house manager and well thought of by everyone. I went to his nephew's funeral. The family was really shaken up. They'd found the boy in some unrented apartment in Belchertown overdosed. No one was with him. The police received a call about him, but could never discover who made the call or determine who he was with. I'll be here for the interview. I'll also talk with Norbie about Liz Abernale, who is his neighbor. Maybe we can go together to speak with the gardener.

"Juan, did you find anything more about Carolina aka Carmen or Vladimir Grant?"

Juan explained Carolina had a green card and had been in the States for about fifteen years. "Captain, that's about as long as Grant has been here."

The Captain mused aloud, "if Carolina's only been here for fifteen years, how could the old lady Mrs. Rojas have helped her out when Carolina aka Carmen was a little girl. It's all bullshit."

Juan also informed them she didn't own the firm, and he could not find any meaningful info on the firm as it was one LLC embedded in another LLC. There was talk she had a boyfriend, and he was older, and very tall and slim. No one knew his name. Rudy asked if Vladimir was tall and thin and was told he was tall but built like a bodyguard; and that no one could ever call him thin.

"I want Grant and Carolina watched. We can't do it. I asked Jim Locke to investigate; get him back on this. He won't bill foolishly. I want it now. Carolina or Carmen was on Silvain Street coming out of the house with the orange cones in front. That house backs up to a house on Spruce Street. Grant got the Garcia women for cleaning ladies through Carolina. It all smells, and maybe there's a link. This spidery guy, well he's tall; what's his nickname again? Maybe he's her boyfriend. And why does she call herself Carmen when her name is Carolina?"

Lilly, ignoring the Captain's meandering, answered with, "'Chavos' is the spider's name, Captain, and everybody's afraid of him. Juan and Petra reported they looked at the census for both of those houses. Carolina sounds classy. Would a classy woman want a spidery type man?"

Lilly got the look from her fellow detectives; the famous look that says you couldn't be that stupid to ask that question. She ignored the look and changed direction.

Lilly asked, instead, that they tell the captain what they found.

Petra said, "The names look made up to me. The one on Silvain Street has an old lady supposedly about 89 years old living there and her name is Sarah Brown. Can't find any Sarah Brown and none of the LLC managers are named Brown; of course, the son could have another name."

Petra was interrupted by Beauregard who said, "Her name, according to what I overheard at the Southern Ladies' house, is Mrs. Rojas. Didn't I tell you that? It's not Brown but Rojas."

Petra continued, saying, "Sorry, Captain, but I didn't have that in my notes. I'll check that name out. Now as to the house on Spruce Street, it shows a man and wife listed there named Cora and Hal Crenshaw, but they must have moved out since the last census. I say that, because that old Puerto Rican man named Alfie lives there and maybe also his son who drives him around. The son is supposed to have a big SUV but he doesn't keep it there regularly. The neighbors don't know Alfie's last name or if they do, they won't say. Another thing I question is what you just said, why does Carolina change her name to Carmen when she's at the 'Southern Ladies' house? Is she trying to fit in ethnically? Those ladies don't seem to care about race or ethnicity."

The captain said, "Listen up. Add 'Discovery of Mrs. Rojas and her son's history and Alfie's surname' to the list. We should know that stuff by now. The problem I think lies in these types of investigation; there are just too many people to investigate. It's all low-lying fruit and we'd better climb the apple tree and get the juicy names."

Mason groaned saying, "Captain, your metaphors are always jumbled, but I know what you mean. Captain, do those kids, who are always found at the murder sites, have more pictures than we've seen so far? Would you consider getting all their cache of pictures?"

"Mason, what makes you think they wouldn't have given me all their pictures in the first place?"

"Because they're kids, Captain, because they're kids. I never would have given up the whole trove. Besides, they think they're artists. Every artist I ever knew kept every photo or drawing of whatever or a copy. It's in their genes. They hoard a little."

A thoughtful Beauregard considered this, saying, "Could be something there, Mason. I'll give it a go. I have an hour before Hank Pimental and Norbie will be here. Let's look at the Las Vegas pictures. And another thing, what's with SUVs? They were used in the dancing-ladies murders; now we're identifying them all over the place in this investigation. Doesn't anyone drive a sedan?"

Ash, attempting to get the captain back on track, said, "Captain, we haven't gone through the Las Vegas photos yet; but we have them here."

He continued with, "Petra and I were just about to analyze them. It'd be better if we all did it together now."

Forty-five minutes went by before the five detectives, after deep discussion, determined they still couldn't decide whether two men in several photos taken with Raymond Losocala were familiar to them. Beauregard thought the tall thin man, always in a dark gray or black suit, fit his mindset for 'Chavos'. He pointed out the guy's long arms, his slim frame and his face that had high cheekbones and lighter skin, saying, "He could be Russian and he's with Losocala in eight photos. He must be important to Losocala. You can see in three videos that the casino staff is giving them high roller treatment. There's a good looking almost handsome man, who might be Italian, who is with them in five of the photos and one video. He moves gracefully. I want to know who he is. Did the casinos identify any of the men in the photos?"

Ash said that they couldn't ask that in advance because there were close to one hundred men in all to identify, but they would send these two back for identification. "It might take two or three days," he said. "They were very helpful when we asked them to pull the video and tapes. I don't think there will be a problem, Captain; it's not local."

Beauregard asked Petra to bring the picture of the tall skinny guy around to Carolina's neighbors and see if he matched the description of her boyfriend saying, "You're not threatening looking, Petra. You'll fit in with the neighbors on Elliott Street. They'll talk to you. Take Jim with you in his car if you agree. I think if you look like a couple, the Springfield Police, if they're called, will accept any story you create. Jim can get creative. I've seen him do it before. He should be writing for fantasy movies. Okay?"

Beauregard, Petra, Norbie, and Hank sat in Interview Room number one. Hank apologized immediately for bringing Norbie into the interview with him, explaining, "Rudy, I may have gone out on a limb with my working with this group. I should have come to see you when Candace and Herbie were murdered, but I thought the little I knew would not be helpful."

Norbie, frustrated his client spoke first when he'd been instructed to keep his mouth shut, moved his hand as if to silence his client. It was effective. Hank immediately stopped speaking. Norbie directed his next words to Beauregard. "My client, Captain, has done nothing wrong. He has just moved information received by him concerning drug activity and immediately gave it to police. He held nothing back and has no knowledge related to the murders of students involved in anti-drug activity."

"Look, Attorney Cull, I have no problems with Hank. I wonder, though, why he thought he couldn't come directly to the police with information on drug activity. Why did he have to resort to this secrecy?"

Again, Hank spoke out, "Captain, the police would have interrogated me to give up the kids. I'm sorry now I didn't, but check on what we accomplished just in West Side. I gave info on sixteen arrests in the last eighteen months. Check with your drug enforcement people. That's a lot of arrests the police would never have known about without my work and the kids' work."

Cull, clearly looking annoyed, criticized Beauregard. "What are you doing, Captain, treating Hank as if he had done something wrong? His motivation is to help stop drug deaths and clearly, he has. Hank is willing to tell you what he knows about the drops, but I think you should respect the work he's done to stop some of this trafficking. You're in homicide and perhaps you're not in the know about those kids who are addicted, but haven't yet met their deaths. Maybe you're only sensitive to those who died."

Petra, appearing to fear some emotional blowout between the Captain and Cull remarked, "No need to go there, Attorney Cull. Captain Beauregard is sensitive to all victims. We understand there is a killer out there targeting young men and women and the captain is sensitive to only that issue now."

Beauregard smirked ending the almost fiasco. He said, "Cull, I have some materials here that show Hank was what is called a COI for courier of information. Is that the correct term, Hank?"

With a nod from Cull, Hank shook his head and said, "Herbie, the young man who died, laid out a whole business plan and it was comprehensive. Have you noticed how all over the area, there have been a lot of small drug arrests? His plan accomplished all of that."

The captain pulled from his folder a folded piece of paper and a few other pieces of normal sized computer paper. He opened the folded piece and it showed a layout of Hampden, Hampshire, and Franklin Counties. There were six COI's labeled, two in each county. Hank's eyes blinked several times before he sighed; leading all present to believe that he had seen the map before. He spoke, saying, "How did you get this? Herbie wouldn't ever let anyone have it. He promised to keep it safe."

"He did keep it safe until he died. He left some cryptic code that one of our detectives figured out. He wanted his work to go on. None of you understood completely what a dangerous game it is, chasing drug-dealers. Now, please tell me about the operation as you understand it. It is apparent you were the COI for all of Hampden County with the exception of Springfield, Holyoke, Ludlow, and Chicopee. You had a big area to travel and for the safety of all the young people who worked the information, I caution you; if you are truthful, we may be able to save lives."

Hank did not know all the names from many of the towns but knew all from West Side, Longmeadow, and East Longmeadow. He did not have the names for initials listed on Herbie's sheet for Southwick, Wilbraham, Agawam, Westfield, Blandford, Holland, Chester, Russell, Monson, Brimfield, and Hampden. He said he had lived in Longmeadow and East Longmeadow and was able to figure out the names from the initials and his sightings of the kids at the drop sites. It was a lot of area to cover and often there was nothing for him at the drop. He was suspicious about Wilbraham and Hampden because he knew from friends that there was a drug problem, but still he'd gone several months recently without a message.

Beauregard asked if he knew who the COI was in Springfield, Holyoke, Ludlow, and Chicopee. Hank did. He said it was the owner of a trucking company in Springfield named John McKinney. He continued talking about his relationship with John. They'd met at a support group for those who'd lost friends or relatives from drugs.

The conversation finally ended with Attorney Cull asking for five minutes alone with the captain. He addressed Rudy. "I know this John McKinney. He's a great guy. Just why would he be involved in this?"

Rudy said, "I think for the same reason as Hank's, Norbie. I ask that you don't share this information with anyone. John may be in great danger if this gets out."

When the visitors left, Rudy sagged almost as if he were recovering from a dental procedure as he rubbed his jaw back and forth. In minutes, Petra returned to the interview room and asked the question she knew to be the question of the day: "What are you going to do now, Captain? Maybe tell McKinney or Loughman or our drug unit; what can you do?"

"John McKinney is now in great danger. Hank thought some of his area has been compromised. That doesn't bode well for the cities that

John is supposed to be COI for. He's risked the task force investigation taking on this endeavor, while working with the Feds attempting to uncover the big drug kingpins. I don't even know, Petra, why he isn't dead. I'm thinking that the perverse killer of the kids may only have a peripheral connection to the drug bosses; maybe he's some sort of hanger on. No drug kingpin allows their people to act out sensational fantasy murders; it brings on too much unwarranted attention."

"It could mean that the Perp and the drug lords don't know about each other's activities, Captain. The Perp could know about John and his role, as a COI, and that it is not as important to him as age and sex in meeting the Perp's needs for a victim. I think Herbie was not killed for the same reason as the other victims. I think Herbie got in the way somehow; perhaps he was too noticeable and too successful."

"So, do I, Petra; so, do I. I hope our thinking is on the right path; otherwise John is a potential victim. In fairness, I'll meet with him. I can't live without warning him. Would you get Mona's sketch of the man in the library and contact the known anti-drug kid activists Hank identified? Do one at a time and see if any of them have ever seen this man. Have you or Ash spoken with them at their homes with their parents? Start with the West Side kids and if we need to include more from other towns, well we will have to seek help from other departments. Don't want to do that unless it's necessary."

Lunchtime found Beauregard back at Eats, the restaurant in Springfield where he had previously met John McKinney. His rather large roast beef with sautéed onions and cheese sandwich pleased his palate and would not be discussed later with Mona. He thought, *Somethings a wife shouldn't know. She'll worry, and after all my diet's been*

decent this week; at least for me.

He was almost finished with his sandwich when John McKinney waltzed in nonchalantly and ordered his usual takeout salad and said while waiting, he'd go outside and have a smoke. The waitress gave some banter about the balance of a healthy lifestyle with smoking and salads apparently equal on the scales of diet moderation. Waiting a minute, Beauregard left cash for his check and tip; he then exited out the back way where he found John.

"I don't like seeing you again, Captain. It's taking a chance and things are getting really hot. I don't think I have any news of value to you. It doesn't mean I don't understand you are really hurt by the shootings of your detectives and your family, but I can't help you."

"John, I'm not looking for your help today. I'm looking to help you. You have been acting as what is called a 'COI' or courier of information for a civilian anti-drug group. Herbert Brent, Jr. organized and managed a specialized drug dealer information flow with you as a major player. I doubt you made this information available to the Drug Task Force and Loughman. They don't work that way; certainly, they wouldn't work with amateurs."

"No, they wouldn't and you're right they don't know about this activity. The problem is that if you know about me, all the work I've done for the Task Force is lost. You know about me; then everyone will soon know about me. I take it you're telling me in an attempt to protect me. I thank you for that, but it won't work. I'm at the crest of our investigation. The new line of trade is through my type of company. I'm scheduled to meet an important player next week; he is perhaps the most important player. If this gets out, shit!!! Shit, all my CI work for the last two years is for nothing."

"John, I'm worried about your life. We suspect there is a person connected to the trade who keeps track of local drug dealings, and unfortunately also tracked the civilian anti-drug group's successes. He is a perverted serial killer and a psychopath. You are out of his age range for murder, but who knows if he'll break that pattern. He's killed both men and women and sexually assaulted both sexes. Age may not be important to him. We think Brent was too visible which called for our Perp to take an interest in him. Also, the arrests resulting from the anti-drug group are almost staggering. Someone would have taken notice. I don't have all the numbers, but in the small towns, the numbers are big for their size."

"Captain, for two years I've talked with all the small fish working my way up to the big guys. Then your detectives, in doing their jobs, prevented me from talking to the supposed big honcho on the day they were shot. Those Dominicans talking to me that day were only a protective detail for the big honcho. I was minutes away from meeting him. He could not have been far away; maybe a block of two. There is a mall nearby. Have you checked cameras? You were close, I know it."

"John, do you really think your meeting was to be with the top guy?"

"I do, and I believe it even more now."

"Why now? What has happened to make you think that now?"

"The shooting at the gas station that included your nephew and sister-in-law as innocent victims was the first in a series of steps instituted to consolidate all of western Massachusetts under one person. That means business and only business is the goal now; nationality is not now as important as it used to be. The potential of very large revenues is what's important. There is a big player out there who seems to be able to work with all groups who are willing to accept the new business model. Those men killed in the gas station fiasco were not willing to make changes."

"Do you think that this kingpin is Russian, John?"

"Why do you say that? Have you heard something? Please, it's of enormous consequences if you have."

"What does the name, Chavos, mean to you, John? Who is he, and would he have the will and the juice to assassinate Sokolov?"

"Where the hell did you hear that name? What do you know about him?"

"John, you haven't answered my question. I asked first."

"I don't know who he is. I'm looking to expose who he is. Maybe that's just a name for the top drug dog. I don't know. I do know whoever is at the top has the will and the juice to have assassinated Sokolov and others who get in his way. And there is reliable info to say it is a man. Now, Rudy, tell me who gave you the name Chavos?"

"We got the name from the street in a whisper and the whisperer was not our man and would not say anything else. What I want to know is whether this top dog or Chavos, or whatever he's called, is he Russian or Spanish? Chavos is kind of a colloquial Spanish word for moola, you know, money. Could Chavos be Russian, and if he is, why would he be called a Spanish name and why would he assassinate his own kind?"

"Rudy, I always assumed he was Spanish. It was a predominately Spanish neighborhood your cops were shot in and where I waited for the big honcho. I never thought about his being Russian, but in retrospect killing Sokolov, with no retaliation against any Spanish group, that I've heard, is an important point. I don't think Loughman thinks he's Russian. He could be. We're all in agreement that the potential revenues from this new drug distribution chain are potentially astronomical; great enough to bring in the most aggressive of criminal elements. I'll tell you right now that Russian dealers, when they're not users, show a tendency to let nothing get in their way; nothing includes murder. I'll have to report this conversation to my handler, Rudy."

"No, you won't and I'll tell you why. If you do I'll take you in under the guise of protective custody. It means I say you are a witness in a murder case who is at risk. You will then lose your value as an asset. Loughman won't know about your arrest until after the damage's been done. I have every reason to do this even with my stringent conscience, John; because you are at risk."

"Fuck it. I can't believe you'd do that; screw up two years of my life and prevent the toppling of the biggest potential drug empire, western Mass and northern Connecticut have ever seen. It'd be such a waste."

"I'm not doing it, John. You are. It's your decision. I don't care about anything other than getting justice for my dead teens. Solving that will also solve your problems. Work with me or don't work with me."

"Your guys threw a monkey wrench into our investigation and interfered in my meeting with the big honcho and I'm to play by your rules?"

Looking annoyed, Rudy answered quietly, "That's how I look at it."

Unhappily, John agreed not to tell Loughman about their meeting today. He further stated he was waiting for a call about the last leg of the distribution chain. The controller of the trucking firm delivering to his company out of New York was to meet with him and the big honcho in less than four days. He did not know the time or place or the exact date. He got a notice he would be notified with a message and a code. The code typed would be 242867. That's all. He was to answer the next call of three calls on his cell. The first call would give a date. The second call would give the time and the third call the place. He had no idea if the calls would be made one after the other or if some would be delayed. He had two burner phones. Loughman planned that John was to make a call to him, after each of the calls, using the second burner phone. John had explained to Loughman that if there was someone with him when he got the calls, he couldn't do that, couldn't just easily call; mainly because no one knew who was involved. It could be someone already on his payroll. Rudy asked John who bought the burner phone. Was it, John, or was it sent to him? John said he bought the burner phones not Loughman. Rudy said, "Good, that way you may call me next and nobody else will know. I think I'm going to be way ahead of Loughman in a couple of days."

John agreed to the plan and they left on good terms with each other.

22

Confabulation and Discovery

sh was impatient and put a push on the city clerk to do discovery for him. The results surprised him, but also gave him an aisle of inquiry which thoroughly pleased him. Adalberto Alonzo lived in Springfield in a high-end condo overlooking the city. It had been developed over twenty years ago in a premiere location. Although well taken care of, it was similar to many twenty-year old multiple condo facilities, now showing some wear, but still a lush address. Ash felt lucky when he got the news; he had friends living there. He'd played often with the husband, his being a horn blower, and felt comfortable calling Donald to question him about his neighbors. His friend was pleased to meet him at Starbucks for a cappuccino.

Ash deliberately took a long time before he started his inquisition. He hoped Donald would not suspect he was investigating Adalberto, if he posed his few questions about him in the midst of thirty other questions about local politics. He knew Donald's wife Cindy was a lawyer practicing locally and had given her musician husband tutelage in the city's activities. The couple had two children and enjoyed their sweet high-end living space. Donald was not put off with Ash's questions. In fact, he appeared to enjoy the attention and interest Ash gave him. He reveled in sharing his views about local politicians and his comfortable lifestyle existence.

Ash asked, "I met a friend through a friend who said he'd been at a nice party with pretty girls at your condo complex, at a unit owned by a guy named Alonzo. He told me the guy's first name, but it was like 'Bert or Albert' or something like that. I guess from his description he's good looking and has many lady friends."

"Ash, I think your friend's trying to impress you with the party idea. I talk with Adalberto at condo meetings. He's tall, dark, and handsome and I would think the girls might like him except that he's cold; kind of a man's man. He has some real European mannerisms. I asked him if he was Puerto Rican or Spanish one day. His answer was really flippant. He said he was ashamed of any Spanish blood in him; that he was a Putin type."

"You mean Russian? Does he look Russian?"

"Well, he has the build and a square and broader face which gives him a non-Spanish appearance. He told me he graduated from Amherst College. I have to believe him, but I'm telling you, Ash, Amherst College didn't rub the street attitude from him. And as far as parties, I've seen him bring a few drunken young things home but there's never any noise there. He's friendly enough, but, you know, not inviting. I've been in every condo in the complex, but not in his. He's good with mechanics. He fixed my car one day when it wouldn't start. He did something with the wires while dressed in a thousand-dollar suit."

Ash questioned, "He's probably what they call a 'metrosexual'? You know, knowing how to do manly things and still able to fashionably dress and go to art galleries. I mean you said he went to Amherst. He had to be bright to get in there."

"Oh, he's smart alright."

"I'll bet he drives a Mercedes or something."

"No, surprisingly, Ash, he has this black Ford Expedition Max. I asked him why he bought an American car, and he told me it doesn't make people jealous and they're not inquisitive in what you do. That car goes for sixty thousand plus dollars. I don't know what he does for a living; he doesn't talk about himself. He does have a few men pick him up at various times, but nothing regular."

Ash finished up with, "Condo living allows you to meet a lot of different types, doesn't it, Donald? Maybe I'll try it."

"There's open house on a really beautiful unit. It's owned by a doctor who's retiring. Come Sunday and take a look."

Ash promised and said his good-byes.

Ash updated Beauregard about Adalberto Alonzo while eating lunch at Luxe Burger Bar. He asked, "Captain, do you think it'd be worth it to track Alonzo during some periods of the day? I know we can't do it, but Jim Locke could if we have the funds. See where he goes and whether he's a connection to the head drug honcho; although I don't think from Donald's description that Alonzo is a druggie. He's too cool."

Beauregard said he would think about some surveillance, pushing forward the thought that he did not want this guy at all suspicious; particularly if he was high up in the food chain. He repeated the theory saying, "I don't want to add pressure at a time when there supposedly is an important meeting coming up, and I don't want John's life put further at risk than it is now. Also, Jim Locke's last report on the St. James Avenue guy and from the gal in One Financial Plaza interview didn't add anything but cost; and we got the information ourselves through other means."

Ash returned to the subject at hand saying, "Captain, I don't have the license plate number yet for Alonzo's wheels. There's nothing in the registry under his name. It's probably in a corporate or other business name. I thought I'd wait around near the condo. It's a residential but fortunately busy area with a small parking lot for a nursing home nearby. I can get lost there and wait for him. Won't take me ten minutes to get back there and Donald says he's often home between two and five in the afternoon. What do you say? I'll just get the plate number, no action, Captain, I promise."

He got the go ahead and drove to the area he'd chosen for surveillance thinking, *I haven't lost it, no sirree. I knew this was a perfect place. Now I hope he'll come sooner rather than later.*

Ash waited an hour while he listened to an old saxophone album on Bluetooth called, "Persuasive Sax" by Russ Procope. The song *Love Walked In* played, Ash's favorite, inspiring him to dream about Martina. His face softened at the memory when his eye caught the large black Expedition turn in. Cursing softly, he drove over to the entrance and was not far behind Alonzo when he was able to spot the Massachusetts plate number. He pulled to the left to the first drive knowing Alonzo would go to the end unit on the right. He waited two minutes and left. Five minutes later, Ash gave Mason the car owner's registration identity. The info given him next from Mason rocked him, making him call the captain immediately.

Beauregard, sitting outside the game store waiting for Him, Me and Paulie, was confused by Ash's call. His thoughts ran the gamut of what could possibly be the connections here while thinking, *there is a connection to Losocala, but how the hell is this guy Alonzo involved?*

He was startled by a knock on his back window, because he was not aware anyone was near. A smiling Jackson moved to his window as he lowered it and said, "Gotcha, Captain, you never saw us coming. When we saw your car, we did a ninja on you."

Beauregard smiled replying, "This time you did. What are you doing right now? Do you have a few minutes to talk about your photos?"

They were happy to jump in his car at his suggestion and were surprised he wanted to look at all their photos of men they saw downtown. Paulie had taken over the task of keeping the photos. Jackson explained, "You can't trust Wayne's mom and my mom. They grab the phones at night and delete what they don't like. We normally use code; you know like we're talking about a movie or a game, but when it comes to pictures, it's a problem. Paulie's mom trusts him and even his step-dad trusts him, but our moms don't."

So, the captain and the kids reviewed all the photos on Paulie's phone. Try as he might, Beauregard could only find two photos of a man who was built like Adalberto Alonzo, but neither photo was full frontal or even one quarter frontal. He thought however that the shape itself was recognizable to him. He asked the boys if they ever saw a man looking like that elsewhere. Jackson and Wayne both said no, while Paulie thought he might have, but could not now think of where or when, saying, "Captain, I'll think on it, okay?"

The captain asked if the boys had ever seen a large black Ford Expedition in the downtown area by the casino. They weren't sure. Jackson explained they had seen at least two or maybe three SUV's; that a black SUV was used by the four men including Mr. McKinney that they took pictures of at the casino.

When the captain drove away, Him, Me and Paulie held a conference in their haunt, McDonald's. Paulie insisted the captain needed assistance from them, but would never ask for it. Wayne wondered what was the big deal on the SUV's and thought they should try to remember the makes of any SUV's they had seen. Jackson reminded them that the old man Alfie who lived on Spruce Street was always driven around by his son in a black SUV. "Did we ever tell Captain Beauregard about that car? The son can't live with his father; I know that. If he lived with him, he'd keep his car there. Should we tell the captain right now?'

Wayne said, "No. We can't call him every minute when we get a little fact. We don't even know if the murders of the girls are related to the cops' shootings, do we? If Alfie's son drives his father around and doesn't live on Spruce Street, then he's probably not connected to the shootings on Spruce Street. He wouldn't be because if he were in the drug business, he'd have enough money to get his old man out of the hood. He has a big SUV, but probably not a lot of money. He's just taking care of his dad."

Paulie suggested they spend a little more time over near Spruce Street and the 'Southern Ladies' house saying, "Let's see how often Alfie's son is over there. I mean he always looks as if he has a suit on when he picks his dad up. At least that's what I see through his car window." The boys divided their time for their new surveillance gig agreeing that there should always be two of them watching at a time.

Detective Lilly Tagliano was reviewing some additional photos the captain had given them. He said they were photos he'd overlooked before. Although new to the unit, Lilly understood his remark was a crock of shit, but of course she couldn't say that to the captain. The broadly built guy in the photos had the stance of the goon who tried to make a meet with her when she was in Vice. She was certain of that. Would that be enough to implicate him? Implicate him in what? So, he's a pervert and maybe connected to some big honchos at the casino. That's not grounds for indictment. Speaking aloud, she asked, "Who is he?"

Ash walked in and hearing her talking to herself, questioned, "Who's who, Lilly. Just who is so important, that you can't keep it in your head but have to talk to the air?"

"Just that guy in the picture is the Who. The Who, who reminds me of that pervert I met while working Vice. Ash, I feel that he is the same guy; but it's kind of a feeling. It's not a logical thought."

He brought Lilly up to date on Adalberto Alonzo who lived in the condos. Lilly questioned whether they had his driver's license photo, saying, "I'd be able to identify his face. I'll never forget him."

Ash said Alonzo did not have a Massachusetts license under that name and birthdate. "I'm waiting to get his social security number before looking nationally for warrants in the triple I's. The trouble is, his car is registered under an LLC. I don't want him to know we're looking at him. I hate these car leases, Lilly. You know I'd have to call the security department at the lease company. Most leasing companies now insist on an affidavit from the District Attorney's office, which then allows an opening for our search getting out. Again, we can't have the DA in the know about what we're doing. Once I get his social, checking for warrants will give me information on him in any state he's been in where there is a record including driver's license. It won't bring up a picture, but I can call on that once I know where to call. It's all much more complicated now. We have the ability to search but with all kinds of legal stops in the system to check on us. Why do you think all the bad guys in the hood drive new rental cars? They know it delays the process of finding them."

"What do you say about us getting a sighting on him at his condo, Ash? I just need to know if he's my pervert. If he is that guy, then I believe he could be our teens' killer."

The two agreed to wait for Alonzo at his condo the next afternoon. Ash would park his car in Alonzo's neighbor's property parking space. It afforded a good look at Alonzo as he drove over to his condo and its parking space. It would even allow Lilly to walk to the corner of the building and watch while Alonzo entered his home. Ash had noticed that Alonzo did not enter by his garage, but parked in his unit's one of three visitor's spaces.

Detective Juan Flores knocked on Nigel Bailey's apartment door. He heard a shuffling of feet before a very tiny but healthy-looking man opened the door. Juan introduced himself and Nigel Bailey smiled and said, "Come in. Liz said you wanted to speak with me. She thought we should meet at her house, but it's better here. She doesn't think my neighborhood is safe; but for me it is very safe. Nobody will bother a man who has reached a hundred years. I'm a star."

And his laugh was almost joyous, making Juan wonder, if perhaps this man had the secret to a long life. He was certain that if he did, it would be in his ability to be happy. He thought, *Nigel has that laid back lovely Jamaican softness to his speech. It allows him to speak slowly giving him time to analyze what he's saying. The kids of today, and maybe me too, could learn from him. He sounds soft but he's checking me out. I can see him. His eyes miss nothing. I think he was much taller when he was younger, but he's strong looking. He has lean muscles on his arms and his face is like a light brown nut with no wrinkles. I thought if you were in the sun all your life that you'd be wrinkled; most of my older men relatives have hard lines from the sun. Here, we have Nigel with skin as smooth as a baby. What do I know about old age? All my older relatives died in their late sixties and early seventies. Not one lived to their eighties. Maybe it's the Jamaican diet. We eat mostly carbs and fats.*

Juan noticed Nigel had also been assessing him. After a long thirty seconds, Nigel said, "Yes, how can I help you, Detective Flores?"

Juan out of respect and his own professionalism started with, "Mr. Bailey, I…"

Before he could finish his sentence, Nigel interrupted and asked Juan to call him by "My Christian name, Nigel."

Nigel asked Juan about being Mexican and being a detective. He wanted to know if there were problems for him serving on a police force saying, "Being a police officer in my home in Jamaica always had problems for the officers. I think it must be the same here."

Nigel spoke slowly, but very distinctly, despite the soft island sound still lingering in his words. It took Juan a few minutes to get Nigel away from talking about himself and his original journey that brought him to western Massachusetts. When Juan finally focused on Nigel, he was forthcoming in discussing the drug problem in his immediate area. He said the Puccini Club was drug free, but that didn't mean that drug sellers or users didn't come in occasionally for a drink or to look around. He said, "The club is on the end of the street and is not big enough to make into one of those warehouse watering holes. It does have a nice parking lot across the street, which is occasionally used by bikers who drink at the club and by some small- time drug dealers. Puccini's manager lived above the bar, and worked for the active board members, all ten of them. She was paid peanuts, but ate for free and was suited for the job." He said, "She's a big woman and nobody would cross her. I've seen her throw out a built biker half her age. She has a baseball bat behind the bar. Everyone knows that."

Juan diligently worked to direct the conversation to houses and residents of Spruce and Silvain Streets. Nigel had no difficulty talking about the cops' shooting, reporting, "Just a dumb thing to do. Those shooters are never in the area. It's all about business. They were just stupid bodyguards that day. The man in there that day is an important white man that they were protecting. Over on Fir Street, they stupidly killed the old man's girlfriend. That normally doesn't happen. That old watchman lives pretty good for just sitting on a porch checking out who's coming and going in the drug house. I think his son must help him with money."

Juan asked if he'd ever been in the old man's house, but was told that in that area, unless you were family or close friends, you didn't go in their houses. Visiting like that with people you don't know was considered 'not smart.' He said, "You let someone in you don't know! They check your house for anything like televisions or computers, and they come back and rob you. It's a close community and we watch out for ourselves and each other. If I didn't know you were coming, Detective, I wouldn't answer the door. I would be ready to run out the back if you knocked too hard."

"What about Silvain Street, Nigel? Do you know Mrs. Rojas and her friend Carmen?"

Nigel really liked Carmen. He would sometimes go to the 'Southern Ladies' parties. Miriam and Sarah were always nice to him and Carmen would get him a tray of food. He did not know Mrs. Rojas, but saw her getting picked up once in a black SUV by her son who looked a lot like the old watchman's son. He said Mrs. Rojas had to be carried out by her son. She was wrapped up in a blanket. He thought she may be heavy because the son who was a big man struggled with her weight. He ended with the thought, "She's probably dead weight, like those paralyzed people. I lived with my friend in 1954 after the war, who was paralyzed in a wheelchair. I was strong and I struggled just helping him get in and out of his wheelchair. He's dead now. He only made it sixty-three years; that's too young to die by my standards."

Juan said goodbye, thanked him, and promised to buy him a drink at the club after Nigel informed him he was there every weeknight from five to seven in the evening for their special dinner of the day; but not on the weekends explaining the club was too crowded.

Juan headed back to the station disappointed he'd not gained any new information. He remembered when Petra detailed the captain's strengths to him. Apparently, going over and over things was okay. He thought, *review and review! Make notes and review again! I'm doing that but there's nothing new here, is there? Bingo, am I stupid that I didn't get it when Nigel said it?*

He drove even faster now that he had two insights, thinking, *two bits of info. The captain's right. Over and over and you see what's there.*

Paulie and Wayne were to meet Jackson at the game store. It was crowded because there was a scheduled event. Paulie was unhappy because he would have been a shoe-in for winning but didn't know about it. He said, "All this investigating is interfering with my playing."

"Paulie, you've got the edge. Don't let one missing chance play with your head. My dad says all insecurities start in our own heads," said a determined Wayne.

Finally, Jackson arrived with a pretty teenaged girl holding on to him like, they thought, a girl friend would. He dragged her over to the other boys and said, "These are my friends. What's your name and what's wrong?"

Before she had any time to answer, Paulie interrupted with, "You live over on the other side of the mall, not far from here. I live on this side. I'm Paulie and you walked in with Jackson and this is Wayne."

She cried, not much, but enough tears for the boys to notice. Wayne said, "Relax. We don't know what's wrong, but if you relax, then you can tell us. If you don't calm down, some adult in here will notice. Do you want that? Do you want us to get the manager to help you?"

The girl stopped with the tears, stood up taller, and said, "I'm Betsy Printer and I do live near here, Paulie. I've seen you around. My problem is that a man tried to get me to go in his car. I'm so frightened. I think he'll try again. I can't tell my mother. She's already wild with fear. Two of my closest friends have been murdered. She thinks I'm next. This man scared me. I've seen him before, but he never stopped his car before. He might just be a pervert, but I'm in jeans and a sweatshirt and jacket. These clothes don't say, 'come on,' do they? Why would he bother me? He must be in his thirties or he could be older. I didn't like his face. He's not ugly, just has that mean look."

Betsy realized the boys looked stunned by what she was telling them. She thought, *they're only about thirteen, probably still in middle school. I've said too much. I can't call my mom; she'll have me at the police station in no time and then permanent home incarceration. The boys maybe can walk me home.*

Before she could ask them to walk with her, Jackson questioned, "Betsy, were you part of the anti-drug group of students along with Candace and Joely and Ollie?"

"How do you know about them? You're kids in a game store."

Paulie said, lying just a little, "I live near here and the police are always asking me questions about who I've seen. I live near Spruce Street where those detectives got shot. Jackson and Wayne's parents know Candace's neighbors. We've heard lots of stuff about the anti-drug kids and that some drug guy must be mad at them for interfering with business. I know there're no drugs going on anywhere near Spruce Street now."

Betsy was now shaking, saying, "I didn't know there was noise about the anti-drug connection to the killings all over the street. I'm not safe if everyone knows. I thought I would be safe if I just stayed clear of side streets, but this weirdo stopped on this mall road. I was just going to CVS to buy make-up. It's daylight. Maybe he's not connected to this. Maybe he's just a pedophile. They're everywhere; at least that's what the internet says. Will you walk me home and not tell my mother?"

The boys went with Betsy, but left it up to Wayne, who at times was noted for his discretion in dealing with difficult situations, to question Betsy. He asked Betsy many questions, but received very little information. The man who accosted her was in a dark and big SUV. She thought it was black or it could have been navy blue. He looked to her like he might be tall, but he was sitting in his car and leaning over from the driver's side talking to her through the window. He said he knew where she lived and would happily give her a ride home. She thought he had a tan and he was wearing a suit jacket. He said he knew her dad. He gave off vibes and she said, "I'm probably imagining the danger, but something about him really scared me; and I've never been stopped by a car whose driver I didn't know before. My aunt says I look twenty-four and had better watch myself. I'm only seventeen. I looked at him and something made me run. I have never been so afraid. I think I'm being silly."

That's when Paulie quoted his step-father saying, "He says, Betsy, to always go with your gut if it's telling you you're in danger. Nothing bad ever happened when you avoid just the possibility of trouble. He would think you did the right thing today. I do too. The man disappeared. He was up to no-good."

After leaving Betsy and waiting a minute to see she went inside the door, the boys agreed Captain Beauregard should be informed. Jackson called and left a long message.

23

Fitting the Puzzle Pieces

Jim and Petra were strolling up Mattoon Street studying the historic brownstone homes, while heading to the turnoff to Edwards Street. One lady exited her home apparently intent on walking her dog. Jim approached her and asked if there were any homes currently for sale, stating he and his wife just loved this area and often went to the Arts Festival held on the street each year. Pleased that they knew about the festival, she said she was active in the neighborhood association and wondered which artist he liked best. Petra interrupted saying, "I love all the jewelry artists and when we're there together, we both love the glass artists; those are the best. I met a woman who lives somewhere here in the area. Jim just loved her, because she told us some of these homes, if you're willing to do some rehabbing, can be affordable. Jim, what was her name again?"

Jim appeared to be searching for a name and finally said, "Carol, no I think Carolina was her name. She was with a tall thin man that day. Which house does she live in; if you don't mind telling me? She told us she would tell us all about the neighborhood when we could find a day off."

"You must mean Carolina Contreau and Albert. I don't know

Albert's last name, but he's quite the gentleman. I think he's European from seeing him with his more formal manners. He's often at her home on Edwards Street, but he doesn't live with her. Come, I'll walk with you up to the home."

Jim and Petra were uncertain about the direction their conversation had taken, causing Petra to say, "What's your name again?"

The woman identified herself as Jordan Logan, while Petra said, "I'm so pleased to meet you, Jordan. We're the Locke's. I think I know which house it is. She said it's the one with all the historic painted wooden privacy panels. I think it's the second one down."

"You're right, Mrs. Locke; that's her home. Good, that will let me go the other way with my little Basil. I stop at the corner store every day when we walk and get him a treat. If I don't, he simply will not take a walk. He walks only for a goodie. 'Basil, you're such a lazy little darling, aren't you?'"

Saying their goodbyes, Petra and Jim headed towards Carolina's home which was not a problem since their car was parked over next to the Catholic Church chancery. In walking by her home, it was quiet. Jim observed in a bit of a whisper, "Petra, these two streets are one way going towards Chestnut Street. It affords an observation perch for seeing unwanted neighbors or folks. You could easily park over by the museums. If you wanted to leave here unseen, you could cut out over behind these houses and get to your car. It's a great location in the city. With limited street and driveway parking, neighbors normally hate regular visitors who park in 'reserved for the neighborhood residents' spaces. If you park in a lot not too far away, neighbors won't know when or if you are there. It's too bad we couldn't get more info on Albert, but she immediately knew him from your description. I wish she knew his name."

"Jim, I wanted to ask her if he was possibly Russian, but was afraid she'd gossip that to Carolina. Well, that's all we could get. Maybe the captain would authorize you to set up a watch to get a picture of this Albert. We could get an ID from a photo maybe? Meanwhile, let's get a nice lunch. We can go to the market in the casino. They have lots of options including a gelato and cappuccino stand that has pistachio ice cream."

Sitting in his grand office chair, Captain Beauregard listened to the call from Jackson. It caused him great consternation. Primary was his concern for Betsy's safety and secondary was his impatience with having to rely on information from Him, Me and Paulie, his informants, but not informants. He cursed the satanic forces at large thinking, *What kind of evil consistently puts me in untenable situations with these kids. Every single time, they give me information I need! In the future, when I speak at the Chamber's luncheon, I will really have to be enthusiastic about civilian involvement. I won't tell them about juvenile involvement; oh no, I won't do that, but I do believe if we all did what these kids and McKinney do, crimes would be solved more quickly. However, I can't under any circumstances knowingly put civilians in danger.*

Beauregard called for Juan and Lilly's presence and told them about the kids and Betsy Printer. He relayed his thoughts. "Look, Betsy lives near the Spruce Street area. I know the other kids live further away from that area. I looked at the notes taken on Ollie Rapusca's family. Ash stated he was a good kid who dabbled in a little pot before getting involved in the anti-drug crusade. His parents thought he looked up to Herbie Brent. At the time they earnestly believed it was a good thing. He used to go to the game store which is not far from Spruce Street. Candace did not go to the game store nor did Joely, but all of them were involved with the anti-drug campaign. This perp knows about the library meetings. I think he haunts this area.

"Our expected reports from the FBI Behavioral Analysis Unit have been delayed. Just when, in multiple, serial murders, isn't the FBI chomping at the bit to take over? I'm beginning to think the delay could be a deliberate slowdown."

Juan replied, "Captain, you're getting like my great aunt Teresa who thinks everything's a conspiracy; especially when we're talking about the government. Do you really think Loughman would slow down a murder investigation of young kids when other teens may still be at risk?"

The captain responded, "I think the FBI has prioritized this big drug push and is considering every other issue as local and not big enough to interfere in the big drug business plan they have. The Agency wants it so badly that nothing else, even public safety for the moment, is quite as important. Loughman has less than four days for his big sweep; that's when he expects to learn the identity of the big honcho or Chavos or the Spider man or whatever. Once he gets him, he won't care what we investigate; he'll then give us all kinds of help. I've never seen such a delay in the BAU before in a multiple murder situation. If you notice, an agent is finally scheduled to be here tomorrow.

"We'll have a meeting with them tomorrow and then every decision will be delayed another day. We'll be almost at their fourth day; the deadline. Yeah, Juan, I think the delay is deliberate. Maybe it's not meant to cause harm, but it has already. If we later find that the FBI's information gives us a perp in a couple of days, then Loughman's delaying actions will have been responsible for deaths. Our job is to find Chavos and whether Adalberto Alonzo has a connection.

"Also, I want to know more about Vladimir Grant. Right now, you are to protect Betsy without being noticed. I want community police involved watching the high school, Amber and Betsy's houses, and reporting on all large black or navy-blue SUV's without, and I say it again, without causing notice. They're to do drive-bys only."

Juan explained his interview with Nigel the one-hundred-year-old Jamaican gardener. Telling Rudy that he enjoyed talking with the old man much more than he had anticipated; he also mentioned he didn't learn too much. The captain told him not to worry, that not every investigation alley is fruitful. He saw the look on Juan's face as did Lilly. The captain said, "Spit it out, Detective; you saw something that didn't fit."

"Captain, Nigel thought that Mrs. Rojas' son looked a little like the old Spanish watchman's son. He said they both wear suits and drive big SUV's. It's his impression, and I'm telling you he notices little things. Could Mrs. Rojas be related to the old man? I was thinking she could own both houses, and that she lets Alfie live in one. Maybe the son is not her son but her grandson; that would make sense. He could be driving his father and his grandmother. We Spanish sometimes don't differentiate family members to outsiders."

The captain thanked Juan and said, "You're on to something. I don't know what it is, but two sons on back to back streets both driving big new black SUV's and shuttling their parents is a tiny wee bit coincidental; and as you know, I don't like coincidences."

As Juan and Lilly exited, they passed Ted entering the captain's office. Lilly, now fully understanding her captain's ways, whispered, "He's on a roll."

Beauregard barely greeted his detective before he was issuing directives to Detective Ted Toddington announcing a plan. "You are to get everything on this Vladimir Grant. I haven't heard from Jim Locke yet on him. I want to know now."

"Captain, I have Jim's report. His office sent it, because he was on a stake-out with Petra you authorized. I've reviewed it and it surprises me. Grant lives in one of the nicer neighborhoods in West Side, right under our noses. A neighbor says he's involved in the almost new-used car wholesale industry in Connecticut. He's lived with a girlfriend for two years now. She's a hairdresser over in Holyoke. The house is nice but not spectacular. Nothing about his lifestyle is out of the ordinary. He drives a black SUV sometimes; then again, he drives all kinds of cars, supposedly from the inventory that's to be auctioned off. I've seen it before with a neighbor who has made big money with the auctions. When he has a big event to attend, he comes home with a BMW or a Mercedes for the event for one night and then, oops, the car goes back to the auction house."

Rudy reviewed the report and asked, "Where does he go in the daytime? Is he a runner for the auction house, bringing cars to and from? Or does he have a regular job as a driver or a bodyguard or as a gofer. Does he look like a principal in any of this and if not, who is he connected with; is it just Carolina or someone else? Also, Losocala says he's invaluable to him. How the hell does Grant get paid? If he's getting paid as a vendor, maybe on a 1099 to a business or corporation, IRS would have info on him. He could be working under an assumed name."

"Captain, I know we're not supposed to be in Springfield, but the only sightings we've had on Grant have been in the area of the casino; that and his address are all we have. He may be here illegally. I have no social, no license. I don't think his connection with the auto auction firm will lead to anything. In fact, I think it's a legitimate enterprise. It's more likely he doesn't work for them but is a middleman vendor of cars from the South and West. I'd like to chase him down. I could start with his house in the morning."

Rudy noticed Ted had not asked his permission, but had just given a presentation unloading what he wanted. He didn't appear for a minute to wonder if he would look stupid by giving his views on the subject. He hung the info idea out there for the captain's taking. Beauregard liked Ted's forwarding what he thought he should do; not asking, but offering what any fool would know was the way to go. So, he told him to take his personal car and to watch himself. Rudy ended with, "Grant's Azerbaijani and supposedly from Russia; I know from one of my kids' friends that most Azerbaijani live in Syria or Turkey. I've no history with any of these people, but if Grant's from Russia then he may be important. What I do know is I am certain he's no fool. Be careful, Ted, when you leave West Side; you'll be just a citizen. Call me at the first sign of trouble. You will not be noticed as police, because you'll have a civilian car and there won't be two in your car. You are there to document, not to intercept. Also, Ted, start now.

"One other thing that really bothers me about this is that Mason discovered Vladimir Grant's car is registered to G-Supply, LLC."

It took a minute before Ted remembered. "You mean, Captain, Losocala's company? How long has he had that vehicle? Losocala's only been in the neighborhood for a couple of years, and Grant's been around for close to fifteen years. Is this a new connection between them and what does Grant do for Losocala?"

"I don't know, Ted, but you are going to find out."

Rudy sat in his chair, drank some cold coffee and coughed at the bitter taste. He knew he didn't like cold coffee, but still sipped wondering why he would do something that went against his nature. He thought, *maybe I'm too lazy to get up and get some fresh java. No, I'm chasing something in my head, a clue possibly? My moving to the kitchen*

would interfere in my thinking process; at least from my way of struggling for a memory or something in my memory. I give up!

He moved to the kitchen, made a fresh batch, and walked over to visit with Detective Mason Smith, who was working on something, saying, "What goes, Mason?"

Mason, with a not so friendly look in his eyes, replied, "I'll tell you, Captain. Every detective is out in the field. You know what happens when this office is empty with the exception of me? I get to field every nonsense call that Millie has not been able to turn away. I wouldn't want her job. She says she's only sent me 10% of what she gets. When is one of them ever coming back to work here and assist me?"

The captain patted Mason on the back and said, "I'll take the next one, Detective. Just let me know. I'm in my office for the duration today. Okay?"

Mason grimaced replying, "Look, Captain, you have three details out there, one including Jim Locke. I know you're fitting pieces together, but it looks to me you're not certain which piece is the big piece or as the British say, 'The Major Line of Inquiry,' except they don't pronounce 'inquiry' the way we do. What's going on?"

Rudy said, "There are some assumptions I'm making based on some ideas my detectives are inferring by putting together little bits of info. I'm feeling like I'm in a contest for puzzle master and I'm missing the big, one, perfect puzzle piece. The puzzle has all four corners built out, but the interior seems to be comprised of funky shades of the same color. One piece, Mason, just one perfect piece is needed." And the captain walked back to his office.

Twenty minutes later Beauregard heard Detective Ash Lent, who had returned, having a debate with Detective Mason Smith over a phone call. He moved from his office and listened. They were discussing a call from a citizen who had heard a shooting next door. He said a patrol car came and went and the officers did nothing; that he tried to wave them down and they ignored him. The detectives checked police calls and saw that it was not a shooting but a carpenter using a nail gun. Mason had diligently explained the situation, but the homeowner wanted him to stop the work next door insisting that, "I should not be in fear in my own house." It took ten minutes for Mason to discretely quiet the resident.

Ignoring Mason's frustration with the city's citizenry, Beauregard asked Ash to join him in his office. He updated Ash about Ted's mission to chase down Vladimir Grant, and Jim and Petra's focus on the Spider's identity, while Juan and Lilly were doing protection duty around the Spruce Street and Mall areas. Ash listened carefully, but stopped the captain when he heard about Juan's question relative to Mrs. Rojas's son and Alfie's son, saying, "Kind of coincidental, don't you think, Captain. I'm surprised you're not on it already."

With an unsuitable smile considering the situation, Beauregard said, "You're wrong there, Ash. Why do you think I'm talking to you? We are on it and I have a plan."

Ash smiled thinking, *of course you and now me, we, have a plan. I shouldn't have doubted that for a minute, but any plan I see is fraught with problems.*

Ash expressed his thought with, "Any plan you could possibly have is problematic. We can't investigate the drug activity or anything related to it. We are only authorized to chase down the teen murders' perverted perpetrator, who most likely is somehow situated within the drug activity in the area. Loughman doesn't know what we know and doesn't think we have information on his undercover guy McKinney. Each avenue we start to investigate, we're stopped from getting quick details by the Feds. Given those constraints, what is your plan?"

"I think if McKinney gets his meet with Chavos, Chavos will be arrested along with anyone connected to him. Once that happens, if our perp is one of Chavos' entourage, then we've lost him for years. I want him. What if the man Lilly insists may be the man in the library, the pervert that she met when she was a prop for Vice, the man who tried to accost Betsy Printer, and maybe is one of the sons on Spruce or Silvain Streets; maybe he's both of the sons on Spruce Street. I know you'll think I'm dreaming, but my gut is talking to me, has been talking to me, and I have not been listening closely."

"Captain, you think this because in every situation, the man, men, in question wore a suit; and in three situations the man, men, drove a black or dark blue SUV. No one is able to assert the SUV is the same make in each case. It's a stretch, Captain. Much as I respect your instincts, it's a stretch and I'm a musician. I'm good at visualizing possibilities."

"What about putting pressure on Spruce Street and ignoring the FBI's thoughts that your and Ted's shootings were not related, and we are not supposed to follow that avenue? Right from the beginning we should have been following that avenue. In fact, Spruce Street may be the best place for Chavos or Spider Man to meet with McKinney. Police aren't near there now. No activity is going on which surprises me, but community police report it's as quiet down there as it is by the mayor's house. Great place to meet. So, just in case I'm correct in my thinking, farfetched as it is, shaking the bushes in that area puts it all out there, giving us time to find our perp first. If I'm wrong, there will be no problem for the FBI or for us."

"Captain, how do we do that without waking the community? Do you want us in the woods watching that house? The meeting won't take place if we do that."

"No, Ash, I want you to knock on doors all around the area with a community police officer. Your story is that the mayor wants to advise the neighborhood that the Department is taking traffic issues and auto break-ins reported by the neighbors very seriously. The mayor has actually made a speech recently he would activate community police to be involved with securing all neighborhoods. He'll love that we paid attention.

"Give each neighbor a community policing card and invite them to the 'Fair on the Green' Police table. Remind them we will be giving out technical information on safety and security issues at the fair. Hit the street behind Spruce Street first. Have a community police car bringing the uniforms to each door. You wait in your personal vehicle while the officers do door to door on Silvain Street, but then have only the community police car go over to Spruce Street. You stay in your car on Silvain Street and wait for any action when the other car hits Spruce Street. I'm hoping someone from the house with the two orange cones will make a move."

A flummoxed Ash asked, "Why would Community Police, who often make neighborhood rounds, especially when there is any negative action in the area, arouse suspicion? Even if their presence worked some people up, what makes you think the son and old lady Mrs. Rojas would care if the police were on their street, Captain?"

"Because, Ash, I just know the 'Southern Ladies' are paid to watch out for the house across the street. If they see the police coming down the street, they will make a call or text to the son's number to warn him. In theory, his mother gets nervous when folks ring her bell and she can't get to the door. Most likely, if he is not tied up, he will come right over. We would then be able to see his car and speak with him. Strike that; don't speak with him. As I remember, you have a camera with a telescopic lens; don't you? Get a picture. Even if we only work to rule him out, it will help our investigation."

Ash left to make arrangements to get that sector's community police officers out there within the hour. The captain said he expected action, if there would be any action at all, immediately. Beauregard called Petra. He asked her to connect with Jim and get over to the parking lot near the Springfield Museums saying, "It's Thursday and they have some sort of lecture and will normally be crowded. By the time you get there, many will be leaving. Wait there. I expect to see someone in a black or navy-blue van parking there, exiting to cut over to Carolina's place on Edwards Street. Jim should bring his best camera. I want pictures of every person in that van. It may take all of this afternoon. If nothing happens, return early tomorrow.

The captain spent fifteen minutes laying out his plan. Finally, Petra cut him off with, "I'm with Jim at lunch now. We'll go right over. You really think that action at Mrs. Rojas house will result in activity over here, Captain? Are we that close? Didn't one of us see Alfie's son when Alfie was questioned about Marisol Garcia and the Dominicans' murders?"

Beauregard swore, and answered, "Juan saw him. I never picked that up. He has actually seen Alfie's son, AJ. Damn, we don't even know if AJ is Alfie Jr. or the J is for his middle name. I'll call Juan to check on his availability, when we have pictures, to see if he would be able to help our sketch artist."

24

Bits for the Fit

Earlier in the day, Detective Ted Torrington enjoyed his coffee at six a.m. watching Vladimir Grant's house. Grant's stunning girlfriend had just put rubbish containers out for collection. It was quite a sight to see, given that her attire was a very short nightie and wrap and fur trimmed UGG's. He understood her wearing the UGG's, but given the cold November morning, he thought, *she must be nuts to come out in the cold in her such scanty clothes.*

Half hour later, Grant opened the left side garage door and with a great deal of noise drove his beautifully trimmed Harley onto the street. Talking aloud, Ted said, "What the fuck! How the hell am I going to follow a motorcycle? Those riders are so much more aware of a trail."

Ted had no trouble following Grant until the 291 turnoff towards the Mass Pike. Grant was three cars ahead and at the last minute moved two lanes over to take the exit while Ted was locked into heading the wrong way. He called the captain explaining his problem, "I can get back there, Captain, but I know he's ditched me."

"Ted, go up towards Saint James over to the trucking depot. There's a biker club just before it. See if his bike is there. You said it's a painted out beauty and you should be able to spot it. I don't know the coverage there, but find a place to park if you can that will allow visibility when Grant leaves. I think he'll be there."

Ted said, "If he's there, your instincts are great."

Within ten minutes Ted was in place and Grant's Harley was parked next to the biker club building.

Beauregard paced around his office and into Mason's with his cell phone in hand thinking, *I hate waiting. It's the worst part of my job. In the field the waiting isn't so bad, but here, it's an invitation to an ulcer.*

Mason tried to soothe his boss by announcing he'd gotten Adalberto Alonzo's baptismal certificate from the Catholic Church offices. "It says his father is Albert with a last name of Sidorov. I checked it out and it's a pretty common name in Russia. I'll do a search. We're finally getting somewhere, huh, Captain."

Smiling for the first time in hours, Beauregard answered, "I think we are. I think we are. I want everything you can find on Albert Sidorov. The baptismal certificate was a great idea, Mason. How'd you know which church?"

"I didn't, but I remember that years ago they had a Spanish mass at the little church in the North End, Blessed Sacrament. It's now a recreation center."

Beauregard replied, "I'll bet anything he doesn't know about it. I'll bet his trail will be minimal at best. Still, I want to know what he drives, if he's ever worked, has he ever owned anything, and when did he come here. How did he come in, directly through some religious agency or through Canada or Mexico? I want it all. I want it soon, even if it won't play a role in what I'm planning, it will be important later."

An hour later Beauregard answered his cell; he was in the other office and had left the cell on his desk requiring him to run. It was Jackson Loyal who excitedly said, "I'm glad you answered, Captain Beauregard. We have news. That black SUV was just on Spruce Street. The driver in the dark suit drove down the street towards the woods, made a U-turn and then dropped off the old man Alfie. It's a Ford Expedition, Captain and we got a look at the guy driving. Paulie's drawing him right now. We couldn't take a picture without them getting suspicious, but Paulie rode his bike by and got a really good look. The guy didn't even glance at Paulie."

Beauregard said, "I want you out of there right now, Jackson, all three of you. I'll meet you over at the game store and you had better be there. Exit the woods at the other end. There's action going on in that area. I want you out and now."

"Are you mad at us, Captain? We were just looking out for the make of the SUV. We knew he'd come around here eventually to get his old man. This is the second day. That's all we've done. We've played it safe, and didn't take any chances."

"I'm leaving now, Jackson, and you had better be there with your friends and bring the drawing."

Before heading to the game store, Beauregard asked Mason, "If I take a picture of a drawing with my cell phone and send it to you, can you send it out for ID to Lilly and see if she can identify him. If she thinks he looks like the john she turned away when she was in Vice, have her call Betsy Printer's mother for Betsy to see the picture."

At the game store, Beauregard had the boys get in his car. He was seriously conflicted. On one hand he was ticked they'd ignored his orders to stay away. On the other hand, in front of him, sat three young boys who deserved a medal for their tenacity and ingenuity; both traits he truly valued. His heart prevented him from giving them hell. Instead he said, "Thank you. You guys have done some great work."

Suddenly, serious faces changed in front of him. Suddenly, three boys had big smiles and Wayne answered, "We did listen to you, Captain, but sitting in the woods and drawing is what we often do. We weren't really disobeying your orders."

The captain could not let this go and spoke very slowly in reply. "It is forty-eight degrees outside today. Don't tell me you sit there regularly in this weather and draw, Wayne?"

Paulie, ever sensitive to changes in adult attitudes, responded, "Captain, don't you want to see the drawing? It's a real good likeness."

Beauregard smiled for the first time thinking Paulie would be a great negotiator someday whether in business or for the police with his obvious ability to suppress tension. Beauregard looked at the man's drawn likeness, got help from the boys in photographing it properly, and sent it off to Mason and Lilly, before ordering the boys to go home.

Within a couple of minutes Lilly called. "That's the guy, Captain, that's the guy. Mason says you want me to get Betsy Printer to look at it. I'll pick up a few other drawings turned into photos plus some photos and let her choose from the group. Juan and I will get right over to her house. I'll call you."

The captain interrupted Lilly saying, "I also want to get this photo over to the librarian and the retail clerks. Maybe, with this drawing of Alonzo's full face, someone will remember him."

Lilly said, "We're on it. By the way, Captain, that was great work!"

Beauregard thought, *yeah, but it's not my great work; it's the work of three thirteen-year old kids who, although they don't listen, do great for us.*

Beauregard remained in his car looking at the drawing thinking, *what the hell do I see in this face? Would I know him as a pervert at first glance? No, I wouldn't. He, if he is the pervert, is deranged. He is the son of the man we think is the Spider Man or Chavos. Did he learn this deviation from normalcy from Chavos? Is he a drug king? I don't think he is. He's a good looking driver and maybe a gofer. He is quite handsome but has a cold look. Could just be the kids' unknowingly interpreting this guy's persona.*

His cell rang. He answered on the first ring hearing Ash report the Community Police Officers were moving down Silvain Street. He said, "Captain, as the officers headed to the house with the orange cones, Miriam ran out of her home and said, 'Don't bother Mrs. Rojas, Officer, she is in her nineties and gets jumpy if anyone rings her doorbell. She has trouble shutting the alarm off and starts crying. Please don't bother her.' And so they didn't. I'll have them check their database later on for alarms going off at that address. I'll bet there's no history there."

Beauregard agreed with Ash's assessment and told him to wait another hour. If anything would happen it would be soon. He also asked, "Did you see a Ford Expedition drive down Silvain Street right after the officers started going door-to-door?"

"No Expedition came down this street yet, Captain."

"Well, the old man Alfie is in his house, so it will be interesting to see if he'll answer the door for the community police officers. I'm hoping he won't. Just watch for a black Ford Expedition. Call me if one comes down. Don't do anything, just watch."

Beauregard headed back to the station with multiple possibilities running through his brain, *something will happen soon, maybe! What will happen, I don't know. If I'm lucky the community police will have spooked the occupants in one of the houses. I like the timing with the Expedition having just been in the neighborhood. My hunch may not be worth shit; still, it could be a good hunch.*

Ash interrupted his reverie. "Captain, Mrs. Rojas' son, driving a black Expedition, just picked up his mother. He got her in a wheelchair from the side door and put her in the back seat. He struggled. That's one big car and she's a big lady all wrapped up like it's ten below zero. He worked to get her in the car and just now drove off. And the SUV's plate is Adalberto Alonzo's."

Beauregard let Ash know the experiment had worked and he could go home. He made a call to Petra and Jim telling them, "There should be a Ford Expedition arriving soon. The problem is I don't know if it will drop someone off at Carolina's house or if it will park in the lot. You have about eight to twelve minutes before it arrives. Can you cover both areas for me and describe what you see. Also, check the license plate. It's Alonzo's plate; of that I'm pretty certain.

"Wherever he drops off his rider, I want him followed. He may go back to his condo, or to the mall area or to another location. Of this much I am certain, if he is our perverted perp, then he's going to feel stress after seeing the community police in the Spruce/Silvain Streets area. I think he is feeling stress today. Call me and let me know what direction he's going."

Reaching the station, Beauregard entered and headed for the MCU kitchen knowing Petra had brought pastry in earlier. He hoped Mason hadn't scoffed them all. Mason was the only detective in the unit who, when he wasn't on a health kick, rivaled Rudy's love of food. Although Beauregard had done little work this afternoon, his detectives had brought his plans to fruition. He was just waiting for the linchpin now and the stress of inactivity and expectation hit his gut. He was starving. He remembered he hadn't eaten lunch today. *when the hell was the last time I missed lunch before? I'm slipping. I wasn't needed for any of the casings today. I was peripheral and unimportant with the exception of intervening with Him, Me and Paulie. Cripes, I'm talking about them the way they talk about themselves, like they're a group of movie stars or the 'Packrat' and I don't think of them as individuals. It's identical to my referencing my unit as the 'MCU' when I mean all the detectives including me; same thing.*

Rudy cut a four inch high three inch wide piece of limoncello cake and with his coffee joined Mason in the murder room. Musing out loud he said, "Mason, Alonzo's our perp, but how and when do we arrest him? Even if I get positive identifications from the librarian, the retail clerk, and Betsy Printer, I only have enough to bring him in as a person of interest and I know that even with the best hustle he won't break. I'll have to wait to hear from McKinney about the meet, that's if McKinney will keep his word. What do I have then, nothing! The FBI will do the arrest and I'm certain Alonzo will be caught up in that and I'll have no juice for arresting a serial murderer. It's time to pray."

Mason responded, "Captain, I worry when you're praying for a solution."

"Well, Mason, it's not always in our hands, is it?"

Before Mason could elaborate philosophically, which he was prone to do, Beauregard's cell beeped. Petra was calling. "Captain, Alonzo is in his SUV with the motor on in the museum parking lot. He dropped a tall thin man off; I think it's Chavos. He seems to be waiting, maybe for Chavos to come back. Jim just called and said the man just keyed himself into Carolina's house. I was going to go get Jim, but he says he'll walk around and get to my car without Chavos seeing us. That way we can follow Alonzo when he leaves."

"Good plan, Petra. Let me know …"

Before Beauregard could finish, he heard Jim open the car door and say, "I'm just in time, Petra, he's moving."

Again, Beauregard was left waiting along with Mason who remarked, "Where do you think he's going, Captain? I better let Lilly and Juan know the watch on Betsy may be really important now."

"It's one of three places he may go to, Mason. One is to Spruce Street, another is to his condo, and the last would be where he keeps his memories of the kills. All these psychopaths have some sort of keepsakes. I don't think he'd keep them in his home. Wouldn't do me any good if he did, I'd have to bring the Springfield Police in to do a search and right now it's not going to happen. I'm thinking of going for a warrant to search the two houses on Spruce and Silvain Streets. It's a stretch, but I have to do something. The trouble is I can't say that Alonzo lives in either house, just that he's connected by what? We now know there is no old lady living on Silvain Street; that Chavos is probably the old lady, and that Alfie is probably Chavos. Of that I'm certain."

Mason took a moment to digest Beauregard's conclusions. "Captain, I didn't think it through; you're probably right. We know Alfie went into the house on Spruce Street dropped off earlier by Alonzo. Mrs. Rojas who is not Mrs. Rojas, but Chavos, came out of the house on Silvain Street and was picked up by Alonzo after they probably heard the police were on the streets. You know, Captain, there's still a possibility Alfie is still in the house on Spruce Street. I mean we can't be certain, can we?"

"Not going with possibles today, I'm certain, Mason, and I'm acting on it."

Beauregard's phone rang again. Beauregard looked at the number and answered, "Petra, which way is he going?"

"Captain, we're in the West Side Industrial Park. You know where they have those office units with shipping bays attached. Alonzo pulled his SUV in the bay and I can see him in his office; well not exactly. I'm able to see his movements through the slats in some window blinds. Shall we stay here?"

"Stay there, no matter how long it takes. I want to know where Alonzo is every minute for the next twenty-four hours."

Beauregard texted the other detectives requesting they return to the station for a meeting ASAP. And again, he was forced to wait while thinking, *again, I must move slowly, while my mind is busting out of my cranium.*

An hour later found the detectives, with the exception of Petra, gathered in the conference room. It was late in the afternoon and Beauregard was acting rushed. He explained in five minutes his problems and asked Ted to go for the warrants on three sites: Spruce Street, Silvain Street; and Industrial Park Unit 78A saying, "Judge Lamborski is there now and is waiting for you. Here's the prepared paperwork, signatures and all. You can thank Millie and me later. The judge will give them to you without much of a fight. He knows two of the families who have lost children. Furthermore, all the addresses are in West Side."

Before leaving, Ted stated, "Captain, I think Vladimir Grant may be undercover. He sneaked through the shrubs and met Mr. McKinney inside one of the trailers in the truck depot and then went back to the biker restaurant."

Beauregard's response was, "Maybe he's undercover or maybe he's making plans for the meet."

Ted left and the Captain explained the warrants should be served at the Industrial Park at five in the morning. He told Juan and Lilly, "Get over there early and relieve Petra, if she'll let you. Make sure the manager of the site stays with you every minute. Take some uniforms but don't use patrol cars. I don't want to wake the dead. I'm thinking that Alonzo, if this is his murder site or even if it's not, is probably keeping the extra clothing there. He's not stupid enough to keep it in his condo. At least I hope he's not."

Mason pointed at a report, requested earlier by the captain, which he placed in front of Beauregard. The captain looked at a list of plate registration numbers with one circled. It was Alonzo's and it was parked on the main access road to Spruce Street on the date and time of Ash and Ted's assaults. Beauregard's response was a query. "Why wasn't he a part of the action? We know that he's Chavos's son and still, he's not a part of the action. It was supposed to be a meet that day according to McKinney. McKinney was there. The Dominican Protective Detail was there outside the third floor apartment. We now know Alfie is Chavos and he was there. Alfie was on the first floor and was probably just about to go to the third floor for the meet when the Dominicans scoped out the detectives entering from the rear. That's why they started shooting; they couldn't understand why the cops were entering the back way. They thought it was a set-up. I still don't understand why the son Adalberto wasn't there. His car was two streets over. How could he help his father escape?"

Ash said, "He couldn't, Captain. I think it's more likely that the father, Chavos, doesn't trust the son; it's not the first time a son is a 'wannabe' but is kept out of action because the father doesn't think he's up to it. Maybe Chavos knows his son is a pervert."

Beauregard answered, "I don't think that, Chavos, who is noted to be only about money, would allow that kind of risk to operate around him. He doesn't know about the son; but my guess is he wants to keep him out of danger. For the son, he would think his father is showing disrespect. I hate using that word. All the punks we arrest say that someone 'disrespected' them and that's their reason for shooting someone. 'Disrespected' is not a word, is it?"

Ash said, "Don't know, Captain, but recently I used it. It's probably new urban language. I do think Adalberto Alonzo has had a complicated background; what with his mother dying when he was ten years old, and his switch from a female household within the Spanish community to a Russian household with his dad. I'm sure he's learned some things he shouldn't have learned. If we get him for these murders, he will make one hell of a study for the shrinks who are interested in sociopathic/psychopathic personalities. He seems so in control, but he's not."

Juan clearly agreed with Ash on Alonzo, saying, "Captain, I don't think Alonzo will go easily. We'll need some uniforms if he's still there at five in the morning. By the way, Ash, the *Oxford English Dictionary* says the verb 'disrespected' has been around since the seventeenth century."

Beauregard groaned but fortunately his cell beeped. The text was from an unknown number and said, "V. Grant dead in shootout near East Springfield."

The captain informed his detectives about Vladimir's death, when Millie walked in and said, "Detective Stellato from Springfield Police wants to talk with you, Captain, and right now."

Beauregard gave orders to Juan and Lilly to be prepared to support Petra and Jim Locke; to Mason, that he should direct the uniforms for the morning; and to Ash, to be on call for his directions in the morning. He said, "I know tomorrow is D-day; I just know it. Despite this Vladimir killing, there will be a meet tomorrow; business requires it. If I know anything about this Chavos, it's that business needs have a priority. He had to have been worried about Grant. Grant is Russian. If for any reason he was suspicious of Vladimir Grant, then Chavos would eliminate him. If he were wrong, he'd make up for it later, but now the meet must happen and remember, Chavos did not kill McKinney, so he's not on to him. The meet is going to be on Spruce Street. Think about it; all attention from the drug people will be on Grant's death. They might even think it's the perfect cover for them. The task force will be scrambling."

Lilly excitedly agreed. "It's like the crime operations we've all read about: the theory is that you point in another direction. Even if Grant is not undercover, he's not important enough to the operation, but is most likely known by the FBI. That's fodder for elimination and a better plan, Captain. And if he is an FBI undercover, well, killing him is what he deserves as far as Chavos is concerned."

Beauregard commented, "How close, I wonder, were Grant and Alonzo? Was there competition there? We have pictures of Grant with Chavos, and the Las Vegas photos have Chavos, the Spider, and Alonzo together. The father plays in the casino in Vegas with his son, but his son isn't with him for the proposed meet on Spruce Street. Grant is a go to guy for Losocala and also for Carolina, Chavos's main squeeze. Now Grant is dead. Grant could be an FBI undercover, and if so how was he compromised? If not, did someone say he was FBI undercover to compromise him?"

The unit broke up to go their separate ways and Beauregard took the call from Stellato. He was apprised by Stellato, "Look, Rudy, Grant lived in West Side. What do you know about him? He's supposed to be a gofer for Raymond Losocala who is in the security business. Do you know anything more about him?"

"Joe, what do you want to know? I want to know a few things too. I want to know why a Springfield MCU detective thinks I know something about the murder of a gofer in Springfield, who just happens to have a house in West Side. As far as I know all his activities were in Springfield."

"So, Rudy, how do you know all about Vladimir Grant who was just murdered? He was on your radar, wasn't he?"

Rudy responded, "Radar for what, Joe? Radar for what?"

Stellato had enough of this game saying, "All right, you win. How important do you think he was in this drug investigation; important enough that he was murdered?"

"Joe, I thought he was one of yours. We've seen him with Losocala, but didn't connect him to the emerging drug empire. Remember, we can't investigate anything to do with drugs."

"Rudy, who are you kidding? I know you. You couldn't leave any of this alone. Your drug unit says you haven't asked about anyone, except that Detective Lilly Tagliano asked about a guy called Spider Man. Where did she get that name from?"

"I don't know, but I'll ask her. She's a brand new appointment to the unit. My guess is she found it in one of the uniform's notes from interviewing one of the witnesses to the shooting scenes over here in West Side. Who is he and is he important?"

Stellato's reply was, as expected, evasive. He said, "Not important, but if you hear anything related to Vladimir Grant, I'd appreciate your help. The girlfriend he lives with is screaming to anyone who will listen that some drug kingpin had him killed."

Rudy answered, "Did some drug kingpin have him killed? Were they Dominicans who did the job?"

Stellato clicked off.

25

Bitter — Bitter - End

At five in the morning on Friday, a search warrant was served on Unit 78A in the West Side Industrial Park. The manager of the leased-out unit knocked on the 78A's door and said a process server was here. Still there was no answer. He gave the keys to Detective Juan Flores, who stood to the side as he keyed the door open and entered with uniforms. Meanwhile on the backside door, Detective Lilly Tagliano with assistance from two uniforms, wrestled with Adalberto Alonzo as he attempted to escape. He had a gun in his hand, but Tagliano kicked it out of his hand and he cursed in what she thought was Spanish. He smacked her hard before the uniforms could cuff him, but not before she got in another good kick, this time to his groin. Once cuffed, he showed no discipline, calling her every perverted name in the books. She was about to bring Alonzo to the station for questioning, when Juan said, "Got it, Detective; got him."

Instead, Lilly read Adalberto Alonzo his rights and put him in the cruiser. He never once stopped his spewing of sexually deviant names related to her gender. She just kept smiling, finally saying, "Lucky you, you got me to arrest you."

Back inside the unit, the detectives found 'The Collection.' Juan said, "The captain was right, he's been active all along. We have the new clothes. There are news articles on the kills in Vegas and Palm Springs; and look, there were kills in Texas, just not in McAllen, Texas. We've got him cold."

Lilly answered, "Juan, over there behind that divider."

The detectives saw a very large photo of a Madonna-like beauty hugging what was surely her son. The boy was around three and he was unmistakably Adalberto as a small child. There was a vase of fresh flowers in front of the photo. Nearby was a plasticized copy of the news of her accident and next to that was a framed letter; it was in Spanish. Juan translated reading the letter aloud. The letter was sent to Adalberto two years after his mother's death in which the aunt told the boy how sorry she was for abandoning him after his mother's death. She wrote that his father would take good care of him, but implied that Albert, her name for him, could not be trusted with her and her family's safety. She ended the letter with, "Alfred is a powerful man and you must do as he says. Never disobey him, and remember we love you." Those words had been underlined by someone.

Lilly broke a lock and opened what she thought was a narrow closet in the back of the office. Pushing the light switch inside the door, the detectives viewed a working office on the left and a bedroom on the right. The space was 50' by 40' and appeared to be a bump out of a garage bay area. They figured this bay was originally meant for storage. A large bathroom was in the bedroom side and had a stainless sink and shower, both oversized. In the middle of the room was a central drain and a large hose on a ring on the side. Juan immediately made the call to the forensics team and told Lilly, "It'll be a long night. We need more help, but we can't get it until the meet is over."

The two started work on the office. Oversized spreadsheets were posted over the immense mahogany desk. The sheets were positioned to allow the person sitting at the desk to see items without moving from his chair. Juan had seen something similar at a trucking firm he worked in as a teenager. The old guy who ran it was not computer savvy. So he sat down and tried to figure out what the abbreviations and numbers listed on the board meant. Lilly pulled up a chair and joined him. She was focused more on the arrangement of the office which appeared to her as more similar to an English aristocrat's library than a storage room. As she turned her head she caught sight of 'TD' listed many times at the end of every third line and then repeatedly at the beginning of every alternated third line. Juan was singing some Mexican tune which he always hummed when he was involved with paperwork. Lilly asked, "Juan, shut up for a minute and tell me, could TD mean Truck Depot?"

Juan looked at the pattern she saw, replying, "On target, Lilly, just look at the starting points. There are three: MCA could be McAllen, MIA could be Miami, and LA could be Los Angeles. Some of the middle abbreviations such as LV for Las Vegas and well I'm not sure of the others; but they are definitely, routes, and I think drug trucking routes. It's dated for next week and seems to be a month's projection. It also says AS is the new czar in large bright green letters with Adalberto's named as assistant to take over.

Lilly said, "Let's hit the desk drawers and the glamourous file cabinet over there. I think we've hit the mother lode; if there's enough here, Juan, it will help the captain bring down the whole system. God, look, Juan, there's a bag of Kennedy coins. Wait till Petra sees this."

It took over five hours more of searching, organizing, and cataloguing before Lilly said, "Eureka, we've got them all. Look at this folder, Juan, it lists hits made and who ordered them by name and date and cost and vendor. This Adalberto keeps copious records. He's their bookkeeper." What struck them both was that Vladimir Grant's name was listed, along with the vendor being from the Dominican Republic, but no name for the one who ordered it. Juan reacted by saying, "He ordered it, Adalberto Alonzo. He had him killed. He's OCD and would never leave a record empty. Everything here is listed. We have all we need for a conviction on them all. It looks as if Raymond ordered the Dominican protection detail for McKinney's meet, but it says here Chavos okayed payment for Ash and Ted's shootings; there's even a negative smiley face next to the payment. The Fir Street hits were authorized by Chavos with Grant as the killer. Grant can't be a Fed. Why was he killed?"

Juan pointed to a line showing Grant authorizing the Dominicans to assassinate the guys at the gas station. There was no evidence that payment was made. "What the hell does this mean; Grant didn't get paid for the kill? Good thing for Grant that he's dead. I'd hate to think what the captain would have done. Well, maybe Chavos killed him for his stupidity. There's nothing here showing who authorized killing Grant."

By lunchtime, the detectives exited the building in time to see the brilliant sunshine on the factory buildings showering their dark straight lines with slivers of light.

By ten-thirty, after the prisoner Alonzo had been booked, Beauregard and Petra met with him in Interview Room 1. Adalberto's whole demeanor cast him as surly and mean; enough to make the detectives wonder how they could have thought him handsome. Alonzo had given the uniforms trouble at his arrest, so he was still cuffed to the chair and looking a lot worse than his usually well-groomed self. His processing also was not an easy task; but the booking officers were used to that kind of trouble.

Adalberto did not ask for an attorney which surprised them. Petra asked him if he wanted them to call his father, Albert Siderov. The prisoner's eyes glazed over and he said, "What are you talking about. I'm Puerto Rican not Russian."

Beauregard excused himself leaving the prisoner with Petra. Back in the unit's murder room, he wondered what he thought about Alonzo's denying his father, thinking, *he knows what's going down today. He doesn't want his father to know he's been arrested. It will interfere with business and that's a no-no. Besides, I don't think his father will support him in this; I could be wrong. We'll have all day with him.*

For the next two hours, Beauregard and Detective Aylewood-Locke, in attempting to interview Alonzo, kept talking about their findings from his rented office. They told him there was DNA that would tie him to the murders. He spoke not a word. A call came in from Ash, and Beauregard took it outside the room. Ash informed the captain that Losocala had just picked Chavos up at the museum parking lot. He said, "I think the meet is soon, Captain. I'm surprised Losocala is involved in the meet. His background is strange, but he doesn't strike me as the kind of guy to get his hands dirty, though you never know. I'd have thought that Vladimir Grant was his guy and yet he's been hit."

The captain mused, "Vladimir Grant was his guy. Chavos didn't order his hit, Adalberto ordered it."

"You got that from the unknown assassin for Grant on Adalberto's chart, Captain? So where is the evidence against Chavos? All the evidence is circumstantial from his son's notes."

"I think we have a witness who will sink under questioning, Detective."

"Who, not Adalberto, you know he'll never talk and neither will Chavos."

"Losocala will talk. We don't have much on him except for his associations, but he doesn't know that. And I'll bet you next week's pay

Raymond is not up to a long jail sentence. Remember, dead bodies were found wherever Losocala lived. I think Alonzo was working for his dad at each of Losocala's locations.

"I haven't seen any evidence that Chavos was in McAllen or Miami or Palm Springs at the times of the murders. He was seen in the Las Vegas pictures. I'm wondering if Alonzo was sent by his father to keep track of business. I don't think Chavos wanted to call attention to his takeover plan's implementation. No! He would not have murdered Grant.

"As to the others, it's possible as part of a business plan, but think of this, he has stayed out of the limelight for over thirty years. Why would he change now? We have nothing on him; no social security, no license, no ownership of anything, and no tax returns. We have a visitor's entry visa thirty-five years ago. He never left, but never did anything to be noticed. At first he loses himself in the Puerto Rican community for ten years and the only trail he left was with Maria Alonzo listing his name at Adalberto's baptismal application. He didn't even know about it."

A message interrupted their call and it came from an unknown number on Rudy's phone. It said, "Today."

Rudy asked Ash to keep following the car but stay far enough back not to be spotted. He reminded him that he thought they were eventually going to West Side; that Ted is not tracking McKinney, because he'll get spotted. However, he told Ted to park at the spot where McKinney would get on the interstate connector to West Side. He said, "It's the best we can do. Wait, here's my second call. It says 'two-thirty p.m.' That's in thirty minutes. In five minutes we'll get the final call."

They waited, Ash in his car following Chavos and Losocala, Ted waiting at the entrance to the interstate, and Rudy in his office. The next call was not a text; instead it was from Lilly and Juan. There was direct physical evidence that Chavos or Alfie, Adalberto's father was the drug kingpin. Five minutes of conversation ended with Rudy calling Ash, saying, "The minute Chavos's car hits West Side and most likely it will be shortly, I want him arrested. Which way do you think they'll cross from Springfield?"

"Over by the green, Captain, and the car will take the street that connects it to the mini-mall road. I think they'll enter Spruce Street from the back."

Beauregard said, "I hope so. There's a detour one block over from the green to that short street with a U back to the route. Traffic practically stops at the turn. Makes it a good place to make the arrest! Neither Losocala nor Chavos has ever been known to appear to carry, but that does not mean there won't be weapons in the car. I'm calling traffic detail now and our tactical support team for backup. We'll be there too."

Beauregard had just finished making his calls, when his cell beeped with a message saying, "Same one." Beauregard said, "Ash, the meet is there. Stop following their car! Go the alternate way. With some speed you'll be there first."

Rudy and Mason headed for the site leaving Petra with the prisoner. It took minutes to reach the short street. With the assistance of the two traffic officers there, they arranged for Beauregard's car to be halfway over the sidewalk in a feigned accident. Two cruisers looked to be investigating the accident. Mason, acting as a driver who had imbibed too much, was propped against a telephone pole. Beauregard thought it looked believable. Seven minutes later, Losocala's car made the turn and was stopped for a minute as every other car before theirs was stopped. Ash and four uniforms with guns drawn came out from houses on both sides of the street approaching the car from the rear. At that moment, Rudy sat up in his car and backed it out on the street to prevent Losocala and Chavos from driving through. Losocala raised his hands as did Chavos and an arrest was easily accomplished.

Beauregard thought, *the ending is often disappointing when it's too easy. In the movies, there'd be a shootout, but not in West Side. These two think we have nothing on them. They for sure don't know about Adalberto's secrets. It's European history all over again with the son betraying the father, but in the modern way by keeping copious records; something the father knew enough not to do. The father is now exposed, after thirty years of living under the radar, by the psychopathic son he created.*

As the excitement of the arrests quieted down, Beauregard headed back to the station, but before he could get a block away, he was waved down by three boys on bikes. He sighed, but stopped to talk to them. Him, Jackson, said, "We heard there's an arrest, Captain."

Before the captain could answer, Wayne said, "My father's police radio said there was an accident over here, and that an arrest was made. Captain, there's no evidence of an accident here, and you wouldn't be here for just an accident."

Paulie closed in with, "Ok, did you get the pervert, Captain?"

Beauregard with a wink and a smile, said, "You know I can't talk about an open case, but if I were you guys, I'd be pleased with my artwork."

All four smiled as Beauregard headed back to the station to face the music with the drug task force and Loughman. He had made the call to Loughman and was greeted by him with expletives. Then with a sigh Loughman announced that the District Attorney and he and the task force were scheduling a press conference in an hour outside the West Side police station to show the arrest was the result of all levels of policing working together. "Do you have a problem with that, Captain Beauregard?"

Beauregard answered, "No, sir, I have the man who murdered my teenaged victims, and the ones who wounded my officers and my family, and the ones who were responsible for other deaths. That's all I ever wanted. You also now have Chavos and the evidence against him in detail. And I think we can turn a witness against him. A press conference will be fine. You direct it. I'm fine with that."

298

299

Acknowledgments

To my husband Joe for his unquestionable
loyalty, kindness, and love.

To my children: The lights of my life.

To my grandchildren: Dream, Endure, and Prevail!

I am grateful for all technical assistance
I received from my good friends:

Police Matters:
Retired Springfield, Massachusetts Chief of Police Paula Meara
Massachusetts State Police Officer John Ferrera
Retired Springfield Police Officer Michael Carney

Attorneys:
Charles E. Dolan
Joseph A. Pellegrino, Sr. (ret. Justice, Massachusetts Trial Courts)
Raipher D. Pellegrino

And to my editors: I thank you for your
editing, support, and counsel.

To all above: All errors on implementation are solely mine.

More Books by K. B. Pellegrino
Kathleen B. Pellegrino – Author & Storyteller

Evil Exists in West Side Trilogy:
Sunnyside Road –Paradise Dissembling (Liferich Publishing)
Mary Lou –Oh! What Did She Do? (Liferich Publishing)
Brothers From Another Mother –All for
One! Always? (Liferich Publishing)

Coming in 2020 another Detective Beauregard Mystery
A Predatory Cabal –Worms in the Apple

You can find K. B. Pellegrino's books on all
major online Book Stores, such as Amazon, Barnes
& Noble, kobo, I Books Store, and SCRIBD.

Follow K. B. Pellegrino on her website. KBPellegrino.com